M000232977

The hoof dug at the ground, splashing mud as the great horse tensed, eager to commence its charge. Ahead stood the official, holding a pennant on high, ready to signal the start. The flag came down, spurs dug in, and sixteen hundred pounds of warhorse sprang forward, pushing its rider back in the saddle. Hooves thundered as the beast tore down the field, throwing clumps of dirt and grass into the air in its wake.

The knight lowered his lance, placing it to the left of his horse's head, straining to keep it level as he closed in on his enemy. Then came the moment of impact, a shattering of wood as lance struck shield and splinters exploded.

The knight felt himself driven backward with the force, but his saddle held him in place, preventing a fall. His opponent, however, was knocked from his horse and crashed to the ground where he lay, unmoving. Men rushed forward, huddling around the unfortunate soul, the crowd falling into a hush. Moments later, the unhorsed knight was hoisted onto a litter and managed a wave, eliciting a cheer from the onlookers.

His warhorse, free of its rider's weight, galloped away, only slowing as it approached the end of the lists.

Ludwig Altenburg watched as the great horse come to a halt, its breath steaming in the chilly morning air. "Magnificent, isn't it?"

"Magnificent?" said Kurt. "A man was nearly killed! I'd hardly call that something to celebrate."

Ludwig frowned. The swordmaster was particularly gloomy this morning. "Come now," the younger man continued, "you must admit it's a test of courage if nothing else."

"Courage? More like stupidity."

"Nevertheless, it's the very reason we came to Torburg."

"We came here to seek employment with the duke," admonished Kurt, "not to watch men almost kill each other."

"How better to gain his attention than by winning the joust?"

"Winning? You've never jousted in your life."

Ludwig summoned up all the bravado his twenty-six years could muster. "How hard can it be?"

ALSO BY PAUL J BENNETT

POWER ASCENDING SERIES

TEMPERED STEEL: PREQUEL

TEMPLE KNIGHT

WARRIOR KNIGHT

HEIR TO THE CROWN SERIES

SERVANT OF THE CROWN

SWORD OF THE CROWN

MERCERIAN TALES: STORIES OF THE PAST

HEART OF THE CROWN

SHADOW OF THE CROWN

MERCERIAN TALES: THE CALL OF MAGIC

FATE OF THE CROWN

BURDEN OF THE CROWN

MERCERIAN TALES: THE MAKING OF A MAN

DEFENDER OF THE CROWN

FURY OF THE CROWN

WAR OF THE CROWN

TRIUMPH OF THE CROWN

THE FROZEN FLAME SERIES

THE AWAKENING/INTO THE FIRE - PREQUELS

ASHES

EMBERS

FLAMES

INFERNO

THE CHRONICLES OF CYRIC

INTO THE MAELSTROM

MIDWINTER MURDER

THE BEAST OF BRUNHAUSEN

WARRIOR KNIGHT

POWER ASCENDING: BOOK TWO

PAUL J BENNETT

Copyright © 2021 Paul J Bennett
Cover Illustration Copyright © 2021 Carol Bennett
Portrait Copyright © 2021 Amaleigh Photography

All rights reserved. No part of this book may be reproduced, stored in a retrieval system, or transmitted in any form, or by any means, electronic, mechanical, photocopying, recording or otherwise, without prior permission of the author.

First Edition: March 2021

ePub ISBN: 978-1-989315-97-2
Mobi ISBN: 978-1-989315-98-9
Smashwords ISBN: 978-1-989315-97-2
Print ISBN: 978-1-990073-06-9

This book is a work of fiction. Any similarity to any person, living or dead is entirely coincidental.

DEDICATION

To my wife, Carol, who gave me wings to let my imagination fly.

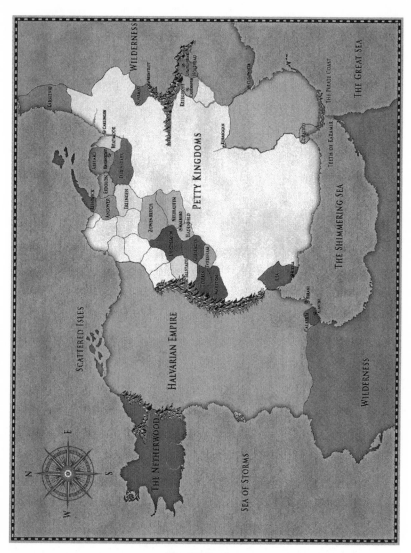

Map of the Continent

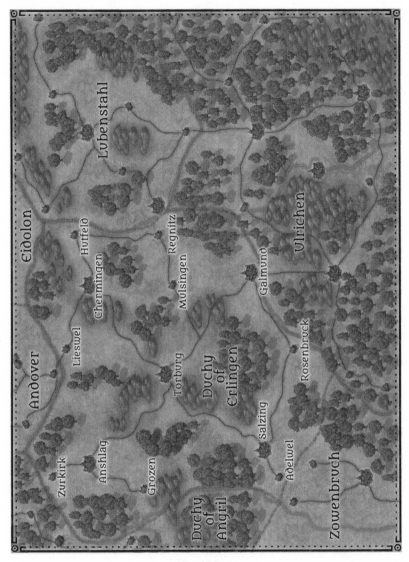

Map of Erlingen

BATTLE OF CHERMINGEN

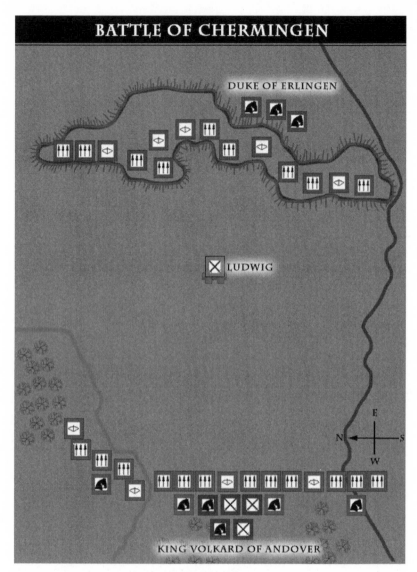

Battle of Chermingen

1

TORBURG

Spring 1095 SR*
(*Saints Reckoning)

The hoof dug at the ground, splashing mud as the great horse tensed, eager to commence its charge. Ahead stood the official, holding a pennant on high, ready to signal the start. The flag came down, spurs dug in, and sixteen hundred pounds of warhorse sprang forward, pushing its rider back in the saddle. Hooves thundered as the beast tore down the field, throwing clumps of dirt and grass into the air in its wake.

The knight lowered his lance, placing it to the left of his horse's head, straining to keep it level as he closed in on his enemy. Then came the moment of impact, a shattering of wood as lance struck shield and splinters exploded.

The knight felt himself driven backward with the force, but his saddle held him in place, preventing a fall. His opponent, however, was knocked from his horse and crashed to the ground where he lay, unmoving. Men rushed forward, huddling around the unfortunate soul, the crowd falling into a hush. Moments later, the unhorsed knight was hoisted onto a litter and managed a wave, eliciting a cheer from the onlookers.

His warhorse, free of its rider's weight, galloped away, only slowing as it approached the end of the lists.

. . .

Ludwig Altenburg watched as the great horse come to a halt, its breath steaming in the chilly morning air. "Magnificent, isn't it?"

"Magnificent?" said Kurt. "A man was nearly killed! I'd hardly call that something to celebrate."

Ludwig frowned. The swordmaster was particularly gloomy this morning. "Come now," the younger man continued, "you must admit it's a test of courage if nothing else."

"Courage? More like stupidity."

"Nevertheless, it's the very reason we came to Torburg."

"We came here to seek employment with the duke," admonished Kurt, "not to watch men almost kill each other."

"How better to gain his attention than by winning the joust?"

"Winning? You've never jousted in your life."

Ludwig summoned up all the bravado his twenty-six years could muster. "How hard can it be? You know how well I can ride."

"Riding is one thing," said Kurt, "but using a lance is a far cry from fighting a duel."

"Nonsense. It merely complicates the matter by adding a horse."

Kurt grabbed his arm, causing the younger man to turn towards him. "I'm serious, Ludwig. If you go out there, you're likely to get yourself killed."

"You've been training me for years. Do you now doubt the usefulness of your own lessons?"

"I trained you to fight on foot, not mounted. There's also the matter of your armour."

"I have plate armour, not to mention one of the finest warhorses you can buy. You saw to that."

Clearly Kurt was upset, but the man took a deep breath, lowering his voice. "You were the one who decided it was time to leave home. All I did was facilitate that by getting your gear together."

Ludwig smiled. "Then consider it fate."

"Fate?"

"Yes, think of it. We leave Verfeld Keep with horses and armour, and what do we stumble across? A tournament, no less. Surely the Saints are looking out for us?"

Kurt shook his head. "Fate had nothing to do with it. Tourneys are a common enough sight in these lands, so it was inevitable we should cross paths with one eventually."

"Look," said Ludwig. "If we're to make a living as soldiers, we must find a sponsor. What better way of doing that than by making a name for ourselves here, in the joust?"

"You don't understand the dangers. I've seen my fair share of these competitions in my lifetime, and someone always gets injured. Go in there unprepared, and you may end up crippled for life."

"I am NOT unprepared. I have, in fact, been paying close attention to the combatants."

"And you believe that's enough to keep you safe?" said Kurt.

"My armour will protect me."

"That armour is meant to protect you in battle, not a headlong charge into a lance."

"But the lances here are made to break," Ludwig persisted. "Can you not see that? Come, let's go and get me registered, then I'll show you just how superior your training has been."

He moved off, forcing the slightly older Kurt to jog in order to catch up. They pushed their way through the crowd as another pair of knights took up their positions.

"Ludwig, wait," begged Kurt. "Surely you can't register now? They've already started."

"That's where you're wrong. These are only practice jousts. The real competition doesn't begin until tomorrow."

"How can you possibly know that?"

"By listening to the crowd. You'd be amazed at what you can learn if you let your ears have free rein."

Ludwig led them towards a tent that was bedecked with flags. Entering, he discovered a well-appointed interior where an older man, dressed in fine clothes, sat in a folding chair, sipping wine as he perused a parchment. At Ludwig's entrance, he looked up.

"Something I can do for you?" the older man asked.

"I'm here to register for the joust."

"Are you, now?" the man replied. "And what name do you go by?"

"Ludwig..." His voice trailed off as he realized his predicament. If he were to reveal his family name, word might get back to his father, a circumstance he would find most unfortunate. He struggled to come up with a solution, then finally spat out his answer. "Alwise, Ludwig Alwise of Garmund."

The registrar looked at him with some amusement. "Garmund? I don't believe I've heard of it."

"It lies far to the southeast," added Kurt, "on the way to Corassus."

"Yes, of course." The man looked eager to hide his ignorance. Setting down his parchment, he then stood, moving to a small table nearby littered with papers, and selected one which was more ornate than the others. With a smile at his success, he moved once more to grab a quill and ink.

Dipping the tip in, he made ready to write, pausing a moment to look this newcomer in the eye. "I assume you have the proper equipment?"

"I do," said Ludwig.

The man began writing with a steady hand. Ludwig waited patiently while his name was placed on the list.

"There we are. You're now officially registered. All that remains is the matter of your fee."

Ludwig felt a knot in his stomach. "Fee?"

"Yes, the funds required to gain entry. A trifling amount, to be sure, but we can't have any old commoner trying to make a name for themselves, now, can we?"

"No, of course not. How much is it?"

"Fifty crowns."

Ludwig looked at Kurt, but all he received was a shake of the head.

"Of course," said the man, "if it's too much…"

"No, not at all." Ludwig withdrew a bulky purse and spilled some coins onto the table, counting out the amount as he went. His task complete, he returned the excess crowns to his purse, then tucked it away.

The registrar scooped up the coins and moved over to a strongbox, taking a moment to undo the padlock and place the coins within. Once done, he turned to face his guest.

"You're all set, Sir Ludwig Alwise of Garmund."

Ludwig was unsure of how to proceed. "When do I start?"

The older man chuckled. "My guess is that this is your first tourney?"

"It is, or rather it's my first as a contestant."

"Well, your initial match won't be until the morrow. In the meantime, you might want to set up your pavilion."

"Pavilion?"

"Yes, your tent, man. Surely you brought one?"

"Of course," replied Ludwig, the lie coming easily to his lips. "Where do I set up?"

"As you leave, turn right. You'll see the area easily enough. You can't miss the pennants."

"Thank you," said Ludwig, who then turned abruptly and left the tent, leaving his companion scrambling to catch up.

"Was that wise?" asked Kurt. "That was a good portion of what we had left."

Ludwig waved away the matter. "It's coins well spent. Now, we must find ourselves a tent if we are to keep up appearances."

Kurt grabbed his arm. "And use up what little we have left? Are you mad?"

The young lord reddened. "I know what I'm doing," he insisted.

"Do you? You could have fooled me. I went to great lengths to help you escape the clutches of your father. I beg you, don't throw it all away by wasting what little we have remaining."

"Nonsense. I've thought this through quite carefully. If we are to win the attention of the duke, we must appear successful. We can't easily do that if we're living a pauper's life."

"Have you no head for finance?"

"Of course I do," said Ludwig. "I helped collect taxes from my father's tenants."

"That's a far cry from understanding the concept of frugalness."

"You worry too much."

"And you, too little. How are we to feed ourselves?"

"Don't worry," said Ludwig. "The rewards will far exceed the cost of the enterprise."

They wandered down towards the line of pavilions, each decorated with coloured standards, displaying the coats of arms or symbols of the knights within.

Those closest to the registration tent were more ornate, some as large as a small house. As they made their way down the line, however, the tents became plainer, many showing signs of prolonged use and ill-repair.

"It appears not all knights are successful," noted Kurt. He turned when Ludwig failed to reply, only to spot him some distance back where a knight sat in front of a tent, his feet resting on a footstool while he oiled his sword. Ludwig, fascinated by the scene, had stopped to take it all in.

Kurt jogged back to join his comrade.

"What do you think?" asked Ludwig.

"Of what?" said Kurt. "His pavilion?"

"No, the man."

Kurt shrugged. "He's a knight. What of it?"

Ludwig failed to answer his question, instead stepping closer.

"Good day," he said. "I am Sir Ludwig of Garmund."

The knight looked up at him, shielding his eyes against the early morning sun. "Greetings, Sir Knight, my name is Sir Galrath."

Ludwig looked at Kurt, but he only shrugged. The younger man turned his attention back to the knight seated before him. "Are you registered for the joust?" he asked.

"I am," Sir Galrath replied. "Is this your first tourney?"

"It is," Ludwig confessed, "and I must admit to being a little over-whelmed."

"You'll get used to it."

"Have you competed much?"

"Indeed. My participation here in Torburg will mark my sixteenth tournament in five years. My experience has made me a wealthy man."

"Whom do you serve?" asked Ludwig.

"I am sworn to the service of the Duke of Erlingen."

"And yet, if I'm not mistaken, you don't display his colours?"

The knight chuckled. "The duke does not wish to be represented in the games he oversees. It might be seen as trying to influence the judges."

"Does the duke employ many such men as yourself?"

"A fair number, although I daresay there are few here this day."

"Why do you suppose that is?" asked Ludwig. "Do they not seek to gain honour in the tourney?"

"Honour?" said Sir Galrath. "Yes, I suppose that's one way to look at it. On the other hand, maybe they don't want to risk their lives on such things."

"Are you saying they're cowards?"

The knight looked him squarely in the eyes. "If I were you, I would guard my tongue. It would not go well for you to spread such false accusations. Someone may take offence and demand to settle the matter once and for all."

"A duel? I would welcome it."

"Then you are a fool, my young friend."

Ludwig's back stiffened. "I take offence at that, sir. Will you retract your words?"

Sir Galrath shook his head. "I meant nothing by the remark, Sir Ludwig. I merely wished to indicate that tournaments are not for everyone." He rolled up the sleeve of his tunic, showing off a long scar. "See this? I got it from the tip of a lance. The thing punched clean through my vambrace, and I was lucky not to lose the entire arm."

"And so your wounds have made you more cautious?"

The knight refused to be drawn into the conversation. "I can see you think quite a lot of yourself. I hope the confidence is warranted."

"It is," assured Ludwig. "Allow me to name Kurt Wasser." He indicated his companion with a wave of his hand.

Kurt bowed. "An honour, Sir Galrath."

"The honour is mine, sir."

"Perhaps," offered Ludwig, "we shall meet on the field of honour."

Sir Galrath rose, moving to stand before the young man. He eyed him up and down, then finally offered his hand in friendship. "I shall look forward to it."

"Might I ask who you're competing against in the first round?"

"I don't know," replied the knight. "At this point, none of us do. Come morning, though, it'll be an entirely different story."

"Morning?"

"Yes, that's when they post the schedule. The jousting is done in rounds. Defeat your opponent, and move on."

"And if you lose?" asked Kurt.

"Then you forfeit your horse and armour."

Ludwig turned pale but soon recovered. "Is this always the way?"

"Of course," said Sir Galrath, "although a knight may always pay out his ransom in coin."

"I thank you for the lesson, sir, but I fear we must be on our way."

"If you must. I shall look for you on the field."

"As will I," said Ludwig, turning abruptly and almost colliding with Kurt. He took a moment to recover, then strode off with purpose.

Kurt followed after him, calling out as he went. "Ludwig, for Saint's sake, man, slow down. This isn't a race!"

"I must find a tent."

"Have we enough for that?"

"I told you, we're fine," said Ludwig.

"So you say, but I'd feel a little more secure if you'd let me deal with our finances."

"Must I remind you again that I am the son of a baron?"

"I'm well aware of that," said Kurt, "but you're no baron's son now. You chose to run away, remember?"

"Which makes it all the more imperative we make a favourable impression with the duke. We can't do that without a pavilion."

"And you expect to find one here?"

"Trust me, I know what I'm doing."

"Do you? I have my doubts."

"There." Ludwig pointed. "You see?"

Kurt swivelled his gaze. A young man, not even twenty years of age, was folding up a worn-looking canvas while all around him were tent poles and rope. They moved closer until the youth was within hailing distance.

"Excuse me," called out Ludwig.

The youth looked up from his work, tracks of tears evident on his face. "Yes?"

"Is something wrong?"

"It is indeed," the young man replied. "My master, Sir Haren, was killed this very morning while he practiced for the joust."

"I'm sorry to hear of it," said Ludwig. "May I enquire as to the manner of his death?"

"He was knocked from the saddle and broke his neck in the fall."

"Didn't he have a helmet?"

"He did, but it helped him not. The body is a frail thing, even when encased in steel, and my master was not well-armoured."

"I take it you'll return home?"

"Home? I have no home, nor did my master. He left there long ago, vowing never to return. For the last ten years, he has been travelling the circuit, earning a living off his martial prowess."

"See?" said Ludwig. "I told you it was possible."

Kurt frowned. "This pavilion is not that of a successful man," he warned.

"It is not," agreed the youth, "but it's all I have left."

"What will you do?" asked Ludwig.

"The only thing I can do—sell this off and seek employment elsewhere."

Ludwig smiled. "Then perhaps fate has brought me to you. How much for this?" He waved his hand, encompassing the campsite.

"Which?" asked the youth. "The pavilion?"

"All of it."

The young man smiled. "Make me an offer."

"Would fifty crowns suffice?"

Kurt covered his eyes, unable to watch the disaster unfolding before him, yet powerless to prevent it.

"More than sufficient," said the youth.

Ludwig found a dry section of canvas and dumped out his purse, counting out the coins. Satisfied, he threw down the purse itself and withdrew five crowns, leaving the rest for his purchase.

The young man scooped the pile up eagerly, filling the purse once more and running off in the direction of the Hammer.

"It looks like we now have a pavilion," Ludwig said with a smile.

"We do," admitted Kurt, "but we have little left in the way of coins. Five crowns, was it?"

"Come now, it's not all bad news. I'll win this back in no time. Now, let's get this pavilion put up, and then go and fetch the horses. There's no sense in paying for another night at the inn."

Kurt moved closer to the pile of canvas, walking around it, trying to make sense of it all.

"Well," he said at last, "we have plenty of rope, and those would appear to be tent poles. How, exactly, does this thing go together?"

"I have no idea," said Ludwig, "but how hard can it be?"

2

PREPARATION

Spring 1095 SR

A drop of water struck his face, and Ludwig opened his eyes. Above him sagged the top of the pavilion, weighed down by the accumulated rain. He sat up on his straw pallet and rubbed his eyes, trying to banish the fatigue. The sound of ripping fabric greeted his ears, and he looked up right as the top of the tent gave way, releasing a torrent of water.

Kurt, who was on the other side of the pavilion, woke with a start. The sight of Ludwig's indignation at being drenched was too much for him to bear, and he burst out laughing.

"It's not funny!" shouted Ludwig.

"Oh, yes it is!" roared his companion. "You look like a drowned rat."

Ludwig stood, shaking the water from his hair. It was a brisk morning, cold enough to see one's breath, and the water had been frigid. Digging through his meagre belongings, he pulled forth a dry shirt and donned it quickly.

From outside drifted the sound of a herald making his way through the camp, calling the participants to gather at the registration tent.

"Looks like I'd better hurry," said Ludwig. "It sounds as if things are starting."

Kurt, who had also risen, was less enthusiastic. "Don't do this, Ludwig."

"What, joust? I told you, I know what I'm doing."

"No you don't," insisted Kurt. "You could get yourself killed."

Ludwig, who was already in a foul mood, quickly turned on the man. "I know what I'm doing!"

"Don't be a fool, Ludwig. You've never fought from horseback, or even held a lance, and you expect to win?"

"Don't tell me what to do. You're not my father!"

"No, I'm not. I'm your friend, and I'm trying to help you."

Ludwig felt his rage building, yet he was unwilling to contain it. "You can help me by staying out of my business."

"This competition will be the death of you, Ludwig. I want no part of it."

"Then leave! No one's stopping you."

Kurt stared back, stunned by the words. "You don't mean that."

"Don't I?" Ludwig took a deep breath, trying to calm himself, but he was furious. He snapped up his tunic, pulling it over his shirt.

"I'm going to find out who I'm fighting," he grumbled. "You'd best be gone by the time I return." Ludwig immediately regretted his words but refused to back down.

"And don't darken my presence again," he shouted over his shoulder as he stormed out of the tent, a blast of cold wind doing little to cool his temper. He stomped past the horses tethered outside on his way towards the registration tent.

A group of knights was gathered here, talking in low tones as they waited. Ludwig's arrival was marked by little more than a cursory glance when he took his place amongst the others, cursing the temperature under his breath while he shivered.

It felt like an eternity passed before the official finally emerged, along with a young lad holding a small pot, and a clerk, carefully balancing a portable table on which rested quill, ink, and parchment. The official lifted his arms to get everyone's attention, and the crowd fell silent.

"I am here this day to draw names for the joust," he announced, "but before I do, I shall go over the rules, few as they are. Combatants will make up to three passes each round, the victor being the individual who accumulates the most points. Any hit with a lance nets one point, whilst breaking said lance is worth two. If you should manage to unhorse your opponent, three points shall be granted. The competition will immediately cease should either person reach five points. Otherwise, the greatest accumulation of points will advance to the next round."

"What of a tie?" someone called out.

The official smiled, warming to the task. "In such a case, additional passes will be run until such time as one combatant gains more points than his opponent. Once all knights have completed their initial rounds, new opponents will be assigned."

"What of ransom?" called out Sir Hendrick.

"Short on funds, are we?" said the official. The knights all laughed, but Ludwig felt sweat begin to break out on his brow.

"The usual rules will apply," the man continued. "Now, shall we proceed with the draw?" Nods of encouragement soon convinced him to continue.

"Each knight's name has been placed in this pot. I will now draw them, two at a time, to determine whom each of you must face in the first elimination round."

He looked at the clerk who, having set down the small table, had taken up the quill and was waiting to record the results. With a nod, the official began the process.

"The first match will be between Sir Hendrick of Corburg and Sir Nathan of Feldmarch."

Congratulations were offered from the rest of the competitors, then all eyes once again returned to the official. The man dipped his hand into the pot once more, pulling forth another pair of names. "The next match will be"—he paused as he read the name—"Sir Ludwig of Garmund, who faces Sir Galrath of Paledon."

"Who?" called out Sir Hendrick.

"Sir Galrath of Paledon," replied the official.

"We all know Sir Galrath, but who is this Sir Ludwig of which you speak?"

"That's me," piped up Ludwig. He held up his arm to make his presence known.

The crowd parted, and Sir Galrath came into view. The large knight looked him up and down in a dismissive manner. "Oh," he finally said, "it's you."

"We met yesterday," said Ludwig.

"So we did, but I'd forgotten your name."

Ludwig felt slighted, and his ears began to burn. Did this man intend to insult him?

"I shall look forward to thoroughly trouncing you," the knight continued.

"It is I who shall trounce you, sir!" countered Ludwig.

Galrath smiled, evidently pleased with the response. Ludwig was ready to continue the debate, but his opponent simply turned, facing forward once more as the official continued. Ludwig fumed, letting the anger build within. It wasn't until they neared the end of the announcements that he resolved to take more immediate action.

The crowd began to thin as most knights returned to their tents to prepare themselves, but Ludwig sought out Sir Galrath. The man was chatting amiably to Sir Hendrick when Ludwig interrupted.

"You owe me an apology, sir!"

The older knight turned to him in surprise, a hint of amusement on his face as he saw his accuser.

"Well?" demanded Ludwig.

"Well, what?" said Galrath.

"Will you apologize for your slight?"

The knight glanced at his companion, who offered a wry smile of his own. Hendrick provided his own observation. "Apparently our friend here is unfamiliar with the etiquette of the tourney."

"Ah," said Galrath, "the passion of youth. Well do I remember it."

"Don't talk about me as if I'm not here," demanded Ludwig.

"My dear fellow," continued the knight, "I can assure you I bear you no ill will."

"In spite of that, you insult me to my face."

"It's naught but friendly banter meant to harden your resolve, common enough at events such as this. You must take no offence."

Ludwig felt his face turn crimson. Was this man mocking him, or had he truly misread his intentions? It was so hard to tell.

"In any case," continued Sir Galrath, "we must both prepare for the joust. You'd best go don your armour and get your horse saddled."

"But we are second up," said Ludwig, struggling with what to say.

The knight chuckled. "You are young, my friend, and inexperienced in such things, so I will forgive your ignorance. A round of jousting is short, seldom lasting more than two or three passes. If you are not ready when your name is called, you will forfeit your placement, and your opponent will advance without challenge. While that might suit some, it does not sit well with me. I prefer to earn my spot at the top, not be handed it by someone's lack of preparedness. Now off with you, and we shall settle our differences later, at the joust."

Sir Galrath turned his back on Ludwig, continuing his discussion with Sir Hendrick. Ludwig felt his pulse quicken but wheeled around, stomping off to his pavilion to prepare.

By the time he got to his tent, his temper had fled, to be replaced by a sense of worry, even fear, although this he fought to control. He wanted to talk to Kurt, but as he rounded the pavilion, only his own horse remained.

Ludwig looked around, desperate to find his friend, but it was useless; he had long since fled. Once inside, he realized with a shock that he had no one to help him armour up. How then was he to dress for battle? It was one thing to put on a tunic, quite another to actually don armour. He stepped back outside, casting his eyes about to see the other knights already dressing, helped by their squires. Ludwig cursed himself for his selfishness. If he hadn't lost his temper, he wouldn't be in this mess.

A man in the brown cassock of Saint Mathew wandered through the tents, offering prayers as the knights readied themselves. He halted before Ludwig. "Is something wrong, Sir Knight?"

"Yes," the young man replied, "I need help getting into my armour. My helper appears to have run off."

"Could I be of assistance?"

"Are you a Temple Knight?"

"Saints, no. I am but a humble lay brother."

"Then I doubt you can help."

"On the contrary, I have two older brothers who took up the lance. I am more than familiar with the armour of knights. Would you accept my aid?"

Ludwig nodded. "Aye, for I have little choice. My name is Ludwig."

"Of Garmund?"

"You know of me?"

"I was reading over the list of competitors just now, and I saw your name. Mine is Brother Vernan."

"Very well, Brother Vernan. Shall we step inside?"

"By all means, Sir Knight."

"Please, call me Ludwig."

Inside the tent, Ludwig began spreading out his armour.

"You'll want to start with the doublet," said the Holy Man, "although this one appears a little the worse for wear." He held it up, examining the cuts and tears.

"I used it when practicing," explained Ludwig. "I'm afraid I left home before I had a chance to have repairs made."

"It matters little. After all, your armour will be worn overtop." He held it as Ludwig slipped his arms into the sleeves and began tying it up.

"So how is it," said the young lord, "that you ended up joining the Church?"

"My father was a knight, as were my two older brothers, but I was never one for fighting, enjoying the simple pleasures of education and intellect instead. It was only natural that I should join the Church. What of you? Did you leave home in somewhat of a hurry? Of course, if you prefer not to talk of it, I shall understand."

"No, it's all right. I left home over a disagreement with my father. It concerned a woman."

"As it so often does," said Brother Vernan. "Might I enquire if she is still with you?"

"She is not," said Ludwig, his cheeks blushing. "She joined the Church. The last I heard, she had left for Eidenburg."

"So she is to be a Temple Knight?"

"A Temple Knight?"

"Yes, that's where they train them, you know."

Ludwig grinned. "That makes perfect sense, now that I think of it. I remember asking her once what she would do if she hadn't been a smith."

"Your lady friend was a smith?"

"Yes," said Ludwig. "Why? Does that surprise you?"

"Women smiths are few amongst the Petty Kingdoms. From whence did she hail?"

"She's a Calabrian."

"Ah, well, that explains a lot."

"What does that mean?"

"Merely that they have different traditions. Will you see her again, do you think?"

"No," said Ludwig, "my father saw to that." He suddenly looked at the Holy Brother with fear in his eyes. "You won't repeat any of this to anyone, will you? I don't want word getting back to him."

"Of course not," said Brother Vernan. "You have my word on it. Speak freely, Sir Knight, and lessen the burden on your soul." He lifted the breastplate, placing the shoulder straps to either side of Ludwig's head, then began buckling it to the backplate.

"I presume your father had some influence," the man continued.

"He's a baron," confessed Ludwig, "and I, his only son."

"I imagine he feels your loss keenly."

"Which is why no word of this should reach other ears. I'm sure he'd send people after me if he knew I was here."

"I gather you are still in love with this woman you mentioned."

"Is it that obvious?"

"No, but then again, I have a keen insight into such matters. You'd be surprised how devastating lost love can be. What makes you think you'll never see her again?"

"One of the conditions of her joining the Church was she be sent far from home. She's probably hundreds of miles away by now."

"Perhaps fate may one day bring her back to you."

"I must say you surprise me," said Ludwig. "I thought Holy Men such as yourself believed such relationships to be beneath them."

"We take an oath of celibacy," said Brother Vernan, "but that does not mean we insist others do the same."

"And the Temple of Saint Agnes?"

The Holy Man chuckled. "Unlike the other orders of Temple Knights, the sisters of the order are free to leave at any time." He reached down, picking up some leg armour. "The greaves next, I should think."

Ludwig waited as the armour was strapped on, his mind racing with the implications. "You say they can leave?"

"Yes, though it's not a common occurrence. When are you competing?"

"My match is the second of the day."

"Then we'd best hurry. Let's get the rest of this armour on, shall we? We still have to prepare your horse."

Ludwig took a moment to place his hand on the man's shoulder. "Thank you, Brother Vernan."

"For what?"

"For offering me solace in my time of need. I'm afraid I have been a bit ungracious of late."

Brother Vernan smiled. "I do the Saint's work. It is he to whom you must give thanks."

A little while later, Ludwig sat atop his horse, his plate armour dull in the overcast sun. He glanced down to where several wooden lances lay.

"How am I to carry all of those?"

"Fear not," said Brother Vernan. "I should be honoured to act as your squire this day."

"Are you sure?" said Ludwig. "Isn't that breaking an oath or something?"

"Not at all. I am forbidden to compete in the tournament, but nothing says I cannot assist a competitor. Now come, I shall gather up your spare lances, and we'll proceed to the field of honour."

They began making their way through the lines of pavilions to the tournament field.

"Is this your first competition?" asked Brother Vernan.

"Why does everyone keep asking me that?"

"It was merely an observation. I sense you are unfamiliar with such things."

"Verfeld was far too small to host such an event, and my father refused to let me travel. I have, however, read extensively on the subject."

"You read?" said Brother Vernan.

"Yes, why? Does that surprise you?"

"I suppose it shouldn't, but I know of many knights who eschew the written word, refusing to learn even the basics of literacy."

"But don't they wish to advance amongst the ranks of nobility?" asked Ludwig.

"Not all do. Many knights are perfectly comfortable with their role in society."

"But didn't all the knights register for this event?"

"They did," replied the Holy Brother, "but unless I miss my guess, it was the registrar who filled in their names."

Ludwig looked around. From his position atop his horse, he had a clear view of the neat rows of tents. At least a dozen knights were in easy sight, each preparing for the coming tournament in their own way. "So you're saying that most of these men are illiterate?"

"I'm afraid so," said Brother Vernan, "though, I would, of course, refuse to name names."

"You mentioned you had two brothers who were knights. Are they here today?"

"No, although both are in service to the Duke of Erlingen. The eldest dislikes these spectacles, whilst I fear my other brother prefers pursuits of a different kind."

"Women?" suggested Ludwig.

"Precisely. A vice, I am told, that is fairly common amongst the lesser nobility."

"Lesser?"

"Yes, knights, barons, and baronets. It is not a term often used in speech, but in written form, it's pretty common."

"Why do you think that is?"

"There are certain social differences. The higher ranks of nobility typically have marriages that have been arranged many years before a child matures. The lesser ranks, on the other hand, struggle to find suitable matches. Knights, of course, aren't hereditary, nor are baronets."

"Barons are, though," said Ludwig.

"That's true, yet on average, few rise to higher positions within society. Here in Erlingen, for example, they often spend more time at each other's throats than seeking advancement."

"Why?"

"A baron is trapped between his obligations to those above him and the management of those beneath."

"Surely that's true of all nobles."

"To a certain extent, yes," said Brother Vernan, "but those of higher status often have more people to rely on for the day-to-day operations. How was it for your father?"

Ludwig grunted. "Much as you've described, if I'm being honest. That's one of the reasons I left home."

"I thought it was because of a woman?"

"Looking back, she was the issue that pushed me over the edge. In any event, it's all over now."

"Yes," agreed the Holy Brother. "And it appears we are now at the lists. Are you ready to gain fame and glory?"

"As ready as I'll ever be."

3

THE JOUST

Spring 1095 SR

L udwig shifted in the saddle, trying to steel his nerves. His horse, apparently as nervous as he, shuffled its hooves and let out a snort. Before him, Sir Hendrick had managed to knock the unfortunate Sir Nathan from his horse, and now the unlucky knight was on the ground unconscious.

The spectators, mostly composed of the wealthy, gaped at the scene, eager for news. Ludwig had to wonder if he might end up in such a way, but quickly dismissed the thought. While it was true he was inexperienced in jousting, he had spent years training for combat. Of course, he also considered himself a fine horseman, but despite that, today his mount was proving difficult to control.

The flock of people around the prone knight grew thicker, and then a couple of them emerged, bearing the fallen warrior away on a litter. The crowd found this highly amusing and applauded their efforts despite the lack of movement on Sir Nathan's part.

Sir Hendrick, the other combatant, rode towards Ludwig with his visor up, his face revealing his anguish. "'Twas a bad hit," he confessed. "I'm afraid my lance was ill-placed, and it struck him low. I fear the wound is mortal."

"Have they no Life Mages here?" asked Ludwig.

Sir Hendrick looked at Brother Vernan with a nod. "The brother would know better than I." The knight rode off in sorrow.

Ludwig looked at his temporary squire for an explanation.

"I myself am a healer," the man began, "but only in the conventional sense. The art of Life Magic is a rare gift, and those who have it are in high demand amongst the courts of the Continent."

Ludwig watched the litter carry the wounded man past him. "And Sir Nathan?"

"I'm afraid his fate rests with the Saints now."

Ludwig was stricken by an image of himself, lying on the ground, dying from blood loss and a broken back. He wanted to cry out about the unfairness of life, but part of him admitted it was his own fault. He had ignored Kurt's warnings, blustering his way through all his objections. Now he was going to die.

He scanned the crowd, desperate to find an official to end this madness, but it was too late. A horn sounded, and his opponent, Sir Galrath, trotted onto the field.

Ludwig swallowed, then urged his mount forward, taking up a position at the opposite end of the field, Brother Vernan at his side. His opponent halted, dipping his head in acknowledgement to the official, then held out his hand. A squire brought forth his helmet, and the great knight donned it, leaving the visor open.

Ludwig felt his own doom circling above him, yet something inside him made him go through the motions. He took his helmet, placing it on his head, then held out his hands as Galrath was doing. Brother Vernan handed him a lance.

"Any advice?" Ludwig asked.

"Aim high," replied the lay brother. "The tip has a tendency to dip as you strike.

Ludwig flipped his visor down, then held on for dear life. He now had a lance in his right hand, and a shield and reins in the other, a most awkward situation and one for which he was ill-prepared. Again he cursed himself for his own stupidity.

An official stepped forward with a small flag raised above his head, holding it still for just a moment, then dramatically sweeping it down.

Sir Galrath burst into a gallop, surprising Ludwig with the suddenness of his response. Digging in deep with his spurs, Ludwig forced his own horse to rush forward, the ground thundering with the sound of hooves. As Galrath drew closer, Ludwig noticed his foe's lance was aimed straight at him. Cursing, Ludwig realized he had forgotten to lower his own weapon and quickly let it drop into place. The action felt unbalanced, and he struggled to keep his shield steady while at the same time controlling his horse. Then came the moment of impact.

Ludwig's lance glanced off Sir Galrath's arm, but the older knight's weapon struck true, hitting the dead centre of Ludwig's chest. After the impact of the initial punch, the next thing he knew, he was flying through the air, and then his back struck the mud, the wind knocked from him. There he lay for a few moments, struggling for breath. His visor was opened, and he saw Brother Vernan staring down at him, mouthing words.

Ludwig waited for the ringing in his ears to cease for Brother Vernan's words to make sense. "Are you all right?" the lay brother was asking.

"I'm fine. I only had the wind knocked out of me." He held out his arm, and Brother Vernan took it, helping him to his feet. "My horse?"

"Someone is fetching it," said the Holy Brother. "Come, let's get that helmet off your head."

Ludwig fumbled with the straps, then removed the helm, shaking his head to clear it. The spectators, appreciative of his efforts, clapped, although he detected little enthusiasm. The official with the flag approached.

"Are you able to continue?" he asked.

"I am," said Ludwig.

The man turned back to the crowd. "Three points to Sir Galrath," he announced.

Ludwig made his way to the end of the field where someone stood by with his horse. He was about to climb into the saddle when Brother Vernan grabbed his arm.

"Are you sure about this?"

"I'm fine," Ludwig insisted.

The Holy Brother peered into his eyes. "You don't look it." He raised his hand, pointing to the sky. "Keep your eyes on my finger, but don't move your head." He moved his hand from left to right, then back again. "You're fine," he announced. "Merely shaken up a bit."

Ludwig returned to the saddle, feeling an ache in his back. At the other end, his opponent had removed his helmet and was taking a sip from a chalice. His break complete, he returned the cup, then replaced his helm and pulled down the visor.

"I shall pray for you," offered Brother Vernan.

Ludwig lowered his own visor, then took a new lance offered by the lay brother. The flag was raised once more, and Ludwig held his breath, gripping the lance tightly. As the flag came down, he dug in his spurs, and his horse responded, charging forward. It quickly built up momentum, closing the distance rapidly, but this time he was prepared. Down came his lance, hovering at chest level, his eyes locked on his target.

He felt his lance strike Sir Galrath's shield, then deflect off to the side.

The force of the impact tore the lance from Ludwig's grip, and he cursed aloud at his misfortune. Sir Galrath's lance, meanwhile, struck him in the shield, driving Ludwig back in the saddle. This time, however, he managed to keep his seat, but his foe's weapon splintered, sending shards of wood flying off into the air.

His horse slowed, and Ludwig turned, pleased with the results. That pleasure soon turned to despair as the herald announced Sir Galrath the winner.

Ludwig trotted back to Brother Vernan. "I don't understand."

"It's pretty simple, really," explained the lay brother. "You were unseated during the initial pass, granting Sir Galrath three points, while you received none."

"But I struck him this time."

"True, and that netted you a point, but his lance shattered, and that's worth two, winning him the match."

"These rules aren't fair."

"That said, you agreed to them when you entered, did you not?"

Ludwig was crestfallen. "I did."

"Then you must learn to be gracious in defeat."

"That's easy for you to say. You're not the loser here."

"Come now," said Brother Vernan. "Sir Galrath approaches."

Ludwig tore off his helmet and watched as his opponent drew closer.

"You did well," said the knight. "Far better than I expected, to be honest."

"I suppose you want the ransom now," said Ludwig, his voice betraying his disappointment.

"We can discuss that later. You should have someone look you over. You took quite a tumble earlier."

"I'm fine," said Ludwig. "It'll take more than a fall from the saddle to put me out of action."

"I shall seek you out this evening, and we can discuss the matter of your ransom."

"I look forward to it," said Ludwig, though he despised the very thought. "Good day, Sir Knight."

"And to you," said Sir Galrath, trotting off to leave Ludwig and the Holy Brother alone.

"It is time to part," said Brother Vernan, "for I must return to my duties, and you must prepare your ransom."

"I'm afraid I lack the funds to pay."

"Then you shall have to forfeit your goods. It is a matter of honour."

"How then am I to feed myself?"

"It is a question, to be sure. Perhaps you should seek employment with one of the free companies?"

"What's a free company?"

"A band of mercenaries," replied Brother Vernan. "They're fairly common in these parts. I expect if you walk around, you'll find two or three represented here at the tournament."

"Do they joust?"

"Saints, no, they're commoners. The only thing they can enter is the grand melee or the archery competition. Have you ever taken up the bow?"

"I can use one," admitted Ludwig, "but I wouldn't stand a chance against a professional."

"A pity. It might have provided you with some extra coins."

"What of this grand melee?"

"You'd need armour for that, and you just lost yours, remember?"

Ludwig felt utterly drained of energy. He had been a fool, and now he was paying the price. Having lost his very first tournament, who'd hire him now?

"Thank you for your assistance, Brother Vernan. It was greatly appreciated."

"You're quite welcome." He paused a moment, possibly seeing the indecision on Ludwig's face. "What will you do now?"

"I shall take my lumps, as befitting the foolish choices I've made."

"In that case, I wish you well. Know that Saint Mathew watches over you, Sir Ludwig. Keep the faith, and he will provide."

"I wish I could believe you."

Brother Vernan smiled. "It is not me who you must believe in, but rather yourself. I sense a great future for you, my friend, but only if you can overcome your own fears."

"I shall take your words under advisement."

"See that you do. Now, I must be off. Come and see me later, if you wish to talk."

"Where would I find you?"

"The mission," replied the lay brother. "Ask anyone hereabouts, and they can give you directions." He left, leaving Ludwig alone with his thoughts.

"Move along," said an official. "The next contestants are coming in."

"Sorry," mumbled Ludwig. He urged his horse into a canter, leaving the field to seek out his tent.

Most of the other contestants were watching the competition, leaving him to wander the camp alone. His thoughts drifted back to the woman who had stolen his heart, and he wondered how she fared. Did it take long to become a Temple Knight? Perhaps he should consider it himself?

Ludwig's thoughts were interrupted by a warrior standing in the middle of the road as he adjusted his belt, leaving scant room for Ludwig to pass.

"Out of the way," he ordered.

The man looked up, revealing the face of a youth. "In a moment."

Ludwig shook his head, for the voice was obviously that of a female.

"For Saint's sake," the woman cursed. Clearly she was having trouble with her buckle, but Ludwig had little concern for such things.

"Can't you do that elsewhere?" he demanded, a sharp tone to his words.

"Hold on to your horse," came the reply.

"Do you know who I am?"

"No, nor do I care. You don't own this road"—she looked around—"not that it's much of a road."

"I have the right of way."

"What makes you figure that?"

"I am a knight," he announced. "Sir Ludwig of..." He struggled to remember his false identity.

She finished fiddling with her belt and looked up at him, hands on hips. "Having trouble with your memory, are you?"

"That's none of your concern," he snapped. "The fact of the matter is I'm clearly a knight, and you should show proper respect."

"Respect has to be earned."

"Just get out of the way, woman."

"Woman, is it now? Didn't anyone ever teach you manners?"

"Who do you think you are, lecturing me?"

"Me? My name's Cyn."

"Cyn? What kind of a name is that?"

"It's short for Cynthia. I'm a mercenary."

Ludwig was overcome with amusement. "You? A mercenary? Don't make me laugh."

She stepped closer, moving to the side of Ludwig's horse. "You think that's funny?"

He stared down at her. "You don't look much like a warrior to me."

"And how many warriors do you know?"

Ludwig waved his hand, indicating the nearby tents. "Look around. This place is filled with them."

Cyn took a quick glance. "Those are nothing but the spoiled sons of nobles. They wouldn't know a battle from a privy."

Ludwig turned in the saddle, bending lower to make sure she heard him properly. "You should watch your tongue. It could get you into trouble."

"Trouble, is it?" She reached out with lightning quickness, grasping his forearm and pulling him from the saddle. He landed in the mud with a splash.

"It's not me who should be minding my manners," she added.

He stared up at her, unable to come to terms with his present circumstance. "How did you do that?"

"Merely something I picked up in Braymoor."

"Never heard of the place."

"It's one of the northern kingdoms. Now, have you something to say to me?"

"I'm sorry?"

"There, that wasn't so difficult, was it?" She extended her hand. "Here, let me help you up."

He took the offer, getting to his feet.

"You're obviously new here."

"I am," he confessed.

"I'm guessing you lost your first fight."

"How did you know that? Were you watching?"

"No, but the mud on your armour speaks volumes."

He felt his face burn with shame.

"Don't worry," she said. "It'll get better. Few knights win their first competition."

"It's not only that," said Ludwig. "I lost my armour."

"Not necessarily," she said, "just pay your ransom. It's bound to be cheaper in the long run."

"I lack the funds."

"Well, don't look at me. I scarcely have enough for drinks at the Hammer."

"The Hammer?"

"It's a big tent over yonder, a makeshift tavern of sorts, where a lot of the competitors go to drink." She paused for a moment, looking him over. "Well, maybe not your lot, but it's good enough for us common folk. Then again, if you've lost everything in a joust, perhaps you are one of us now. I tell you what, if I see you over at the Hammer, I'll buy you a drink. How's that sound?"

"I'm already spoken for," said Ludwig.

"I wasn't offering anything other than a drink. Shame on you."

"Sorry, this is all so overwhelming."

"I'd love to stay and chat, but I've got to meet Siggy."

"Siggy?"

"Yes, a good friend of mine."

"And is she a mercenary as well?"

Cyn laughed. "Yes, as a matter of fact, HE is."

"Siggy's a man?"

"Yes, his real name is Sigwulf, and only I get to call him Siggy, but I've already said too much. I'm late now, thanks to you."

Ludwig managed a nod of his head. "Then good day to you, Mistress Cynthia."

She managed a clumsy curtsy that looked ludicrous in her armour. "And a good day to you, Sir Knight."

Ludwig climbed back into the saddle and sat still, thinking things over. He would soon find himself bereft of his trappings, and with few coins to his name, what was he to do? His spurs kicked back, urging his mount forward while he pondered his situation. He hated admitting it, but Kurt had been right all along.

His tent soon came into view, but it was not what he had expected, for the poles that held the top in place had failed, leaving little more than ripped canvas and broken wood.

Ludwig dismounted and tied off his horse, then meandered over to examine the ruins, but there was little that could be salvaged from the remains.

He cleared away some debris, exposing the pallet that served as his bed. Miraculously it was dry, and he gave a silent prayer of thanks to the Saints. Taking a seat, he began pulling off his gauntlets, tossing them to the ground, no longer concerned about their upkeep. If Sir Galrath were to take his armour, then to the Afterlife with them.

Ludwig sat for some time. Off in the distance, he heard the roars of the crowd, but each cheer reminded him of his own disgrace. Slowly, he unbuckled his vambraces, then began the laborious task of removing the rest of his armour. It was a difficult task without an assistant, and he briefly thought of seeking out Brother Vernan, but the Holy Man had been quite insistent he was needed elsewhere.

So slow was his progress that it was mid-morning by the time he was done. He stared at his sword, fondly remembering the day he had received it. It had been a gift from his father, but it was the dark-haired woman who had delivered it that had caught his attention.

"Charlaine," he muttered, feeling the word caress his mouth. He had known a few women in his time, but she was the only one who had somehow captured his heart. His relationship with her had led to his current circumstance, yet, try as he might, he couldn't fault her. He knew, deep inside, he would carry her memory with him for the rest of his life. The thought gave him a sense of satisfaction. He stood, taking in the discarded armour.

"This won't do," he said. "What would Charlaine think?" He began picking it up.

4

RANSOM

Spring 1095 SR

S ir Galrath arrived late in the afternoon, walking right up to what was left of the tent and looking around at the mess.

"It appears your pavilion has seen better days," he remarked.

"So it has," replied Ludwig. "But you have not come to comment on my tent, but to collect my ransom."

Sir Galrath rubbed his hands together. "I have indeed."

"Then you may take it, Sir Knight."

"Gladly will I relieve you of your purse, Sir Ludwig, but I see no sign of it."

Ludwig pointed at the armour, laying neatly on the nearby pallet. "It's there."

Sir Galrath frowned. "I was hoping for coins."

"I am afraid I lack the funds to comply with your request."

"Come now, surely you have a little? What if I were to reduce the ransom to, say, five hundred crowns?"

"Five hundred or five, it makes little difference, for I have neither."

The knight's face fell. "Are you saying you're penniless?"

"I have enough for one more meal, two if I'm lucky."

"Had I known, I would have refused to countenance the match."

"It's my own fault, Sir Galrath. I let my pride get the better of me. Take my belongings. It's only right."

"Your horse I'll take, for I can always use a spare, but what am I to do with your armour? It definitely wouldn't fit me."

"Then sell it and receive the coins you covet."

The older knight wandered over to stare down at the neatly laid-out armour. He picked up a piece, examining its workmanship. "This is fine work."

"Yes, made by my father's smith, though I daresay his weapons were not as ornate."

Sir Galrath lay down the piece, selecting Ludwig's sword in its place. He pulled it from the scabbard and held it before him, examining the blade. "You say his weapons were not decorative, yet this blade says otherwise."

"That weapon was made by another, a smith from the town of Malburg."

"I've never heard of the place, but this sword is the work of a master. How did you come by it?"

"It was a present from my father."

"He must be extremely fond of you. Does he still live?"

"As far as I know. He and I are estranged."

Sir Galrath placed the sword back in the scabbard and set it down with great care. "Come, let us talk."

"Aren't we already talking?"

"Look, it's clear you're on your last legs here. What will you do now?"

"I have no idea," said Ludwig. "I had thought to compete further, maybe in the melee, but with no weapon or armour, I cannot."

"What if I left you something?"

"What are you suggesting?"

"I'll take your horse, but leave you your sword and a bit of armour as well."

"How much armour?"

"The padded doublet that goes beneath the plate, a helmet, and maybe even the breastplate. The rest I'll attempt to sell, although it pains me to do so."

Relief flooded through Ludwig. "Thank you," he said. "I shall not forget this kindness."

"There's a further price, however."

"Which is?"

"You must promise to never enter the joust again."

Ludwig laughed. "I promise."

"Good. Now, have you any ale?"

"No."

"Then let us go and find some so you can drown your sorrows."

"But I have so few coins as it is."

"Fear not," said Sir Galrath, "for you are not the only knight I have vanquished this day." He patted the purse which hung from his belt. "And unlike you, the other contestants were amply financed."

Ludwig swept his eyes over what was left of his camp. "What about the armour?"

"Don't worry, I'll send someone by later to take care of it. Now come. A drink will do you well, I'd wager."

The Hammer was nothing more than a tent with kegs nestled beneath the canvas, while the majority of the patrons sat outside, soaking up the occasional ray of sun that poked its head through the clouds. Several wooden benches had been laid out alongside some rough-hewn logs that served as tables. Sir Galrath took a seat, then motioned for Ludwig to do likewise.

"A couple of ales, Millie," he called out.

"This is quite the place."

"Yes," said the knight. "I suppose it is."

They waited as the barmaid brought them two flagons, then drank deeply.

Sir Galrath placed his cup on the table, gazing across at Ludwig. "You mentioned a place called Malburg earlier. Is that where you're from?"

"Not quite. I hail from Verfeld. It's a small village close by."

"You're obviously well-bred. Is your father a noble?"

"He is, but I really don't want to talk about him. Tell me of yourself. Did you always aspire to be a knight?"

"I did, as a matter of fact, and I am the first in my family to do so. My family have been soldiers for generations, but I'm the first to rise up to such heights."

"So you just woke up one morning and decided you wanted to be a knight?"

"Not exactly. My father taught me to ride when I was young. Once I became a man, I joined the king's army as a horseman. Of course, that was back in Talyria, before the troubles."

"Troubles?"

"Yes. When the king died, he left a young prince as his heir. The chancellor was named regent until the princeling was of age. It was at that time I was knighted."

"For guarding a prince?"

"No," said Sir Galrath, chuckling. "We had some troubles on our southern border, and then Marston invaded, thinking the young prince weak."

"So you won your spurs in battle."

"I did, though my service didn't last long. The prince died before he could be crowned. They say he was sick, but I believe he was poisoned by the chancellor. Of course, I couldn't prove it. Things got exceedingly uncomfortable for me after that."

"What happened to the chancellor?"

"He still rules. He's given up pretending to be a chancellor, calling himself king instead. That's when I decided to leave."

Ludwig took another swig, finishing his cup. "How long ago was this?"

"Just over five years. I've been travelling the circuit ever since, competing for coins."

"But you serve the earl here, don't you?"

"I do," said Sir Galrath. "It puts a roof over my head and food in my belly, but doesn't offer much in the way of funds."

"Are you successful at it? Jousting, that is."

"I've made a fair sum, but I can't say I would recommend it as a way of life."

"Why not?"

"Age catches up with all of us, Ludwig, and there's always someone ready to take your place. You'd do better to find yourself a wealthy benefactor."

"How about you? I could work as your squire?"

"I admire your pluck, but I already have one, and in any case, I couldn't see myself having a noble's son as a squire, can you?"

"No, I suppose not."

Sir Galrath noted his empty cup and called out for two more. "You know," he said, "you should enter the melee."

"Why? So I can lose even more?"

"No, it doesn't work like that. They don't charge an entry fee."

"That means anyone can fight?" said Ludwig.

"That's right, it does, but knights see it as beneath them. After all, we have appearances to keep up. Good thing, too, not many people have weapons that could penetrate our armour."

"Tell me more about how the melee works. Is it fought in rounds like the jousting?"

Sir Galrath watched as Millie dropped two more tankards on the table. He tossed her a coin, then took a sip, leaving Ludwig waiting.

"Well?" pressed the younger man.

"Well, what?" said the knight.

"You were going to tell me about the melee?"

"Ah, yes, the grand melee. It's quite a sight to see, let me tell you. All the contestants are led onto the field, and then it's last man standing."

"All of them?" said Ludwig. "Isn't there a limit?"

"Only by the number of competitors. The largest I've ever heard tell of was last year, in a place called Lonkirk over in Eversham. Are you familiar with the place?"

"Can't say I am. How many contestants were there?"

"I've heard conflicting accounts, but rumour has it there were well over a hundred."

"Do you suppose there'll be that many here, in Torburg?"

"No," said Sir Galrath. "This is a much smaller affair. I would be surprised if there were more than forty."

"Still," said Ludwig, "a lot of people to beat. How do they manage?"

"You make temporary alliances," offered the knight. "Stand shoulder to shoulder with them, understanding that eventually, you'll have to fight each other."

"And people truly do that?"

"They have to. It's the only way to get through it. It's also an extremely demanding trial, far more difficult than using a lance. Not only do you have to attack, but you have to defend as well. How's your swordplay?"

"I would have said excellent, but after the thrashing you gave me today, I shouldn't be so sure of myself."

"Nonsense. You did well."

"You unhorsed me on the first try," said Ludwig. "In what sense did I do well?"

"You came back and scored a point. That shows you think on your feet... or maybe your back." Galrath chuckled. "Either way, you stood your ground, and that's something to be proud of."

"I appreciate you saying so, but it doesn't feel like it."

"I know you're down on yourself right now, Ludwig, but you'll get over it. I did."

"You lost your first competition?"

"Of course," said Sir Galrath. "My first five, if the truth be known. Jousting isn't easy, by any means. First, you have to control your horse while the enemy thunders towards you. Next, you have to keep your shield well-placed, or you can suffer a serious hit. Lastly, you have to balance the twelve-foot pole we call a lance."

"You mastered it."

"Only after making many mistakes. Tell me, why did you want to compete?"

"To gain notice," admitted Ludwig.

"To what end?"

"I'm not sure what you mean?"

"I mean," continued the knight, "what type of notice did you seek? Are you in it for the glory, or are you looking to gain employment with a noble?"

"The latter."

"Then jousting is a poor way to go about it."

"But jousting is the most popular contest."

"It is," admitted Sir Galrath, "but it does little to showcase battlefield skills. If you want to seek employment as a knight, you need to show how well you can do in an actual battle."

"You mean go to war?"

"Precisely."

"And how do I do that?"

"Well, admittedly, this region is peaceful of late, but you know the Petty Kingdoms. It won't take long for old disagreements to surface once again. Keep your eyes open, Ludwig. There's bound to be employment sooner or later."

"And in the meantime?"

"Earn a little to keep you going. Entering the melee is a good start."

"I thought of that," said Ludwig, "but others are likely to be far more experienced."

"Winning the melee isn't about fighting ability, not entirely, at least. A lot of it's about strategy. Try to pick out the weaker opponents and let the veterans take care of each other."

"And if someone comes after me?"

"Parry, parry, and then parry some more. It's all about outlasting your opponent. Have you a shield?"

"Not anymore. You took mine."

"Ah, yes," said the knight. He paused for a moment, evidently thinking things through. "I tell you what, I'll lend it back to you. If you do well, then you can keep it."

"Don't I have to win to get coins?"

"No, not at all. They award prizes to the top three competitors."

"How does that help you?"

Sir Galrath smiled. "I'll place a wager or two. Who knows, you might even make me a wealthy man."

"Not if you're betting on ME."

The knight drained his cup, then stood. "Much as I'd like to continue this discussion, I said I'd check in on poor Sir Nathan. He took quite a hit this morning. Good luck in the melee, Ludwig. I'll keep an eye out for you."

Ludwig raised his tankard. "Thank you." He watched Sir Galrath leave, then turned his attention back to his own drink, staring into it as he tried to think things through. Could he survive long enough to win something in the melee? This morning he would have had no doubt, but his experiences in the lists had shaken his confidence. He shrugged off his fears, then lifted the tankard to his lips, pouring the rough ale down his throat.

Millie appeared as soon as he set down his cup. He noticed the drink in her hand.

"No, thank you," he said. "I've had my fill."

"This one's free," she said.

"Free?"

"Yes"—Millie nodded at a distant table—"courtesy of her."

Ludwig looked over to see the woman he had encountered earlier. Her dark hair reminded him of Charlaine, but while his love had long hair, this woman's was short and cut to fit beneath a helm. Charlaine had joined the Temple Knights of Saint Agnes and he now wondered if she, too, now wore her hair in a similar manner. His musing faltered as he remembered the serving girl waiting for an answer. He looked up at her.

"You can leave it here."

Millie placed it on the table, retrieving the empty cups. "Is there anything else?"

"No, thank you."

Off she went, back to the waiting patrons, leaving Ludwig alone with his thoughts once more. He cast his eyes around, wondering which of these patrons he might face in the melee. They were, for the most part, rather common. Sir Galrath had cut a fine figure as a knight, but these others were clearly cut from a different cloth. Indeed, their clothes revealed their more modest upbringings.

A shadow loomed over him, and he looked up to see a giant of a man with a bushy brown beard standing to his side.

"Can I help you?"

"Are you Ludwig," boomed the voice of the newcomer.

"Yes. What of it?"

"My name is Sigwulf."

"Should that mean something to me?"

In answer, the giant looked across the room to the dark-haired woman. She shrugged and then got to her feet and started making her way to the table.

Sigwulf moved to the other side, taking what had been Sir Galrath's seat. "I hear you were in the joust," he said.

"I was," said Ludwig with a wince. "Did you see it?"

"No, but I heard you lost."

"Well, that part, at least, is true."

Cyn appeared at the table, giving Ludwig's memory a jog. "Ah, yes," he said, "now I remember." He turned to the giant. "You're Siggy."

Sigwulf's face reddened. "No one calls me that except her."

Now it was Ludwig's turn to blush. "Sorry, I meant no offence."

"Cyn tells me you were pretty rude to her earlier."

"For which I apologized."

The big man grunted, leaving Ludwig wondering what it meant.

"I see you met Siggy," said Cyn, obviously enjoying his discomfort.

"I did," said Ludwig.

"So, have you lost any more competitions yet?"

"No, I'm still recovering from my first failure, though I do intend to enter the melee." He wasn't sure why he was telling her this, but he couldn't help himself. Perhaps he was only lonely.

"The melee?" said Sigwulf, with a chuckle. "You're too scrawny to do that."

Cyn smacked him on the arm. "Don't be rude, Siggy. He's a knight." She turned to Ludwig. "Isn't that right, Sir Ludwig?"

"Yes," said Ludwig, "though my name is not well-known."

"Not well-known?" added the big man. "That's an understatement. Tell me about yourself, Sir Ludwig. You came from Garmund, didn't you? What's that like?"

Ludwig's nerve began to falter. He felt intimidated but held his ground. "It's on the way to Corassus."

"Is it, now? I'm quite well-informed in regards to the Petty Kingdoms. Where, precisely, is it?"

"As I said, between here and Corassus."

Sigwulf leaned back, crossing his arms. "Sure it is."

Ludwig found his irritation mounting. He was not used to being treated like this. "What does it matter to you, anyway?"

"I'm not a big fan of people who misrepresent themselves."

Sweat started to bead on Ludwig's forehead, so he changed subjects. "Where are you from?"

"Me?" said Sigwulf. "I hail from Abel... I mean Braymoor."

The slip grabbed Ludwig's attention. Now it was his turn to sit back and cross his arms with a smug look. "Oh, yes? Braymoor, you say?"

The tactic worked. The man visibly paled.

"Look," said Ludwig. "You keep to your story, and I'll keep to mine, agreed?"

Sigwulf nodded.

"Well, now that you two are done," said Cyn, "what brings you to the Hammer?"

"Just this," said Ludwig, lifting his tankard.

"Who was that I saw you with earlier?"

Ludwig felt the affront. He wanted to lie or tell her it was none of her business, but there was something to that penetrating look that told him he wouldn't get away with it. "Sir Galrath," he said at last.

"Isn't he the one who beat you?" she said.

"Indeed."

"An interesting turn of events. Tell me, are you still determined to enter the melee?"

Ludwig thought it over once more, but his eyes tracked to Sigwulf. The man was easily a head taller and significantly broader in the shoulders. "Not if he's in it."

The giant barked out a laugh. "Me? Enter the melee? I think not!"

Relief flooded over Ludwig. "In that case, I'm in. Why?"

"I'm entering myself," said Cyn. "Maybe we can work together?"

"Why would I do that?"

"It helps to have allies."

"But you're a woman." As soon as the words left his lips, he realized his mistake.

"You don't know Cyn," offered Sigwulf.

"I tell you what," said Cyn. "Why don't you come by our camp tomorrow morning and watch me practice? Maybe you'll learn a thing or two."

Sigwulf smiled. "Unless you have something better to do?"

Ludwig shrugged. "I might as well. I've nothing else to pass the time."

Cyn was obviously upset by the slight, but Siggy put his massive hand on hers. "Good, then we'll see you tomorrow. Now, let's drink!"

5

MERCENARIES

Spring 1095 SR

With his tent in shambles, Ludwig had no choice but to wake with the morning sun. Stumbling out of bed, he squinted up at the sky where the clouds that had plagued them for days had finally drifted off, revealing a pristine blue horizon.

Still half-awake, he fumbled with his clothes and then pulled out his few remaining coins. For the first time in his life, Ludwig Altenburg had to consider the cost of a meal and what it would do to his remaining funds.

To make matters worse, someone within the tent lines was cooking sausages, and the smell caused his stomach to grumble. He picked up his waterskin, determined to fill it at a stream. If he was lucky, he could grab some bread for a few pennies, and that should be sufficient to hold his hunger at bay.

Ludwig's wanderings took him some distance from the tournament, but he finally managed to find a babbling brook winding its way through a small copse of trees. He knelt down to fill the waterskin, then caught his reflection.

Staring back at him was an unkempt ruffian he barely recognized. His hand automatically went to his face, feeling the stubble. When he was at home, he had shaved regularly, a mark of his civilized nature. Here, however, he felt no such compunction and, if truth be known, had thought it gave him a roguish countenance. Now, however, he came to the realization he looked more like an escaped galley slave than a debonair adventurer.

He splashed some water onto his face, trying to wash the image from his memory, but it persisted. Was he losing his mind? If he kept going as he was, he would soon be a pauper, begging on the streets for scraps of food.

His thoughts drifted back to the previous evening. He had drunk deeply, probably more so than he should have, and his head suddenly screamed for more. Instead, he dipped the waterskin into the stream and began filling it, turning his mind to thoughts of Charlaine. He wondered what her training would be like. Did Temple Knights undergo the same kind of weapons training Kurt had given him? He doubted it. The Temple Knights were said to be the most disciplined warriors on the Continent. She would not be wallowing in misery as he was.

Suddenly he was struck by the thought that, in joining the order, she was displaying more nobility of character than he was despite her common birth. Ludwig stood, capping his waterskin. If Charlaine could prosper in her new life, then he must do no less. He started making his way back to camp, resolved to get his life in order.

He passed a knight who was out in the field practicing runs with a lance. His squire had placed a simple wooden post with a square of wood atop it, and the horseman was galloping back and forth, attempting to hit it dead centre. It reminded him of his promise to visit the mercenaries, so he altered course, steering for the open fields off to the east where he spotted the distant smoke of campfires.

The mercenary camp was nothing like he expected. Instead of a ragtag bunch of wild men, he found a haphazard arrangement of tents guarded by alert sentinels. As soon as he drew near, they challenged him, but the mention of Cyn's name allowed him passage. He wandered through the camp to an open area in its centre. This had been a farmer's field at some time in the past, for it was bordered by the remains of a wooden fence on which leaned Sigwulf, who was watching Cyn spar with an opponent, while other pairs practiced their techniques nearby.

Ludwig moved closer, leaning on the fence like his new acquaintance, his gaze drifting to the fight beyond.

"You're up early," said Sigwulf, keeping his eye on Cyn. The woman was using a mace and shield, but her jacket surprised him.

"Shouldn't she be wearing armour?"

Sigwulf chuckled. "She is. It's a brigandine—there are metal plates sewn into it. Not as good as plate, mind you, but better than nothing."

"She's quick on her feet. Has she been at it long?"

"Ever since she was little."

Now it was Ludwig's time to laugh. "No, I meant today."

Sigwulf grinned. "Aye, she's been at it since breakfast."

Ludwig's stomach growled, causing the big man to look at him.

"Have you eaten?"

"I haven't had time," said Ludwig. "I had to get this." He held up the waterskin.

"Well, we can't have you fighting on an empty stomach." Sigwulf turned, nodding in the direction of a nearby fire. "Get yourself over there and tell Dorkin I sent you. He'll take care of you."

"Thank you," said Ludwig. "I don't mind if I do." He began making his way over to the fire.

"And eat well," called out Sigwulf. "You'll need your energy if you're going to be fighting Cyn."

The smoke of the campfire drifted closer, bringing with it the smell of fresh bacon.

"Are you Dorkin?" asked Ludwig.

An old warrior looked up from where he crouched, tending the fire. "That's me. Did Sig send you?"

"He did."

The man fetched a wooden bowl and then used a knife to pick out some bacon strips from the pan and handed it to Ludwig. Next, he cut off some bread from a nearby loaf, dropping it into the grease.

"What are you doing?" asked Ludwig.

"Have you never had barn bread before?"

"Can't say I have. What is it?"

"We take older loaves and cook up slices in bacon fat."

"How does it taste?"

"Greasy, as you might expect," said Dorkin, "but it'll help fill you. Care to try some?"

In answer, Ludwig held out his bowl. He watched the bread begin to sizzle, then the cook used his knife to deftly flip it over. All the while, the smell of bacon set Ludwig's mouth to watering. He picked out a strip from the bowl, popping it into his mouth. Dorkin had cooked it lightly, making it somewhat chewy. The pig that sacrificed itself was likely old, the meat tough, but the taste was like manna from the Saints.

He swallowed down the bacon, then watched as Dorkin fished out the barn bread, dropping it into his bowl.

"Make sure you use your knife," said the old man. "It gets fairly messy."

"Tell me, why is it called barn bread?"

"They say it was invented by mercenaries who were low on food. All they had was three-day-old bread and some stringy rations of bacon."

"I'm not sure I see the connection," said Ludwig.

"They were holed up in a barn at the time, you see?"

"Now I understand." He withdrew his own knife, stabbing the bread and lifting it to his nose for a tentative sniff. "It smells like bacon."

Dorkin looked incensed. "What else would it smell like? Fish?"

Ludwig took a bite, feeling the grease dribble onto his stubbled chin. It warmed him, and the taste was incredible, leading him to smile as he ate.

"What did I tell you?" said Dorkin.

"How old is the bread?"

"Five days or so."

"You wouldn't know it," said Ludwig. He scarfed down the rest, then finished off his remaining strips of bacon. "I feel full," he announced, "though admittedly a little thirsty."

"The bacon is salted. You'll get used to it in time."

"Oh, I'm not joining the company. I'm just visiting it."

"Sure you are," said Dorkin. "You just haven't realized it yet."

Ludwig set down the bowl. "Thank you for the food. I suppose I must now go and earn it." He wandered back over to the fence where Sigwulf and Cyn were chatting.

The big man turned to their new visitor. "All set now?"

"I am," said Ludwig, "thanks to that cook of yours."

Cyn laughed. "He's not a cook, he's a mercenary."

"He's tending the fire. I naturally assumed…"

"Everyone in this company fights," said Sigwulf, "and we all take turns cooking. It just happens to be Dorkin's turn today."

"Well," said Cyn, "I can't stand here and talk all day. I need to practice if I want to win the melee." She donned her helmet, picked up her mace and shield, then strode back into the field where her opponent waited.

"You know," said Ludwig, "I don't believe I've ever watched a woman fight before."

"She's not much different than a man when it comes to battle," offered Sigwulf, "but she tends to be a little more nimble than most."

They watched her spar for a while as the sun grew higher, the day turning warmer. Ludwig could feel the sweat building under his arms.

When Cyn took a break, Sigwulf turned to him. "Well? What did you think?"

"Not bad," said Ludwig, "but she gives away her moves."

"I'm not sure what you're saying?"

"If you watch her footwork, you can predict when she's going to attack. She also lets her guard down when she strikes."

"She's beaten all her opponents," said Sigwulf.

"No doubt, but she's likely familiar with their weaknesses. Does she always practice with the same people?"

"She does."

"There you have it, then. She needs fresh blood."

"Do you believe you can beat her?"

"I can give it a try," said Ludwig, "but I didn't bring my gear."

Sigwulf moved aside, revealing a half-dozen swords leaning against the railing. "Pick one," he said.

"What's this, now?"

"These are blunted swords like they use in the melee. After all, the competitors aren't trying to kill each other."

"A blunt weapon can still kill someone," said Ludwig.

"True, but it lessens the odds."

"Odds?" Ludwig said. "What a strange thing to say. I didn't take you for someone with an education."

"What makes you guess I'm educated?"

"Your turn of phrase. You come across as somewhat of a barbarian, but you speak as if you've been raised at court."

"Perhaps I should play the fool," said Sigwulf.

"It's not a criticism, merely an observation."

"Are you going to fight Cyn or not?"

"I am," said Ludwig.

"Then choose your weapon. One of these must be suitable. Do you prefer one or two-handed?"

Ludwig looked them over, finally selecting a sword with a three-foot blade. He swung it around experimentally, then nodded his head. "This one will do."

"Did you bring your armour?"

Ludwig frowned. "I'm afraid not. The truth is, I didn't even remember I was coming here till I was out of camp."

"Not to worry, we have spares." Sigwulf nodded at a pile of jackets. "Pick yourself out a gambeson."

Ludwig moved over to the jackets and fished through them. They were a motley collection of long-sleeved, padded jackets, all in various states of disrepair. Many had cuts and tears while others were stained dark by blood. He selected one that looked like it might fit and began pulling it on. Once dressed, he turned to Sigwulf, who tossed him a helmet.

"Do you use a shield?"

"I do," said Ludwig.

Sigwulf moved farther down the fence, retrieving a shield. He returned, handing it over.

"This is wooden," said Ludwig. "Have you no shields of steel?"

"Not for you," said Sigwulf.

"We save them for battle," called out Cyn. "Now, are you ready to fight me, or are you just going to stand there and chat with Siggy all day?"

Ludwig moved away from the fence and took up a defensive position, his sword in middle guard, his shield held to his front.

Cyn moved in quickly, using her shield to deflect his sword while her mace struck out against his own shield. Stunned by the speed of the attack, Ludwig backed up.

"Come on," she urged. "Show a little spirit."

He took a breath, then advanced, remembering his training. Cyn's attacks were quick, but he soon realized they lacked strength. By watching her feet, he could predict her movements, and soon he was winning each bout. She shifted her tactics, relying instead on the use of her shield to bash him, even going so far as to use its edge against him. Her tactics baffled him, for he was used to the duels of court, not the 'anything goes' tactics of a real battlefield.

By the time they halted at noon, Ludwig felt utterly exhausted, but Cyn was full of energy, rushing over to Siggy, but slowing when she saw him talking to a well-dressed, older man.

"Who's that?" asked Ludwig.

"Captain Ecke," she explained, "the company commander."

"I wonder what he wants?"

Cyn smiled. "Let's go and find out, shall we?"

They made their way to the fence, but the captain left without acknowledging them.

"What was all that about?" asked Cyn.

"The captain was watching you two fight." He turned to Ludwig. "He wants to meet you."

"Well then," said Cyn. "You'd best clean yourself up, and then I'll take you there."

"You?" said Sigwulf.

"Yes," she replied. "Why not me?"

"Well, for one thing, you've been sweating all morning and could use a wash."

"Then you take him."

Sigwulf looked put out, but then smiled. "I see what you did there. Very clever."

"Oh?" said Cyn. "And what is it you think I did?"

"You manoeuvred me into taking him. That was your plan all along, wasn't it?"

In answer, she smiled. "I can't help it if I sweat while I fight!"

The office of Captain Waldemar Ecke was a simple tent, nearly the same size as a knight's pavilion, but whereas a pavilion was often decorated with furniture and carpets, Ecke's abode had little save for a pallet, chest, and a small foldable table with two stools.

The captain stood as they entered. "Sir Ludwig, good of you to agree to see me."

"I wasn't aware I had a choice," replied the young noble.

Ecke looked at Sigwulf. "It's all right, I won't be needing you." The great man bowed, then left.

"Can I offer you a drink?"

"No, thank you all the same," said Ludwig. "I'd prefer to keep my wits about me. I'm afraid I've had more than my fill in the last day or so."

The captain appeared amused. "Still feeling the effects?"

"Let's put it this way, I've learned an important lesson."

"Meaning?"

"You can't drink away your memories."

Ecke chuckled. "Many have tried. Now tell me, what do you know of the Grim Defenders?"

"Nothing much," said Ludwig, "other than the fact you're mercenaries."

"I formed this company almost a year ago. Does that surprise you?"

"I would imagine it took a lot of coins to do so."

"It did at that, and in all that time, I've never had a problem finding recruits. Do you know why?"

Ludwig took a guess. "Because there are a lot of unemployed soldiers?"

"I suppose that's true to a certain extent, but no, that's not the reason why. I handpick my people, Sir Ludwig, and they know they can trust me."

"What has that to do with me?"

"You're a knight, and I've heard you're low on funds."

"Meaning?"

"Knights are well-trained warriors, even the bad ones, just the type of man who's needed to whip others into shape. I saw you today, sparring with Cyn. You're good."

"Thank you. I had an experienced swordmaster."

"Are you proficient in other weapons?"

"I am," said Ludwig. "My training included mace and hammer, though not to the same degree. Why do you ask?"

"The sword is seldom used against a heavily armoured opponent. What of polearms? Ever use them?"

"Never," spat out Ludwig. "They're the weapons of peasants."

"I should not dismiss them out of hand if I were you. When properly employed, they can wreak havoc amongst well-armoured foes."

"Are you trying to recruit me?"

"Not at this time, no. However, do well in the melee, and I may change my mind."

"And you called me here to tell me that?"

"No," said Ecke. "I called you here to assess you. Sigwulf tells me you're entering the melee. It's important for me to know what Cyn's up against."

"Why the interest in Cyn? Surely you have other entries amongst your ranks?"

"Captain Hoffman, Cyn's father, was a good friend of mine. He led a free company called the Crossed Swords. Ever heard of them?"

"Can't say that I have," said Ludwig. "Why?"

"Last year, they were under contract to a baron in Braymoor; I shan't mention his name. After serving him for some months, the fool withheld payment, forcing them to disband. Well, as you can imagine, they were forced to ravage the countryside, looking for anything they could eat. Eventually, the king sent royal troops to restore order. Captain Hoffman was hanged, along with several others."

"Let me guess, Cyn and Sigwulf escaped."

"They did," the captain confirmed. "You see, Cyn was raised amongst the Crossed Swords, spent her whole life learning the ways of warriors. I hired them on as soon as I learned of their misfortune, so you can understand why I have a vested interest in her success. Who knows, maybe one day she'll form a mercenary band of her own."

"Or take over this one?" suggested Ludwig.

Ecke shrugged. "Perhaps. After all, I can't keep this up forever."

"If you're not recruiting me, what exactly are you proposing?"

"That I put a few coins in your purse. All you'd have to do in return is help Cyn prepare for the melee."

"But I want to compete myself!"

"Go ahead, I won't stop you. Anyway, the grand melee isn't for another two days, and I can offer you coins upfront if you're interested?"

"How much?"

In answer, the captain reached into his own purse and tossed some coins onto the table. "How's that for two day's work?"

Ludwig scooped them up. "In that case, I agree."

6

THE GRAND MELEE

Spring 1095 SR

T he Hammer was a busy place. With the grand melee only a night away, contestants were eager to drown their nerves with ale. Ludwig sat at a table, feasting on a large bowl of stew while Sigwulf and Cyn were opposite him.

He looked across at the huge man. "Are you not having a bowl?"

"No," said Sigwulf. "The bowls here are too small for my appetite."

Right as he finished, Millie arrived, depositing two bowls of stew before the man and a plate of chicken in front of Cyn.

"I thought you weren't having any?" said Ludwig.

"No," corrected Sigwulf. "You asked if I was having 'a' bowl, and I'm not. I'm having TWO." He roared out with laughter.

Cyn shook her head and started tearing the leg off her chicken. "Tell me," she said, "who taught you to fight?"

"My father hired a swordmaster named Kurt Wasser," said Ludwig. "He came highly recommended."

"Well," she replied, "he certainly earned his keep today. You surprised me with some of those techniques."

"Yes," agreed Sigwulf. "Too bad he didn't train you properly in the use of a shield."

Ludwig snorted, almost choking on his stew. He caught his breath, then continued. "I was trained for courtly duels, not actual battle. They frown on shields in such a fight."

"I'll never understand why," offered Sigwulf.

"You have to understand courtly etiquette."

"What makes you assume I don't?"

Ludwig stared at the man, trying to determine if he was being duped. "You've been to a court?"

"I have," said Sigwulf, his voice betraying no deception. "Does that surprise you?"

"It does. I didn't think mercenaries favoured such places."

"They don't, but I wasn't always a mercenary."

"You have intrigued me," said Ludwig. "Tell me, are you a noble?"

"Do I look like a noble?"

"You might if you cleaned yourself up a bit."

Sigwulf turned red. "You think I look unclean?"

"Take it as a compliment, Siggy," suggested Cyn. "I'm sure that's how it was intended. Isn't that right, Ludwig?"

"Of course. I meant no disrespect. So you served in Braymoor," continued Ludwig. "Is that where you two met?"

"It was," said Cyn. "Siggy here joined the Crossed Swords. I took a liking to him right away."

"So it was love at first sight?"

She sent a quick glance Sigwulf's way. "Not exactly. Let's just say it took a few months for him to come around."

"You can't blame me," the big man interjected. "She was the captain's daughter. That's a mite intimidating."

Cyn burst out laughing. "I still recall the time he caught us in a tent together. Do you remember?"

"I could hardly forget," said Sigwulf. "He had me on sentry duty for two months!"

Ludwig smiled. "Let me guess, he didn't approve?"

"He came around eventually," said Cyn, "but it took a lot of work."

Someone appeared behind Ludwig. He craned his neck around to see Brother Vernan, waiting patiently.

"Am I interrupting?" asked the lay brother.

"What brings you to the Hammer?" asked Ludwig.

"I was, in truth, looking for you. May I sit?"

Ludwig shuffled along the bench. "By all means."

Brother Vernan eyed the small band. "I see you've made some new friends."

"I have. Allow me to introduce you. This is Sigwulf, and this is Cyn."

"And you are?" said Cyn.

"Brother Vernan. As you can plainly see by my cassock, I am a lay brother of Saint Mathew."

"I hope you're not here to lecture us on morals," she said.

"Not at all."

"Ludwig has been helping me with my melee skills."

"Has he, now?"

"Yes," added Sigwulf. "We were just saying how he needs help with the use of his shield. I don't suppose they teach such things in your order, do they?"

"Saints, no," said Brother Vernan. "I'm not a Temple Knight, merely a lay brother. Normally I assist down at the mission in Torburg, but my fellow brothers and I are here to help with the wounded."

Ludwig swallowed a mouthful of stew. "Do Temple Knights ever participate in tournaments?"

"No, it's forbidden."

"Lucky for us," said Cyn. "I'd hate to go up against one in the melee."

"On that, we are in full agreement," said Sigwulf. "One of those Temple Knights of yours would likely defeat us all without breaking a sweat."

"Possibly a slight exaggeration," said Brother Vernan, "but not too far from the truth."

"The Temple Knights wear that expensive plate armour," said Sigwulf. "Far better than the gear we can afford."

Ludwig remembered his own armour, now mostly in the possession of Sir Galrath. He had been a fool to risk it and had ultimately paid the price. "I suppose you could always have some made?"

Sigwulf frowned. "Have you any idea how much that stuff costs? If I had that much, I could retire."

"Not to mention the nobles," added Cyn. "They don't look kindly on common folk having access to such things."

"I suppose," said Ludwig, "you could always get yourself knighted, then a wealthy patron would equip you."

Cyn raised her cup. "Now that's a thought. Here's a toast to a wealthy benefactor."

As they all raised their drinks in salute, Ludwig realized Brother Vernan had no cup. "My apologies, Brother, it seems we've forgotten you." He raised his hand, catching the attention of the server. "Two more, Millie," he called out. She nodded, then disappeared into the tent.

"Are you sure it's wise, drinking the night before the big competition?" asked the Holy Brother.

"I'm taking it slowly," explained Ludwig. "And in any case, I can't leave you to drink alone. That would be rude."

Millie soon appeared, depositing two tankards. The foam sloshed over the edge, soaking the table, but everyone ignored it.

"Here's to the grand melee," said Brother Vernan.

They all raised their cups, knocking them together and causing more ale to spill. Everyone drank deeply, then lowered their cups.

"You said you were looking for me," said Ludwig. "Was it for something specific?"

"I thought you'd wish to hear of Sir Nathan."

"And how is our gallant knight?"

"I'm afraid he passed away this afternoon."

The table fell silent.

Ludwig set down his drink. "He was alive when they carried him from the field," he said. "I'm surprised he couldn't be helped."

"He died from internal bleeding," explained Brother Vernan. "I'm afraid there was little we could do for him other than make him comfortable while life remained within him."

"A grim fate for a noble warrior," said Sigwulf. He looked at Cyn, worry on his face. "Fighting in such competitions can be particularly dangerous."

"I'll be fine," she reassured him. "I've been training for this, and anyway, it's not the first melee I've entered."

"True," replied the giant, "but it's the largest. They say there'll be more than fifty contestants tomorrow."

"More like sixty," corrected Brother Vernan. "I saw the list this very afternoon." He turned to Ludwig. "Did you decide to compete?"

"I did, although the closer we get, the more I fret over my choice. Have you any advice for us?"

"You must be vigilant," offered the Holy Brother, "and keep the faith. Saint Mathew will watch over you."

"Is that all you've got?" asked Cyn. "No disrespect, but don't the Saints watch over us all?"

"They do."

"Then how do they know who to help?"

The Holy Brother's face betrayed his confusion while everyone else broke out into fits of laughter.

"Don't worry," said Cyn, finally catching her breath. "I know you mean well."

"Are you coming to the match tomorrow?" asked Ludwig.

"Definitely," replied Brother Vernan. "I wouldn't miss it for anything."

. . .

Ludwig stared up at the sky. Rain had come overnight, drenching the field, but at last, it was clearing. He stood in line, along with Cyn, waiting to enter the competition. A rough circle had been marked off in front of the stands, a low fence denoting its perimeter. Into this area were four gaps, each crammed with contestants eager to begin.

Someone in the stands was talking, likely the duke himself, but Ludwig could make out none of his actual words. He stood on his toes, trying to see the man, but the press of warriors in his group was too tight, so he had to make do with waiting patiently.

"For Saint's sake," he cursed.

"Swearing won't do you any good," said Cyn.

"What are you, a Holy Sister or something? It makes me feel better."

She forced a smile. "In that case, keep on cursing. Not that it'll help speed up any of this."

"When are they going to start? It feels like we've been standing here the best part of the morning."

"Hush now. It won't be much longer."

A cheer erupted from the crowd, marking an end to the speeches. At the sound of a horn, their line began creeping forward. Each group started making their way onto the field, though perhaps mud pit would have been a more apt name. The grass had been worn to dirt over the course of the tournament, and the overnight shower had turned it into a boot-sucking mess.

The grand melee was an affair of honour, and competitors were required to leave the field should they fall, but with so many coins at stake, Temple Knights had been enlisted to enforce the rules. Should someone refuse to leave, they would drag the hapless fool out.

As Ludwig passed through the gate, he was finally able to see the Temple Knights up close. He had expected them to be wearing the dark-grey of Saint Cunar but was surprised to see the distinctive scarlet of the Sisters of Saint Agnes. The sight made him think of Charlaine, and he paused, only to be pushed forward by Cyn.

"Keep moving," she said. "You're holding up the entire line."

He chided himself for losing focus as he stepped onto the field. His fellow competitors began milling around, forming small knots of warriors, no doubt teaming up to last longer. He thought he spotted at least three other women, but it was difficult to tell with their helms in place. As to his own equipment, he had chosen to wear his own breastplate over the padded doublet supplied by Sigwulf, along with his helmet. The blunted sword he gripped was borrowed from the Grim Defenders, its edge dented and scratched. They had also loaned him a wooden shield, and this he hefted, testing its balance.

Another horn sounded, calling everyone's attention to the stands. A herald stood front and centre, announcing the competition was about to begin. Next, he read off the rules, few as they were, and then told everyone to take up their places.

Ludwig looked around. Outside the ring, commoners were packed up against the fencing, eager to watch the competition. On the field itself, many little groups had formed. He moved back towards the fence, pulling Cyn with him. When this thing started, it would be chaotic, and he didn't want to be overwhelmed by the press of competitors.

The herald raised a flag on high, waving it around to get everybody's attention, then swept it down, signalling the battle to commence.

A group of six warriors rushed across the field in a line, taking down two men before they even had a chance to ready themselves. They soon reached the other end of the field, only to come into sharp conflict with another group, hardened warriors by the look of them.

Ludwig cursed as he put his shield up just in time to block a swing, but his distraction had cost him, and he felt the blow knock him back into the railing. Planting his feet, he struck out with his sword, thrusting it into his attacker's stomach. The man let out a grunt, then backed up, allowing Ludwig room to step forward with a slash of his sword. His foe stumbled, and when his boot sank into the mud, the unfortunate man fell onto his back, knocking him from the competition.

Hearing a noise to his left, Ludwig wheeled around only to find Cyn using her shield to protect herself from a rain of blows. He struck while her opponent was distracted, swinging out at the man's legs. He felt the blade scrape along metal greaves, then the man fell, forced from his standing position.

Someone bumped Ludwig from behind, and he stumbled forward, desperate to stay afoot. His opponent pushed him again, but Ludwig managed to turn in time to see Cyn strike the man's helm with her mace. It rang out like a bell, and then the man turned on her. She, however, struck again with lightning speed, using her shield to smash into his gut and push him backward.

Ludwig reacted instantly by sidestepping, then thrust his leg out, trying to trip the fellow. The tactic worked, and the warrior fell face-first into the mud as Ludwig turned, ready to face a new opponent. Even though his helmet protected him, it severely restricted his vision, causing him to struggle for a moment to find a suitable foe.

A shield smash against his back forced him forward, his boots sinking into the mud, threatening to topple him. He managed to extricate his right foot, planting it before him to avoid catastrophe. He turned to see Cyn's downed opponent once more on his feet.

Ludwig raised his shield while readying his sword for a blow, but the Temple Knights had witnessed the exchange, and two of them pushed through the crowd, grabbing the man by the arms and hauling him away.

The press of combatants was getting fiercer. Ludwig had hoped to stay near its periphery, but the battle appeared to have a mind of its own. Every time he attempted to move outward, someone else would attack, forcing him back into the melee. He tried to keep close to Cyn, but she was having troubles of her own as the mud was treacherous, churned up by the warriors' heavy boots as they all fought for the prize.

Ludwig struck out, driving a foe backwards, and then advanced to take his place. The strategy was to outlast all the others, and so to this end, he placed his back to his ally; she doing the same.

A man barrelled into him, knocking him from his feet. Only his back hitting that of Cyn's stopped him from tumbling into the mud. He spread his stance, trying desperately to gain more solid footing.

His shield splintered as a blow landed, the jolt of the impact running up his arm. Shaking it off, Ludwig gripped his sword in both hands and swung, feeling the shock as his blade struck that of his attacker's. Back and forth went their blows, the sound drowned out by the hue and cry of the grand melee. Ludwig's opponent lunged forward, but then his feet went out from under him, and he fell to the ground with a splash.

A yell from Cyn caused Ludwig to whirl about only to find she had been driven to her knees under the relentless assault of a man with a great sword, and even as he turned to help, she went sprawling. Not content with simply eliminating her from the tournament, her attacker stepped forward, raising his sword for a devastating overhead blow.

Down came the weapon, but Ludwig was there, deflecting the assault with his own blade. They both stumbled back, trying to gain some traction in the endless muck and mire, and then the Temple Knights appeared, dragging the warrior away.

Wildly looking around, Ludwig spotted Cyn, limping from the field, and then his attention shifted back to the great melee. The battleground was clearing rapidly, the fighting growing less intense. Ludwig's arms ached, and his breath came in ragged gasps. Moving through the cloying mud was almost as tiring as the fight itself, and he cursed himself for agreeing to enter in the first place.

A warrior stumbled by, his leg bleeding profusely. Ludwig watched him as he reached the fence, and then returned his attention to the fray. His distraction cost him dearly, though, because someone, taking advantage of his lapse, leaped onto his back and starting raining down blows upon his helmet.

Ludwig staggered, doing everything he could to remain on his feet. He tried crouching, then turned suddenly, throwing his attacker off his perch. He saw his foe land with a splash, the man's part in the competition now at an end.

With his ears still ringing from the blows to his head, he spotted another warrior heading directly for him. Ludwig raised his sword yet again, feeling the burn in his muscles as he took a step, meeting the man halfway, their weapons striking each other in unison. The dull clang rang out, and then they were sword to sword, each trying to force the other back through brute strength.

Ludwig sidestepped, sweeping his blade down, forcing his opponent's weapon aside to leave the warrior open to attack. Ludwig quickly struck, his sword crashing into the man's shoulder, but only glancing off his pauldron. Even though his strike was weak, his foe had apparently had enough and dropped to his knees, calling for quarter.

A yell came from Ludwig's left, and he twisted as a warrior in a blue surcoat barrelled into him. Ludwig tried to step back, but the mud sucked at his feet, and he lost his balance, feeling the squish of mud as he landed flat on his back, where he remained, overcome with emotion. The fight was over, and he had lost.

When the crowd suddenly roared, he lifted his head to see what the commotion was all about. The blue surcoat was bashing away at a warrior in a chainmail jacket. The two traded blow after blow, each weaker than the last, until the one in chainmail finally knelt in surrender.

Ludwig got to his feet and started making his way over to the perimeter. Just as he was about to exit, a Temple Knight directed his attention to the stands where a herald waited by the edge of the field. Before him stood the man in the blue surcoat, ready to receive his prize, along with his chain-clad opponent who had obviously come in second. As Ludwig approached, it dawned on him that no other warriors were present—it appeared he had managed to fight his way into third place.

He swayed, barely able to stay on his feet as the announcements were made, then a purse was thrust into his hands, the crowd exploding into a cacophony of cheers. His knees weakened, and then he was surrounded by people slapping his back and offering congratulations. Desperate to suck in some fresh air, he pulled off his helmet, and Sigwulf grabbed his arms to steady him.

"You did it!" the man bellowed.

Ludwig was too tired to reply.

7

CELEBRATION

Spring 1095 SR

L udwig took another swig of ale, desperately trying to remain awake. Surrounding him were the Grim Defenders, celebrating his accomplishment. His winnings had been small, enough to last him a month if he was lucky, but many of the mercenaries had wagered on his success, and they were now in a good mood and wanted to spend their ill-gotten gains.

Sigwulf slapped him on the back. "That was quite the fight. I've never seen anything like it."

"So it was," added Brother Vernan. "Saint Mathew certainly had you under his gaze this day."

"It wasn't Saint Mathew," said Cyn. "It was me!" They all cheered, raising a cup once more.

Ludwig felt his head nodding and quickly snapped his eyes open, but then the faces surrounding him began to turn fuzzy. Slowly, his head tilted back, a loud snore escaping his lips.

He awoke to see Brother Vernan looking down at him. "How are you feeling?"

"Better," said Ludwig. "How long have I been out?"

"All night, and the better part of this morning."

Struggling to sit up, he looked around to see he was lying on a rough straw mat in a small tent. "Where am I?"

"In the camp of the Grim Defenders. They brought you here after you passed out."

"Am I sick?"

"No," said Brother Vernan, "merely tired from your exertions. The melee took a lot out of you."

Ludwig reached for his purse, only to find it missing.

"Fear not," said the Holy Brother. "Your winnings are secure. We thought it best to hide them away while you slept."

"Where are they?"

"Safely locked up in the captain's strongbox. I witnessed it myself. Your armour is there as well, along with your sword and the rest of your meagre belongings."

"I-I don't understand," Ludwig stammered out.

"You were brought here after you passed out. These people look on you fondly, Ludwig. They have only your best interests at heart."

"I must find some way to repay that friendship."

"You can start by talking to Captain Ecke. He's asked to see you."

"I doubt he needs me to train Cyn anymore. The competition is over."

"I cannot speak of his motives, but I believe it's in your best interest to hear the man out. You may discover he has something else in mind."

"What of you, Brother Vernan? I suppose with the tournament over, you'll be returning to the mission in Torburg?"

A smile crept over the lay brother. "My superiors have other things in mind for me, but there are more important things for you to consider at this moment. We must get you cleaned up so you can see what Captain Ecke wants." He shuffled across the room, returning a moment later with a bowl of water and a towel. "Here, have a good wash and clear your head. I shall wait for you outside."

Ludwig took the offering, splashing some water onto his face. Though his muscles ached, his recent success had given him a sense of accomplishment. For the first time in months, he felt ready to take on the world, come what may. He towelled himself off, then rose, making his way outside.

Brother Vernan was in conversation with Cyn, but his arrival put such thoughts from their heads.

"The captain wants to see you now," said Cyn. "Are you ready?"

"As ready as I'll ever be. Lead on."

They made their way through the camp, Brother Vernan lagging slightly behind. Several mercenaries waved as they passed, but Ludwig's attention was on the distant tent occupied by the commander of this company. They soon arrived, and Cyn pulled back the canvas, allowing them entry.

Captain Waldemar Ecke sat, looking up as they entered. "Sir Ludwig, good of you to come and see me. Can I offer you a drink?"

"No, thank you," said Ludwig. "I'm told you wanted to see me?"

"Ah, straight to the point, I see. When we last spoke, I told you how this company came to be."

"Not exactly," corrected Ludwig. "You told me WHEN you created it, not the details of how or why."

Ecke smiled. "I can see you're a man of intelligence. What do you know of the free companies?"

"Not much, I must confess. They're all mercenaries, each under the command of a different leader. Of course, the term company is almost meaningless since they range in numbers so greatly. Some of them are said to be the size of small armies."

"All of that is true. The Grim Defenders, for example, number some seventy warriors of late, although they have, at times, been almost twice that number."

Ludwig showed surprise. "You've taken losses?"

"Not precisely. Some men join to earn a few coins, others to travel. I generally don't care what a person's reason is for becoming a member of our esteemed group, as long as they pull their weight. In times of relative peace, such as we find ourselves in now, some get bored and leave us, travelling instead to a place of greater conflict in the hopes of gaining more profitable employment."

"In other words," said Ludwig, "the company is currently unemployed."

"Indeed it is, but I'm hoping that will soon change. I have, this day, received word from someone named Lord Gebhard Stein. Have you heard of him?"

"I can't say I have."

"He's the Baron of Mulsingen, a town that lies some eighty miles to the east. It would appear he has a dispute with one of his neighbours over something or other. To be honest, the letter doesn't go into any specifics, but he wishes to discuss terms of employment. To that end, I shall be marching the Grim Defenders in a few days. I'd like you to accompany us."

"You wish me to join?"

"Not precisely," said the captain. "I lack the funds for that, but your expertise might prove to be of some use."

"Might I offer a solution?" said Cyn.

Ecke looked at the woman, leaving Ludwig to wonder if this interaction had been planned all along.

"Speak your mind," said the captain.

"Why not take him into the fold as an apprentice? The company would be responsible for feeding and clothing him but wouldn't have to put out any coins until we get a signed contract with the baron."

Ecke pursed his lips. "I might consider it." He turned to Ludwig. "What are your thoughts on the matter?"

"I'm of two minds," said Ludwig. "On the one hand, I have to wonder why you would be making me this offer. I hardly have the experience to warrant the attention."

"I saw you in the melee," said the captain. "You proved you can handle yourself in a fight. And on the other hand?"

Ludwig smiled. "I find myself with nothing to do for the foreseeable future, so I am available."

"Then you are amenable to the matter?"

"I am, though I would know at what rate I would eventually be paid."

The captain grinned. "As a new recruit, you'd receive one share of whatever I manage to negotiate with the baron."

"That doesn't sound so bad. How many shares are there?"

"One per member of the company."

"And ten for the captain," added Cyn, "but that's after expenses, of course."

"Expenses?" said Ludwig.

"Yes," agreed Captain Ecke. "We still need to eat, and that means purchasing food. Of course, then there's upkeep and maintenance."

Ludwig's face betrayed his ignorance.

"We have to pay smiths," offered Cyn, "to maintain the weapons and armour, not to mention all the others a company needs to survive."

"Others?"

"Yes," added the captain. "Drovers, so we have fresh meat, men to drive the wagons that haul our supplies, fletchers and bowyers to maintain our weapons..."

"Now you're making things up," said Ludwig. "I've seen this camp of yours, and I know you don't have archers."

"That's true, at the moment, but I'm hoping to expand in the future."

"So what you're really saying is after all that, whatever's left gets divided up amongst us according to our shares?"

"Precisely."

"That doesn't sound like a lot."

"It's not," said Cyn, "but it pays for the occasional ale. What we honestly need is a nice war, then the coins will start flowing."

"Yes," agreed Ludwig, "but so will the risk. I gather a free company is only as good as its last battle."

"I see you've thought this through," the captain remarked.

"How many battles have the Grim Defenders seen?"

"Three," said Ecke. "Though I must confess, two of those were more like skirmishes. Still, it was enough to get us the attention of the baron."

"But you've had experience with other companies?"

"I have, too many to count, in fact, but I grew tired of the way they were conducting themselves. That's what led me to form the Grim Defenders."

"Just so I'm clear," said Ludwig, "how does this company run?"

The captain looked puzzled. "I'm not sure what you're asking."

"What is the command structure?"

"It's quite simple, honestly. I'm the captain. Everyone else is next in line."

"And if you should be injured or killed?"

"Then it shall no longer be my problem," said Ecke.

"Hardly a way to run a company."

The captain fidgeted. "And what would you know of such things?"

"I've read many historical accounts," said Ludwig. "It's somewhat of a passion of mine. I've always wanted to be a soldier."

"I see. What would these stories of yours tell you?"

"You need a rank structure. At the very least, you should appoint a few sergeants to keep everyone in line. Of course, that means you'd have to pay them a little more, perhaps an extra share each?"

"That would cut down on profits," warned Ecke.

"Yes, but it would make you more flexible when it comes to deployment. You can issue orders to the sergeants and know they'd be carried out properly."

"Were you a professional soldier before you were knighted?"

"No," replied Ludwig, "merely passionate when it comes to warfare. Luckily, my mother encouraged the interest."

Ecke leaned back slightly, crossing his arms and looking at Cyn. "It appears we have a scholar amongst us."

"I would hardly call myself a scholar," countered Ludwig. "I've read a few books, that's all."

"I dare say that's more than most of our lads. You'd be hard-pressed to find one here who is even literate."

"How many can read?" asked Ludwig.

"Why should that matter? I need them to fight, not read bedtime stories."

"Because sergeants should be able to read written messages. Find out who can read, and you've found your sergeants."

"I might remind you this is MY company," said Ecke.

"It's merely a suggestion, sir. You may take it or leave it at your discretion."

"You've given me much to think on," the captain continued. "In the meantime, you must decide whether or not you will take us up on our offer."

"I shall," said Ludwig.

Ecke grinned. He stood, offering his hand. "Excellent! Welcome to the Grim Defenders."

Ludwig peered down at the tent: a modest affair, consisting of two short poles with a rope connecting them at the top. Other lines held the structure in place, and a strip of canvas was placed over the taut rope, creating just enough room to lie down.

"Well? What do you think?" asked Cyn.

"It's pretty small, isn't it?"

"It's the standard size for such things."

His indignation was highly evident. "There isn't even enough room to get dressed."

She laughed. "It's only for sleeping. You get out of the tent to get dressed. Haven't you ever seen one before?"

"I'm a knight, remember? The only tents I'm familiar with are pavilions." He knelt, peering inside. "Where's my pallet?"

"There is none. You sleep on the ground, or on some skins if you can manage it. Mind you, if we're on a battlefield, we normally find an old house or something for shelter."

Ludwig shook his head. "I suppose it will have to do."

Cyn's annoyance was unmistakable. "Have to do? You're lucky to even have something like this. Other companies would make you sleep in the open air."

"They would?" said Ludwig. "Why's that?"

"Do you have any idea how much was spent to provide this shelter? Most mercenaries would prefer to pocket the coins."

"Was it like that in the Crossed Swords?"

"It was," said Cyn, "though admittedly, my father had a pavilion."

"I thought you said your father found you and Sigwulf in a tent?"

She laughed. "I did, didn't I? The truth is mercenaries are free to spend their earnings however they see fit. Most choose to waste it all on ale, but some of us use it to buy things like tents. They're much more convenient than trying to build a shelter in the middle of Saints-know-where."

"What about my armour?"

"What about it?"

"Where do I keep it?"

"That's easy," said Cyn. "You wear it."

"No, I mean when I'm not fighting."

"So do I. We're a company that moves around a lot, so we don't have room for armour stands. I suppose you could throw it in a sack if you wanted to, but I'd hate to see it stolen."

"Stolen?" Ludwig said. "Are you saying you have thieves in the company?"

"Not that I'm aware of, but the same can't be said of the locals."

"Surely your guards keep them at bay?"

"Guards can't watch everything, and when night comes, it's easy enough for people to sneak into camp."

"You speak like someone with experience."

Cyn chuckled. "I'll admit I've come in late once or twice."

"Are there rules concerning such things?"

"No, as long as we're all ready to march when the time comes."

"Or fight?" said Ludwig.

"Yes, that too."

He gazed once more into the small tent. "Well, I might as well give it a try."

"Here," said Cyn. "Let me help."

"I can manage to get into a tent by myself."

"Fair enough, but if I were you, I'd take off my sword belt first. Your scabbard will get in the way."

He stood, removing his weapon. "Anything else?"

"Yes. Always remove your helmet before entering. You'd be surprised the damage that thing can do to the tent poles."

"I'm not wearing a helmet."

"True, but that won't always be the case."

Ludwig tossed his sword inside, then crawled in and lay on his back. "The ground here is cold," he remarked.

"I would suggest lying on something. Have you a cloak?"

"I do."

"Then lie that down when you're ready to sleep."

"It's not long enough to do that."

"Then you'll have to let your feet hang over the edge."

He looked up at her. "Won't they get cold?"

"Not if you keep your boots on."

"What if my boots are wet?"

"Honestly," said Cyn, "must you complain about everything? Did your mother teach you nothing?"

Ludwig fumed. "What's that supposed to mean? My mother taught me plenty."

"Sometimes," said Cyn, softening her voice, "you must simply make do with what you have. Look on the bright side, Ludwig. You have shelter, you have comrades, and you have two full meals a day. What else could you need?"

"I honestly don't know," said Ludwig. "Perhaps something to read?"

"Don't look at me. Books are expensive."

"Does no one here have any?"

"I believe the captain might. Why don't you go and ask him? I'm sure he'd be willing to share."

"Maybe later," said Ludwig. "I need to get settled in first."

She crouched, looking around the inside of his cramped compartment. "Settled? What is there to settle into? It's a bed, not a house."

"Then what am I supposed to do with myself?"

"That's simple," said Cyn. "You come and hang out with the rest of us."

"The whole company?"

"If you want to. Most of us have our own little groups, but you're more than welcome to make friends with others. Shall I make some introductions?"

"That would be nice," said Ludwig. "Thank you."

"In that case, come out of that tent." She waited as he extricated himself from the tiny space. He stood, stretching his back like an old man.

"All done?" she asked.

"Ready when you are."

"Good, then follow me."

She led him through the camp. "Dorkin over there, you already know. He's the man to go see when food gets scarce."

"Does he have a secret stash?"

"No, but he knows what kinds of plants you can eat without getting sick. A useful skill when the company's coffers are low."

"Does that happen regularly?"

"Thankfully, no," said Cyn, "but then again, I've only been here for a few months."

"How many months?"

She thought for a moment. "I'd guess about eight, but I'm not one for keeping track of dates." They passed a trio of men standing by the fence that marked off the practice field.

"Who are they?" Ludwig asked.

"The tall one is Odo. You want to avoid him if you can."

"Why's that?"

"He's a notorious gambler," said Cyn. "He'll cheat you out of what coins you have at the drop of a hat, any hat."

"What about the other two?"

"Quentin and Emile. They're actually twins, though obviously not identical. Usually, they hang around with Baldric. I'll point him out later."

"Strange names," said Ludwig. "I take it they're not from around here."

"Very observant of you. They hail from the west."

"How far west?"

"Within the area that's now occupied by the Halvarian Empire. Their parents fled the region years ago, but the naming tradition continues."

"Anyone else I should watch out for?"

Cyn halted, taking in her surroundings. "Yes, let me see..." She pointed. "See that man over there?"

Ludwig rotated his gaze to take in a dark-haired mercenary with a vicious scar on his chin. "Yes, what of him?"

"That's Baldric. I'd watch myself around him if I were you. He angers easily."

"What of it?"

"We don't know much about him before he joined, but there are some who reckon he's wanted for murder."

"A murderer?" Ludwig said. "Here in the company?"

"Don't look so surprised. The captain doesn't care much about people's backgrounds, as long as they know how to fight."

"And can Baldric fight?"

"Oh, yes," said Cyn. "He's one of the toughest warriors I've ever seen, and that's saying something. Trust me, you don't want him on your bad side."

"I'll remember to keep my distance," said Ludwig.

"Good," said Cyn. "Now, let's get on with the tour, shall we?"

8

SECRETS

Spring 1095 SR

The early morning sun poked in through the end of Ludwig's tent, waking him. He opened his eyes only to stare up at the canvas above him, damp with dew, and his aching back was a testament to the nearby tree whose root had somehow found itself beneath him.

Sitting up, he grabbed a spare shirt and then crawled over to the opening. Once outside, he shivered in the early morning chill, donning his clothing as quickly as possible. Around him drifted the smells of campfires, and for the briefest of moments, it reminded him of the kitchens back home. That reminiscence was soon put to rest by the sound of someone urinating.

He turned, determined to investigate the source, only to see Baldric loosing his piss against the side of some poor fellow's tent. Ludwig shook his head, remembering Cyn's warning. Determined to avoid any such unpleasantries, he set out in search of his friends.

He soon found Sigwulf. The bear of a man stood at a campfire, stirring a pot that dangled over the coals.

At his approach, Sigwulf turned. "How was your first night in a tent?"

"Fine," replied Ludwig, "as long as you don't mind sleeping on the root of a tree. I swear it wasn't there last night."

His companion chuckled. "It's not the worst thing that could be in your tent."

"What could be worse?"

"A badger," said Sigwulf. Ludwig opened his mouth to speak but was cut off. "Don't ask!"

Ludwig shrugged his shoulders, turning his attention to the pot. "What have you got there?"

"Gruel."

"What's that?"

"You've never heard of gruel?"

"Can't say I have," said Ludwig. "Care to enlighten me?"

"It's a thin porridge," said Sigwulf, "made from oats."

"It doesn't smell like porridge."

The giant sighed. "No, it doesn't, does it? I'm terrible at this sort of thing."

"Then why are you cooking it?"

"It's my turn."

A yawn drew their attention. Dorkin approached the fire, took one sniff and winced as the aroma met his nostrils. "Let me guess," he said. "Sig's been cooking again."

"It's gruel," offered Ludwig.

"It certainly doesn't smell like it."

"It's not my fault," repeated Sigwulf. "I never learned how to cook."

Dorkin frowned. "I can tell." He turned to Ludwig with a smile. "He's the only person I know who can burn water." Returning his attention to the pot, he peered inside. "You better let me take over there, big man."

"Be my guest," said Sigwulf. He took a seat on the ground, soon joined by Ludwig.

"That's one more thing I know about you," said Ludwig. "You never learned to cook."

"I confess, it's true. What about you?"

"What about me?"

"Did you ever learn to prepare food?"

"Alas, no. Our household had a cook, quite an accomplished one, I might add. Often was the night my father would entertain guests. I had my issues with the man, but I have to admit he set a fine table."

"Do you miss it?" asked Sigwulf.

"I miss having nice meals, but that's about it. There's nothing back there for me anymore."

"What about your mother?"

"She died some years ago."

"I'm sorry," said Sigwulf. "That must have been difficult."

"It was. What of your folks? Are they still alive?"

"I wish they were. Things would be a lot different."

"Different, how?"

"Well, for one thing, I wouldn't be here in the middle of nowhere, serving in one of the free companies."

"Then where would you be?"

"Back home."

"In Braymoor?"

Sigwulf eyed him warily. "You have an excellent memory."

"I know. It's a curse."

Sigwulf shrugged. "You might as well know. You'll find out eventually. The truth is, I was born in Abelard."

"Why hide that?"

"Oh, there's more to it, trust me."

"I'm all ears," said Ludwig.

"My family were lesser nobility, my father being a baron and all."

"Something we have in common," said Ludwig.

"Indeed. The politics of the kingdom were, at best, twisted, and I'm not sure I fully understand them now, even after all these years, but the long and the short of it is, the people rose up in rebellion."

"What happened?"

"They assembled an army but were defeated in battle, at a place called Krosnicht. Unfortunately, my father was on the losing side."

"I presume he died?" said Ludwig.

"He did, in battle. The rest of his army scattered to the four winds. I wasn't there, mind, but my older brother was. In the aftermath, they stripped the family of its lands, and we fled to Braymoor. So you see, I didn't exactly lie when I said that was where I was from."

"And your brother? Does he still live?"

"No," confessed Sigwulf, "though I do have a sister that's out there somewhere, assuming she's still alive."

"But if your father was a rebel, wouldn't his name be recognizable?"

"Yes, but my sister took another name, as did I."

"So Sigwulf isn't your real name?"

"It's my middle name. My first name is actually Lucius."

"And your family name?"

Sigwulf looked around, but only Dorkin was within earshot, and he was busy with the gruel. "Marhaven," he whispered, "but if you tell anyone, I'll have to kill you."

"Don't worry," said Ludwig, "your secret is safe with me. Does Cyn know?"

"Yes. I told her long before we came to Erlingen."

"I can see why you'd want to keep quiet about it."

"Indeed. What about you? What's your story? You didn't murder your father, did you? I mean, it's no business of mine if you did. It's not like you're the only murderer around here."

"I did not murder my father!" insisted Ludwig. "And what do you mean by that, anyway? Are you saying there are murderers nearby?"

"Never mind that," said Sigwulf, "continue with your story. You obviously didn't get along with your father. Was it always so?"

"Not while my mother lived, no, but after her death, he turned in on himself and mostly took to avoiding me."

"You likely reminded him of your mother. Was there a resemblance?"

"To a certain extent, I suppose. We both had the same colour hair."

"Did she die in childbirth?"

"No, of a fever," said Ludwig. "I was fifteen at the time."

"Just on the cusp of manhood."

"I suppose. In any event, it hit me hard."

"Did things get worse?"

"They did. I could get used to being mostly ignored, but then he went on a trip at the behest of my cousin."

"Your cousin?"

"Yes, King Otto."

Sigwulf's eyes went wide. "Your cousin's a king?"

"Well, second cousin, we share a great grandfather. Didn't I mention that?"

"You most certainly did not!"

"Yes, well, the king sent my father on a diplomatic mission to Reinwick, and he came back with a new wife."

"Ah, yes," said Sigwulf. "The complex diplomacy of the Petty Kingdoms at work again. You know, sometimes I think all nobles do is marry off their sons and daughters to make alliances."

"That's precisely what they do."

"Yet you're not married, or are you?"

"No, I'm not," said Ludwig. "Though I wanted to be."

"Ah," said Sigwulf. "I sense a story here. Who was she?"

"Her name was… IS Charlaine. She's the daughter of a swordsmith and is a master smith in her own right."

"Let me guess: your father forbade you to marry her?"

"He wouldn't even allow me to see her."

"And would you have married her, had your father approved?"

"Yes," admitted Ludwig, "I believe I would have. She was unlike any other woman I'd ever been with."

"Where is she now?"

"Far from here. She became a Temple Knight of Saint Agnes."

Sigwulf looked into his eyes with a penetrating gaze. "You're still in love with her."

"I suppose I am, not that it matters. She serves her Saint now."

"I win," said Sigwulf.

"You win what?"

"I have the worse story."

"I have a lost love," defended Ludwig. "How can it get any worse than that?"

Sigwulf poked himself in the chest with his thumb. "I have a price on my head." He saw the look of defeat on Ludwig's face. "See? I told you mine was worse."

"All right, you win... or lose, depending on your point of view."

"Are you two done babbling?" asked Dorkin. "'Cause if so, the gruel is ready. Pass me those bowls, will you?"

Ludwig reached forward, fetching the requested items and passing them to Dorkin. The man ladled some gruel into them before handing them back.

Sigwulf scooped up some with his fingers, pouring it into his mouth. "Wow," he said through a mouthful, "that's hot."

"What did you expect?" said Ludwig. "It just came off the fire."

"He never learns," added Dorkin.

"You be quiet," snapped Sigwulf.

Ludwig chose to let his food cool. "Where's Cyn?"

"The captain wanted to see her."

"Is that typical?"

"Not particularly," said Sigwulf. "Why? Are you worried about something?"

"No, merely curious. I suppose I'm simply used to seeing you two together."

"She's more than capable of looking after herself." Sigwulf tipped up the bowl, pouring the gruel into his mouth to finish it off. The bowl came down again, and he looked at Ludwig, then at his breakfast. "Are you going to eat that?"

"Yes," said Ludwig. "I'm waiting for it to cool."

Sigwulf's eyes wandered past him. "You'd better not wait too long. Here comes the captain now."

Ludwig turned, his meal forgotten. Captain Ecke was walking at a brisk pace, collecting men as he went. Cyn followed in his wake, along with the others. "This doesn't look good."

"Nonsense," said his companion. "He doesn't look mad." Even as he spoke, Sigwulf rose, prompting Ludwig to do likewise.

"There you are," called out the captain. "I've been looking for you, Sig."

"Me? What for?"

"You'll find out in a moment." Ecke looked around, taking in the crowd and raising his voice. "I was hoping to gather the entire company, but this will have to do. I've been thinking things over and have decided to implement a few changes around here."

Grumbles erupted from the crowd, and he held up his arms to halt it. "Now, I know what you're thinking, and I'm here to tell you you're wrong. These changes will make it easier for you to have your say, not to mention easing the strain of getting your pay."

"Go on, then," called out someone. "Get on with it!"

Ecke smiled. "As you know, I organized the Grim Defenders along military lines."

"Tell us something we don't know," came another voice.

The captain ignored the jibe. "I have decided to create the rank of sergeant to better enable me to keep my eye on things. As such, I have picked three people who will, as a result, receive an extra share when it comes time to divide up the pay."

The crowd fell quiet.

"The first person to be elevated to the rank of sergeant is..." He paused, drawing it out for dramatic effect. "Sigwulf."

"Me?" the big man replied. "Why would you do that?"

"He offered it to me," said Cyn, "but what do I know about reading?"

Ecke held out his hand. "What do you say, Sig? Will you take the offer? It doubles your pay."

"Of course."

Everyone cheered, for Sigwulf was known as a fair man, the perfect candidate for such a position.

"The second person to receive the rank of sergeant is Baldric." The captain scanned the crowd. "Where is he?"

"He's indisposed," called out Emile.

"Hungover is more like it," added Quentin.

"Then I'll let you give him the good news."

"And the third?" asked Sigwulf.

"The third I shall hold off on for now. I'd like to see how things work out for the next week or so before making an announcement. Now, are there any questions?"

Ludwig stepped up to the challenge. "How will the command be split?

Will each sergeant command half the company, and if so, how do people know which half they're in?"

"All good questions," replied the captain, "but I've only just announced the rank. Fear not, gentlemen, you shall have your answers in due time."

Dorkin cleared his throat. "Any word on this new contract?" he asked.

"I am awaiting a reply from the baron. Once he gives us leave to march, we shall travel to Mulsingen. There, he will review the company and decide whether or not he will employ us. Until that time, he's putting us on half pay, to guarantee we don't find employment elsewhere."

A cheer went up, for half pay was better than none at all.

"Now," continued the captain, "I have better things to do than spend all morning chatting with you lot. Congratulations, Sigwulf, and pass on my regards to Baldric."

He turned to leave, but Sigwulf caught him by the arm. "Excuse me, sir, but what do my new duties entail?"

"Come by my tent this afternoon, and I shall be happy to explain it to you. In the meantime, you should celebrate while you can."

"While I can?"

"Of course," said Ecke. "Once you're a sergeant, you'll be far too busy for such things." He strode off, an enormous grin on his face.

Sigwulf looked at Cyn. "What have you gotten me into?"

She simply smiled back.

"I suppose," said Dorkin, "we'll have to get him a bigger helmet?"

Sigwulf shot him a look, but the cook clearly missed it.

"You know," the man continued, "to go with his swelled head!"

The crowd burst into laughter, causing the giant of a man to turn a bright crimson.

"Don't worry, Siggy," said Cyn, taking his arm. "It's all for the best."

"Yes," added Ludwig. "You can save up all the extra pay you'll get and buy a nice big castle for yourself."

"Very funny," said Sigwulf. "You'd better watch yourself, my friend. Knight or not, you're under my command now."

"We don't know that for sure," said Ludwig, grinning, "but let's hope so. I don't much fancy my chances under Baldric."

"Well said," added Cyn. "Now, who's for that celebration?"

Ludwig passed the jug across, watching in disbelief as Sigwulf emptied the entire contents down his throat. Half of it dripped down his chin, but the amount the huge man could imbibe was still impressive.

"Is he always like this?" asked Ludwig.

"No," said Cyn, "sometimes he really lets loose."

He wasn't sure if she was serious and was about to say so, but then a familiar face came into view. "Brother Vernan?"

The lay brother smiled, moving to join them at their table. The Hammer was busy, this being the last day of the tournament, and the ale flowed freely. Vernan had to push hard to break through the throng of people.

"What are we celebrating?" he called out, raising his voice to be heard above the din.

Ludwig put a mug in the good fellow's hand. "Sig here's been promoted to sergeant."

"Is that a good thing?"

"Yes," said Ludwig, "yes, indeed. How's the mission?"

"It's doing well, my friend."

"But?"

"What makes you believe there's a but?"

"Simple," said Ludwig, "your manner. You have a look of melancholy about you."

"Do I? I definitely didn't intend to."

"What is it, then? Come on, out with it."

"They're sending me to Eidenburg."

Ludwig grinned. "They're not making you into a Sister of Saint Agnes, are they?"

Brother Vernan appeared upset but relented when he saw the look of mirth on Ludwig's face. "Very funny. No, they're sending me to be ordained."

"They're making you into a Holy Father?"

"So it would seem."

"Why, that's wonderful news, isn't it?"

"I suppose it is."

"Then why so glum?"

"I find I've come to like it here," admitted Brother Vernan, "and a Holy Father has so many more responsibilities."

"Nonsense," said Ludwig. "It's a step up, and make no mistake, you'll make a great father."

"What did you say?" said Cyn.

"I was talking to Brother Vernan."

"Did I hear you say he's going to be a father?" she continued. "I didn't think they allowed lay brothers to have children."

"No," said Ludwig. "I meant he'll make a good HOLY Father. By the Saints, woman, he can't have children; he's celibate." He turned to Brother Vernan. "You are celibate, aren't you?"

Vernan blushed. "Yes, of course. It's a requirement of our order."

"There, you see?"

"Come now," said Cyn, "can you honestly say that out of the thousands of lay brothers who work for Saint Mathew, not one of them has lain with a woman?"

To Ludwig's amusement, the Holy Brother turned an even darker shade of crimson. "First of all," started Vernan, "brothers' vows only apply AFTER they have joined the order. Many had families before they found their true calling."

Cyn was obviously relishing the conversation. "And second?"

"We do not 'work' for Saint Mathew. We follow his teachings."

"No wonder he has no descendants. You wouldn't catch me joining the order."

"Women can't join the Order of Saint Mathew, can they?" asked Ludwig.

"No," said Brother Vernan, "at least not in an official capacity."

"What does that mean?"

"Well, as you know, we have missions spread throughout the Continent to help the needy. We often treat women in such places, and occasionally they stay on to assist with other patients, but I can assure you we treat them with the utmost care and respect."

"Do they sleep at the mission?" asked Cyn.

"Most assuredly not!" replied Brother Vernan.

"She's only teasing you," soothed Ludwig. "Pay her no attention."

The Holy Brother took a cleansing breath. "I shall try."

"So tell me more about Eidenburg. That IS where they train Temple Knights, isn't it?"

"It is, in fact. I'm told the seminary where I'll be staying is in close proximity to the commandery of Saint Agnes."

"I assume a seminary is where they'll bestow your new rank?"

"Yes, after a suitable period of time, although we prefer to use the term 'elevated' rather than bestowed, and it's a position, not a rank."

"I stand corrected," said Ludwig. "Why do they make you wait?"

"What gave you the impression I would be waiting?"

"You said 'after a suitable time'. I merely assumed that meant there was a delay."

"Ah," said Brother Vernan, "I see the confusion. When one becomes a Holy Father, one must be trained. This, in turn, takes time."

"Trained? But I thought all Holy Brothers knew the teachings of Saint Mathew?"

"We do, but a Holy Father must perform ceremonies like weddings and funerals. That requires much more than mere reading."

"So what happens after you're ordained? Do you get to pick where you go?"

"To be honest, I have no idea. I suspect they will send me where I'm needed most, but hopefully, I will have some say in the matter."

"I wish you well," said Ludwig. "It's been a pleasure to have made your acquaintance."

"Thank you," replied Brother Vernan, "and I hope you find the peace you seek."

"What makes you suppose I seek peace?" asked Ludwig. "I'm a mercenary now."

"I know. I was referring to finding inner peace. You are a wandering soul, Ludwig. May Saint Mathew watch over you and keep you safe."

9

A SOLDIER'S LIFE

Spring 1095 SR

The sword's edge scraped along the grindstone, smoothing out the nicks and scratches. Ludwig paused long enough to run his thumb down the blade, then nodded to Sigwulf, who was turning the wheel using his hands.

"This would be much easier if we had a foot pedal to rotate it."

"It would," agreed Sigwulf. "We used to have one, but then Baldric broke it."

"Can't it be replaced?"

"Do you see a carpenter in camp?"

"Why not hire one?"

"Do you have the coins for that?"

"I suppose I see your point," said Ludwig. He lowered the sword once more, listening as the sandstone wheel ground out the imperfections. Three more revolutions, and then he pulled it up, this time looking over the steel for any remaining nicks.

"That will do nicely," he announced.

Sigwulf stretched his back. He was a big man, and stooping to turn the wheel had been uncomfortable for him, although he was loath to admit it. "What are we up to today?" he asked.

"You tell me," said Ludwig. "You're the sergeant."

Sigwulf smiled. "I don't know if I'm ever going to get used to that."

"So? What's your decision?"

"The camp has grown lazy. We need something to keep us active."

"Well," said Ludwig, "the tournament's been done for a week now. What did you have in mind?"

"A battle?"

Ludwig laughed. "That's all well and good, but we need a war for that, don't we?"

"Not at all. We can fight amongst ourselves."

"Are you mad?"

"No," said Sigwulf. "Hear me out. We divide the company into two groups."

"Already done," said Ludwig, "or did you forget you're only sergeant to half the men?"

"I suppose I did."

"Go on, then. What's the rest of your plan?"

"Simple," said Sigwulf. "We take blunted weapons and have a go at each other."

"Like the grand melee?"

"In a sense, only instead of each man fighting for themselves, we work in teams."

Ludwig smiled, something he was doing a lot lately. "That's a marvellous idea. Do you believe the captain would approve?"

"I don't see why not? If nothing else, it'll keep our fighting skills sharp."

"When do you propose we have this mock battle?"

"This afternoon," said Sigwulf, "but I'll have to clear it with the captain first."

"Best get a move on then before half the company disappears into town."

The sergeant hurried off, leaving Ludwig alone with his sword. His peace was short-lived, though, for Cyn soon arrived.

"Have you seen Siggy?" she asked.

"He's off to see the captain," said Ludwig. "He wants to arrange a mock battle."

Her eyes lit up. "A mock battle? How exciting! Who'll be fighting?"

"The entire company, if he has his way."

"How would that work? Who would we attack?"

"Each other. He intends to divide the company up into two groups and let them fight it out."

"Ooh," said Cyn. "I hope I'm on Siggy's team."

Ludwig let out a laugh. "I imagine you will be. After all, he's your sergeant?"

"He's yours too."

"Yes, I suppose he is."

"So what's our strategy?"

"Strategy?"

"Yes," she pressed, "for winning the battle?"

"It's far too early to worry about such things. We don't even know where we'll be fighting."

"Still," Cyn said, "we should come up with some tactics, don't you think?"

"The only tactic we need is to beat the other side."

"Don't be ridiculous," said Cyn. "There's lots of things we could do to ensure victory."

"Like what?"

She thought a moment. "Well, for one thing, we could group people together, like you and I did in the grand melee."

"That didn't help us win," Ludwig reminded her.

"True, but you did come in third. How far do you reckon you would have gotten without me watching your back?"

"I suppose that's a valid point."

"Come on, let's go get our gear."

Ludwig stared at her, trying to determine if she was serious. Her eyes betrayed no sign of humour. "You're pulling my leg, right? The competition likely won't be until this afternoon."

"You can never be too prepared!"

Ludwig stood ready, sword in hand, shield to his front, while to his left, Dorkin nervously clutched his axe. Sigwulf was on his right, and just past him stood Cyn, dwarfed by the sheer size of the man. More men filled out the line, creating a wall of warriors thirty strong.

Across the field, some distance off, Baldric led his own group, equal in number to theirs. Captain Ecke had come to witness the fight, aided by three others who were too sick or lame to participate in the spectacle. Blunted weapons had been the order, and Ecke had been sure to inspect all blades as the two forces assembled.

They would meet in the middle of a field, really little more than a grassy patch, though there was, they were told, a small stream that managed to meander its way through the clearing.

Sigwulf doubted it would make much difference, but Ludwig wasn't so sure. Even a minor obstacle could play havoc with plans. Not that there had been a lot of planning. He suspected the entire exercise was simply to let the Grim Defenders release some of their pent-up energy.

Captain Ecke gave a shout, gathering everyone's attention. Drawing his sword, he held it aloft, waiting as all eyes were trained on him. Moments later, he swept it down, indicating the battle should commence.

Across the way, Baldric gave a yell, and his men surged forward. There was no organization to it, only a wild pack of raving warriors rushing into the fray.

Sigwulf gave the order, and his group began an orderly advance. They were shield to shield, taking small steps to keep their line intact. Each warrior gripped their weapon of choice, ready to strike should the opportunity present itself.

The distance closed far too quickly, to Ludwig's mind. He was just getting used to their steady cadence when the first of Baldric's warriors hit them. A large brute named Kerwain smashed into Cyn, knocking her back with the force of his assault.

Sigwulf was quick to react, turning with a fury and driving his huge club into the man's back. Kerwain's padded jacket helped to absorb part of the strike, but the warrior still called out in pain and collapsed.

"Stay down," ordered Sigwulf. He continued his advance, Cyn rushing back into place. Ludwig looked to his front in time to see Quentin and Emile bearing down on him. Each was armed with a great sword, and it was clear they were aiming for him. He raised his shield higher as they approached, then struck low with his sword, smashing into a pair of legs.

Emile went down, but Quentin redoubled his efforts, bringing his sword down onto Ludwig's shield with a clash that sent a shock up the young knight's arm. Ludwig countered by kicking out, his boot impacting the man's shin. The twin's leg gave out, sending him tumbling to the ground beside his brother.

Sigwulf, meanwhile, had three men on him. The first swung his sword directly at Sigwulf's head, and as the mighty warrior retaliated, the other two rushed forward, seizing his arms and holding on tightly. Sigwulf struggled with the two clinging to his arms but finally went down beneath their combined weight.

Cyn took on one of them, using her mace to smash the man three times in quick succession. Her foe cried out on the third and released his grip, allowing Sigwulf to struggle to his feet.

Ludwig saw an opportunity and struck, delivering a blow that rang off an enemy helmet. The next thing he felt was a solid hit to his own stomach, knocking the wind from him. He had fallen to his knees, gasping for air, when a shadow loomed over him.

Baldric drove his knee into Ludwig's face, a hit that would have broken his nose had his helmet not been in place. As it was, Ludwig's head snapped back, and for a moment, he lost sight of his foe. Another blow struck him, this time in the chest, and he staggered back, shaking his head to clear his vision. He cursed the narrow view of his helmet and swore never to wear it again, then a kick to his knee knocked him prone.

Baldric moved closer, delivering a violent stomp to his head. Ludwig's ears rang, and he rolled onto his back, staring up at his attacker. The sergeant drew back for another kick, and Ludwig struck out with his sword's hilt, connecting with his attacker's groin.

Baldric hunched over, letting out a high-pitched scream. The pause gave Ludwig enough time to scramble backwards and then move into a crouch to deliver a kick to the man's stomach. Baldric toppled backwards, landing with a thud, and there he lay, clutching himself.

Ludwig turned to rejoin his line, but with their leader's defeat, the opposing force began to flee. He felt Sigwulf's hand slap his back in congratulations, but Baldric, having torn off his helmet, stared at Ludwig with pure malice in his eyes.

Cyn, ecstatic and bouncing around in glee at their victory, jumped into Sigwulf's arms, and the big man blushed profusely.

"Well done," called out the captain. "You all did magnificently. Now, let's go and celebrate, shall we? I have a keg of ale with your names on it."

A cheer erupted from both sides, and they all began flooding back towards the camp. Ludwig kept an eye on Baldric. As the man was helped to his feet, he whispered to Quentin and Emile, but Ludwig couldn't hear anything from his position. One thing that was clear, however, was the look of hatred Baldric sent his way.

It was well into the night before people started drifting off to their tents. Ludwig had drunk more than his fair share and was feeling the effects as he stumbled back to his own modest home. A figure unexpectedly appeared in front of him, causing him to halt to avoid running into the fellow. Ludwig squinted, trying to identify the fool in the dim light, but as he leaned forward for a better look, a fist came out of nowhere, slamming into his jaw. Thrown off-balance by the assault, he fell to the ground. Almost immediately, a boot took him in the side.

"That'll teach you," came the voice of Baldric.

Someone else snorted, and then another boot struck Ludwig's arm, this time from the right. He scrambled to his hands and knees, desperately trying to stand upright, but a leg tripped him, sending him back to the ground. Baldric towered over him, soon joined by the faces of Quentin and Emile. They were all grinning, and then the boots started stomping him.

Ludwig rolled up into a ball, determined to avoid serious injury, but the blows didn't stop. Another boot struck his head, and blood trickled down from his forehead, but he refused to give in. With a glimpse of someone at his side, he launched himself into whoever it was, gouging at their eyes in a last-ditch effort to save himself from almost certain death.

His foe stepped back, and then men were pulling him away.

"What's going on here?" bellowed the voice of Captain Ecke.

"This man here, Ludwig, assaulted Sergeant Baldric," accused Quentin.

Ludwig tried to speak out, but between the beating and the drink, he could barely take it all in.

"It's true," added Emile. "I saw it myself."

"What about you, Sergeant?" asked Ecke.

Baldric was wiping blood from his face. "Yes, Captain. Ludwig attacked me as we passed. He was in a blind fury. It must have been the drink."

The captain leaned in close to Ludwig's face. "What have you to say for yourself, man?"

Ludwig spat out blood but said nothing. The witnesses had already condemned him.

"This is bad, Ludwig," continued the captain. "Baldric is a sergeant, and this is a serious breach of discipline. I have no choice but to impose punishment. When you joined this company, you agreed to its rules. Will you now subject yourself to our discipline, or will you leave the Grim Defenders, never to show your face again?"

"This is my home now," spat out Ludwig. "I shall face whatever punishment you deem necessary."

"Then you leave me with no options," said Ecke. He turned to his men. "To the pillory with him. Let him remain there until noon tomorrow."

They dragged Ludwig off, his head still spinning from his ordeal. He silently thanked the Saints for the ale, for without its dulling effect, the pain would have been excruciating. His side ached, and he wondered if they had broken his ribs, but there was no way to tell, for they pinned his arms to his side.

Others followed as he was taken through the camp, and he soon found himself before a wooden pole. Attached to this was a cross plank with holes for his neck and wrists. They pushed him down into an uncomfortable crouch and placed his head and arms within while a similar plank was laid above him and then secured in place, preventing him from moving.

Captain Ecke stood before him, staring down at Ludwig. "You have brought this on yourself," he announced, then turned to face the crowd. "Let this be a lesson to you all. Behaviour of this sort shall be dealt with swiftly and firmly. Now get to your beds, all of you!"

The men disbursed while Ecke looked at Ludwig one more time, shaking his head, then turned, disappearing from view.

The night wore on, and Ludwig ached all over. The blood on his forehead had run into his eyes, making it difficult to see. It would have been bearable had the pillory been at a suitable height, but crouched as he was, he could neither stand nor sit, leaving him in the most uncomfortable of positions.

He lost track of time. A dim light permeated the sky, signalling dawn's approach, and still he hunched over, his legs quivering with the effort.

Someone appeared before him, and he squinted through a swollen eye to see Emile. The man held a stone, tossing it from one hand to the other as he stared at Ludwig. Evidently, he had made up his mind and stepped back, readying for a throw, but a massive hand yanked him from view.

Ludwig heard some sounds but couldn't raise his head enough to see what was happening. Things went quiet, and then the figure reappeared. He took a breath, trying to anticipate the hurled stone, but then a hand touched his face with a damp cloth to wipe away the blood.

"Ludwig? Can you hear me?" Cyn's voice was hushed, no doubt because of the proximity of the captain's tent.

Ludwig tried to speak, but his throat was too dry. He nodded instead.

"Don't worry," she soothed. "We'll keep an eye on you. Here, let me help." She scooped the dried blood from his eye, then wiped off the rest of his face. Her hand moved to the side, and someone handed her a bowl. She lifted it to his mouth. "Here, drink. It's water."

He lapped up the water like a dog, unable to turn his head.

"We heard you attacked Baldric," she said. "Is that true?"

"They ambushed me," Ludwig managed to squeak out. "There were three of them."

"Let me guess," came Sigwulf's voice. "Quentin and Emile were with him?"

"They were."

"I'll kill them," the big man promised.

"No," said Cyn, "not now, at least. We must bide our time, get them when they least expect it."

"But they must pay for this," Sigwulf objected.

"They will, but we'll pick them off one by one, destroying Baldric's power before we deal with him ourselves."

"No!" said Ludwig. "This is my battle. I'll deal with it."

"Baldric and his cronies attacked one of my men," swore Sigwulf. "That makes it my business."

"Yes," added Cyn, "and if it's Siggy's business, then it's mine too!"

· · ·

The morning wore on. Others wandered by, but the sight of Sigwulf standing guard kept them at a distance. Ludwig felt as though every muscle in his body was on fire. He tried to sit, but the pillory wouldn't let him. He tried stretching a leg, but it unbalanced him, making things even more painful. All he could do was hang on and pray this torment would come to an end.

Captain Ecke finally arrived. He looked at Ludwig, then at Sigwulf and Cyn, who stood watch. "Release him," he commanded.

Cyn removed the latch and lifted the top bar while Sigwulf moved around the back. Ludwig, now free of the punishment, felt his legs give way. Sigwulf lifted him, carrying him two-handed.

Ludwig tried to take in what was happening but struggled to understand. Sigwulf stared at the captain, though to what end he couldn't say. Ecke finally turned and walked off, then Cyn led them back towards their tents.

Cyn lifted his shirt, examining the wounds beneath and grimacing. "That looks bad."

"You've taken quite a beating," added Sigwulf. "It'll take you some time to recover. You say there were three of them?"

"Yes," said Ludwig, gritting his teeth as Cyn pushed on each rib.

"Nothing looks to be broken," she said. "You're lucky."

"Lucky? It sure doesn't feel like it. I can hardly move?"

"I'm afraid you're going to have to."

"Why?"

"We're setting off for Mulsingen tomorrow."

"He's in no shape to march," said Sigwulf. "We may have to leave him behind."

"No," said Ludwig. "I'll manage somehow."

"I'll go into Torburg," offered Cyn, "and hopefully, I can pick up some numbleaf."

"It's worth a try," said Sigwulf, "but do we have the coins?"

Cyn shrugged. "What if we can find Brother Vernan?"

"He's probably left by now," said Ludwig.

"Maybe," she agreed, "but we could at least mention his name?"

"I suppose," agreed Sigwulf. "In the meantime, you'd best rest, my friend. Your body needs to heal."

"Certainly," said Ludwig, "but do you suppose you can convince Cyn to stop prodding me first?"

10

THE MARCH

Spring 1095 SR

The next day, Ludwig had expected to march at first light, but it took far longer than that to take down the camp. Halfway through the morning, the Grim Defenders still weren't ready, and Captain Ecke looked as though he was going to throw a fit.

Finally, just before noon, the first mercenaries began the trek eastward, clearing the city of Torburg as the bells tolled midday. The captain had reckoned the distance to Mulsingen to be no more than a week away, but if today was to be any measure of their progress, it could easily take twice that long.

Ludwig struggled. His muscles ached, covered as he was in bruises, and although the numbleaf helped, it soon became apparent his own footwear was not up to the task of a prolonged march. As a noble, he had been used to riding anywhere he went, resulting in expensive but comfortable boots to help keep his feet warm. Now that he was on foot, like the others, he began to realize a more firm-footed sole would have been far superior.

"Come on," urged Sigwulf, "we've miles to go yet."

"Yes," agreed Cyn, cheerful as ever, "and this is a slow pace compared to what the Crossed Swords used to do."

Ludwig grimaced. "You call this slow? My feet are killing me."

"Try some more numbleaf," she urged, "but keep an eye on your feet."

"Why, will they drop off?"

"No, but blisters can form and with the numbleaf in you, you'd never know."

"Blisters don't scare me," said Ludwig.

"Nor me, but if they burst and you keep going, you could turn your feet into a bloody mess, then they'd have to amputate. I don't know about you, but I'd prefer to keep my own feet intact, thank you very much."

Ludwig laughed, but even that small action sent him into a spasm of pain. Sigwulf and Cyn both looked at him in alarm. Seeing their reaction, he dipped into his belt pouch, pulling forth a small, pale-green leaf. He popped it into his mouth and bit into it, releasing the taste of mint. Almost immediately, he felt the aches and pains wash away, and his speed noticeably improved.

"That's better," said Sigwulf.

"How long does this stuff last?" Ludwig asked.

"It varies by individual," said Cyn, "but they say the more you use it, the heavier the dose that's required."

"Which means?"

"You'll probably need to take some more by mid-afternoon."

"I can deal with that," said Ludwig. He looked around. They were passing farmland now, and the fieldworkers were out, sowing their crops. It made him think of Verfeld, and he suddenly felt homesick.

"You all right?" asked Sigwulf.

Ludwig coughed to cover up his emotional state. "I'm fine," he answered, although his voice was hoarse. "This place kind of reminds me of back home."

"You lived in farm country?"

"Is there any other type?"

"Yes," said Sigwulf, "you might be from one of the major cities."

"Not me. I've never set foot in a city."

"Not true," said Cyn. "You've been to Torburg."

Ludwig smiled. "So I have. And now you mention it, I have been to Malburg, so I suppose that counts as a city, or at least a large town."

"There, you see? You're more widely travelled than you thought."

"So I am. Though in those days, I spent more time on a horse."

"You should thank us," said Sigwulf.

"For what?"

The big man smiled. "This march will toughen you up. Before you know it, you'll be as big as me."

Ludwig couldn't help but laugh. Sigwulf was the largest man he'd ever seen, but inside he had a soft heart, likely due to Cyn's influence.

"How long to Mulsingen?" asked Cyn.

Now it was Ludwig's turn to impress. "Eighty miles or so, the captain indicated. That should be about a week's march, shouldn't it?"

"Not at this pace," said Sigwulf. "We'll be lucky if we make five miles today."

"Five miles? Is that all?"

"What can I say? The company has been idle for the last month. There's also a lot of new recruits who haven't been hardened to the march. You should be thankful. In your condition, you're lucky to make even this slow pace."

"It's not my fault I was beaten black and blue."

"Isn't it?" said Cyn. "I warned you about Baldric, yet you insisted on humiliating him in the battle."

"I had to. He was coming after me."

"True," said Sigwulf, "but did you have to go for the groin? That unsettles a man."

Ludwig sighed. "I suppose you're right." He looked over his shoulder, wondering how far back his nemesis was.

"Don't worry," said Cyn, "he's bringing up the rear. I heard the captain issuing the orders. I doubt we'll see him again until we make camp."

"And when will that be?" asked Ludwig.

"Why? Getting tired already?"

"I can't help it. It's this cursed numbleaf. It steals the very blood from my veins."

"No, it doesn't," she chided. "Stop being such a baby about it."

"I still say it makes me tired."

"Perhaps, but at least we didn't have to leave you behind."

Ludwig turned to Sigwulf. "Do you still believe we can make Mulsingen in a week?"

"Yes. I suspect we'll increase our pace each day, breaking in the new recruits gradually. Were it up to me, we'd set a brisker march, but showing up with the company strung out along the road wouldn't set a good precedent. I might remind you we still haven't officially signed a contract with the baron."

"Speaking of which," said Ludwig, "how does all that get settled?"

"Simple," said Cyn. "Once we arrive, the baron will probably want to take a look at us, even if it's only from his keep. If he's impressed with what he sees, he'll make an offer to Captain Ecke."

"And then?"

"If the offer is agreeable, we'll be gainfully employed."

"And if not?" asked Ludwig.

"Then negotiations will begin, but hopefully it won't come to that."

"You've seen this type of thing before?"

"I was raised in a free company," said Cyn. "This was a common enough occurrence. Unfortunately, it can be a lengthy process if they can't agree on a fee."

"Let's hope that isn't the case here," said Sigwulf. "Then we can just concentrate on whatever it is the baron wants us for."

"Surely it's to fight?" said Ludwig. "Why else would he hire mercenaries?"

"Fighting's not the issue. It's the details. Are we to fight a battle in a field, or conduct a siege?"

"Does it matter?"

"It certainly does," said Sigwulf. "A field battle would likely be over in a week, but a siege... that's a far different situation."

"So you're saying a siege is preferable?"

"Only from the perspective of pay. Have you ever been in a siege?"

"Can't say that I have."

"From what I've heard, they're terrible things. Weeks of digging siege lines, enduring rain, even the threat of fever. I wouldn't wish it on my worst enemy."

"And if we're called on to do just that?"

"Then we follow orders," said Sigwulf. "It's what we signed up for after all."

That night they made camp in an empty field. The tents were spread out, with little thought to organizing anything. Ludwig shook his head, and Sigwulf noted the action.

"You disagree with something?"

"The camp is disorganized," said Ludwig. "It's a wonder anyone can find anything with this layout."

"Why is that so important?"

"What if we were attacked? How would the men know where to form up?"

"But we're marching in friendly territory," argued Sigwulf.

"True, but it won't always be that way. If an enemy were to attack us under these circumstances, there'd be little we could do to stop it. What we need is more discipline. I've read that's important in battle."

"You may be right. I heard tell that was the reason the rebellion failed in Abelard. The real question is, where do we start?"

"You start by organizing the troops," offered Ludwig.

"Organizing, how? We've already split into half companies."

"And that's good, but we need to go farther. Look at these tents. They're all over the place."

"What are you suggesting?"

"I'd lay them out in two lines, facing each other. That would keep them close together. The end of the line would be the assembly point in the event of an emergency."

"A fine idea," said Sigwulf, "but far too late to implement today. I'll bring it up with the captain, and if he's amenable, we could try it tomorrow night."

"Do you think he might agree?"

Sigwulf shrugged. "I doubt it. He shows little interest in such things. On the other hand, he did like your idea of creating sergeants."

"You don't seem to have an extremely high opinion of our glorious leader," noted Ludwig.

"He's not the most inspiring of men. Then again, I've heard of worse."

"Not Cyn's father?"

"No, Captain Hoffman was a decent fellow, with years of command experience under his belt."

"Are you saying Ecke has no experience?"

"Yes, at least not as a leader. Oh, sure, he's seen his fair share of battle, but not as a captain."

"But I thought this company had some battles under its belt?"

"It does," said Sigwulf, "but they didn't require a lot of leadership."

"Tell me about them."

"The first was right after Cyn and I joined the Grim Defenders. We were under the employ of a man called Lord Rossdale. Have you heard of him?"

"Can't say I have. Is he local to Erlingen?"

"No," said Sigwulf, "he hailed from Ulrichen, the kingdom that lies to our southeast. In any event, he hired us to escort a merchant train from Rosenbruck to Kurslingen, the capital of Zowenbruch."

"An entire mercenary company to escort a merchant? What was he carrying, a king's ransom?"

"As a matter of fact, yes. You see, the King of Ulrichen was waylaid on his way home by Zowenbruch forces. Being an impoverished nation, their king, Konrad III, decided to hold him for ransom. The problem was Konrad didn't want Ulrichen troops anywhere near his border, thus necessitating the hiring of mercenaries to escort the payment."

"Something obviously went wrong," said Ludwig, "otherwise you wouldn't be bringing this up."

"King Konrad decided he'd take the ransom for himself and keep his prisoner locked up. He actually crossed the border into Erlingen to ambush us."

"So he sent his own troops against you?"

"He did, though it didn't go well for him. We beat off the attack and retreated to Ulrichen, along with the ransom."

"And Captain Ecke was in command?"

"He was, but I would say we survived despite his attempts to command us, rather than because of them. It was a chaotic, bloody affair, and he lost his head. If it hadn't been for the fact that most of us were veterans, it would have turned out far differently."

"But if you feel that way, why not seek employment elsewhere?"

"That's easier said than done, my friend. Free companies aren't as common as you might think, and it takes coins to travel around looking for them. Besides, what would I do without Cyn?"

"Couldn't you simply take her with you?"

"There aren't many bands who will take women, and I'd never expect her to give up the life of a warrior. It's too important to her."

"So you're stuck here, in the Grim Defenders," said Ludwig, "just like me."

Sigwulf nodded. "It appears we share a similar fate."

"Wouldn't it be better to seek employment in the service of a lord?"

"With a price on my head? I consider that unwise, don't you?"

"I suppose that's true. Mind you, you're a trustworthy fellow. I'd hire you in an instant."

Sigwulf laughed. "Then when you inherit your father's barony, you can hire us on."

"Agreed," said Ludwig. "I'd hire you and Cyn, although maybe not the entire company."

The big man grinned. "I'll hold you to that promise."

"I wouldn't have it any other way."

Sigwulf, true to his word, sought out Captain Ecke, but the man had little interest in Ludwig's suggestion. He did, however, give the sergeant free rein to try it himself. Consequently, Ludwig, Cyn, and Sigwulf spent the best part of the next day planning out the camp as they marched.

The pace was brisk on the second day, and they covered a far greater distance than they had the day before. By the time the halt was called, Ludwig was exhausted. Sigwulf, however, was far too keen to start organizing the tents, something that required Ludwig and Cyn's help.

The first step was to mark out spaces for tents. This was easily accomplished by having Ludwig pace off the distance. He would take five steps, then Cyn would put down a stake to mark the spot. With the first row marked off, men began setting up their tents. A second row was then erected facing the first.

There was some confusion as the half company began taking up their positions, but with guidance and some shouts from Sigwulf, they all fell into place. By the time the fires were started, the men were in a better mood. The place looked professional, leading the captain to come and see what all the chatter was about. He walked up and down the line, hemming and hawing but saying little. Finally, he grumbled something that sounded like 'well done', then wandered off to his pavilion.

"High praise from Captain Ecke," said Cyn.

"That was praise?" asked Ludwig.

"Oh yes," added Sigwulf. "He was positively chatty."

"I'd hate to see him when he's in a foul mood."

"You have, remember?" said Cyn. "That's how you got put in the pillory."

Ludwig felt the ache in his bruised chest and winced. "I'm not likely to forget."

Sigwulf looked down the line, taking pride in their work. "It's nice, isn't it? Highly professional."

"You'd think we had an army," noted Cyn. "I wonder if the Church does something like this?"

"Probably," said Ludwig, "though I would suspect Temple Knights have much nicer tents."

"Yes," added Sigwulf, "and they're all mounted troops, remember? They'd need an area for their horses."

Cyn looked at Ludwig. "Ever considered joining the Church? I hear the Temple Knights of Saint Cunar are always looking for experienced horsemen?"

"No," replied Ludwig. "I imagine I'd find their lifestyle too restricting. I'll stick with being a mercenary for now, thanks."

"Have it your way," said Cyn, "but at least they'd give you some really nice armour."

"I had one of the finest sets you can buy, but I was a fool and lost it... well, most of it."

"You're no fool now."

"That," said Ludwig, "remains to be seen."

They set out on the march again the next morning. Having the half company all together made it easy to gather the men and even easier to load up the wagons with their tents. They were soon on the road and setting a brisk pace, causing the rest of the company, under Sergeant Baldric, to rush to catch up.

By midday, they had covered quite a distance, and even Captain Ecke was getting tired. He called a halt, allowing men to rest their weary feet and eat what rations they carried.

Ludwig, spotting a nearby stream, elected to go and refill his waterskin. He had taken only a few steps when Cyn appeared at his side.

"Where do you think you're going?" she asked.

Ludwig produced his skin. "Fetching some water. You?"

She held up her own. "Same."

"I saw a stream off in this direction." He pointed.

"Come on, then," she urged. "I'll race you."

She burst into a run, leaving him struggling in her wake. Up ahead, a babbling brook meandered its way across a farmer's field. The land to one side had been freshly ploughed, while the other was naught but wild grass. They knelt by the bank and began filling their waterskins, but then a sound off to the right drew Ludwig's attention. Three men were running back to the roadway, each carrying a dead chicken by the neck.

"What's this?" called out Ludwig.

Cyn looked up. "Baldric and his friends," she said as if that explained everything.

"He's stealing."

"What of it?"

He turned to her in shock. "The people hereabouts eke out a living. They can't afford to have their stock stolen by thieves."

"You know the people around here, do you?" she asked.

"No, but I know their type, and I doubt they appreciate having their food stolen."

"There's not a lot we can do about it," warned Cyn.

"I should report this to the captain."

"Are you sure that's what you want to do?"

"Don't you?"

She shrugged. "It makes little difference to me, but if you want to lodge a complaint, I'll back you up."

"Good," said Ludwig. "Let's head back to the road."

They joined up with the rest of the company, but before they could begin looking for the captain, the Grim Defenders were ordered to their feet, and the march continued.

. . .

They ended up having to wait until evening to lodge their complaint, and so it was they found themselves staring across the small table at Captain Ecke.

The man looked displeased, for in addition to Cyn, Sigwulf, and Ludwig, he had called Sergeant Baldric, along with Quentin and Emile, the better to judge the complaint.

Ecke, who had remained quiet as they arrived, looked up at Sigwulf. "I understand these two lodged a complaint, but what are you doing here?"

"I'm their sergeant. I should be present when one of my men…" His eyes flicked to Cyn. "I mean people, lodges a complaint."

"This is none of his concern," said Baldric. "Sigwulf should mind his own business. There's nothing wrong with soldiers supplementing their food ration. It is, in fact, expected."

"You are depriving the locals of their livelihood," said Ludwig. "Can you not see that?"

The captain held up his hand to interrupt. "I've heard enough." He looked at Ludwig. "It's clear to me that you are only trying to get even with Baldric for your earlier punishment. You have a bright future ahead of you as a mercenary, Ludwig, but you must learn to live within the confines of this company. I shall not countenance any further discussion of this matter."

"But I—"

"But nothing," roared Ecke. "It is my decision that you shall stand watch this evening."

"Which shift?" asked Sigwulf.

"All of them," spat out the captain. "That's right, you heard me. You shall stand watch all night, and by the Saints, if I catch you sleeping, I shall have you flogged! Now get out of here, all of you."

Ludwig fought to keep his anger in check. Stepping outside, he took in a deep breath of the chilly night air and let it out slowly. Baldric appeared at his side, giving him a dirty look.

"No one likes a rat, Ludwig. You should have kept things to yourself."

"Piss off!"

"No," Baldric replied. "It's you who'll piss off. I'm a sergeant now, and that makes me untouchable, you hear me?"

Sigwulf intervened. "Move on, Baldric."

The two stood, staring at each other with absolute malice in their eyes. Ludwig was sure they were about to explode into action, but Baldric finally backed down, slinking off into the night.

11

THE BARON

Spring 1095 SR

Mulsingen was a small town surrounded by outlying farms. The Grim Defenders marched through, knowing their true destination was the keep that lay on the far side. The villagers watched them, keeping their faces neutral.

Sigwulf smiled as they passed by, content in the knowledge they were close to their destination. "Just like last time," he remarked.

Cyn turned to Ludwig. "We passed by here on the way to Torburg," she explained.

"Is Mulsingen a free city?" asked Ludwig.

Both Sigwulf and Cyn gave him a blank look.

"A what?" asked Cyn.

"A free city? Malburg was given a charter by the king to govern themselves, electing a council of commoners to do that very thing."

"Why?"

"Yes," agreed Sigwulf, "why in the Continent would a king agree to something like that?"

"My cousin, King Otto, needed more funds for his coffers. The townsfolk convinced him that in the guild's hands, they would prosper."

"And did they?"

"Yes," said Ludwig, "and far in excess of what was expected. I would go so far as to suggest it's the way of the future."

"Don't be ridiculous," said Sigwulf. "No king in his right mind wants to give up control of a city."

"Cousin Otto did."

"Tell me more about this cousin of yours," said Cyn.

"What would you like to know?"

"You can start by explaining where Malburg is."

"It's in Hadenfeld," said Ludwig.

"And where's that?"

"South and a little west."

"Can you be more specific?"

"Well," said Ludwig, "Zowenbruch lies to the south of Erlingen. You'd have to travel through that kingdom, then to Neuhafen beyond. Hadenfeld lies on its western border."

"So it's three kingdoms away?"

"Yes, I suppose it is, but I wouldn't ride through Neuhafen if I could avoid it."

"Why is that?"

"They used to be part of Hadenfeld, but they rose up in rebellion and broke away to form their own country."

"That happens a lot in the Petty Kingdoms," mused Sigwulf. "Do they give you trouble?"

"Nothing we haven't been able to handle. Mind you, their king is always talking about claiming our throne, so I imagine it'll lead to war eventually."

"Aren't you worried?" asked Cyn.

"About what?"

"Your family?"

Ludwig waved off the concern. "No, my father's a stubborn man. And in any case, it would take a sizable army to wrest control of Verfeld Keep from his hands."

"It sounds like your father's relatively wealthy," said Cyn.

"Yes," agreed Sigwulf, "and likely powerful if your cousin is the king."

"I suppose that's true," said Ludwig. "Not that I spent much time thinking about it."

"So why is it you left?" asked Cyn.

"A woman," interrupted Sigwulf. "It's all quite romantic."

Cyn looked at him in surprise. "You're showing your soft side."

In answer, Sigwulf coughed. "Look," he said, "we're clearing Mulsingen. We should be able to see the baron's keep shortly."

She turned to Ludwig. "He's always trying to swallow his feelings."

"I'm a sergeant now," insisted Sigwulf. "I have to set an example."

The village gave way to the fields beyond. Atop a small hill in the distance was a square keep, much like Verfeld, but with a curtain wall that surrounded an outer bailey. This arrangement was topped off with a gate-house that was basically a small tower with a portcullis and a gate leading through it.

Ludwig wondered what the inside was like, but they were not to find out, for as they drew closer, they were ushered into an adjacent field by two men wearing mail coifs and padded gambesons.

Cyn and Ludwig immediately began marking off the area while Sigwulf assigned duties to the men. They were half done when Ludwig spotted Baldric yelling at Quentin and Emile about something. Ludwig paused, watching the drama unfold.

Cyn, who was still pacing off the distance, looked back at Ludwig, waiting for him to place a stake. "Are you coming?" she asked.

"Just a moment," he replied. "It looks like Baldric is up to something."

She moved closer, following his gaze. "What are they doing?"

Ludwig chuckled. "I imagine the captain must have told him to line up his tents like we do."

"What makes you say that?"

"Look at those two fools trying to pace off the distance."

Quentin was taking exaggerated steps, making the whole effort appear ludicrous. It looked like their hosts agreed, for the two men who had directed the company to the field were staring at him, laughing their arses off.

"Should we help?" asked Ludwig.

"No," replied Cyn. "Let them sink or swim on their own."

"Sink or swim? We're on dry land."

She chuckled. "Sorry, it's an expression I picked up in Braymoor. They're known for their warships, you know."

"No, I didn't. Tell me, what was it like up there? Is it cold?"

"No more so than here, although if you live on the coast, the wind can be brutal."

"Is that where you served?"

"No. We were in the southern region, well away from water, thank you very much."

"You don't like water?"

"I have nothing against it," said Cyn, "but that doesn't mean I want to set foot aboard a ship."

"Why? What's wrong with a ship?"

"What if it sinks? I don't want to drown."

"I'm sure plenty of ships ply the waterways of the Continent without sinking."

"I'd prefer not to hazard the risk. Now, enough of this banter; let's get back to work, shall we?"

Ludwig tore his gaze away from Baldric and his cronies. "All right."

By nightfall, they had settled in while Captain Ecke disappeared into the keep along with two warriors, but little was said to the rank and file. The next day was no different nor the day after. For five days, the same dull routine repeated itself.

Ludwig grew bored. It was one thing to march around the countryside, quite another to be stuck in a muddy field for days on end with nothing to do. He was looking forward to the prospect of battle if only to relieve the tedium.

He took to the habit of rising early each morning, ensuring he had unfettered access to the nearby stream. It wasn't that people prevented him from using it, but far too many mercenaries were content to relieve themselves in the water. As a consequence, Ludwig had to make his way farther and farther upstream to find a supply suitable for drinking.

Today the weather was clear, a pleasant change from the damp, windy days that had preceded it. He re-entered the camp to see Sigwulf casting his gaze about.

"Ah," the big man said, "there you are, Ludwig. Grab your armour. You're coming with me."

"To where?"

"We're escorting the captain today."

"Into the keep?"

"So it would seem."

Ludwig rushed to his tent, pulling out what armour he had. He stepped back out into the sun and began dressing. "It would be nice if the company would equip us," he commented.

"That would cost a fortune," replied Sigwulf, "and, quite frankly, I'd prefer to have the coins."

"But we look so... ragged."

The sergeant looked around. "Why would you say that?"

"No two mercenaries look the same. It's hard to tell we're even in the same company."

"What would you have us do? Wear surcoats like some noble's household?"

"It couldn't hurt."

"We're mercenaries, Ludwig, not a garrison. We fight those battles no one else wants to. Do you think they care a whit about what we look like?"

"No, I suppose not, but I can't help but feel it would make us look more professional."

"There you go with that word again," said Sigwulf. "I tell you what. When you raise your own company, you can decide what everyone's going to wear. Fair enough?"

Ludwig chuckled. "I'll hold you to that."

"Now, come on," the big man urged. "The captain's waiting." They made their way towards the command tent where Ecke stood waiting.

"Finally," said the captain. "Come along, you two; we've work to do."

He led them towards the gatehouse, setting a brisk clip. Two of the baron's men stood watch, leaning on their spears, and watching as the small group passed. Ludwig gave the guards a quick glance, noting the poor condition of their armour. It didn't bode well for the future.

Across the inner courtyard they walked, past another group of disinterested soldiers. Many were overweight as evidenced by their bulging armour. A gambeson was a thick, padded jacket, often making a man look bulkier, but in this case, Ludwig noticed the material straining at the seams. Apparently, the baron's soldiers ate well.

They entered the keep, where a well-dressed servant led them into the great hall. Lord Gebhard Stein was, like his soldiers, a somewhat portly individual. Beside him stood a man, tall and thin, wearing a younger version of the baron's face.

"Good morning, Captain," said the baron. "I trust you slept well?"

"I did," said Ecke. "And yourself, Lord?"

"Very well, indeed. Shall we continue our discussion?"

"By all means."

"Now, let's see; where were we?"

"We had finally agreed on payment," said Ecke.

"Yes, of course. With that out of the way, we can now concentrate on the matter at hand. As I have mentioned previously, I've had some issues with one of my neighbours, Lord Wulfram Haas, Baron of Regnitz."

"So you indicated yesterday," said Ecke. "I assume you wish to lure him out to fight?"

"That would be preferable," replied the baron, "but I doubt we'll get the chance."

"Then what, pray tell, are you proposing?"

The baron smiled. "I mean for us to capture his keep."

"A siege?"

"No, an assault," the baron clarified. "An attack meant to quickly overwhelm his defenders."

"And might I ask what we can expect in the way of defences?"

"Regnitz is much like Mulsingen, a square keep with an enclosed court-yard adjacent. Of course, there's also the matter of the moat."

"He has a moat?"

"Yes, although it's not deep."

"That presents a formidable obstacle," said Ecke, "and an assault would be costly."

"Precisely why I have hired on the Grim Defenders. Your men ARE up to the task, aren't they?"

"They most definitely are," said Ecke. "Still, I think it wise to get more information about the place if we can."

"Nonsense," said the baron. "Lord Wulfram has few enough troops. I know for certain that he can't man the entire wall."

"He doesn't have to, my lord. He only has to defend whatever wall section we attack. We lack the manpower to surround the place, even with the help of your household troops. And what of the duke?"

"What of him?"

"Won't he object to his nobles fighting?"

"No, he pays little heed to such things. It has ever been thus."

"Good to know," said Ecke. "What can we expect in the way of defenders?"

"His forces are decidedly limited. At last count, he had but thirty men, and only one-third of them archers."

"And the village of Regnitz?"

"Lies a little to the south of the keep, several hundred yards from its walls. The ground thereabouts is clear in all directions."

Ecke visibly paled. "So we have to assault across open ground, then wade through a moat?"

"Precisely. Don't worry, though, my men will be backing you up."

"When you say 'your men,' how many are you talking about?"

"I have gathered a force of one hundred, with thirty of those yeoman cavalry."

"Of little use in a siege, my lord."

"True," agreed the baron, "but priceless as we approach. If we're lucky, we can catch some of them before they withdraw inside their defences."

"And the rest?"

"Of my remaining men, fully a third are bowmen, the remainder being foot."

"So let me get this straight," said Ecke. "You're marching with thirty horsemen, two dozen archers, and about forty-odd foot?"

"In addition to your company, yes."

"And you consider that sufficient to take the keep?"

"I can assure you it is," pressed the baron. He noted the dismay on Ecke's face. "Come now, Captain, I've seen the state of Lord Wulfram's men. The only question now is whether I can count on the support of your company?"

Ecke stiffened. "We are mercenaries, my lord. You pay the fee, and we shall march and fight."

"Good. Then we have an agreement?"

"We do," said the captain, "though there are some more things I should like to hear of."

"Certainly," said the baron. "What would you like to know?"

"Have they a gatehouse?"

"Yes, remarkably similar to ours, in fact, except for the drawbridge."

"They have a drawbridge?"

"Of course, how else would they get across the moat?"

"Have you conducted a siege before, my lord?"

"No," admitted the baron, "but I am not without my own resources. I have hired on an expert, Captain Gottfried Jager. Do you know him?"

"I'm afraid I don't."

"He is a master of siege warfare. I doubt Lord Wulfram will stand a chance against that kind of experience."

Ludwig watched as indecision wracked the face of Captain Ecke, but the man would never back out of a deal. "Very well," he said at last. "When shall we march?"

"Tomorrow," said the baron. "Regnitz is nearly forty miles away. I expect we shall be there in three days. Let's hope, if we're quick about it, we can take the keep before he knows what hit him."

"While that would be preferable," said the captain, "let's not count on it. Instead, we should make plans for the assault."

"Yes. Ideally, I'd like to see the assault carried out the same day we arrive."

"I'm afraid that won't be possible, my lord. We'll need ladders, and those take time to produce. We also need to take into account the weather."

The baron grew impatient. "We can deal with all that once we arrive. You'd best get back to your men, Captain. I'm sure there are preparations to be made."

Ecke bowed. "Of course, my lord. We shall march first thing tomorrow morning."

"Excellent. Then we shall be feasting in Regnitz by the end of the week."

The captain turned, leaving the room with Sigwulf and Ludwig falling in behind. It wasn't until they were clear of the keep that Ecke finally spoke again. "The blasted man's a fool!" He turned to Sigwulf. "What did you make of him?"

The sergeant cleared his throat. "I think he overestimates the chances of success."

"And you?" said Ecke, looking at Ludwig.

"He's being overly optimistic if he believes he'll be within Regnitz Keep by week's end."

"There is good news," offered Sigwulf.

Ecke halted, turning to face his sergeant. "Which is?"

"If this turns into a long siege, as I suspect it will, it'll cost the baron a fortune. Good for us."

The captain smiled. "Yes, but at what cost? Sieges are terrible things, Sigwulf, make no mistake. If the assaults don't kill you, the pestilence likely will. Have you ever been in an army when the plague visits? It's not something you'd want to see, believe me."

"Are you saying you don't believe we can take Regnitz Keep?" asked Ludwig.

"No," said Ecke. "We can take it all right. I'm just concerned Lord Gebhard will force us to take all the casualties."

"Isn't that what we're paid for?"

The captain resumed his walk. "I suppose it is, but I don't have to like it."

"We could always refuse the commission," suggested Sigwulf.

"No. If we did that, word would get around that we're unreliable. We'd never get another contract again. We can't back out now."

"What can we do to help?" asked the sergeant.

"Get back to camp and make sure no one gets drunk tonight. I need them ready to march at the crack of dawn."

"That early?" asked Ludwig.

"The sooner we get there, the sooner we'll fully understand what we're up against."

Cyn was waiting for them upon their return.

"How was it?" she asked in her typical cheerful manner. Her smile soon turned into a frown as she beheld the grave face Sigwulf wore. "What is it?"

"We're marching in the morning," he replied.

"That's good news, isn't it?" She looked at Ludwig for an explanation.

"It looks like we're marching towards a siege," he explained, "and we'll likely bear the brunt of the assault."

"A siege, you say?"

Ludwig nodded. "Yes, and the defences are, perhaps, better than we had anticipated. Have you ever been in a siege?"

"No," said Cyn, "but my father often talked of his time in the east."

"The Crusades? I've always thought of travelling there."

She frowned. "No, not the Crusades, but close. The Realm of Novarsk lies on the far eastern edge of the Petty Kingdoms. He took the Crossed Swords there, long before I was born. The first crusade had just ended, but the influx of warriors had overwhelmed the inhabitants. Some of the local barons rebelled, leading to all sorts of troubles."

"I take it they hired him to pacify the region?"

"They did. Of course a large crusader army was present, but they were needed to hold on to the strongholds. The Swords ended up being assigned the job of recapturing a place called Halmund. It was a bloody affair."

"It must have been quite the company to take a city," said Ludwig.

"They weren't alone. There were four other mercenary groups. The initial assault against the city walls failed, and they settled in for a siege. Unfortunately, it was late in the year, and winter came early. Some died from the cold, but many more succumbed to fever."

"Did they ever manage to capture the city?"

"They did, eventually, but not until the spring. By the time they broke the walls, they were in a fearful rage. I'm afraid they committed unspeakable acts once they got inside. It was always my father's greatest shame."

"Despite that, he told you about it?" said Ludwig.

"He did. My father always insisted on telling me the truth of such things. We mercenaries lead a grim life, Ludwig; never forget that."

"But it doesn't have to be that way."

She shook her head. "It has always been so, and we are powerless to stop it."

"No, I refuse to believe that. Life is different now than in the days of our ancestors because people resolved to change things. The same is true today. We can make a better life for our descendants, Cyn. I know it."

"Descendants now, is it?" said Sigwulf. "Do you have a son tucked away somewhere?"

Ludwig blushed. "No, but maybe someday. What about you two?"

"What about us?" said Cyn.

"Have you ever considered having children?"

Her mood soured. "Stop talking such nonsense." She turned, leaving the area at a quick pace.

Ludwig watched her go, noting how she wiped her eyes. "Did I say something wrong?"

Sigwulf rested his hand on Ludwig's shoulder. "No. There are some things Cyn doesn't like to discuss. She'll talk about it when she's ready."

12

ON THE MOVE

Spring 1095 SR

The march began with little fanfare. The company formed up on the road, and then the captain ordered them forward, wagons in the rear. The morning air was crisp, but the cloudless sky promised a warm day. They were fully a mile down the road when Sigwulf noticed Ludwig glancing over his shoulder.

"What are you doing?" he asked.

"Looking for the baron's men. We're not attacking all by ourselves, are we?"

"They'll be along soon enough. They're probably still having breakfast."

"That must be nice," said Ludwig. "All I had this morning was some stale bread."

Sigwulf smiled. "Be thankful you had that. Back in Braymoor, we often went for days with no food. Why, I remember one time when we had to resort to eating rats."

Ludwig looked at him in surprise, but the big man couldn't maintain the facade. He broke into a laugh. "Well, maybe I'm exaggerating a little."

"A little?" said Cyn. "How about a lot? When did you ever eat rats, Siggy?"

Sigwulf looked offended. "What about Walgarten?"

"That wasn't a rat," she replied, "that was a stoat."

"They're similar?"

"No they're not," said Cyn, fighting to suppress a grin. "They're 'stoataly' different!" She let out a laugh, unable to contain it any further.

"Are you done?" said Sigwulf.

She halted to catch her breath, leaving her to fall behind them, if only momentarily.

"Is she always like this?" asked Ludwig.

"Yes," said Sigwulf. His tone was serious, but the look on his face said otherwise. "It's one of her most endearing qualities."

"Is it normal for us to march first? I would have thought the baron would have liked to lead us."

"His Lordship doesn't want to leave us alone in Mulsingen, even for a morning."

"Does he not trust us?"

"No. There have been too many incidents of free companies turning against their employer."

"I thought mercenaries were highly regarded."

Sigwulf let out a guffaw. "Surely you jest?"

Ludwig was confused. "But aren't we professional warriors?"

Cyn chose that moment to catch up to them. "What are we talking about?"

"Ludwig here was under the impression mercenaries were held in high regard."

"Some are," she said, "but even the best-intentioned of captains can let their troops get the better of them."

"I'm not sure I follow?" said Ludwig.

"She means the troops get out of hand."

"Yes," said Cyn. "Like at Halmund. It very nearly brought the wrath of the Church upon them."

"The Church?"

"Yes, the Temple Knights take a dim view of such things amongst the cities of the Petty Kingdoms. Mind you, they have no such qualms about doing the same to their enemies."

"What enemies does the Church have?"

Cyn frowned. "Where have you been for the last few years? Forgotten the Crusades, have you?"

"Oh yes, of course," said Ludwig. "I wasn't thinking."

"A common trait, it would appear," muttered Cyn.

"Pardon?"

"I said we set a fast rate. The sky is clear. What was it you wanted to know?"

"I was curious about the Crossed Swords," said Ludwig. "From your description, they'd obviously been formed some years ago. Was your father always their captain?"

"No," replied Cyn. "He was there when they first formed and more or less worked his way up to captain."

"What happened to them? I heard they were forced to disband."

"Where did you hear that?"

"Captain Ecke."

"I suppose most of what he said was likely true, but I'll give you the story from my perspective. At the time, the company was in the employ of a baron, much like we are now. He'd hired us to put an end to a group of bandits who had been terrorizing the area."

"And were you successful?" asked Ludwig.

"We were, actually, but when it came time to collect what we were due, His Lordship refused to pay. The company had been waiting for three months, and the stores had run low, so my father did the only thing he could; he raided the local countryside looking for food."

"I'm sure the baron didn't appreciate that."

"That's putting it mildly," said Cyn. "Next thing you know, the baron's complained to the king, and then royal troops were sent to chase us down."

"That must have been awful."

"Awful doesn't begin to describe it. They captured my father and several others. Have you any idea what it's like to watch your own father hanged?"

"No," said Ludwig. "It must have been terrible."

"It was," said Cyn. "Shortly after that, Siggy and I fled Braymoor."

"What brought you here to Erlingen?"

"Chance, mostly. As we got closer, we heard tell of the Grim Defenders and sought them out. It just happened Captain Ecke had served with my father years ago."

"A happy coincidence, then?"

"I don't know if I'd call it happy," said Sigwulf, "but it gave us some stability. There's not many employment opportunities for a pair of sell-swords in these parts."

"I would have thought a position as bodyguards would have been ideal," said Ludwig.

"Probably, but people want someone they can trust in such a role, and, being foreigners, we had little in the way of reputation."

"And that brought us here," said Cyn. "Now you know everything."

"Everything except where my next meal is coming from."

"Now, that," said Sigwulf, "I can answer. The baron has wagons full of food that he's providing for us. I hear he sets a fine table."

"If he does," said Cyn, "it's not likely one we'll be invited to."

Sigwulf turned defensive. "What's that supposed to mean?"

"Only that those wagons are probably for the baron's men, not us."

"But he wouldn't sit back and let us starve, would he?" said Ludwig.

"Wouldn't he?" said Cyn. "I'm not so sure of that."

"I can understand your distrust of nobles," said Ludwig, "particularly taking into account your father's story, but to hire a company and then not feed them feels unlikely, to say the least."

"We're not his household troops. I doubt he even cares. He's paid us, and now he wants us to fight—nothing else matters."

"For what it's worth," said Sigwulf, "I disagree. I think it likely food will be provided. After all, the baron wants this whole situation resolved before the end of the week. He can't do that if we're half-starved."

"Can't he?" said Cyn. "Care to place a wager on that?"

"Come on, you two," said Ludwig. "Let's not argue over something that's out of our hands."

"I'm not arguing," said Cyn, "merely stating a point of fact."

"As am I," added Sigwulf. He turned to look at Cyn. "Does he honestly believe we're fighting?"

"He does."

"I shall have to have a talk with him."

"I'm right here," said Ludwig.

They both looked at him as if seeing him for the first time.

"So you are," said Sigwulf.

Ludwig shook his head. This was going to be a long march.

That evening they were fed bread along with cheese gathered from local farms. It was not the freshest of food but more than sufficient to fill them, and they went to bed with their stomachs full.

Morning came far too early for Ludwig's liking. He had his tent packed up in record time, but the company was told to hold back.

"What's happening?" he asked as Captain Ecke approached.

"We're waiting," their leader replied. "This road takes us into the Barony of Regnitz, and Lord Gebhard wants to be the first to cross into his enemy's lands."

"And where is His Lordship?"

"Behind us," said Ecke. "Likely still having breakfast." He wandered off, far too preoccupied to continue with the conversation.

"What do you make of that?" said Cyn.

Sigwulf shrugged. "It makes no difference to me. If the baron wants his fat arse to cross the border first, then so be it."

"It's not a border," corrected Cyn. "Both barons are still in the same kingdom."

"Well, whatever you call it, it's still fine."

"Look at that," said Ludwig, pointing. The baron's men had finally appeared. They were shuffling along the road, sweating in the early morning sun despite the cool air.

"They look like they're ready to die," said Sigwulf.

"They're not used to marching," said Cyn. "I doubt they march more than a few hundred yards when they're in garrison."

Sigwulf laughed. "Yes, the distance between their rooms and the dining hall."

"Now, now," said Ludwig. "We shouldn't disparage them. They are our allies after all."

Sigwulf sobered. "You're right, Saints help us. This doesn't bode well." He turned to Cyn. "Can you imagine any of those men climbing a ladder to assault the wall?"

"I can barely imagine them marching," she replied, "yet here they are."

They watched in silence as the men passed by.

"I suppose we should get moving," said Ludwig.

"There's no hurry," said Sigwulf. "We'll catch up to that lot in no time."

A bellow urged them to move, and then Baldric and his men began marching by.

"I suppose this means we're bringing up the rear," said Cyn.

Sigwulf waited until they had passed, then assembled his half company. They marched out at a slow pace, determined to conserve their strength for the afternoon.

In theory, the road between Mulsingen and Regnitz was straight, but whoever had mapped the area had made no allowance for the hills that dotted the region. As a result, the road wandered, never going straight for more than a mile.

The weather warmed considerably, giving the first hint that summer was right around the corner. All in all, it was a good day for marching: not too hot and not too cold.

Late in the afternoon, Sigwulf halted his men. They had picked up the pace considerably, but now the baron's men were lagging, causing the mercenaries in the rear to bunch up, interfering with their march. Baldric kept pressing on, cursing and swearing to no end, but Sigwulf decided to halt his men and give them a rest.

Thus it was they found themselves sitting by the roadside when the newcomer arrived seated upon a dappled grey mare, dressed in grey himself, making him look like some form of ghostly apparition. Upon spotting the resting mercenaries, he slowed, then turned his horse towards them.

"Hello?" he called out.

Sigwulf stood. "Can I help you?"

"I would most definitely hope so," the man replied, his voice betraying his educated manner. "I seek a man named Gottfried Jager. I understand he's a captain?"

Ludwig turned to Sigwulf. "That's the siege expert the baron hired."

"He's up the road," said the sergeant, "but you'll have to pass through this army to find him."

"A pity," said the newcomer. "I was hoping to get something to eat."

"And who are you, exactly?" asked Cyn.

"My name is Linden Herzog. I'm an Earth Mage."

Ludwig laughed. "An Earth Mage? Why don't you simply conjure yourself a rabbit to eat? That's what you people do, isn't it? Work with animals?"

The man chose to take offence. "Is that what you think? I'll have you know the magic of the earth can do much more than summon animals."

"Oh, yes? Like what?"

"Well, for one thing, we can manipulate stone. What would you prefer to do, climb a wall or have it turn to dirt?"

Ludwig's eyes widened. "You can do that?"

"I can do a great many things."

"If I give you some food, will you tell me more?"

The man grinned. "I would be delighted."

"Shouldn't we send him up to the baron?" asked Cyn.

Sigwulf shrugged. "We can't very well send him off hungry, now, can we?"

Ludwig dug into his sling bag, producing some bread. He offered it to Linden.

The mage took it, breaking off a small piece and popping it into his mouth. He barely chewed it before swallowing. "Ah," he said at last, "manna from the Afterlife."

"I don't reckon he's eaten in days," noted Cyn.

"You would be correct," said Linden. "I have been riding hard, and Clay is as exhausted as I."

"Clay?" she said.

"Yes, my horse." He saw the look of confusion. "Note the colouring?"

"Yes," said Ludwig. "We can all see your horse is grey. Nevertheless, you must admit Clay is an unusual name."

"Agreed, but it suits her. Like Clay, she has a malleable personality."

Linden Herzog dismounted, allowing Ludwig to take the reins.

"She's a fine beast," said Ludwig. "Have you had her long?"

"Nearly a year. Why do you ask?"

"I have a passing familiarity with horses."

"And yet you march on foot," said the mage. "I sense there's an air of mystery to you." He broke off another piece of bread.

Sigwulf laughed. "You might say that of everyone in the Grim Defenders."

"The Grim Defenders? Who are they?"

"That's us," explained Ludwig. "We're a mercenary group."

"Indeed? How fascinating." The mage chewed some bread, then swallowed. "Have you anything to drink?"

"Here," said Ludwig, passing him a waterskin.

The mage unstoppered it, then drank heavily.

"Does your horse need water?"

The mage belched. "My pardon. No, my horse watered itself at a stream."

"And you didn't think to water yourself?"

"And drink from runoff from these fields? Have you no sense, sir?"

Ludwig wanted to tell him he had likely filled his waterskin from the exact same stream but chose instead to withhold that information.

"So if you can manipulate stone, why does the baron need us?"

Linden handed back the waterskin. "Someone has to get me to the wall and then protect me while I work my magic."

"I'm not sure I follow. Don't you just cast a spell, and the wall comes down?"

"My good fellow, you know nothing of magic."

"Feel free to explain."

The mage looked pleased. "I should be delighted. You see, a spell like that requires me to be in close proximity to the target."

"How close?" asked Ludwig.

"I must be able to touch it."

"And then you can collapse it?"

"No, pardon me if I gave you that impression. The spell, when cast, softens the stone, allowing me to manipulate it."

"Softens it?"

"Yes, it takes on the consistency of clay."

"Then why couldn't we dig through it?"

"No, it's much more complicated than that. You see, I, as the caster, am the only one who can perceive that change. To anyone else, it would still appear as solid stone."

"So then you have to shape it?"

Linden smiled. "There, you have it now. I can only manipulate a small amount at a time, so I can't just open up an entire wall."

"But you could create a hole big enough to crawl through?"

"Exactly."

"I can see why the baron called on you."

The mage blushed. "Ah, well, therein lies the rub. It wasn't the baron who sent for me. Rather, it was Gottfried Jager. I have no idea if the baron wishes to employ me or not."

"But surely if he were aware of your powers?"

"They are spells, not powers, and require a significant amount of concentration, not to mention years of study."

"Still," pressed Ludwig, "if you can get us inside…"

"Let us hope the baron sees reason. In the meantime, I shall have my horse back, if you would be so kind."

"Certainly," said Ludwig, passing over the reins, "and good luck with the baron."

Linden Herzog climbed into the saddle. "Thank you. Now I must be off. I shall look you up once the siege begins. Our co-operation will be the key to victory, I think." He rode off without further discussion.

"What do you make of that?" said Cyn.

"An interesting individual," said Ludwig. "I wonder what the baron will make of him?"

"Let's not get our hopes up," said Sigwulf. "I have a feeling Lord Gebhard will not be easily convinced of his value."

The first sign they were nearing their destination came late in the afternoon when thick black smoke billowed in the sky off in the distance, far more than could be expected from campfires. As they rounded a hill, a burning farm came into view, with a couple of the baron's men taking an axe to a cow, while the rest stood around watching, perhaps mesmerized by the flames.

As they passed, Ludwig noticed the bodies of the poor peasants who had lived there. They had been slaughtered by the baron's men, and he wondered what anger Lord Gebhard must have against his neighbour to conduct war against him in such a manner.

Cyn saw him staring. "Terrible, isn't it?"

"Unfortunate to be sure," added Sigwulf, "but it's the fate of peasants to live or die at the whims of the nobility."

"What is it that drives the baron to take such action?" asked Ludwig. "If he means to capture the keep, wouldn't he want the farms to continue to produce?"

"I doubt he intends to hold Regnitz Keep," said Sigwulf. "More likely, he wishes to destroy it, hence the carnage here."

"So he's simply going to lay waste to everything?"

"We are mercenaries. We hire on to whoever pays us. It's not our place to question the motives of nobles."

"I disagree," said Ludwig. "War brings unnecessary cruelty. We should fight with honour."

"Honour? You know so little of battle," said Sigwulf. "Honour has no place there. It's a cesspit of murder and mayhem."

"But it doesn't have to be."

"He's right," added Cyn. "War should be between soldiers, not taking things out on poor farmers."

"We live in an age of near constant warfare," said Sigwulf. "People are inured to it."

"Yes," Ludwig agreed, "but they shouldn't have to be."

"A noble sentiment," said Cyn. "I wish more thought as you do."

"That might put us out of work," warned Sigwulf.

"No," said Ludwig, "on the contrary. You'd be hired to fight warriors, not burn the huts of farmers."

The great man turned red. "I might remind you it wasn't me who torched that farm."

"True, and I don't blame you, my friend. I am merely considering how things might be... different."

"He's full of ideas, this one," said Cyn. She turned to him, amusement in her eyes. "One more thing for you to change when you're baron," she remarked.

"Not me," said Ludwig. "I'm content to be a mercenary."

"Are you?" said Cyn. "Truly?"

13

ARRIVAL

Spring 1095 SR

The village of Regnitz had been hastily abandoned as evidenced by the open doors and discarded tools. Captain Ecke marched the Grim Defenders right through the centre of town, while it soon became apparent Lord Gebhard's men intended on taking up residence.

As they cleared the village, Ludwig noticed a body hanging from a nearby tree. He had seen executions in his time, but it was clear this unfortunate soul had choked to death rather than suffering a broken neck.

Two of the baron's men mocked the body, prodding it with the ends of their spears, and Ludwig suddenly felt ashamed to be a soldier. For years, he had aspired to be a warrior and lead a life of adventure, but here, in this place, he felt nothing but shame over his chosen profession.

The company was led past the dangling body into the open field that faced the keep of Lord Wulfram. To the left of the road, Baldric's half company had already begun marking out their tents while a small group began erecting the captain's pavilion.

Sigwulf led them just south so that the captain stood in the middle of the two halves of his command. Cyn and Ludwig began pacing off the camp while their sergeant conferred with the captain. Soon a fire was going, and soldiers gathered to cook their evening meals.

Cyn stirred the pot, then noticed her sergeant approaching. "Siggy, anything to report?"

The big man came closer to the fire, warming his hands. The air was turning chilly, the sky overcast, and it was beginning to look more and more like it might rain on the morrow.

"I imagine we're going to be here a while."

"Why? What's happened?"

"I have word Lord Gebhard wants to parley with his esteemed adversary. He's of the opinion the baron might give in to his demands."

"What are his demands?" asked Ludwig.

"I have no idea," replied Sigwulf. "Nor, I fear, does our captain. I'm beginning to wonder if the Baron of Mulsingen has any idea what he wants to do at all."

"Come now, it can't be as bad as that? Surely he wouldn't have marched all the way here if he didn't intend to follow through with the assault?"

"Oh, I believe he wanted very much to carry it through, only now he's getting cold feet. There's a big difference between threatening something and actually carrying it out."

"Where does that leave us?" asked Ludwig.

"Well, for one thing, it means we're not assaulting right away. The truth is, it'll probably be several days before we see any action."

"And in the meantime?"

"We're to gather wood for assault ladders."

"What about the moat?"

"Apparently," said Sigwulf, "our siege expert feels it's not much of an obstacle—at least that's what Ecke relayed."

"I wonder if he's met his Earth Mage yet?"

"If he did, it wasn't brought up."

"So when are we supposed to start cutting down trees?" asked Cyn.

"We'll leave that for tomorrow," said Sigwulf. "For now, we just rest and take it easy."

"That's it?" said Ludwig.

"Oh, we're also not allowed to go into the village."

"There's not much left of the village," said Cyn. "It's been abandoned."

"True, but the baron has claimed what's left to house his men."

Ludwig peered over towards the hanged man. "And that?"

"That remains. It's meant to upset the defenders, convince them we mean business."

"If we meant business, we'd already be attacking," complained Cyn.

"Hey, now," said Sigwulf. "I'm merely the message carrier. I didn't make the rules."

Ludwig smiled. "Did he say anything about going to look at the keep?"

"No, why? What have you got in mind?"

"I thought we might wander over there and see what it looks like. It might give us some idea of what we're up against."

"That's a great idea," said Cyn.

"Sounds reasonable," grumbled Sigwulf, "but can we eat first?"

Cyn laughed. "Make it quick. We want to see the place before it gets too dark."

Regnitz Keep consisted of a square tower, much like the keep in Mulsingen. It also had a curtain wall built around a bailey or inner courtyard, but there the resemblance ended. Whereas Lord Gebhard's residence had a simple tower as a gatehouse, Regnitz had a properly fortified structure, complete with drawbridge and moat. The walls were also manned, each warrior keeping a constant vigil, lest the attackers begin their assault.

"How deep do you reckon the moat is?" asked Ludwig.

"Impossible to say," said Sigwulf, "although it is wider to the east."

"Yes, I'd noticed that. Do you suppose that makes it shallower?"

"I doubt it."

"Look at that drawbridge," said Cyn. "There's no way we're equipped to take on that place. What do you think, Siggy?"

"The plan is to employ ladders. That means we'll be assaulting to the left of the gatehouse."

"I don't like that," said Cyn. "Their arrows can reach us from both the western tower and the gatehouse. Are you sure there isn't an easier approach?"

Sigwulf frowned. "I'm afraid not. The captain says that's the narrowest part of the moat."

"Meaning that's where they'll be expecting us," added Cyn. "It'll be a bloodbath."

"It could be worse," offered Ludwig.

Cyn turned on him. "How in the Afterlife could it be worse?"

"It could be raining."

"Look at you," she said. "Always looking at the bright side of things. How many defenders did you say they have?"

"Lord Gebhard reckoned they had no more than thirty."

"That's definitely not the case now," said Cyn. "Look at the churned-up mud in front of the drawbridge."

"What of it?"

"That would indicate heavy traffic. I bet most of the village is now safely behind those walls."

"But they're not soldiers, are they?"

"It doesn't take much to toss a rock from the walls. Let's face it, sieges are desperate affairs."

"Yes," agreed Sigwulf, "and remember, Cyn's always looking on the bright side of things."

"Now you're making me feel depressed," said Ludwig. "Isn't there any good news?"

The sergeant grunted. "I have an idea. Come on."

They made their way back to camp. Upon their return, Sigwulf began looking around as if searching for something on the ground.

"What is it you're looking for?" asked Cyn.

"A stick," he replied.

"Any old stick, or one in particular?"

"One about four or five feet in length."

"What for?"

He grinned. "I want to visit that moat tonight. A stick would be useful to test the depth of it."

"And you figure there'll be one around here that will do?"

"I saw one earlier."

"Don't be silly, Siggy. Someone would have taken it for firewood. If you want something like that, we'll have to go find a tree."

"How about a spear?" suggested Ludwig.

"We don't use spears," said Sigwulf.

"No," said Ludwig, "but they do." He pointed at the hanged man and the two guards who stood watch.

"Are you suggesting we steal one of their spears?"

"I prefer the term 'borrow,'" said Ludwig.

Sigwulf grinned, his teeth shining brightly in the light of the fires. "All right, let's go."

"Hey, now," said Cyn. "I'm the stealthy one, remember? You're not going without me."

"Come along, then. We haven't got all night."

They headed south, towards the lights of the village. Once they were closer, they skirted its edge, approaching the hanging tree from the west.

The two baron's men who stood watch looked uninterested in their surroundings. One leaned against the tree, his helm pulled down over his eyes, while his companion stared off longingly at the lights of the village. Cyn crept forward, following the field's natural indents while Sigwulf and Ludwig stood ready to help, should the need arise.

They could see her clearly from their position, but the closer she drew to their target, the harder it became to make out her shape. Soon she disappeared from sight, leaving them wondering where she had gone.

The staring soldier suddenly turned southward, alerted by a sound. Even as they watched, Cyn rose up from behind him, using some force to tap his helmet with her mace. The man staggered forward, dropping his spear and clasping his helmet with both hands, trying to stem the ringing.

The spear quickly disappeared, and then Ludwig spotted Cyn rushing towards them, the weapon firmly in hand.

"Good job," said Sigwulf. "Now, let's get out of here before he raises the alarm."

They made their way back towards the keep, slowing their pace as they neared. Atop the curtain walls, they could see sentries marching back and forth, their faces illuminated by torches.

Sigwulf shook his head. "The fools are not used to this."

"Why do you say that?" said Ludwig.

"The sentries are carrying torches," he replied. "Not only does it give away their position, but it destroys their ability to see in the dark."

"But you have to be able to see," said Ludwig.

They crouched, preparing to move closer. "No, you don't understand. If you stand within the light of a campfire, everything around you will look darker. If, however, you step outside that light, you'll be able to see more of what lies outside the lit area."

"That's unusually clever, Sigwulf. Wherever did you come up with that?"

"From me," said Cyn, grinning.

Sigwulf urged them to silence, then waved them forward. The moon was out this night, giving them barely enough light to stumble their way over to the moat.

Crouching by the water's edge, Sigwulf poked the spear into the depths. Satisfied, he stepped into the water, which promptly rose past his shins. He waved back at the others to stay put, then prodded again with his makeshift staff.

He was fully halfway across when a shout erupted from above. Ludwig looked up to see someone staring directly at him, unaware of Sigwulf's presence. The yell was soon replaced by a bell, and then others began running to the wall.

Sigwulf, alerted by the alarm, began moving back to the moat's bank, but the muddy bottom slowed his progress. An arrow flew, a wild shot, to be sure, considering the darkness, but even an archer could get a lucky hit. Ludwig moved out along the edge of the moat, trying to draw their attention away from Sigwulf.

Ludwig felt an arrow sail past his head, and then more splashed into the moat. Sigwulf gave a grunt as he extricated himself from the water, and then Cyn gave a yell, signalling their retreat.

Ludwig turned and ran, pumping his legs for all they were worth. More arrows flew towards them, but where they landed was anybody's guess. Soon, the fires of the camp drew nearer, telling them they were beyond effective range. Ludwig slumped to the ground, his breath ragged.

"That was close," he said.

Sigwulf waved it off. "That was nothing."

"Did you get what you wanted?"

"Yes," the man replied, "but it's not the best of news."

"What is it?"

"The moat is crossable, but it'll take some work."

"Too deep?"

"No, too muddy. The bottom is hard to navigate. It sucks on the boots, making progress difficult. The only saving grace is the fact that the water is only chest deep."

"Yes," added Cyn, "but that's your chest, not ours. If I were to try to ford that moat, the water would be up to my neck."

"Could we use boats?" asked Ludwig.

"Do you see any hereabouts?"

"What about filling it in?"

"And with what would we accomplish that? Shovels?"

"Yes, as a matter of fact."

"A good idea," said Cyn. "Do you have any in your tent? No? How curious, I thought everyone travelled around with a shovel."

"Hey, now," said Ludwig, "don't get upset with me. I'm merely making suggestions."

Her tone softened. "Sorry. I know you're trying."

"What about the baron? Does he have shovels?"

"I doubt it," said Sigwulf. "That would have required planning and foresight. Neither of which Lord Gebhard has demonstrated, to my knowledge."

"The problem," said Cyn, "is getting across the water."

"Can you swim?" asked Ludwig.

"Not in armour, and especially not while under a barrage of arrows."

Ludwig snapped his fingers as a ghost of an idea came to him. "I have it."

Sigwulf looked at him with interest. "Go on."

"How wide was that moat?"

"Fifteen, maybe twenty feet at its widest."

Ludwig grinned. "Then we make a bridge."

Cyn frowned. "I thought you had an actual idea."

"I do. Bear with me for a moment. We find ourselves a nice long log, long enough to span the distance. Men carry it forward, much like you would a battering ram, except instead of using it to batter down the door, we drop it in the water."

Sigwulf warmed to the idea. "Yes, and then we have the largest men pull up the other end onto the inner bank."

"Is there one?" asked Cyn. "I thought the moat went straight up to the castle walls."

"No, there's a small gap between the moat and the water," the sergeant insisted. "Once we have it in place, others can cross quickly and begin putting up their ladders."

"I don't know about this," said Cyn. "It sounds foolhardy."

"You know what they say," said Ludwig, "faint heart never won fair maid."

"Where did you hear that?"

"I don't remember. I suppose I read it somewhere."

"He has a point though," said Sigwulf. "And it would allow succeeding waves to cross the moat quickly."

Ludwig and the sergeant both looked at Cyn. "Well?" they said in unison.

She surrendered. "I suppose it's worth a try."

"Good," said Sigwulf. "I'll go see what the captain thinks."

"Perhaps we should all go," suggested Ludwig.

"Do you feel that's a good idea, Ludwig?" asked Cyn. "You and the captain haven't always seen eye to eye."

Ludwig paused, thinking things over. "You have a valid point. I guess we should leave it to Sigwulf."

"Or think it through a bit more," suggested Cyn. "After all, there won't be an assault for several days at least. The baron still wants his parley, and we have ladders to build."

"In that case," said Sigwulf, digging into his bag, "let's have a drink and work this thing through." He displayed a clay bottle for their inspection.

Ludwig leaned closer. "Where did you get that? It looks expensive."

"Does it?" said Sigwulf. "What makes you say that?"

"The bottle itself. I've seen ones similar to that in my father's keep."

"I gather your father likes to drink?"

"Does a fish swim?"

Sigwulf pulled out the cork, passing the bottle to Cyn. She sniffed it experimentally, then smiled. "It smells good. Where did you get it?"

"Back in Torburg," said Sigwulf. "To be honest, I won it."

"Won it?" she said. "From who?"

"A merchant, if you must know."

"And what was it you were wagering on?"

"You and Ludwig, in the melee competition."

"What did I tell you about gambling?" she said. "We'll never get any savings at this rate."

"True," Sigwulf replied, "but at least we have some nice wine for a change. Now, will you join us? Or will it be only Ludwig and me who will partake of this particular delicacy?"

She tipped back the bottle, taking a mouthful. "Very nice," she said. "I suppose you're forgiven... for now." She passed the bottle to Ludwig.

He, too, took a sip, savouring the taste. "I've had something like this before, back in Verfeld. It reminds me of apples."

"Does it?" said Sigwulf. "Let me see." The sergeant reached across, taking the bottle from Ludwig's hand. Tipping it back, he guzzled down what must have been half before lowering it and letting out an enormous belch. "You know, it truly does."

A man loomed out of the dark. Ludwig recognized him from back at the baron's keep.

"My lord?"

"Where's your captain?"

Ludwig pointed towards Captain Ecke's tent, and the man stomped off.

"Who was that?" asked Cyn.

"I think that he's Lord Gebhard's son. He certainly resembles the baron."

"What's he doing here?"

"You heard him as well as me. He's looking for the captain."

"You don't think they're planning a night attack, do you?"

"He can't," offered Sigwulf. "We have no ladders yet, remember?"

She frowned. "I doubt that would stop him."

They all stared at the captain's tent. The interior was lit by candles, allowing them to see the baron's son and their captain silhouetted. Their discussion looked to be intense, and then the noble left, heading back towards the village.

Moments later, Captain Ecke exited, looking left and right, presumably to find his sergeants. Upon spotting Sigwulf, he came closer.

"Get out the sentries," he commanded.

"Trouble, Captain?" said Sigwulf.

"Yes, it appears Lord Wulfram sent out a raiding party. They attacked one of the baron's men."

"How many?"

"Only the one," said Ecke. "Over there, by the hanged man."

Sigwulf closed his mouth, afraid of condemning himself by his own words.

"And signs of numbers?" asked Cyn.

The captain seemed to suddenly notice her. "He estimates at least half a dozen. They wouldn't sally forth with any less."

"Was anyone killed?"

"No, thank the Saints, but we must be vigilant." He returned his attention to Sigwulf. "Get the sentries out, Sergeant. I shouldn't like to have enemy troops make their way into our camp."

"Yes, sir," replied the big man, trying to sound as alarmed as his superior.

"I'll have Baldric do the same." The captain headed north, quickly disappearing from sight.

"Well, I'll be," said Cyn. "That's the first time we've ever had to guard against ourselves."

"You two better take up your positions," said Sigwulf. "I'll send replacements once I rouse them."

"You'd better get changed first," suggested Cyn.

"Why?"

"You're soaking wet, Siggy. You don't want to catch yourself a chill."

He waved her off. "Don't be silly. It's not that cold."

She moved to stand before him, her hands instinctively going to her hips. "You listen to me, Sergeant. I won't have you getting sick, do you hear me?"

Ludwig found the scene quite comical. Her short stature was dwarfed by Sigwulf, yet somehow, her presence seemed superior.

"All right," conceded the sergeant. "I shall do as you ask."

14

REGNITZ

Spring 1095 SR

Morning came far too quickly to Ludwig's mind as he struggled out of bed into the early morning sun with bleary eyes. The smells of the campfires drifted towards him, and he found himself drawing closer.

Dorkin noted his approach. "Hungry?"

"Famished," replied Ludwig. "What have you there?"

"Porridge and barn bread."

"No bacon?"

The man chuckled. "Where in this Saints-forsaken place would I find a pig?"

"And yet you cook barn bread?"

"That's because I saved up a supply of lard. Do you want some or not?"

Ludwig found his mouth watering. "I'm most happy to take you up on your offer."

He waited as Dorkin ladled out some food into a bowl, then fished a piece of bread out of the frying pan.

Ludwig picked it up gingerly, the hot grease burning his fingers.

"You in a hurry?" asked Dorkin.

"Only to fill my stomach." He took a bite, savouring the taste.

Off in the distance, half a dozen horsemen were riding towards the drawbridge.

"What's that?" asked Ludwig.

Dorkin glanced up from his work. "I imagine that's the baron and his entourage. Likely heading off in the hopes of negotiating the defender's surrender."

"That young fellow," said Ludwig, "is he the baron's son?"

"Yes, Hagan Stein, at least that's what I'm told. The other one is Gottfried Jager, the so-called siege expert."

"You sound like you know a lot about them."

"I might have heard Captain Ecke talking to them earlier."

Ludwig watched, his meal forgotten, as the riders drew nearer to the drawbridge. They halted just south of it as soldiers appeared on the top of the gatehouse. Words were obviously exchanged, though, from this distance, nothing could be made out.

Shortly thereafter, a small door opened in the gate, and three individuals exited. There could be no mistaking Lord Wulfram Haas, for he wore a distinctive-looking suit of plate armour. Ludwig had thought his own armour to be decorative, but even from the campfire, he could see its detailed design. Meanwhile, his companions were outfitted in more common armour, replete with the baron's coat of arms upon their breasts.

There was an exchange of words, and Ludwig wished he was closer, listening to their conversation. Suddenly he was struck by the realization that his own fate might be inextricably tied up in whatever it was they were talking about. Not that they would mention him by name, but their decisions could mean the difference between a negotiated peace and a bloody, prolonged siege.

Whatever they said did not go down well, for Lord Wulfram grew more aggressive in his stance. It finally culminated in him shouting, "Never!" the word carrying easily across the field.

Haas turned, seeking the shelter of his gatehouse once more. Lord Gebhard and his party waited until the door was shut, then turned around slowly and began cantering back to the village of Regnitz.

"I suppose that means we're going to fight," said Dorkin.

"So it would seem," agreed Ludwig. He remembered his meal and took another bite of his bread, chewing absently. "How long do you reckon it will take to make our ladders?"

"Not long. I suspect they'll be ready by dark."

"Is that the normal time to attack?"

"Yes," said Dorkin. "The darkness will keep the archers at bay. Best eat up if I were you," he added. "You'll need all your strength for cutting down trees."

. . .

The axe sunk in deep, and Ludwig had trouble extracting the blade from the trunk. Finally, he pulled it free, then stepped back, wiping the sweat from his brow. "This is hard work."

Sigwulf laughed. "This?" he said. "This is nothing!" He was hefting the largest axe Ludwig had ever seen, his bare chest covered in sweat.

"Doesn't he ever tire?" asked Ludwig.

Cyn was staring at her man. She suddenly became aware that she was being watched and turned to Ludwig with a blush. "Sorry," she said. "I got a little distracted."

"Aren't you supposed to be tying off those rungs?"

"Yes, I am."

"Then you'd best pay more attention to it," he added, "else the ladders will collapse when we're trying to climb them."

She bent to the task, tying off some more rope to secure the rung. "How many of these do we need?"

"As many as we can manage," explained Ludwig. "Ideally, one for every five men."

"That's more than a dozen," noted Cyn. "Why so many?"

Sigwulf, upon hearing her query, halted his work. "The baron will probably want some for his men as well," he explained.

"So we're manual labour now?" she complained.

"Would you prefer to be risking your life in the assault?"

She shrugged. "I suppose not. Still, it would be nice if some of his men would lend a hand instead of standing around mocking us."

"They're not mocking us," said Ludwig. "They're guarding us."

"From what?"

Ludwig grinned. "From those raiders that were out last night."

Sigwulf frowned. "If I'd known it would have caused so much trouble, I wouldn't have bothered." He stopped, picked up a waterskin, drank thirstily, and then poured some over his head and shoulders.

"You know," said Ludwig, "you never told me about those other battles the Grim Defenders were in."

"You mean the skirmishes?" asked Sigwulf.

"Yes, the very same."

Sigwulf stoppered the waterskin, tossing it to the ground. He picked up his axe again, testing its weight. "Cyn can tell you all about it. I have to get back to work."

Ludwig turned to Cyn. "Well?"

"All right, but only if you come here and hold this in place while I tie it off."

Ludwig set down his own axe, crossing the distance quickly. Anything was better than burning his muscles chopping down trees. He took the rung, putting it in place as Cyn began wrapping the rope to secure it.

"The first took place some four months ago when we were camped in a field near Anshlag. The captain sent out a small patrol to see what the area was like, and we came across a bandit camp."

"Is that common in these parts?"

"I can't really say," said Cyn. "We only ran across it the once, but then again, we hadn't been with the Grim Defenders long."

"So what happened?"

"There were three of us to begin with: Siggy, Dorkin, and, of course myself. We were, in fact, looking for a stream to gather water when we were accosted by a group of armed men. They wanted all our coins, but the joke was on them. We hadn't been paid for some time."

"What happened?"

"They didn't believe us. The next thing we knew, we were carrying out a fighting withdrawal. Eventually, we got close enough to camp that others could hear us. The bandits scattered soon after that."

"Did anyone get hurt?"

"Only minor cuts and bruises on our side, but two of the bandits died."

"And you say this was your only run-in with bandits?"

Cyn nodded. "It was."

"Then what was the other skirmish all about?"

"Now, that," she replied, "is a bit more complicated." She finished tying off the rung.

Ludwig grabbed another stick, repeating the process. "It appears we have plenty of time."

She selected another length of rope, using her knife to cut it, then began the process of tying off the next rung. "We had an altercation with another mercenary company."

"When you say altercation…"

"I mean a fight. Right after we arrived in Torburg for the tournament, another free company, the Blades of Vengeance, showed up. They felt we had taken their field and insisted we leave. Well, as you can imagine, that didn't go over well."

"And so a skirmish broke out?"

"I wouldn't call it a skirmish so much as a brawl if I'm being honest. It started innocently enough, with their captain asking ours to move the company."

"And he refused?"

"Naturally. Things escalated quickly after that. The fighting didn't die down until nightfall, and it took the threat of the duke's interference to break up the brawl."

"But you won, didn't you?" asked Ludwig. "After all, you had the field when I first met you."

"We did, though it wasn't as easy as you might think. In the end, it had to be settled by arbitration. Once the Church got involved, there could be no arguing the matter."

"So what happened to the Blades of Vengeance?"

"I imagine they're still around. They marched out of Torburg just before the tournament started."

"I suppose they didn't want to hang around after their defeat," suggested Ludwig.

"Likely not, but I'm sure that won't be the end of it."

"You figure they'll carry a grudge?"

"I know they will. People like that live for their reputation. Us winning the dispute gave them a bloody nose. They'll want to get even."

"You can't possibly believe they'll turn up here?"

"No," said Cyn. "Given their reputation, I doubt Lord Gebhard could afford them."

"How about Lord Wulfram?"

"They number close to one hundred. If they were here, we'd have seen some sign of them."

"Not if they're inside those walls."

"We'd have to make the assumption Lord Wulfram knew Stein's army was coming and had enough time to hire on mercenaries. I figure we can safely rule that out." She finished with the rung, then stood back, admiring her handiwork. "Well? What do you think?"

He joined her, looking down at the ladder. "It looks solid enough."

"We need to test it," she said. "Let's head over to the village and lean it up against the tavern. That ought to be tall enough."

"I thought going to the village was forbidden."

"Nonsense," said Cyn, "and in any case, we're not going INTO the town, we're merely going ADJACENT to it. We'll put up the ladder, and then you can climb up to the top to test it."

"Me?" said Ludwig. "Why do I have to test it?"

"You're heavier than me, and we have to see if it'll bear the weight of an armoured man. Unless, of course, you'd prefer to wait till you're up to your armpits in an assault?"

"No," said Ludwig, "I concede the point." He moved to one end, lifting it while Cyn struggled with the other.

He grunted with the effort. "This is heavier than it looks."

Being so long, it was awkward to carry, but they managed to cross the field with only a few missteps.

"This would be much easier with more men," observed Cyn.

"We can call some over if you like."

"No, my stubbornness has kicked in. We'll get it in place. Just you wait and see."

They drew closer to the tavern and dropped the ladder to the ground. Ludwig looked up at the nearest window.

"This," he said, "is more difficult than it looks. How are we to get this to stand on end?"

"Brute force," said Cyn. She struggled to lift her end up over her head, but to no avail. Soon she was sitting, staring at the ladder with a look that could curdle cheese.

"Problem?" called out Sigwulf.

Having observed their situation, the man had wandered over, and now he stood, looking at them both.

"It's too heavy," said Cyn. "How are we gonna get it against the wall?"

"What we need," said Sigwulf, "is a pole with a crook in it. A branch would do, providing it's the right length."

"How will that help?" asked Ludwig.

"Simple. You lift up your end, then we use the pole to push it higher, using Cyn's end to anchor it to the ground."

"And do we have such a branch?"

"Stay here, and I'll find one."

Ludwig sat, catching his breath as their sergeant ran off.

"He seems confident," he said.

"He knows what he's doing," she replied.

Cyn stood, making her way to the back of the tavern and peering in through the window.

"Busy?" Ludwig asked.

"There's quite a few people, but not much is happening. I suspect the baron has taken this place as his lodgings."

"Do you see him?"

"No, he's probably upstairs."

Sigwulf returned bearing a long branch and a look of enthusiasm. "Let's give it a try, shall we? You hold the base of the ladder, Cyn, about three paces out from the wall. Ludwig, you lift up this end, and I'll use the branch."

Ludwig lifted the ladder's end over his head while Sigwulf used the crook in the branch to hook the top rung. The sergeant gave a mighty heave, and then the ladder rose.

"Give me a hand," grunted Sigwulf.

Ludwig moved to his side, grasping the branch and putting his weight into it. It resisted at first, but as they lifted it higher, it became easier to raise. Finally, it was upright, and they felt the weight release as it came loose, falling against the tavern's wall with a thud.

"That appears to have worked," said Cyn. "Up you go."

Ludwig stepped up, grasping the rails and putting a tentative foot on the first rung. He put all his weight on it. Then, secure in the knowledge it could handle it, he began to climb. The ladder held, the bindings keeping the rungs in place, but the spacing was uneven, requiring him to pay close attention lest he hit his shins. He soon became accustomed to them, and before long, he was at the top.

Looking down, he gave Cyn and Sigwulf the thumbs-up. They smiled back, and he prepared to descend, but the sound of voices drew his attention. It was then he discovered he was beside an upper-floor window. He leaned closer, careful not to lose his footing, the better to hear what was being said, and instantly recognized the voice of Lord Gebhard.

"The fool refuses to see reason," the baron was saying.

"Then we have no option, my lord," said a slightly younger man, likely the siege expert, Captain Jager. "We shall commence operations in the morning."

"Will we be ready?" asked Stein.

"Yes," replied the captain, "though I wish you'd reconsider the use of Herzog, my lord."

The irritation in Stein's voice was clear. "Do not bring the man up again, Captain. We shall rely on the cold press of steel, not the unsaintly use of magic."

"My lord," pressed Jager, "I can assure you the use of Earth Magic is not unsaintly."

"Say what you will, Captain, but the result is the same. I will not countenance it."

"And if the assault goes poorly?"

"Then I might consider it at a future time, but until we have tested those defences, I shall make no such commitment."

"That is all I ask, Lord."

A younger voice intervened. "May I have the honour of leading the attack, Father?"

"No, Hagan, that's the responsibility of our mercenaries. Once they seize the gate, however, you shall have the honour of leading the cavalry through."

"I would urge you to reconsider," said the captain. "Your heir should remain safely behind our lines. To have him take forward the horse exposes him to an unacceptable level of danger."

"Even riding a horse has its dangers, Jager, yet you do not countenance its abandonment."

"True, my lord, but then again, a horse does not plot your death, whereas the enemy does."

"And I appreciate your concern," said the lord, "but my son must earn his place as my heir. I would not have him cower in the safety of the village while my men are risking their lives in the taking of the keep."

"Then at least allow me to surround him with trusted men, men who can keep him from harm."

"That I shall allow," said the baron. "Now, let us get on to other things. What do you make of our mercenaries, Captain?"

Jager paused before answering. "They shall do," he said at last, "though I cannot speak to their effectiveness."

"Meaning?"

"I have heard little of their reputation, my lord. Their captain gives a good accounting, but their manner is... rough."

"Rough?" said Stein. "What's that supposed to mean?"

"They are rabble," continued Jager. "Recruited from the dregs of society if I don't miss my guess."

The baron snorted. "Can't the same be said of all mercenaries? In any case, what of it? They're at least good enough to storm the walls, aren't they? Or are you saying they're not up to the task?"

"I think them more than adequate, but I fear their losses will be high."

"That's hardly any concern of mine. I have hired them to take the keep. I'm more than willing to lose a few during the assault, providing we are successful."

"Yes," added the younger Stein. "And what does it matter? We don't intend to pay them anyway."

"My son has hit on a salient point," said the baron. "In fact, it's better if their casualties are high. It means there is less to deal with when this is all over."

"I must object," said Jager. "If you refuse payment, they may go on the rampage. We all know how badly that can turn out."

"Nonsense. They'll be tired from the battle. It won't take much to scatter what's left."

Ludwig, engrossed in the conversation, leaned over farther, but the ladder slipped, scraping along the wooden wall. He hastily regained his position on the rungs to steady it.

"What was that?" said Jager.

Ludwig climbed down as quickly as possible, jumping the last few rungs. "Come," he said. "Let us hasten from this place."

"Why?" said Cyn. "What happened?"

"I believe I overheard something I wasn't supposed to."

He stepped beneath the ladder, pushing with all his might. Sigwulf, seeing his action, reached out, hooking it near the top and lowering it using the branch. It came down quickly, then they picked up either end, rushing headlong into the trees.

15

PREPARATIONS

Spring 1095 SR

"Are you sure about this?" asked Captain Ecke.

"I heard it as clear as day," said Ludwig.

"And tell me again how you came to be listening at the window?"

"We were testing one of the ladders, sir, and needed to make sure it could take the weight of a man. The tavern is the tallest building in the village and thus offered us the perfect opportunity."

"You were specifically told that Regnitz was off limits."

"Not quite," piped in Cyn. "We were told not to ENTER the village, and we didn't."

Ecke gave her a withering glare. "I did not ask for your opinion, nor do I wish to hear it. The fact of the matter is you disobeyed orders."

Ludwig had had enough. "No, Captain. The fact of the matter is Lord Gebhard isn't going to pay us. You would do well to remember that."

"You dare cross me?" countered Ecke. "I can have you whipped for your insubordination."

"No," said Sigwulf, "you can't. The company won't tolerate that, and you know it. You stand here and belittle those under your command when you should be fighting for them. You're the captain of the Grim Defenders. Now act like it, or step aside and let someone else take the reins."

The captain's voice grew louder. "And who would do so? You? Don't stand there and lecture me, Sigwulf. I made you, and I can unmake you. Do you hear me?"

The sergeant's fury had been unleashed, and now nothing could contain it. "What's the matter with you? You're the commander of this company. Nothing else should matter. It's your job to look after our people, not berate them for bringing you timely information. These men you have made a deal with intend to double-cross you, sir. What will you do about it?"

"And what would you have me do?" shouted Ecke. "Shall I go to the baron and tell him we were spying on him? By the Saints, we would never get another contract again. It would be the end of the company."

Sigwulf persisted. "Then maybe it's time for the Grim Defenders to disband! Would you have us risk our lives in battle for no reward? If the baron means to betray us, it's best it comes to light now, rather than later when we are too weakened from battle to argue."

Ecke stared back, but the fire was gone. Instead, he wore a defeated look. "I'm afraid there's nothing I can do."

"You mean," pressed Sigwulf, "there is nothing you are willing to do. There's a difference."

"Could you not hold back on the assault?" suggested Cyn.

"Yes," added Ludwig, "at least until he advances us some of our payment?"

The captain sat, regaining his composure to a degree. "It might be possible," he said at last. "I could, perhaps, explain that we have incurred costs, but only at the risk of upsetting him."

"Then upset him," said Sigwulf. "What have we got to lose? He knows full well he can't assault the keep without us."

"Yes," added Ludwig. "There will never be a better time to renegotiate."

"I realize now I might have overreacted," said Ecke. "I will see what I can do. Thank you all for bringing this to my attention, but I must take it from here."

"Then we will leave you to it," said Sigwulf. He bowed his head in respect, then turned and left, the other two following suit.

Cyn looked at Sigwulf, concern on her face. She placed a hand on his arm, causing him to look at her.

"Are you all right?" she asked.

He forced a smile. "I'm fine."

"No you're not," she pressed. "You never lose your temper like that."

Sigwulf took a deep breath, letting it out slowly. "He infuriates me, that's all."

"He's doing his best."

"Is he? Sometimes it doesn't feel like it. Captain Ecke is not your father. I fear he's losing his respect for the company."

"How so?" asked Ludwig.

"He's become obsessed with his position of power. Now it's more to do with being in command than actually leading the men. I hate to say it, but appointing sergeants has allowed him to become even more detached from the company's affairs."

"But nobles run companies all the time," insisted Ludwig. "It's how most armies are organized, isn't it? Or are you suggesting nobles don't pay attention to such things?"

Sigwulf frowned. "I'm sure many of them do, but you must remember they owe service to those above them, such as dukes or kings. Our company has no such allegiance, so that makes the captain the ultimate authority."

"We need a charter."

"Like that city of yours? What was it called?"

"Malburg?"

"Yes," said Sigwulf, "although I don't see how that would help us."

Ludwig laughed. "A charter is simply a system of rules put in place to limit and define what responsibilities are necessary to get things done."

"You make it sound so complicated."

"But it doesn't have to be. A company charter would lay out what each rank is responsible for, and it would put limits on what captains and sergeants could offer in terms of punishment. It would also formally describe the pay structure and what's expected of each member of the company."

"But we have a pay structure," said Cyn. "Remember the shares?"

"Is it written down anywhere?" asked Ludwig.

"No," she replied, "but we all know it."

"But if the captain were to die, there would be nothing to guide his replacement."

"True, but the company IS the captain, isn't it? Once he's gone, the company would fold."

"No," said Ludwig. "Look to your own father's life. You said he worked his way up to command the Crossed Swords. That could only happen if the company were run efficiently. Captain Ecke might mean well, but he lacks the experience of command. Such a document would explain what's required of him."

"You make a valid point," said Cyn. "What do you think, Siggy?"

"It makes sense, I suppose," said Sigwulf, "but I hardly think this is the time to be introducing the concept. If we survive this contract, we should bring it to his attention."

"And therein lies the rub," said Ludwig. "We must somehow survive the contract. Not so easy to do if our employer is plotting against us."

"We have to hope the captain can sort things out," said Cyn. "In the meantime, we must prepare to carry out the assault."

"And if he's unsuccessful?" asked Sigwulf.

"Then maybe it's time to reconsider our service in the Grim Defenders."

Ludwig looked down at the log. It was twelve paces long, easily long enough to span the moat, yet still he worried. Across from him stood Sigwulf, ready to lift it when the command was given. Behind them, ten more men took up similar positions, set to lead the charge. Their job was to secure the log on either side of the moat to enable those behind to flood across with their siege ladders.

Baldric was to their left, leading another such group, while Cyn, being lighter of frame, would come forward with the rest of the troops, ready to climb once the ladders were in place.

The sky was growing darker, evidence that night was coming, but clouds were also rolling in, and Ludwig feared rain would soon be upon them, making the assault even more difficult.

"This will be the end of us," he said.

"Fear not," said Sigwulf. "We shall see this through."

"How can you be so calm?"

"We have the simple job, you and I. All we have to do is place this log. It's the others you should be worried for."

"They'll be throwing everything they have at us," warned Ludwig, "and we'll be hampered by the log, not to mention the moat."

"Yes, but the darkness will hide us."

"Yet one more thing to complicate matters."

"Have you never gone into battle before?" asked Sigwulf.

"No," confessed Ludwig, "nor have I killed a man."

"And here I took you as an experienced warrior."

"I can fight, it's true, but I fear my training has ill-prepared me for what is to come. My bowels feel as though they will soon loosen."

"Set your mind on the task ahead," urged Sigwulf, "and put all other matters from your mind. Those who fear death often bring it upon themselves. Think, therefore, on the immortal words of my father."

"Which are?"

"Get your arse moving and don't stop unless you have to."

Ludwig laughed, feeling some of the tension drain away. "Wise words. I wish I could say the same of my own father. I feel like I was an embarrassment to him."

"Men often find it hard to say what their heart feels. I'm sure he loved you in his own way."

"If he did, I saw no sign of it."

"That sword of yours," said Sigwulf. "Was that the work of your smith?"

"Charlaine? Yes, why?"

"A weapon like that is worth a lot. Did she gift it to you?"

"No," said Ludwig. "My father commissioned it."

"Ah, so your father did show his affection for you, then."

Ludwig's eyes drifted to the hilt of his sword. "I suppose he did."

"It's a fine blade," continued Sigwulf. "A princely gift if ever I've seen one."

"If you're trying to make me feel bad about leaving home, it won't work."

"Not at all. I'm merely pointing out that some people are not good at expressing their feelings. I was the same way myself."

"You?" said Ludwig. "I hardly see you as being a man who talks of such things."

"And before I met Cyn, I would have said the same thing, but things change when a man finds the right woman."

"I found one, but then I lost her, all because of my father."

"That relationship was doomed from the start," said Sigwulf, "and well you know it. Nobles and commoners don't mix."

"But you found Cyn, and she's a commoner."

"She is, but then again, I gave up any claim to being noble."

"As have I," insisted Ludwig.

"Have you? I very much doubt that."

"What's that supposed to mean?"

"Merely that you still have the outlook of a noble. You want the world to be a better place, Ludwig, and that's not a small thing. People like you can use their influence and power to accomplish great things, yet you spend your time slumming with mercenaries."

"A man must make a living."

"True, but there are easier ways of doing that than joining a free company. Don't get me wrong, we're glad you're here, but don't try to pretend this is your home. You have the wanderlust within you, like the knights of legend."

Ludwig's eyebrows shot up, not that anyone could see them beneath his helmet. "You honestly think so?"

"I know so. You are destined for great things, my friend. You have that indefinable quality that sets you apart. Our job is to keep you alive long enough for you to achieve your destiny."

Ludwig scoffed. "I don't believe in destiny."

"It doesn't matter whether you do or not. What matters is whether destiny believes in you."

"You're beginning to sound more like an old woman."

Sigwulf smiled. "With age comes wisdom. I'll take that as a compliment."

A shuffling off to their right revealed the baron's bowmen moving into position.

"Looks like the assault is getting ready to begin," offered Ludwig.

"So it does."

"Do you think the captain has spoken to Lord Gebhard?"

"I hope so," said Sigwulf, "but we must put such things from our minds. We have work to do."

Ludwig looked right, watching as the commander of the bowman gave the order to loose their arrows. The light was fading fast, but the archers needed to get the range right before darkness engulfed them. They would keep up a steady barrage until the ladders were brought forward, then it would be up to the Grim Defenders.

Time seemed to stretch on forever until finally, off in the distance, the first torches were lit atop the curtain wall, revealing a mass of warriors waiting to repulse the assault. Ludwig, finding his courage tested, forced himself to look away, staring instead at the log beside him. They had looped a rope around the trunk with the two ends hanging loose to enable it to be picked up.

Ludwig grabbed his bit of rope, with Sigwulf copying his actions on the other side. Those behind followed suit, each taking up the loops that had been prepared and then waiting a moment longer as the sun finally hit the horizon, sending the field into a land of twilight.

"Lift," called out Sigwulf. Everyone heaved at the same time, raising the log off the ground. Ludwig closed his eyes, counting slowly, trying to keep his mind from wandering.

"Advance," came the command, and then they started moving forward. It was awkward, to say the least. With both hands on the rope, Ludwig could only shuffle along, taking short, measured steps to keep pace with the rest of them. That meant no drawn sword, and, even more importantly, his shield must remain slung on his back, bouncing against him as he moved forward.

To his right, the archers kept up their attack, loosing arrow after arrow into the gathering darkness. The sun finally disappeared behind the horizon, and then there was little to see, save the distant torches amongst the defenders.

He felt his feet stumble across the uneven turf, then someone behind him tripped, sending the log crashing to the ground. Ludwig let out a curse.

"Watch your footing," roared Sigwulf, "and prepare to lift on the count of three. One… two… three, heave!"

Ludwig pulled up on the rope, and the log rose again.

"Small steps," called out the sergeant. "Don't rush it."

All that existed in the darkness was the rope, the log, and the ground beneath his feet. Ludwig stared ahead, focusing on the distant wall, fighting down the fear that an arrow would take him in the eye. He tried to tell himself it was just nerves, but he couldn't shake the feeling that disaster was about to befall them.

On and on they went until the weight made his muscles protest. Ludwig considered himself in fighting shape, but his back ached, and he found himself thinking back to his home in Verfeld Keep. His father had been wracked with back problems for years, the result of a fall from horseback. Most of the time, he'd managed to hide his pain, but on the rare occasion, it was difficult to ignore. Ludwig now felt more sympathetic towards what his father had been forced to endure.

Something whistled past his ear, and then the man behind him let out a scream. The log threatened to tear itself from his grasp, but Ludwig held on as if his life depended on it. They slowed, then picked up the pace again as others moved past the wounded man.

Another step, and then Ludwig lost his footing, having reached the edge of the moat, only to have the ground collapse beneath him. He sank up to his ankle, instinctively letting go of the rope. A curse from Sigwulf revealed he'd made a similar discovery.

"We are here," the sergeant called out. "Wade in and keep pulling."

Ludwig turned, struggling to find the rope in the inky blackness. Finally, he found it and then pulled, turning to move farther into the water, which was cold, much colder than he expected. He felt the shock of the frigid liquid as he sank up to his groin.

"Heave!" called out Sigwulf.

Ludwig pulled, and the end of the log scraped along the ground while the front was over the water. He pulled again, and it dipped down, sinking beneath the surface, if only for a moment.

Taking another step, the water rose to the middle of his chest, and the silt beneath him was slippery. He struggled to gain traction. Another tug on the rope brought the log sliding forward.

Sigwulf called out the cadence now. "Heave-ho," he shouted, desperate to get the men working in unison.

Slowly, the log edged forward as Ludwig half-swam, half-walked across the moat until his toe struck a stone. His waist finally cleared the surface as the bottom began angling upwards. He pulled once more, hauling with all his might.

The log was almost at its destination. All that was required was to lift the end up out of the water. Ludwig and Sigwulf abandoned the ropes, choosing instead to stand on either side, facing the log. They put their hands beneath it, lifting with every ounce of strength they had left.

It rose a fraction, and then the end stuck fast to the mud and silt of the moat's bank. They heaved again, but between the weight of it and the effect of the cold water, their strength was waning. More men appeared behind them, lifting in unison, and the log finally came free, and they swung it forward, then dropped it, their job complete.

Now relieved of his burden, Ludwig lifted himself from the water and leaned against the curtain wall. More dark shapes appeared, and then he spotted Baldric and the others sliding the second such log into place beside the first. They lashed them together, then made haste to the wall, desperate to avoid being spotted.

Things quieted down until the ladder teams gave a roar as they rushed forward, obviously trying to overcome their fears. The first group misplaced their feet, falling into the moat as they attempted to navigate the makeshift bridge in the dark. The second fared much better, splashing into the water only as they got within three feet of their target.

A ladder was hoisted up, and the first warrior took his position at its base, ready to climb. It was then the defenders struck.

16

ASSAULT

Spring 1095 SR

A burning bale of hay was tossed from the heights, falling at the base of the wall to light up the assault for all to see. Moments later, a hail of stones and rocks followed.

Ludwig pressed himself against the wall when a stone struck the ground near his foot. He watched as a fellow mercenary reached a hand out towards the ladder, and then a rock smashed into his shoulder, ripping his arm clean off. The man fell back with a splatter of blood, his cries of anguish silenced as he sank beneath the surface of the moat.

More rocks fell, splintering a ladder and sending bits of wood flying everywhere. Two men ascended a ladder near Ludwig, the first giving a yell of triumph as he reached the battlements, only to be silenced as a spear stabbed out, taking him in the throat. The unlucky footman fell backwards, taking out the next warrior on the ladder.

Smoke burned Ludwig's eyes, nearly blinding him. He moved along the wall, desperate to escape into the darkness. Arrows thudded into the ground beside him, and then he heard the sound of steel on steel. A couple of warriors had managed to reach the top and were now fighting for their very lives.

Ludwig raced to the nearest ladder, then waited as the man ahead of him began climbing. He feared a rock would come crashing down at any moment, and then finally, it was his turn to ascend. Placing his foot on the first rung, he paused when a scream from above caused him to clutch the ladder in panic as a body hurled past, thudding into the ground. Ludwig, desperate to suppress his fears, forced his legs to obey his commands.

He looked up to see an enemy looming overtop, a stone held high. Pressing against the ladder, he prayed to the Saints to protect him. There was a whiff of air as the stone passed by, and then he rushed up the last few rungs. He was almost at the enemy when he realized he had yet to draw his sword.

Pausing, he pulled forth his blade, then found his legs had seized. Panic had overtaken him, and he struggled to remember the words of Sigwulf. Ludwig stared at his sword, his mind a whirlwind of emotions as the light from above illuminated the scrollwork on the hilt. Garnering the last of his bravery, he gritted his teeth and launched himself upwards.

Another stone flew past, glancing off his shoulder and threatening to knock him loose. He took a breath and stabbed out with the tip of his sword as he reached the top. It had been a gamble, for he could see naught of the defenders, yet his wild attack caught someone in the chest.

His foe staggered back, giving Ludwig time to get onto the top of the wall. He struck again, sinking the blade into a shoulder. The man screamed in pain and then toppled into the courtyard below.

Ludwig's mind was racing now, trying to make sense of the chaos and confusion of the fight on the wall. A blade scraped off his breastplate, and he instinctively lashed out, slicing across an arm.

Twisting around, he saw an axeman, his weapon raised on high for the killing blow. Ludwig took a step and sank his sword into the man's chest, stumbling forward as the blade caught and his foe collapsed to his knees. The man sighed out a last breath, the smell rank in Ludwig's face. He scrambled to his feet in time to parry another attack, then slashed out, feeling steel hit flesh.

He tried to orient himself, but in the confusion of the melee, he had strayed from his initial position, and now enemies converged on him from all directions, their weapons at the ready. Clearly, he was outnumbered, and so he raced for the parapet and leaped, hoping the Saints would see him safe.

He flailed around as the air rushed past, twisting as he plummeted, only to hit the water with his back. The impact was jarring, but as fortune would have it, it saved his life. A cold embrace enveloped him, then strong arms lifted him to the surface.

"Back," the man was yelling. "Retreat. We cannot take any more of this."

Ludwig was dragged across the moat, and then firm hands pulled him from the water. Staggering to his feet, he cast a glance over his shoulder; the ladders were all either destroyed or ablaze. The eerie glow of the burning straw lit the area like a scene from the Underworld while dead men lay strewn about, several floating in the water, face down, victims of the ferocious defence.

His eyes sought out Sigwulf, but he could find no sign of him. Ludwig followed the other Grim Defenders as they streamed south, desperate to escape the enemy's arrows and stones. Finally, he collapsed to the ground, gasping for breath as around him stood others, many covered in blood. The attack had been an unmitigated disaster.

Somehow during the escape, he had managed to hold on to his sword. He stared at its blade, stained with blood, and started shaking uncontrollably. Voices rose around him, then someone shook him. He tore his gaze from his sword to see Cyn standing over him.

"Where's Siggy?" she pleaded.

"I don't know," he found himself saying. Rising unsteadily, he looked back towards the carnage of the assault. His grip grew stronger, his voice more sure, and then he managed to get control of his trembling.

"Come on," he called. "Let's go find him."

They made their way back to the slaughter. The bundles of hay were now burning low, no longer illuminating the area as they once did. On the wall above, the defenders had ceased their counterattack, instead peering down to survey the damage they had wreaked.

Ludwig ran to the edge of the moat calling out for Sigwulf. Jeers came from the wall, but the defenders withheld their stones and arrows, no doubt conserving them for the next attack. He splashed into the moat, turning over a body to see a mangled face. The bile rose in his throat, and then Cyn called out, "Over here."

He made his way towards her, spotting Sigwulf lying on his stomach, half out of the moat. It looked as though he had been retreating, exiting the water as an arrow took him in the back. Cyn was pulling with all her might, but the sergeant was too big for her to budge.

Ludwig jumped into the water and lifted his friend's legs, pushing as hard as possible to get him onto the bank. Sigwulf let out a groan, and Ludwig redoubled his efforts. He was alive!

Climbing out, he then lifted Sigwulf's arm, attempting to put it around his own shoulder. He glanced back at the wall to see an archer taking careful aim. Illuminated by the few fires that remained, Ludwig had no doubt he was a dead man, but before the arrow could sail forth, Lord Wulfram appeared on the wall.

"Let him go," he commanded. "There has been enough death this day."

. . .

Sigwulf groaned as they rolled him over. They were back in camp, having laid out their sergeant on a cloak, the better to examine his wound. Ludwig held a torch as Cyn probed the injury to Sigwulf's lower back, thankful it had missed any vital organs. She cut away his shirt to reveal the arrowhead protruding from his front, and they thanked the Saints for the minor miracle.

"We shall have to remove it," she announced.

"I know nothing of such things," confessed Ludwig. "Have you done this before?"

"I have, twice, but one of those died, so I'm no expert."

"Yet you're all he has right now. What do we do?"

She wiped the tears from her eyes, then cleared her throat. "We must cut off the tip, then pull the arrow from his back, but one false move, and it might kill him."

A large hand shot out, gripping her arm. "Do it," grunted Sigwulf.

"We need something for his pain," she said.

"No you don't," the big man persisted. "Just get on with it before I change my mind."

"We need to roll him onto his side."

Ludwig called over Dorkin, and between them, they manoeuvred their patient into position.

"This is going to hurt, Siggy," warned Cyn.

Sigwulf nodded, then she grasped the head of the arrow, giving it a twist. The shaft split but refused to part. She twisted it again, eliciting a cry of pain from her patient. One more time, and the head came clear. Blood started to ooze from the wound, and she stuffed a torn shirt against it.

She looked at Ludwig. "Take the shaft," she commanded, "then pull. You'll need to extract the whole thing in one go, understand?"

He nodded, taking up a position at Sigwulf's back. His hands went over the fletchings, and he gripped the arrow tightly. "Whenever you're ready."

She nodded her head, and he pulled with a firm grip. At first, there was resistance, and then the shaft came free, sending Ludwig tumbling to the ground. Blood gushed forth, staining the cloak red as Dorkin stuffed a shirt up against the wound.

Cyn wore a worried look. Leaning forward, she placed her face close to that of her patient. "Siggy, can you hear me? Talk to me, Siggy, for Saint's sake!"

Ludwig held his breath, fearing the worst.

Cyn forced Sigwulf's eyelid back, then breathed a sigh of relief. "It's all right," she said. "He's simply passed out."

Ludwig let out his breath. "Thank the Saints for that."

. . .

Ludwig peered into the tent. Sigwulf was lying on his back, his features drawn and pale, while Cyn wiped his brow.

"How's he doing?"

"He has a fever," she replied, "but I have hope he'll pull through."

"He has a strong constitution and the best of care. I brought him some ale if he's up to it?"

"I'll take that," said Sigwulf, his voice reedy.

Ludwig passed over the bottle. "Is there anything I can do to help?"

"Not at the moment," replied Cyn. "But check in with us later. I may need a break."

"I will, I promise."

He left them, seeking out the nearest fire. It was mid-morning, the day after the attack, and the mood in the camp was sour. The company had lost twenty men, and a further twelve were wounded to some degree or another. In addition, the ladders had all been destroyed, setting them back in their plans. The only saving grace had been the fact that the logs had worked well to breach the moat. Of course, they were useless now. The defenders had seen to that. Shortly after the retreat was completed, they issued out, dragging the logs back inside the defences. It would not work a second time.

Ludwig warmed his hands by the fire, staring into the flames, reliving the horror of the attack. A movement to his left drew his attention, and he saw Dorkin stepping out of the captain's tent.

"Trouble?" asked Ludwig.

"The captain wants to see you."

"He wants to see ME?"

"Unless you know someone else in this company named Ludwig?"

"No, I suppose not."

"He's in a foul mood today," warned Dorkin. "You'd best get moving."

"I will," promised Ludwig. He walked over to the captain's tent, his mind in turmoil. Upon arrival, he paused, wondering how best to proceed, but the decision was soon made for him.

"Ludwig?" called out Captain Ecke. "Is that you?"

"It is, sir."

"Come in. I need to speak to you."

He stepped inside to the smell of stale wine. Captain Ecke sat at his table, drink in hand, staring down at a list of names, many of which were now crossed out.

Ludwig couldn't help but feel pity for the man. Ecke looked worn out, his eyes showing dark circles from lack of sleep. The burden of command obviously weighed heavily on him.

His captain gulped down the contents of his cup, then looked at Ludwig. "How's Sig?"

"Feverish."

Ecke grimaced, then refilled his cup. "He's a good man. I'd hate to lose him."

"Is that why you wanted to see me? To tell me how much his loss will mean?"

"No. Sigwulf's loss will be keenly felt, but the company must endure, and to do that, it needs its sergeants." He looked Ludwig in the eyes. "I'm offering you the position."

"Me? Surely there are others with longer service."

"This isn't about time," said Ecke. "It's about character. I've been watching you, Ludwig. You're a pain in the arse, it's true, but you have a good head on your shoulders. The truth is, we need more like you. Tell me you'll accept the position."

"I'm not sure I'm ready."

"Nonsense. I'm told you managed to reach the wall during the assault."

"I did," Ludwig confessed, "but I couldn't hold it. I ended up having to jump into the moat to escape."

"By the Saints, that was a desperate gamble. Had you landed on the ground, you would have broken your legs, if not your neck."

"That thought didn't occur to me at the time."

"And a good thing too," said the captain. "Had it done so, you would have died on the wall. It looks like you have luck in spades. How many battles have you been in?"

"This was my first, sir."

"Your first? Truly?"

Ludwig nodded. "The truth is, I came to you untested, Captain."

"Well, you definitely proved you're up to the challenge."

"If you say so."

"I do say so. Now come, you'll accept the position of sergeant, won't you?"

"It belongs to Sigwulf."

Ecke sat back, looking Ludwig over with a critical eye. "I tell you what, let's call it a temporary appointment, shall we?"

"Temporary?"

"Yes. You can hold the position until Sigwulf recovers from his injuries. Will that soothe your ego?"

"It's not my ego I'm concerned about. Rather, I am worried I'm not up to the job."

"Ah," said Ecke. "But don't you see? The very fact you're concerned is proof you're worthy."

"I'm not sure I follow?"

"Some people are born great, Ludwig, while others achieve it through happenstance. You, my friend, are destined for something, though I can't for the life of me figure out what that something is. I do know, however, that you'll have to be dragged there, kicking and screaming all the way."

"You don't make it sound appealing."

"You're an educated man and a fine swordsman. Add to that your natural ability to lead, and you'll be unstoppable."

"I would hardly call myself a leader," said Ludwig. "What have I accomplished that would indicate I could pull off something like this?"

"You have a sense of justice," said Ecke. "Don't get me wrong, it's a royal pain to work with, but it garners you respect amongst the company. You also have some good ideas." He held out his hand, counting off on fingers as he talked. "You organized the camps; you suggested using sergeants; you came up with the idea of using the logs to cross the moat—"

"Yes," interrupted Ludwig, "and what did that get us except a lot of dead and wounded."

"You feel responsible for the losses, don't you?"

Ludwig lowered his head in shame. "I do."

Ecke smiled. "That's another point in your favour." He leaned down, rummaging through a sack that lay beside him, then extracted a purse that he set on the table. "Do you know what's in here?"

"Coins?"

"Indeed. And do you know why they're here? Because you warned me of the baron's treachery. I might be an obstinate fool when my temper's up, but I do care about the Grim Defenders. I visited Lord Gebhard before we began the assault and told him we wouldn't participate unless he coughed up some coins. As you can see, it worked, and I owe that to you."

"And Sigwulf," added Ludwig.

"Of course, and I suppose Cyn had something to contribute as well. Look, I know I'm not the most dynamic of captains. I need men like you and Sig to keep the others motivated. We suffered a defeat last night, and you know as well as I do that our employer isn't about to give up his dreams of conquest. We can't just try the same tactic again. It's too costly." He pointed in the direction of the keep. "That fortification will be the death of us if we don't come up with something better. Take the sergeant's position, I beg you."

"I accept," said Ludwig, "but only until Sigwulf is recovered."

"Agreed."

Ludwig turned to leave, but the captain wasn't quite finished.

"Oh, and Ludwig?"

"Yes, Captain?"

"Put your mind to our present circumstances, will you?"

"To what end?"

"We need a new plan to assault the keep."

"You want me to plan the next assault? Why?"

"You're an educated man, Sergeant, and I'm guessing you're well-read?"

"I never really thought about it," said Ludwig, "but my mother did encourage me to read."

"Good. Then give some thought to our current problem, and see if you can't come up with a better plan, will you?"

"I will," promised Ludwig. "Though I cannot for the life of me imagine what that might be."

17

LESSONS

Spring 1095 SR

The sky, which had been threatening rain for days, finally let loose with a downpour, the likes of which was seldom seen in the Petty Kingdoms. The entire camp was drenched, turning the field into a sticky, muddy mess. To make matters worse, a cold front moved in from the north, bringing with it unnaturally bitter winds.

Ludwig had been a sergeant for three days now, and he began to wonder if the promotion had been worth it. It felt like all he did was run around looking after his men. Thankfully, the wounded had been moved westward to a slight rise that avoided the flooding of the field, and it didn't take long for the rest of the company to follow.

He walked across the field, his boots ankle-deep in mud and water. Food was running low, and the captain had sent him into the village to seek what supplies he could. His clothes were thoroughly soaked, and his hands frozen despite the fact it was spring. For a brief moment, he wondered if they had somehow misplaced summer, but then common sense took hold. This weather would pass in time, but until then, it must be endured.

One of the perks of his new position was it allowed him into the village, and although he felt guilty, nothing cheered him like the thought of an ale before a roaring fire.

He stepped inside the tavern, taking a moment to shake off his sodden cloak. The customers were few this morning, so he made his way to a table, taking a seat. A young man soon approached, a soldier by the look of him. When they had arrived, the villagers had fled, but Lord Gebhard had assigned some of his men to run the tavern, a welcome respite to the inevitable siege.

"An ale," said Ludwig, "if you please."

"Certainly," the man replied, heading towards the back room.

Ludwig stared at the fireplace, soaking in the heat of the flames. Suddenly overcome with weariness, he stretched out his legs, letting out a big yawn.

"May I join you?" a voice asked.

He looked up to see none other than Linden Herzog. "Of course."

The mage sat. "I trust things are going well for you?"

"They are," said Ludwig. "They made me a sergeant. You?"

"Lord Gebhard has put me on half pay to keep me around, but so far, he isn't amenable to any of my suggestions."

"You'd think after the failure of the first attack, he'd be a bit more sympathetic."

"Barons can be stubborn folk on occasion," replied Herzog, "particularly when their pride is at stake."

Ludwig leaned forward, his interest piqued. "His pride, you say?"

"I can see no other explanation."

"Then you know what this dispute is about?"

"No," said Herzog. "I fear it is merely speculation on my part, but it seems clear, given his actions, that some grave insult occurred."

"We may never know," said Ludwig. "And in any case, it has little effect on you and me."

"On the contrary. It's of vital interest."

"It is?"

"Of course," said the mage. "The baron has brought us here because of some perceived slight. Whatever it is, it must be serious."

"Yet not so serious as to warrant more troops."

"Precisely. I, therefore, conclude it must be something he doesn't want known, something personal."

"Like what?"

"I have no idea, and I suspect we never shall. In the meantime, let it suffice for us to sit here, drink ale, and warm ourselves by the fire."

"Easy for you to say," said Ludwig. "Your men aren't freezing in the rain."

The server reappeared, carrying a tankard that he dropped on the table before looking at Herzog. "Something for you, sir?"

The mage pointed at the cup. "I'll have one of those."

Back to the kitchen went the server.

"Is it bad?" asked the mage. "The camp, I mean."

"It's the wounded I'm most concerned with. A good friend of mine took an arrow."

"The large fellow?"

"Yes, Sigwulf."

"Did you get it removed?"

"Yes," said Ludwig, "but he's developed a fever. I fear he won't last much longer, and this weather clearly isn't helping."

A nearby soldier stood, his chair scraping the floor.

"You need to submerge him in cold water," suggested Herzog. "They say it helps."

"I thought to give him numbleaf, but he insists he has no pain."

"I suppose he's in the Saints' hands now."

"Excuse me," came a voice.

They both looked up to see a heavily built soldier standing before their table.

"Did you say someone had a fever?"

"I did," said Ludwig. "A friend of mine took an arrow. Why?"

"What you need is warriors moss."

"And you are?"

"Sorry," the man said, extending his hand. "Let me introduce myself. Name's Karl Dornhuffer. I'm one of the baron's men."

"So what's this warriors moss you speak of?"

"It's common enough in these parts. It typically grows in the shade of trees. Look for a green moss with blue flakes in it."

"And that cures the fever?"

"Not precisely," said Dornhuffer, "but it draws out the pus."

"And does he drink it?"

"No, you mix it into a paste and apply it as a poultice."

"Mix it with what?" asked Ludwig.

"Pretty much anything will do. The point of the poultice is to hold the moss on the wound. You can use milk, water, even mud if you like."

"And what's the secret to finding this moss?"

"It's typically just a matter of searching the woods. You'll find it at the base of a tree, somewhere damp or shady."

Ludwig looked at Linden. "Are you familiar with this?"

"I've heard of it," replied the mage, "but never had to use it."

"I shall start looking immediately," said Ludwig. "What of you, Linden? Care to lend a hand?"

"And go traipsing off into the woods? No, thank you, but if you do find some, I'd be happy to assist in the application of the poultice."

"Thank you," said Ludwig, "and to you too, Karl."

"Not at all," remarked the soldier. "Just trying to help a fellow warrior."

The edge of the woods had largely been cleared when they'd cut down the trees to make the ladders. Now Ludwig would have to go farther afield. He had returned to camp, roping in Dorkin to lend a hand, so it was that they meandered through the trees, looking for signs of the warriors moss. The air was still chilled, but at least the boughs gave some respite from the constant rain.

Ludwig found the woods oppressive as if the very trees themselves were crowding in on them. For his part, Dorkin looked unconcerned with such things and spent most of his time gathering herbs and plants. As the light of day started to wane, it began to look like they had wasted their time. Dorkin, however, stopped, plucking some mushrooms from the soil.

"Look at this, will you?" he said. "I've never seen them of such size. This must be rich soil, indeed."

Ludwig watched absently as the man placed his discovery inside a small sack.

"That'll be dinner," Dorkin announced.

"Is that all you can think about?" asked Ludwig, his frustration growing as the sun lowered.

"I can't help it," explained Dorkin. "I used to be a cook, you know."

"A cook? For who?"

"A man by the name of Adler Bonn. Have you heard of him?"

"Can't say I have," said Ludwig. "Is he a noble?"

"No, although I'm sure he wouldn't object if he were given a title. He was a wealthy merchant who made his living in spices."

"How does one make a living with spices?"

"By shipping them in from the south. They say they grow in abundance on the southern continent."

"But that's mostly desert, isn't it?"

Dorkin smiled. "Depends what you mean by desert. I'm told the areas near the coast are nothing but sand and stone but go farther inland, and you'll hit thick vegetation, much thicker than what we have here."

Ludwig glanced around the area. "This is thick enough for me. I couldn't imagine anything worse."

"Then best not travel south."

"So what happened?"

Dorkin looked up from his work, a puzzled look on his face. "With what?"

"How is it you're no longer a cook?"

"Ah, well, that's not entirely my fault."

Ludwig watched the man, waiting expectantly.

"Well, you see," Dorkin continued, "I was a great believer in fresh food in those days, so I used to go out each morning and gather what I needed from nature."

"And?"

Dorkin blushed. "It was the mushrooms, you see. They turned out to be poisonous."

"Tell me you didn't kill your employer?"

"Of course not, but he did get pretty sick. After that, I was dismissed."

"And so you found your way to the Grim Defenders?"

"Not quite. There was some wandering in the middle there. I'd been on the road for, oh, I don't know, maybe six months? I happened to find myself in Anshlag while the Defenders were visiting."

"What made you decide to become a mercenary? It's a far cry from being a cook."

"It is, but I was desperate. My funds had run out, and my clothes were a ruin. I only narrowly missed being arrested for vagrancy. The Defenders offered me a place of refuge."

"Did they teach you to fight?"

"I'd spent some time in the town militia growing up, so I wasn't completely useless. They'd recently returned from the south, down near Salzing, where they'd had a run-in with some noble. As a result, they had some spare equipment. They gave me a padded jacket, a hatchet, and a wooden shield. Later on, I managed to acquire a helmet, then I was all set."

"And how does life in the Grim Defenders compare to your previous position?"

"Let's just say it keeps me fed. Given a choice, I'd much prefer to be working in a kitchen, but I doubt anyone would hire me after what I've done."

Ludwig looked down at the mushrooms. "Are you sure those aren't poisonous?"

Dorkin laughed. "Yes. I'm not foolish enough that I would make the same mistake a second time." He began gathering more of the fungi.

Ludwig sat on a fallen trunk, breathing in the musky scent of the woods. "You know, this place reminds me of home."

"Oh? How so?"

"There are woods near Verfeld Keep much like this, though the trees are a little less dense. I would often ride there."

"You had a horse? You must have been wealthy indeed."

Ludwig suddenly realized he had said too much. He had already revealed his heritage to Cyn and Sigwulf. If he kept this up, the entire company would soon know of his background, and then word might get back to his father. He decided to change the subject.

"How did you become a cook?" Ludwig asked.

"I took after my mother."

"What did your father do?"

"I never knew my father," said Dorkin, "though I was told he was a soldier. Maybe that's why I fit in so well with the company. What about your da? What did he do?"

Ludwig cursed his luck, for his attempt to distract had merely returned the discussion to his own past. "He was a soldier as well," he replied. In fact, it was a partial truth, for Lord Frederick had seen battle under Ludwig's cousin, King Otto, but that had been years before Ludwig came on to the scene.

"It sounds like we have something in common," said Dorkin. He stood, placing the last few mushrooms into his sack, then let his eyes wander the forest floor one last time.

"I suppose we should be getting back to the camp," said Ludwig.

"What did you say that moss looked like?"

"It's green," said Ludwig. "Then again, most moss is green, isn't it?"

"Yes, but didn't you say something about there being flecks of blue?"

Ludwig's interest was piqued. "I did. Why?"

Dorkin pulled his knife, then crouched, pointing with it. "Look here."

Ludwig came closer, mimicking the cook's actions. "Well, I'll be," he said. "Can that be it?"

In answer, Dorkin took the tip of his blade, scraping it along the top of the moss. Sure enough, they could see a faint blue sheen. "Do you think this will be enough?" he asked.

"It will have to," said Ludwig. "I don't see any more around here, do you?"

His companion started gently prying up the moss, working carefully to keep it as intact as possible. He then set it aside, digging through his bag to retrieve a small scrap of cloth approximately the size of a kerchief. This he placed on the ground, then commenced the process of gently wrapping his prize. Ludwig watched as Dorkin lifted it, placing it carefully within the bag as if it were a Holy Relic.

"We'd best get going if we're to help Sigwulf," said the cook.

"Yes," agreed Ludwig. "Let's hope we're not too late."

. . .

Ludwig watched as Linden Herzog used the pommel of his dagger to grind up the warriors moss. Occasionally he would pause, test the consistency, and then add a bit more mud to the mix and continue working.

"How thick does it have to be?" asked Ludwig.

The mage frowned. "Thick enough it'll stay in place. The idea is to make a compress or a poultice. Something that will cling to the wound if we are to draw out the pus."

Ludwig looked down to where Sigwulf tossed and turned. His fever had worsened since last Ludwig saw him, and he worried for the man's life. Cyn, normally the tough one, was shattered, barely holding herself together as her Siggy lay dying.

Linden Herzog placed his knife aside and lifted the bowl, sniffing it and wrinkling his nose. "This stuff stinks, but let's hope it works. Did you bring those linens?"

"Linens? You mean these scraps of cloth? Yes, I have them here."

"Good. Now we have to pack the wound on both sides. I'll smear on this stuff"—he held up the bowl—"and then you push the cloth up against it and hold it tight. Once both sides are done, we can start wrapping his torso to keep everything in place."

"And that will cure him?"

"Let's not get ahead of ourselves," warned the mage. "Neither one of us is exactly an expert in treating a wound of this nature. We shall have to trust in Karl's advice."

Ludwig looked at Cyn. "You should hold on to his hand. He might feel some discomfort with us moving him."

She nodded, unable to speak, her cheeks tear-stained.

"Right," said Herzog. "Let's get to work, shall we?"

They rolled Sigwulf onto his side, then gently cut away his shirt, revealing the wound. The mage used his fingers to scoop out the paste, then began liberally applying it to the patient's wound. When he was done, he nodded to Ludwig, who pressed a cloth into place.

"That went well," said the mage. "Now let's see to his back, shall we?"

He moved, getting into a better position, then examined the wound, but it was not looking good. Grey-green pus oozed out, and with it, a terrible stench. Herzog looked around, spotting the damp cloth Cyn had been using to mop Sigwulf's brow. "Pass me that," he said.

She handed it over, and he used it to wipe away the corruption as best he could. Sigwulf muttered something, obviously in pain, but his words were impossible to decipher.

Linden scooped out more of the mixture, then laid it over the wound, pressing it with a firm but gentle hand. He nodded to Ludwig, and then another cloth was pressed against the poultice.

The mage sat back, taking a breath. "There," he said at last. "Everything's in place. All we have left to do is bind him." He lifted his knife and began cutting the spare cloth into strips.

Ludwig's hands, which had been applying pressure to the wound, were beginning to ache, yet he dare not release them for fear the paste of warriors moss might come loose. Linden Herzog began threading the strips around Sigwulf's chest and stomach, lifting the giant man as best he could to get beneath him.

The task was time-consuming, and Ludwig found himself looking at Cyn to distract him. She followed the entire ordeal with devout attention, but Siggy's illness had left a marked effect on the woman. Her eyes were sunken and her face devoid of emotion as if life itself had been sucked out of her. He was struck by the sudden realization that if Sigwulf's fever did not abate, it might claim the both of them.

"You can let go now," said the mage.

Ludwig withdrew his hands and sat back, his back cracking as he straightened.

"Well?" said Ludwig.

"I have done all I can," said Herzog. "Once again, I must remind you I am an Earth Mage, not a healer. Now come, let us step outside. I need some fresh air."

"I will stay," said Cyn, her voice convincing them there could be no argument.

Ludwig stepped outside. The rain had ceased for now, but the dark clouds promised more on the morrow. He turned to his companion. "I thought Earth Mages were nature experts?"

"Earth Magic is a complex subject," replied Herzog. "Would you say all warriors can use an axe?"

"No, I suppose not."

"It's the same way with us. While it's true some Earth Mages tend to the ways of the living world, that is not my calling. Instead, I favour the magic of earth and stone."

"But doesn't that limit your magic?"

"My dear fellow, we all face limitations to what we can do. Take yourself, for example. Have you a horse?"

"No," said Ludwig, "though I had one. Quite a nice one it was too."

"And while it was in your possession, would you have called yourself an expert at mounted warfare?"

"Possibly, when I first arrived in Torburg, but I have come to realize it's not my strength. I am, it seems, better suited to fight on foot."

"And so you, in your own way, are realizing you're better working with swords, just as I am more comfortable working stone."

Ludwig nodded his head. "I see now. I suppose I never honestly thought of magic that way."

"Have you no mages back home?"

"No, at least none I'm aware of."

"We are typically found at the courts of kings or princes," noted Herzog. "Though some, like me, prefer to travel the Petty Kingdoms instead."

"And do you prosper?" asked Ludwig.

"Not particularly, but at least it allows me to ply my trade."

18

THE PLAN

Spring 1095 SR

L udwig took a sip of ale and stared across at Linden Herzog. The mage was carefully sipping some wine, but suddenly he put down his goblet.

"I have an idea," he announced.

"About what?" said Ludwig.

"How we might gain entrance to the keep."

"I believe you might be a little late in that regard. The baron has already decided to starve the place out."

Herzog chuckled. "We can't, don't you see? The baron has few enough troops as it is. There's no way he could completely encircle the place."

"Yet that's what he intends to do."

"I have another idea," said the mage, "and I think it would work too."

"You must tell me more," pressed Ludwig. "Is it something to do with your magic?"

"It is, in fact. Of course, I'd need to get close to the wall, and that would require a frontal assault."

"We tried that. It didn't work."

"No, wait. Hear me out. If I can get close enough to the wall, I can use my magic to create a doorway into the courtyard."

"That doesn't win us the keep," said Ludwig.

"True, but if we can get even half a dozen men inside, maybe they can rush the gatehouse and open the doors."

"And lower the drawbridge, don't forget that."

The mage looked at him with an inscrutable gaze. "What do you think? Could half a dozen men take the gatehouse?"

"It might work," mused Ludwig, "but if you're going to open up a hole in the wall, wouldn't it be better to seize the courtyard?"

Herzog smiled. "Yes, I suppose it would, wouldn't it? That's a splendid idea. Now, how do we get me to the wall?"

"Under cover of darkness. We'll send a small group to protect you with shields. How long would it take for your spell to work?"

"The spell itself would weaken the stone in no time, but then I'd have to use my hands to reshape the stone."

"I assume that's when you'd be at your most vulnerable?"

"It would indeed."

Ludwig looked up towards the ceiling, going over things in his head. In answer, Linden leaned forward, craning his neck to see the object of his companion's fascination.

Ludwig's eyes came back down. "What are you doing?"

"I was going to ask you the same thing. Is there something up there?"

"No, I was just thinking. Sometimes it helps to stare off into the distance to focus my mind."

"That's a bizarre custom, my friend."

"What do YOU do to think?"

"Thinking has never been a problem for me," confided the mage. "To be honest, I have a harder problem trying NOT to think."

"Why would you not want to think?"

"Sometimes my mind is too active, and then I lie awake at night, unable to sleep."

"Have you tried ale?" said Ludwig, grinning.

"It doesn't work."

"Then maybe you need the warm embrace of a woman?"

"That would be a distraction of another kind," remarked the mage. "And in any case, this camp has few on offer."

"Few?" said Ludwig. "More like none, from what I've seen."

"What about Cyn?"

"What about her?"

"Ever thought of trying your luck with her?"

"First of all," said Ludwig, "she's a friend, and she's with Sigwulf. Also, when did this conversation become about me? You're the one who said you had trouble sleeping?"

"So I did," said the mage. "I'm sorry, I seem to have gotten us off topic. Let's go back to my plan, shall we?"

"Good idea."

"You were in the first assault, weren't you?"

"I was," said Ludwig. "What do you want to know?"

"What was the opposition like?"

"Deadly and well-prepared."

Herzog frowned. "Can you be more specific?"

"What are you looking for?"

"What were their defences like?"

"They had bundles of oil-soaked hay ready to light and toss over the wall."

"Hmmm," said the mage. "Leaving no place to hide, I'd warrant."

"Yes. They were also waiting on the wall and certainly didn't seem to have a shortage of troops. I did manage to get to the top, you know, but then I was overwhelmed by their soldiers. I only escaped by leaping into the moat, and that's not something I'd care to do again."

"Could archers not keep them busy?"

"Perhaps," said Ludwig, "but we attacked at night. Any daytime attack would leave us vulnerable during the advance, not to mention getting across the moat."

"You can swim, surely?"

"In armour? I think you underestimate the challenge. You're the Earth Mage. Couldn't you fill the moat with dirt?"

"Possibly, but it would take some time."

"Time," said Ludwig, "is the one thing we seem to have in abundance."

Herzog took a sip of wine. "I don't think that's such a good idea."

"Oh? Why?"

"Magic is a rare gift," the mage continued. "Its use in battle should be saved for the moment where it can be most effective. Any use of magic to fill in the moat would alert our enemies to my presence."

"What if it does?"

"Well, for one, you can forget about me getting us through the wall."

"I'm not sure I follow," said Ludwig.

"Let me explain. If Lord Wulfram or any of his people have heard of Earth Mages, they'll know that coming through the wall is a distinct possibility."

"But your type are rare, aren't they?"

"They are, but we must not underestimate our enemy. Should they get wind I'm present, they might have people watching for just such an attack."

"So what are you suggesting?" said Ludwig.

"Merely that we may only get one chance at this. The objective here should be to make the most of that opportunity."

"In that case, we have to assault the wall again. Only a direct attack will keep them busy enough to ignore you."

"You could try using a siege tower," suggested Herzog. "I hear they're extremely effective against prepared defences."

"And how, pray tell, would we get them across the moat?"

The mage frowned. "A valid point, I think. It's looking more and more like a nighttime attack."

"I suppose we could try a bluff?"

"What do you mean, a bluff?"

"It's quite simple, really," said Ludwig. "We stage a pretend assault against another section of wall. Then, while that attack is underway, we make our way to wherever it is that you can get us through."

"I like it," said the Earth Mage. "How many men do you believe you can spare for the diversion?"

"We'd need to send the bulk of our troops," said Ludwig. "Otherwise they'll see it as a ruse, and for that, I'll have to speak with my captain."

"Do you suppose he'll be amenable to the idea?"

"He did task me with coming up with a plan."

"And if he approves?"

"Then he'll likely have to broach the subject with the baron. After all, it's Lord Gebhard who hired us."

"We should go and see him," said Herzog. "Maybe together we can convince him it's a good plan."

"Sounds like a good idea. When would you like to go?"

"How about right now? It's not as if we're doing anything else important."

In answer, Ludwig downed the rest of his ale, then nodded towards the door. "All right, then. Let's go, shall we, before I lose my nerve."

Captain Ecke proved highly receptive to the idea, so much so that he insisted they accompany him to visit the baron. Lord Gebhard Stein sat at a table when they entered, pulling apart a roast chicken with his bare hands. He tucked a morsel of meat into his mouth, looking up as his visitors entered.

"What's this, now?" he asked.

The captain bowed his head. "My lord, we believe we may have found a way in."

"Another assault?"

"In part," said Ecke, "but only as a diversion."

The baron swallowed his food, then wiped his hands on his kerchief. "You have me intrigued. Tell me more."

"The plan was hatched by Sergeant Ludwig here, with the assistance of your Earth Mage, Linden Herzog."

Stein frowned. "Oh, it uses magic. I must say that's a bit disappointing."

"What does it matter," said Ecke, "as long as you're victorious?"

"I suppose you have a point. Very well, tell me of this plan."

"I shall let the sergeant explain." The captain turned to Ludwig who, caught by surprise, was at a loss for words. Linden, on the other hand, was ready with an explanation.

"As you know, my lord," the mage began, "I can manipulate stone. It is our intention to get a small group of warriors past the curtain wall. From there, they could seize the gate, or clear the walls, depending on what they find once they're in."

"And how, exactly, would you 'manipulate stone'?"

"I anticipated your request," said Herzog. "I thought a little demonstration might be in order." He reached into his shirt, producing a flat stone approximately half his palm in size. "Would you examine this, my lord?" He handed the stone to Lord Gebhard.

The baron held it up but could see nothing of interest.

"You will note," said the mage, "it's an ordinary stone, unremarkable in any way."

Stein frowned, but then Herzog took it back and held it before him, uttering strange words. The room seemed to buzz as if a swarm of bees had entered, and then the mage's hands began to glow ever so slightly.

The words ceased, and the mage grasped the stone with both hands, twisting it. To Ludwig's amazement, it did nothing to resist the effort, moving as if it were made of clay.

His task complete, Herzog held out the stone in one hand. "Would you care to examine it, my lord?"

Stein looked pale. "Hagan?" he called out. "Get in here!"

The door behind him opened, revealing the baron's son.

"Is something wrong, Father?"

"Take that stone," the baron ordered.

Hagan, unaware of what had transpired, crossed the room, taking the strange object in hand.

"What do you make of it?" snapped the baron.

"It's a strange rock, to be sure. Where did you find it?"

Linden Herzog merely smiled. With no answer forthcoming, Hagan Stein looked at Ludwig.

"Master Herzog used his magic on it," he explained.

Hagan smiled. "Remarkable. Tell me, can he do this with any stone?"

"Stone, brick, or mortar," said Herzog. "The material matters not."

"Yes," agreed Ludwig. "You might say it's immaterial."

Herzog let out a laugh, then looked at Ludwig. "I must say that was quite clever."

The baron was not at all amused. Instead, he was turning red, a sure sign he was upset.

Ludwig cleared his throat. "You can see, my lord, how easily Master Herzog can manipulate stone. This same technique can be used to get through Regnitz's walls."

The tactic worked, and the baron's attention returned to the task at hand. "And how many men can you get inside?"

"That largely depends on how many are on the other side," said the mage. "I can open up a man-sized breach, but the first people through must secure the other side."

"I estimate a dozen," said Ludwig, "maybe a few more, then the defenders will realize what's happened. Of course, we could increase our chances by a diversion."

"What sort of diversion?"

"Another attack against a wall."

Stein frowned. Ludwig couldn't help but notice it reinforced the wrinkles on the man's face, leading him to conclude it was a common occurrence.

"The first assault cost us dearly," said Stein. "And you want to repeat that fiasco?"

Ludwig was incensed, for it was the Grim Defenders who had taken the losses, while the baron's men had been left unscathed. He wanted to argue the point, but realized a more diplomatic approach was needed here.

"The attack is a ruse," he finally said, "and as such, it's only being staged to attract attention. The plan would call for an advance on the western wall, but to halt shy of actually scaling it."

"And this would give you enough time to get inside?"

"It should," said Ludwig.

"I'm afraid that would be difficult. The weather is turning, and the clouds will smother the moonlight."

"Then we attack during the day," said Ludwig.

"But won't they see us coming?"

"That's precisely what we want, my lord."

Hagan interrupted. "But won't they see your group getting into position?"

"No," said Ludwig. "We'd already be in place by the time the sun comes up."

"Yes," agreed Herzog. "But the diversion must begin at first light. We need to keep them occupied."

Stein turned to his son. "What do you think?"

"It's a courageous plan," said Hagan, looking at Ludwig. "Are you sure your men are up to it?"

"He is," added Captain Ecke, "as am I. We have a chance to bring this conflict to an end, my lord."

"We'll try it," said the baron. "Who knows, if it works on the curtain wall, we might be able to use it on the inner keep as well."

"We shan't disappoint you," promised Ludwig.

Captain Ecke led them from the room. He paused as they closed the door behind them. "Assemble your team," he said, "and choose wisely. We won't get a second chance at this."

Ludwig poked his head inside the tent. "How's he doing?"

Cyn looked up, wearing a glazed expression. "His fever still rages."

"It will likely take some time for the warriors moss to work," offered Linden Herzog. "Is he conscious?"

"Not at the moment, but his ramblings are becoming less chaotic."

"A good sign. It means his mind is still working."

Ludwig crawled into the cramped confines of the tent. "Go and get some sleep, Cyn. You'll be no good to Sig in your current condition."

"My place is here!"

"No, you need to be strong for him. You can't do that when you haven't slept. Besides, when was the last time you ate?"

"I can't remember."

"Go," Ludwig commanded. "At least get some food into you. I'll sit with Sigwulf."

He noticed the hesitation in her face. "GO!"

"Come," said Herzog, "let's get you fed." He reached out, taking her hand and leading her away like a small child.

Ludwig made himself as comfortable as he could in the tiny space. He looked down at his friend. Sigwulf lay still, his breath rasping, and Ludwig reached out, feeling the clamminess of the skin.

"Come on, Sig," he said. "You've got to pull through. We're all counting on you."

He sat for a while, and then he found his thoughts drifting to matters divine. Did the Saints truly watch over them? Ludwig had never considered himself a religious man, but now, facing death in the form of his dear friend lying before him, he had to wonder. He considered praying, but to whom? If anyone had asked him before this, he might have prayed to Saint Cunar, but he was the patron saint of warriors, not the sick. To whom, then, should he pray for the life of his comrade who lay dying?

A gentle breeze swept through the tent, bringing the fresh scent of grass. It reminded him of home, and he was suddenly struck by the image of Prior Yannick sitting at the dinner table at Verfeld. Was this a sign?

He took Sigwulf's hand, cold as it was, and placed it between his own. Closing his eyes, he said a silent prayer to Saint Mathew. It felt as if time stood still. Ludwig had no idea how long he sat thus, but then Sigwulf shifted, breaking his concentration.

"I hope this doesn't mean we are to be married?" said a raspy voice.

Ludwig looked down in shock. Sigwulf was staring up at him, his haggard face pale, yet the hint of a smile played at the corners of his mouth.

"You'd best not mention this to Cyn," Sig added. "You know how jealous she is."

Ludwig couldn't help but smile. "You gave us quite the scare there."

"Speaking of Cyn, where is she?"

"Getting something to eat. She hasn't left your side for days."

"I must get back to work," insisted Sigwulf.

Ludwig let go of his hand. "You're not going anywhere until you're fully recovered, my friend."

"How long have I been out?"

"Three days," said Ludwig.

"What have I missed?"

"That depends. What do you remember?"

"The assault went badly," said Sigwulf. "I recall taking an arrow in the back as I was making my way across the moat. Then Cyn did something that hurt a lot."

"That arrow almost killed you," said Ludwig. "She had to break off the head so we could pull it out."

Sigwulf shifted slightly, obviously in some discomfort. "I remember now. Did you get it all?"

"We did, but you took ill with a fever."

"And yet I live?"

"Yes, thanks to warriors moss."

Sigwulf raised his head, trying to view his bandages, but Ludwig used a hand to force him back down.

"You covered me in moss?"

"More or less. In any event, it appears to have done the trick. Now, you need to rest until your strength recovers."

"How's Cyn?"

"Uninjured, if that's what you mean, but she hasn't slept much since we discovered you, nor eaten, to be honest. She's definitely in no fit shape for the next attack."

"You plan to scale the walls?"

"Actually," said Ludwig, "we've come up with something a little different this time. I think you'd be impressed."

"Would that I could join you, but I fear my strength has been drained."

"It'll recover in time, my friend. You must rest for now, but I'll tell you all about it once we're victorious."

"You'd better," said Sigwulf.

19

THE GATEHOUSE

Spring 1095 SR

Dawn. The sun stretched out its rays, bathing the land in a golden hue. Ludwig, up to his waist in water, and in the shadows, shivered. They had advanced under cover of night and now stood beneath the raised drawbridge, huddling in water that sapped their strength. He looked at the others: twelve hand-picked men, all of them shivering like him, waiting on the order to begin.

"Soon," he whispered. This was the most difficult part, the waiting. In order to get close to the wall, they must stay put until the diversionary attack began. Only once that commenced could they risk the rush of the last few yards to get the Earth Mage into position.

The gatehouse projected out from the curtain wall, forming a corner of sorts, and it was where these two structures met that was the intended point of entry.

Ludwig felt confident. Once Linden Herzog opened up the wall, it would be a simple matter to get inside the gatehouse and lower the drawbridge. Their task complete, the cavalry under Hagan Stein's command would rush across, securing victory, providing, of course, Ludwig and his group could get into position without being seen.

From the west drifted the sound of warriors charging forward, steeling themselves for the assault on the wall. Ludwig closed his eyes and started counting, trying not to rush. When he finally reached fifty, he looked at Herzog and the others.

"Ready?" he asked.

They all nodded, and then Ludwig moved to his left, navigating his way around the base of the drawbridge. He scanned the curtain wall but spotted no sign of soldiers. Closer he crept, then began climbing out of the water. The moat's bank was steep here to allow the drawbridge's massive counter-weight room to swing. It also made navigation far more difficult. He struggled for a moment, then managed to grasp a tuft of grass and haul himself onto his stomach.

His task complete, he turned, offering his hand to the next in line. As they exited the moat, each man made their way to the curtain wall, pressing themselves up against it. Ludwig soon joined them. Linden Herzog was pushed up against the corner where the wall met that of the gatehouse.

The mage rubbed his hands, trying to warm them, then placed them against the stone. Clearly, he was looking for something, for he moved them several times, then smiled.

"What's wrong?" whispered Ludwig.

"I have to find just the right spot," replied Herzog. "I don't want to tunnel right where a support sits."

"Why? Would that bring down the wall?"

"No, but it would mean displacing more stone, and we don't have the time for that. Now, let me concentrate on the task at hand."

He began mumbling something, and then Ludwig felt the air come alive as if a swarm of insects had come upon them. The hair on the back of his neck rose as the mage's hands began to glow with a faint yellow light. Herzog was sweating now, and the strain was clearly visible upon his face as the words kept flowing and then abruptly ceased. The yellow light faded into the stone, and the mage lowered his hands.

"What's wrong now?" said Ludwig.

Herzog turned to him, grinning broadly. "Nothing. It's worked like a charm."

"But the wall is unchanged."

"I suppose it would look that way to you, but in reality, it is now ready for me to manipulate. Watch closely, Ludwig, and see how real power works." Herzog pushed his hands into the stone, which parted under his touch.

Ludwig couldn't believe his eyes. It was one thing to see him bend a pebble, quite another to see a stone wall part beneath his very fingers. The mage worked slowly, pushing in and then scooping out the stone. Those around him watched in fascination, for their eyes could not grasp what was happening as the stone parted beneath Herzog's fingers like clay.

Another scoop, and then his hands were knuckle-deep. More stone came loose, dropping to the ground in small blobs, and still he worked on. Ludwig held his breath, then forced himself to breathe.

The work continued until Herzog's arms were up to the elbows in the stone. He stepped back, revealing a small hole that penetrated the wall.

"I'm through," he announced. "Now comes the job of widening it."

Time dragged on, and Ludwig began to worry it was taking too long. He glanced up to the top of the wall, but no one had yet taken any notice of them. Off in the distance, the sounds of the assault were dying down, a sure sign their time was running out. He looked over Herzog's shoulder, trying to gauge the mage's progress, but all he could see was a dark hole, hidden in shadows, and the mage's arms, nearly shoulder-deep as he worked to push the stone to either side.

Fearful that they would soon be discovered, Ludwig turned to the man behind him. "Take this," he said, passing over his shield. "It will only get in my way." He stepped to Herzog's side. "How goes it?"

"It is far more difficult than I anticipated," revealed the mage. "The wall is thick, and it's resisting my efforts. I am unable to press it aside and must, instead, scoop out the stone to make the opening wide enough."

The odd sounds of fighting were still drifting in from the west, but Ludwig knew it wouldn't last much longer. "As soon as you have a small opening, I'll crawl through."

"Are you sure you wouldn't prefer to wait?" said Linden. "You could become trapped on the other side."

"We have no choice. If we don't secure the chamber beyond, they'll be able to pick us off as we come through."

Herzog knelt, his hands working feverishly. The hole had become more of an oblong, and he worked to form it into a vertical opening.

Ludwig peered through the gap, careful not to get in the mage's way. Beyond, the room was lit by a torch, but he could see little other than the flickering of the flame on the opposite wall.

The Earth Mage was sweating profusely now. He shook his head, though to what end, Ludwig couldn't say. Wider and wider grew the gap, and then the mage took a step back.

"Do you think you can get through?" Herzog asked.

"There's only one way to find out," said Ludwig. He poked his sword in, then, leading with his right hand, began squeezing through the opening. He flattened himself as best he could and moved sideways to reduce his surface area.

His arm soon cleared the opening, but then his chest caught on the stone. Ludwig exhaled, driving the air from his lungs, and pushed harder, finally clearing the wall. Casting his eyes around the room, he discovered he was in a small chamber, not more than three paces deep. To his left was a door, and he moved towards it quickly, pressing his ear to it.

He had just settled into position when someone pushed on it, throwing him backwards and causing him to fall. A guard gave a startled cry as the door flung open, and he spotted Ludwig sprawled there, then backed up, giving himself room to draw his sword.

Ludwig jumped up and rushed through the door, striking out with his own weapon, but the soldier's chainmail surcoat resisted his efforts. He was in the inner courtyard now, and the duke's men looked to be everywhere. The surprised defender's cry had alerted the keep, and now a half-dozen men began running towards him, spears in hand.

Ludwig cursed, for the plan had gone awry from the start. The false attack had ended, releasing the soldiers into the courtyard. The first guard struck with his sword, but Ludwig managed to parry the blow. He swung, but his blade once more scraped across the superior chainmail.

Someone stabbed at him with a spear, and he jumped back, narrowly avoiding the attack. He parried, then attempted to close the range, only to find the fellow was using his weapon like a staff, driving the butt of it into Ludwig's groin. Pain shot through him.

Ludwig fell to his knees as men rushed past him. He tried to reach out with his sword, anything to buy his men time, but the end of another spear struck him in the helmet, causing his head to ring.

Men swarmed him, seizing his arms. Ludwig fought with all he had to free himself, but their grip was solid, and they quickly pinned his arms in place. He looked back into the entryway in time to see a soldier pushing a spear through the hole in the wall. Someone on the other side let out a terrible scream as the warrior pulled back his spear, blood dripping from its tip. Ludwig knew in his heart that Linden Herzog was dead.

Others flooded into the room, and then two of them held shields up to the gap, preventing any further infiltration. A figure loomed in front of him, blocking his view as a sword hilt smashed into the side of his face, his head swimming for a moment before everything went black.

Ludwig awoke to the feeling of damp straw pressed against his cheek. Somewhere off in the distance was the drip of water, and his first thought was to wonder where he might be. Rolling onto his back with his head throbbing, he struggled to breathe. His hands clawed at the dried blood that had flooded from his nose.

Above him, a faint light reflected off the arched ceiling, possibly denoting a cellar of some sort. He lifted his head to look around, noticing the iron bars that defined his cell. Sitting up, he took stock of his situation. He was in a small room, barely long enough for him to lie down, but someone had at least tossed in some straw. Why go to such lengths for a prisoner, he wondered.

The cell took up roughly a third of the circular chamber. Across from him sat a torch in a wall sconce, the only source of light in the place, while a nearby door indicated the only exit. Pressing his ear to the bars, he was desperate to hear any distant sounds that might give him some clue of how the attack fared. It was a futile attempt, revealing nothing but the drip of water and the crackle of the torch.

Ludwig had heard of the kind of treatment that might be afforded a prisoner. Had he identified himself as a noble, he might expect a comfortable imprisonment, but as a common soldier and a mercenary at that, he could expect little, save for perhaps torture and death.

His thoughts drifted to Linden Herzog. Was he the one who had taken the spear? He hoped not, and yet he could see no other explanation. The mage would have been working to enlarge the gap, so there was little chance it could have been anyone else.

Ludwig examined his legs. They appeared uninjured, and he wore no shackles. For that, at least, he must be grateful. Moving to the far wall, he sat with his back against the stone, facing the iron bars that kept him prisoner, and waited.

Sleep claimed him at least twice, but he had no concept of how much time had passed until, finally, footsteps approached and then came the sound of keys turning in the lock. Moments later, the door swung open, revealing a man in the livery of the Baron of Regnitz.

"Ah," the man said. "I see you're awake."

"Where am I?" asked Ludwig.

"Where do you think? Under the baron's keep, where else?"

"Why am I still alive?"

The guard looked amused. "Why? Would you prefer to be dead?"

"No, merely curious."

"His Lordship was most intrigued by the method of your attack. I expect he'll want to talk to you about it."

"I shall say nothing," swore Ludwig.

The guard shrugged. "It makes no difference to me. Are you hungry?"

"Yes," said Ludwig, "though thirst is of more immediate concern."

"I detect an air of education to your manner. Are you a knight?"

Ludwig was caught. He could reveal his noble lineage, but to do so risked his father hearing word of his whereabouts. "No," he finally responded, "merely well-read."

The guard grunted out, "Wait here," then disappeared back through the doorway, only to return a moment later, a ladle in hand. He approached the door to the cell with caution, then reached out with it. "Here, have some water."

Ludwig took the ladle, eagerly downing the brackish liquid. "Thank you."

"Don't thank me," said the guard. "I'm only here to keep an eye on you until the baron's ready for you."

"What of the attack?"

"You mean the feint against the wall or your little escapade?"

"What do you mean, feint?" asked Ludwig.

"Come now, it was pretty clear that the attack from the west was only designed to keep us busy. I'm guessing your infiltration was the real plan."

Ludwig felt the defeat well up inside him.

"Well," said the guard, taking back the ladle. "I'll go and scrape up something for you to eat, shall I?"

"To keep me full for my execution?"

"Who said anything about an execution?"

"I'm your prisoner. Why would you deign to keep me alive?"

"What do you take us for, Orcs?" replied the guard. "Lord Wulfram would never countenance such a thing." He shook his head. "What strange ideas you have. Tell me, how long have you been in service to Lord Gebhard?"

"I'm not," said Ludwig. "I'm a Grim Defender."

"Oh, yes? What's that?"

"A company of mercenaries."

"I suppose that explains how he raised an army so quickly," noted the guard. "Now, let me go and dig you up some food before it's all gone."

He left the room, closing the door behind him, leaving Ludwig to ponder his fate.

Sometime later, the door opened, revealing visitors of a different sort. In addition to the guard, the baron himself was present, along with a young woman with hair of spun gold. Lord Wulfram stared at Ludwig, though to what end, the prisoner couldn't say.

"So you're the one who broke through the wall," he finally said. "What's your name?"

"Ludwig."

"Wait," said the baron. "I know that name. Didn't you compete in the tournament at Torburg?"

Ludwig blushed. "I did, my lord."

"Yes, I remember it now. You went down fairly quickly at the hands of Sir Galrath, if I recall."

"I did."

"And now you're a mercenary?"

"Yes," said Ludwig. "I'm a member of the Grim Defenders."

"So I've been told. That was quite the daring feat, coming through the wall like that. I doubt many men would have had the courage to do what you did."

Ludwig shrugged. "I was merely doing my duty, my lord."

"Duty? Don't make me laugh. You're either exceedingly brave or extremely foolish. I can't quite make up my mind which." He turned to the young lady. "What do you think, my dear?"

Her face was unreadable. "I believe he's an enigma, Father. On the one hand, he's obviously noble-born, or he wouldn't have been able to compete in the jousting. On the other, he has sunk to the level of becoming a sell-sword."

"And what conclusion do you make from that?"

"I sense his fortunes have turned sour."

"You must pardon Rosalyn," said the baron. "My indulgence of her literacy has led her to flights of fancy."

"And yet," said Ludwig, "she is, in essence, correct."

"Is she now?" The baron stepped closer. "Tell me more. Perhaps I shall take pity on you and let you live."

"Father!"

"Hush now," said the baron. "I spoke in jest only." He returned his attention to his prisoner. "Are you, in truth, a knight?"

"No," said Ludwig, "though my family is noble."

"Who is your father?"

"I would prefer not to say, my lord. There is an estrangement between us."

"Ah, that would explain why you joined the mercenaries, I suppose."

"It would."

"Well, it's of no concern to me." The baron turned to leave, but Ludwig, desperate for anything to give him hope, tried a different approach.

"My lord?"

Lord Wulfram craned his neck around. "Yes?"

"Why does Lord Gebhard hate you so much?"

"That," said the baron, "is between him and me and is not for others to discuss."

Lord Wulfram stepped towards the door, then turned once more unexpectedly. "It's clear you are a man of refinement," he said. "I shall arrange a blanket for you, along with some decent food, but I'm afraid you must remain here in the dungeon, for the time being. Perhaps, in time, I might change my mind, but you are still my enemy for now. Of course, your noble birth should warrant better treatment, but we are a bit... strained at the moment. I shall assign Rosalyn to keep an eye on you and ensure you are treated with the dignity and respect due your station." He turned to his daughter. "I assume that is acceptable to you?"

"It is, Father."

"Good. Then the matter has been decided."

"Yes, Lord," said Ludwig.

The baron turned to the guard. "You can return to the walls, Horst. Rosalyn can handle this."

"Are you sure that's wise, my lord? She is but a maid?"

"And he is behind bars. I can assure you my daughter is more than capable of dealing with this fellow. Now, come along, Rosalyn. We have much to discuss before you take up your new duties."

They exited the room, the door slamming shut behind them, leaving Ludwig alone with his thoughts once more.

20

PRISONER

Spring 1095 SR

He had no idea how much time had passed when the torch finally went out, plunging him into inky blackness. Ludwig considered himself a brave man, for in his mind, any man who fought on a wall must indeed be made of stern stuff. Yet now, alone in the dark, even the smallest of sounds made him shudder, and the scrabbling of what he had to assume were rats drove him to distraction.

The mere thought that his straw might also be infested with insects drove him to lie on the cold stone floor, and thus it was that Rosalyn and her two servants found him curled up in a ball, looking like death warmed over, the heat sapped from his very bones.

"Fetch the key," she ordered, and one of the servants ran off in a hurry. She stepped closer to the bars, seeking to determine if he was still even alive. Her aide quickly returned, key in hand. When he fumbled with the lock, she pushed him aside, doing the work herself. A click announced her success, and then she stepped inside. Ludwig had a sense of her bending over him but was unable to respond.

"Lay out that blanket," he heard her say, "and we'll place him upon it."

They struggled to lift him. He could feel his arms flailing around, but he didn't have the strength to control them. Instead, they rolled him onto the blanket, then covered him with a second one, tucking it beneath his arms. He felt himself being lifted, but still he was numb and unable to speak.

"Is he dead?" said a voice.

"No," said Rosalyn, "but he has lain on a cold floor in wet clothes. Did no one think of such things?"

Ludwig's head lolled to the side, and he struggled to right it. Remembering the butt of the spear ringing his head, he felt a slight moment of panic. Had it done more damage than he thought?

"Bring him this way," he heard her say, and then came the gentle swaying as the servants each held on to an end of the blanket and carried him from the cell with awkward steps.

A bright light shone over him. Slowly, his eyes adjusted until he could make out the face of the young woman peering down at him, the lantern appearing halo-like over her head.

"Can you hear me?" she asked.

Ludwig tried to answer, but the words came out all jumbled. He cursed his stupidity as he shivered. If only he had seen fit to lie on the straw, he would not be so terribly chilled. They bore him up a set of stairs, having to set him down several times, the cold stone hard upon his back. Up and up they went, farther and farther, until he lost track of where he was.

Finally, he heard the jingle of keys. They carried him through an open door, but his head banged loudly against the doorway, and he thought he heard Rosalyn curse. Once again, he was set down on the floor. This time, two soldiers moved to stand over him, one lifting him under the arms while the other grabbed his feet. They dumped him onto a bed, and then a couple of blankets were thrown over him.

Ludwig tried to keep his mind alert, his eyes focused, but it was all such a struggle. Again, Lady Rosalyn looked down upon him, concern written on her face.

"Bring some broth," she commanded, "and more blankets."

"Maybe some rum?" suggested one of the soldiers.

"A good idea. Please see to it." Ludwig heard her pacing the room. "What else can we do?" she asked.

"A brazier?" suggested a soldier.

"Have we one?"

"We do," the warrior answered, "though it hasn't been used in years."

"Then fetch it."

Ludwig once again succumbed, and as he closed his eyes, he felt Lady Rosalyn take his hand in her own.

. . .

He opened his eyes as light streamed in through a small window. His action alerted a young woman who sat beside the bed. She immediately hopped up and ran from the room, calling for her mistress.

Ludwig lifted his head, taking in his surroundings. He was in a small room somewhere in the keep, although judging from the sun, it was high up rather than ground level. He strained to hear any noises that might reveal more, but all he could make out was the distant sound of chopping wood.

The blankets felt heavy against him, and for a moment, he thought he might be restrained, but a quick flick of his arm told him otherwise. Footsteps approached from the hallway, and then Lady Rosalyn appeared, her golden hair glowing in the early morning sunlight.

She smiled. "I see you're awake. How do you feel?"

Ludwig struggled to answer, but his voice only came out as a croak.

Rosalyn came closer, pouring him some water. "Here," she said. "Drink this."

Feeling the cup put to his lips, he drank thirstily.

"Thank you," he managed to squeak out.

"You had us very worried there for a while."

"What happened?"

"The dungeon can get quite cold. I'm afraid it sapped your strength."

He tried to focus on his memories but found it difficult to concentrate. "How long have I been unconscious?"

"It has been two days since we brought you here," she said. "For a while there, we thought we were going to lose you, but you seem to have recovered."

"Am I sick?"

"No, merely overcome by the severe conditions of our dungeon. Did you not think to use the straw?"

"It was overrun with vermin," said Ludwig, "or so I believed."

"And you thought the cold floor preferable?"

He felt the blood rush to his face. "I must confess I didn't think it through."

Her face softened. "Well, it's a good thing we came back when we did, or you might not have made it."

"Am I now to be returned to the dungeon?"

"No, at least not for the present. My father feels you may yet have value to him as a hostage."

"I'm afraid I have little to offer in that regard."

"But you are a noble. Would you not be worth ransom?"

"A noble I may have been," said Ludwig, "but my fortunes have turned. I am naught but a mercenary now."

"Yet still of noble character, judging by your manner."

"True, but there are none here I am aware of that might pay for my freedom."

"You have family. Would they not pay to see you safely returned?"

The question forced Ludwig to think. Would his father wish to see him safe?

Rosalyn noticed the look of concentration on his face, mistaking it for sorrow. "I'm sorry," she said. "I didn't mean to pry."

"You have a right to know if only to realize I am worthless to you. The truth is, my father knows nothing of my whereabouts nor, do I suspect, does he care to."

"He is your father. How can he not care?"

"We parted under the worst of circumstances," said Ludwig. "For you see, I ran away from home." As soon as the words left his mouth, he realized his mistake. He felt so childish as if the entire episode had been little more than a tantrum on his part.

"May I ask why?"

He gazed at her, unsure if he should reveal the truth.

"Why do you want to know?"

"You seem a man who bears a heavy burden. I seek only to relieve you of it."

"And how will my talking to you do that?"

"Sometimes it helps to talk of things," Rosalyn suggested. "It helps us overcome a loss."

"What would you know of loss?" Ludwig noticed her face darken and immediately regretted his choice of words.

"You are not the only one to lose a loved one," she said.

"Who said anything about losing someone?"

Her surprise was easy to read. "I just naturally thought…"

"You thought wrong."

"Then what is it that vexes you so? Did you have a falling out with your father? You mentioned an estrangement betwixt the two of you. What, I wonder, could cause such a rift? Your mother?"

"My mother died years ago," said Ludwig. "And my father remarried."

"A stepmother, then?"

"If you had asked me that some months ago, I would have agreed, but I have come to see her as a caring person. No, the truth is it was an affair of the heart. My father and I did not see eye to eye on the matter."

"But didn't he want to see you married?"

"Most assuredly, although not to the woman I chose." He felt his cheeks burning. "I'm sorry, it's not something I am prepared to speak further of at this time."

"I understand," she said. "The heart is easily wounded and takes time to heal."

"How is it that one so young is full of such wisdom?"

Rosalyn bristled. "Young? I am not much younger than you, sir, yet you dare to treat me as a child?"

"I apologize if I gave offence. It certainly was not my intention."

She calmed herself, smoothing the front of her dress with her hands. "I accept your apology, my lord."

"Please," said Ludwig, "don't call me that. I've given up that life."

"Then what shall I call you?"

"Just Ludwig will do."

Rosalyn smiled. "Very well, Just Ludwig."

He laughed, causing her own smile to widen.

"There," she said. "That wasn't so difficult, was it?"

"No, I suppose it wasn't."

"Now, why don't you share a little more about yourself?"

"Such as?"

"Do you ride? Have you fond memories of childhood? Those sorts of things."

"Riding gives me pleasure," said Ludwig, "though I have not done so for some months. You saw me in the tournament. I lost my horse there."

"An unfortunate turn of events."

"What of yourself? Do YOU ride?"

"I do, though not, of course, under our present circumstances."

"And did you take to the saddle at an early age?"

"No," said Rosalyn, "the reverse, in fact. I found horses to be thoroughly frightening as a child."

"Frightening?"

"Oh, yes. My mother died after falling from a horse, you see. She broke her neck."

"How old were you at the time?" he asked.

"Five. I barely remember her, if truth be told, but the mere thought that a horse killed her haunted me for years."

"And what changed your mind?"

"My father," she admitted. "He took great pains to help me overcome my fears, even going so far as to travel all the way to Anshlag to buy me the most docile horse in the realm."

"And that worked?"

"It did. Now I regularly ride across my father's lands, or at least I did before this whole unfortunate business came to pass."

Ludwig's ears pricked up. "What business is that?"

She laughed. "The siege, of course. What else?"

He felt duly chastised. "I should have realized that. What's the nature of this feud between your father and Lord Gebhard?"

"I'm afraid that's entirely my fault."

"Surely not?"

She nodded. "Yes, you see, Lord Gebhard came to visit my father nearly six months ago and proposed a union of our two houses."

"So you're saying he wanted you to marry his son, Hagan?"

She nodded again but remained quiet.

"I'm guessing you didn't agree with the idea?"

"No, the very idea repulses me."

"Is Master Hagan so villainous a figure?"

"The truth is I know almost nothing about him, but if he's anything like his father, I should prefer to die a spinster."

"Have you ever met the man?"

"I have not. Have you?"

"I have, as a matter of fact," said Ludwig. "He seems a decent enough fellow."

"Is he now? Tell me, is he like his father?"

"I can't say I've been in his company long enough to make that determination." The implications began to sink in. "Are you saying this whole siege is because you refused to marry him?"

"Yes," said Rosalyn. "Terrible, isn't it?"

"It's horrifying. Men are dying out there, and all because Hagan Stein couldn't take being refused?"

"I believe it more his father's doing, to be honest. Gebhard Stein was never a man to take no for an answer."

"But aren't there other women who would make a good match for his son?"

"Indeed, but none so well positioned geographically."

"I'm not sure I follow," said Ludwig.

"It has always been Lord Gebhard's ambition to raise his family name amongst the ranks of the nobility. If he were to marry off his son to me, our child would inherit both baronies."

"How does that elevate the family?"

"He would be doubling their land, don't you see? That would warrant a higher title, maybe even an earldom."

"But Erlingen is a duchy. There are no earls."

"Stein, and others, have been pressuring the duke to declare himself a king for some time now."

"What difference would that make?" asked Ludwig. "He'd still rule the same realm."

"It's a matter of prestige. Wars have been fought for less."

Ludwig shook his head. "This is madness."

"And what of your own situation? Is it not madness to run away from a life of privilege?"

Ludwig felt the shame again. "You make a valid point."

"I do not mean to mock you. People often make decisions based on their emotions, even though they deny that's the cause. You yourself ran away, and it has made you the man you are today. Had you the chance to do it all over again, would you decide any different?"

Ludwig thought it over. His thoughts naturally drifted back to the woman with dark hair and almond eyes. "No," he declared at last. "I wouldn't."

"Then you should come to peace with your decision rather than be ashamed of it."

"Who said I was ashamed?"

"Your features betray you, Ludwig, and you are not the only one who has had to make difficult decisions."

"What of yourself?" he asked. "Would you change your mind knowing that your refusal of Hagan Stein led to your current circumstances?"

"No, I suppose I wouldn't."

"Then we must both accept our fate."

"Fate?" she said. "Are we all mere pawns in some grand scheme?"

"I used to think so," said Ludwig.

"And now?"

"I think what we see as fate is merely the result of happenstance. It's easy to see patterns in things that have already passed, quite another to think something else controls our future."

"What of prophecies?" asked Rosalyn.

"Prophecies? Now you're getting into all sorts of strange subjects. Do you spend all your time reading?"

"As much as I can. How about you? Do you read?"

"I do," said Ludwig, "though admittedly not so much in the last few months. Believe it or not, books are scarce in a mercenary camp."

"You are in no camp now," said Rosalyn. "Would you like to read one of my father's books?"

"It would definitely help pass the time. Which would you suggest?"

"Now that presents an interesting quandary. On what subject do you like to read?"

"Anything concerning armies," said Ludwig, "or knights."

"I'd have thought you had seen enough fighting by now."

"Truthfully, I've seen little. The initial assault on the wall was my first battle."

"Truly?"

"Yes, but I've always wanted to make a name for myself as a leader of men."

"So you led the attack?"

"Hardly," Ludwig said. "I'm a simple mercenary who follows orders."

"Yet they let you be the first into the courtyard?"

Ludwig grinned. "Aye, it's true, but only because Linden and I hatched that crazy scheme."

"Linden?"

"Yes, the Earth Mage who opened up the wall."

"Ah, yes. I'm sorry to tell you, but I believe he was killed in the counterattack."

"I had expected as much. Can you tell me any more?"

"I'm afraid there's little more to tell. Your fellow soldiers were beaten back at the west wall even as your mage was working his magic. Then again, I imagine that was your plan."

"It was," said Ludwig. "And it would have worked had the spell not taken so long."

"Magic is a fickle thing," said Rosalyn. "That's why so few warriors rely on it."

"Yet mages are common enough amongst the courts of the Petty Kingdoms, are they not?"

"They are, or so I'm led to believe. What of your own home? Did it have mages?"

"None that I'm aware of," said Ludwig, "though, in truth, I spent no time in the capital. Have you been to the duke's court?"

"I have, in fact, quite recently. We stayed there while the tournament was running."

"Is that a common thing for you?"

"To see the tournament? Most certainly. It's the highlight of the year. Do they not have them where you're from?"

"They do, although nowhere near as large, from what I've been told. Malburg tried to host one once, but there weren't enough competitors to make a go of it."

"Why?" asked Rosalyn. "Do knights not seek to make names for themselves in Hadenfeld?"

Ludwig felt the colour drain from his face. "How did you know I was from Hadenfeld?"

She chuckled. "I know the Petty Kingdoms well. You gave it away when you mentioned Malburg. If I recall, there's a barony around there somewhere." She placed a finger to her chin as she thought. "Varfield, perhaps?"

"Verfeld," corrected Ludwig. "It appears you have uncovered my identity."

"It was you who revealed it. Don't worry, I shan't mention it to anyone else, but tell me, why is it so important that nobody knows?"

"I fear my father would seek me out should he learn of my location."

"Even here? In a besieged keep?"

"He can be stubborn at times."

"Well," said Rosalyn, "our present situation prevents any word getting out, even if we wanted it to. I'm afraid we've no choice but to keep it to ourselves."

A maid appeared at the door, beckoning to the baron's daughter. Rosalyn made her way over, listening carefully as the older woman whispered something in her ear.

She turned back to Ludwig. "I'm afraid you must excuse me. It sounds like my father is asking after me."

"Will you be back?" asked Ludwig.

She smiled. "Of course."

21

HONOUR

Spring 1095 SR

A cool breeze blew in from the east, ruffling Ludwig's hair and bringing with it the fresh scent of pine. He gazed out the window, watching the movement below. The besieging army was settling in for the long haul, and the sounds of axes drifted up to him from the distant trees. No doubt they would soon be building engines of war. Hearing footsteps, he turned to see Lord Wulfram Haas.

"My lord," he said, bowing his head.

"You're looking much better," said the baron. "One might even go so far as to say you're thriving under my daughter's care."

Ludwig blushed. "I am," he said. "And I must thank you for your kindness. Were it not for your generosity, and hers, I would likely be dead."

Lord Wulfram made his way to the chair, then sat, waving his hand at the bed. "Please, sit."

Ludwig did as he was asked. The Baron of Regnitz stared at him for a while. Ludwig felt the intensity of the man's gaze the entire time.

"Tell me of yourself," his host finally commanded.

"There is not much to tell," said Ludwig.

"Rosalyn says you're from Verfeld, in the Kingdom of Hadenfeld. Is this true?"

Ludwig felt the anger build. "She promised she wouldn't speak of it," he spat out.

176 | WARRIOR KNIGHT

Lord Wulfram held up his hand. "Do not fault my daughter," he said. "She did what she felt was right. Now answer the question."

"It is," Ludwig finally admitted, surrendering to the inevitable. "My father is Lord Frederick Altenburg, Baron of Verfeld. Do you know him?"

"No, but then again, the Petty Kingdoms have hundreds of barons. Does King Otto still rule in that part of the Continent?"

"He does."

"I knew him years ago, at the court of King Ebert of Deisenbach."

"I know of it," said Ludwig. "It rests against the northern border of Hadenfeld."

"Of course he wasn't a prince back then, merely the spoiled son of a wealthy baron, much like you." He held up his hand to prevent any argument. "Not that I'm suggesting you're spoiled in any way."

"I can understand Otto being sent there. I hear it's a common enough practice, but why you? Weren't there closer kingdoms for your father to send you to?"

"There were," said Lord Wulfram, "but they were all neighbours of our realm and, as such, might covet our land. One can hardly blame him for not wanting to send his sons to a potential foe."

"Sons? You have a brother?"

"I did, but he died some years ago. I was never supposed to be the baron —that was Lothar's fate. Have you ever spent time at court?"

"No, I was born and raised in Verfeld."

"I'm surprised. Sending away a son to another lord's court allows him to learn the way of things. It also forms lasting friendships that benefit the Petty Kingdoms."

"You have me intrigued," said Ludwig. "I knew that Cousin Otto was the son of a baron, but my father never spoke of how he came to sit on the throne."

"That," said Lord Wulfram, "is a long story. I shan't bore you with the details other than to say it was a combination of war, illness, and maybe even a little murder. In those days, the land was in constant strife, much as it is now, come to think of it. He was, I believe, something like the seventeenth in line to the Crown. In any event, there was that nasty little war of yours. That's what finally propelled him to the throne."

"You mean the civil war?"

"Yes, I understand some of the barons rose up in rebellion?"

"It was much more than that," said Ludwig. "They broke off and formed their own kingdom. Neuhafen, they call it. That was before I was born, of course, but they still cast a shadow over the entire kingdom."

"From what I heard, it was a bloody affair," continued the baron. "Otto's father was killed in the fighting, and so he became the baron. If I recall, there was a massive battle, somewhere near Harlingen, your capital."

"I've heard tell of it," said Ludwig. "The rebels won the field but took too many casualties and lacked the men to capture the throne. It marked the end of the war."

"Yes, and almost the end of the Royal Line too. By nightfall, Otto was the next in line to the throne. When the king died five years later, Otto was given the crown."

"Remarkable."

"It was," agreed Lord Wulfram, "yet many of the other Petty Kingdoms have suffered similar fates. We live in a land full of petty rivalries and unbridled greed. Some might say it's our fate to be forever at war with each other."

"Surely there's a better way?"

"I wish there were, but we must learn to live with the hand we are dealt. Do you play cards?"

Ludwig frowned. "I never developed a taste for them, much to my father's disappointment. I would prefer to be outside, riding."

"Well, I'm afraid under the present circumstances, that is entirely impossible. I might, however, be able to find some cards if you were to change your mind."

"Rosalyn tells me you have a large selection of books."

The baron smiled. "I do. Do you read?"

"Rather avidly, though not, of course, of late."

"Have you read Marroch or Allard?"

"I'm afraid those names mean nothing to me," confessed Ludwig. "Were they military leaders?"

"No, poets, philosophers even."

"Their names sound foreign."

"That's because they hailed from lands that were overrun by the Halvarians decades ago."

"And yet they offer advice?"

"Advice?" said Wulfram. "Is that what you think poets do? No, they entertain."

"I always thought the purpose of books was to educate."

"Wherever did you get that idea?"

"My mother."

"Did she not read you stories?"

"She did. Quite a few, in fact. My favourites were those concerning the knights who lived in times of old. That's how I learned my history."

"My dear fellow," said the baron, "those aren't historical texts. They're only stories. Knighthood has only existed for a few centuries and is nothing like those ancient tales."

Ludwig was crestfallen. He had looked up to these valiant warriors all his life, had even modelled his own behaviour after them. To find out they were nothing but flights of fancy shook him to his core.

The baron noticed his look of dismay. "Don't be disheartened," he said. "Those stories are meant to inspire people, even if they aren't true. They speak to your soul."

"But they are false!"

Lord Wulfram leaned forward. "They are not false so long as you hold them here." He gently prodded Ludwig over his heart. "You found them inspiring, yes?"

Ludwig nodded.

"Then they have done their job. The future changes, my young friend, because of people like you."

"Me? Whatever gave you that idea?"

"You took these writings to heart, and that shows a concern for your fellow man. I might remind you of your earlier words. You said, 'Surely there's a better way,' indicating you are willing to change things to achieve your goals. I should be keenly interested to see where you are ten years from now."

"Knowing my luck, I'll be dead by then."

"That, I highly doubt," said Lord Wulfram. "Of course, it's not impossible, but I expect you have a strong survival instinct."

"What makes you say that?"

"I'm not sure, just a feeling I have. Any other prisoner would have died of the cold down in the dungeon, but you… somehow you survived. That's a rare gift, Ludwig. Don't waste it."

"You seem to assume I'm some kind of chosen one."

The baron chuckled. "Ah, yes, the ancient prophecies: Someone will unite the Petty Kingdoms; the Saints will be reborn. I've heard many over the years, and every one of them is complete rubbish. They've been saying those things for centuries. Surely, if any of that was going to happen, it would have occurred by now?"

"One would think so," agreed Ludwig. "I suppose that means you don't hold the same beliefs as your daughter?"

"Rosalyn? Why? Did she say something to you?"

"We may have discussed the concept of fate."

"Ah, yes, fate. One of her favourite subjects. She can talk all evening on the topic. It can grow most wearisome."

"She also told me this dispute with Lord Gebhard was her fault."

The baron looked surprised. "She told you about that?"

"She did, my lord."

"Well, that's a bit of a surprise. I suppose, from a certain point of view, she has a point. After all, it was her refusal to marry Hagan that led to our current circumstances."

"You could have pressed her to marry," said Ludwig, "yet you didn't. I'm curious as to why?"

"My daughter means the world to me, as you've probably already guessed. Her mother died some years ago, and ever since then, she's been my life. I couldn't bear to see her married off to a man who wouldn't think the same of her."

"And so we are at war," said Ludwig.

"We? I don't remember your name coming up in the dispute. You apparently happened to be in the wrong place at the wrong time."

"Perhaps not," pressed Ludwig. "It occurs to me that this is precisely where I'm meant to be."

"Don't tell me Rosalyn has convinced you of her nonsense?"

"It's not her, at least not just her."

"Then what is it?"

"Something strange happened to me recently. Something I'm not sure I've completely come to grips with yet."

"This sounds intriguing. Would you care to elucidate?"

"A good friend of mine took an arrow to the back in the initial assault, and we had to carry him back to camp."

"Wait a moment," said Wulfram. "Did you say to the back? I saw you from the wall. One of my men wanted to finish the poor fellow off, but I stopped him. I had no idea that was you carrying him away."

Ludwig nodded. "That was me all right. In any event, we took him back and removed the arrow, but then the wound festered, and it brought on a fever."

"Did he survive?"

"He did, eventually, but it was what happened next that shook me. We applied a poultice to draw out the pus."

"Let me guess, warriors moss?"

Ludwig looked up in surprise. "You know of such things?"

"I have a passing familiarity, but please, continue your tale. You were saying you gave him warriors moss?"

"Yes, but it didn't seem to be working. When he was at his lowest, I prayed to Saint Mathew."

"And?"

"He recovered."

Lord Wulfram smiled. "That was merely a coincidence."

"Was it? Somehow I have my doubts. You weren't there. You didn't feel the sudden breeze, the scent of grass that so reminded me of home."

"And you attribute that to a dead Saint?"

"It reminded me of the prior, back home. You can't believe that a coincidence?"

"You were camped in a field, were you not?"

"We were," admitted Ludwig. "What of it?"

"Well, you were surrounded by grass. What else would you smell? You were lucky enough to catch a breeze, that's all. The rest is due to your imagination."

"They say the Saints work in mysterious ways," countered Ludwig.

"Of course they do. How else can they peddle their beliefs?"

"You don't believe in the Saints?"

"Don't let me give you the wrong impression," said Lord Wulfram. "I believe the Saints existed, but I don't think they're somewhere in the Afterlife, guiding us to join them. It's Humans who shape the Petty Kingdoms, not some long-dead prophets."

"What about the other races?"

"What, Elves? They had their chance. The Continent belongs to Humans now. That much is clear."

"How about the Dwarves?"

"Now, they are an interesting race. Unlike the Elves, they've learned to live amongst us, plying their trade."

"Do they not have kingdoms of their own?" asked Ludwig.

"They do, but they're small compared to those of Humans. They also live in mountainous terrain, so they are little threat to us. Have you ever met a Dwarf?"

"I can't say I have."

"They are a capricious people."

"Capricious?"

"Yes, contrary and unpredictable," said the baron. "They are masters of their craft, yet often refuse the offer of trade. I certainly have a hard time understanding them."

"Have you met many?"

"No, thank the Saints, and I have no inclination to do so in the future. I'll stick with our own race if you don't mind."

"I saw Orc tracks once," said Ludwig. "What do you know of them?"

"Orcs? Precious little, other than what I've been told. They are, apparently, a savage race, unused to the ways of civilization. I'm told they eat Human flesh, although that may just be stories meant to frighten children.

It matters little, for there are none of the green-skinned folk in these parts. They were wiped out generations ago."

"After the Therengian Wars?"

"You know of those?"

"It's a particular fascination of mine. I'd be delighted to hear your take on them."

Lord Wulfram frowned. "They are not a people to idolize, Ludwig. Their rule of the Continent was one of military occupation."

"In what way?"

"At their height, they organized their kingdom into a series of provinces, each with a military governor. It's said only the elite members of their society were allowed to govern."

"But that's no different than us, is it?" said Ludwig. "They might have used their military, but we use the noble lines. I fail to see any difference."

"The nobility of the Petty Kingdoms has a long and storied past," explained the baron. "They rule by right of blood, not on the whim of some military appointment. The very fact the Therengians were defeated shows the superiority of our system. Nobles are meant to rule, Ludwig, never forget that. It is their place in the world... and yours."

"It appears you've given me much to consider."

Lord Wulfram stood. "It also appears I have stayed longer than I had anticipated. You must excuse me. I have things to attend to."

Ludwig's eyes drifted to the window, and he remembered what he had seen. "They're cutting down trees, you know. It won't be long before they start using catapults."

"Indeed, but that's my concern, not yours. I have no doubt Lord Gebhard will eventually take this keep."

"Then why resist?"

"Honour," said the baron. "I refuse to give in to the demands of others."

"At the cost of your own life?"

"If need be. We must all take our own measure, Ludwig. Do you consider yourself a man of honour?"

"To be truthful, I don't think I've given it much thought."

"Do you stay true to your word?"

"I do."

"Then, by your own admission, you are an honourable man. The Continent needs more like you, my young friend. See that you live long enough to do good."

"Is that what I'm doing now?"

"I don't know; you tell me. Earlier, you said you thought you were right where you were needed to be. What did you mean by that?"

Ludwig waved him off. "I was simply rambling."

Lord Wulfram sat. "No, tell me, I beg you. It may be important."

"Very well. It occurred to me that my being here might allow this situation to be resolved."

"Are you a diplomat now?"

"No," said Ludwig, "but I'm now familiar with both sides, and I have the advantage of being an outsider, which gives me an unbiased view of things."

"Unbiased? I doubt that. The same mercenaries you serve are under the employ of Lord Gebhard, are they not?"

"They are," Ludwig confessed, "yet I've always felt apart from them in some way."

"That's your noble upbringing. It's to be expected."

"No, it's more than that. Don't get me wrong, I've made friends, but I'm beginning to feel the mercenary life is not for me."

"Look here," said Lord Wulfram. "I know we captured you, but that's no reason to go all morose on me."

Ludwig chuckled. "I promise you, I'm not sad. No, it's more a dawning realization I have yet to find my path in this life."

"I sense you've been speaking to a Holy Father. They'll talk your ear off if you're not careful. A 'path' as you put it, is nothing more than a series of choices, choices that you yourself have taken. There's no such thing as predestination."

"How can you be so sure?"

"If such a thing as fate exists, then what is the purpose of life? Are we merely the playthings of the Saints, to wander this mortal realm and carry out their will?"

"No," said Ludwig. "A wise woman once told me the Saints offer us guidance in our daily lives, allowing us to live life to its fullest."

"It amounts to the same thing, doesn't it?"

"Does it?" said Ludwig. "The nice thing with advice is you can choose to ignore it. Do we not already benefit from the advice of those older than ourselves?"

"Most do," said the baron. "Does this mean you've decided to join the Church now?"

"No," said Ludwig. "Though at one time, the notion of being a Temple Knight appealed to me. Now, I'm content to remain outside the direct control of the Church."

"And all this is because some woman spouted off the teachings of Saint Mathew?"

"Actually, it was Saint Agnes," said Ludwig, "although I imagine the teachings of Mathew are similar. I understand the two orders work together often."

"I would have taken you for a follower of Saint Cunar," said Lord Wulfram. "After all, he's the patron saint of warriors."

"What can I say," said Ludwig, grinning. "The Saints move in mysterious ways."

22

COMFORT

Spring 1095 SR

The lone window became Ludwig's link to the outside world. He would stand there, gazing out to the east, wondering what Sigwulf and Cyn were up to. He knew they would attack again, but not before the catapults began their incessant pummelling of the walls.

He turned to his bed, picking up a book entitled *Honour to the Brave* that the baron had left for him. He wondered if it were meant as some type of hidden message, but then his thoughts were interrupted by Rosalyn's entry.

"How are you feeling?" she asked.

"I'm fully recovered, as you well know," said Ludwig. "What I don't understand is why I'm still here, in this room, instead of back down in the dungeon?"

"My father has sent me to make you an offer," she said. "One that he hopes you will find satisfactory."

Ludwig tried hard to think what that offer might be but came up empty. "Please continue," he prompted.

"He believes you to be a man of honour, and so extends to you the freedom of the keep, provided you promise not to escape, nor interfere with its defence in any way."

"And if I choose not to accept?"

"Then you shall remain here, in this room, as a prisoner."

"Then I accept."

Rosalyn smiled. "I was hoping you'd say that."

"So what happens now?"

"I am to give you a tour of the keep, modest as it is."

"Modest it may be, but it's still larger than Verfeld where I grew up."

"In that case," she said, "will you follow me?"

"Most certainly, fair lady."

She led him out into the hallway. It wasn't much to look at, but to Ludwig's mind, it represented freedom.

"How old is the keep?" he asked.

"It was built by my great grandfather. Of course, back then, they didn't have the curtain wall or the outer courtyard; those were added by my grandfather."

"And did your father expand on the defences?"

"He did," she replied. "He was the one who added the moat and drawbridge."

"Ah, yes," said Ludwig, "and that was my undoing. If it hadn't been for the gatehouse, we wouldn't have attempted the magical attack."

"I'm not sure I follow. Wouldn't the drawbridge have the opposite effect?"

"No, for you see there was a weakness. We gained entry where the gatehouse poked out from the curtain wall—it created a blind spot."

"Why are you telling me this now?" said Rosalyn. "Is that not counterproductive to the plans of your allies?"

"Not at all. The attack failed, so they won't try it again."

"You have a lot of faith in your friends."

"It's not only that," said Ludwig. "Your father's men killed the Earth Mage, remember? I doubt they'll find another, and even if they did, what Druid in his right mind would attempt something that's already failed?"

"I suppose you have a valid point." Rosalyn began leading him upstairs.

"Where are we going?"

"I thought we might start at the top. The roof gives a commanding view of the countryside."

She took him up the spiral staircase, emerging onto the flat roof. A pair of archers noted their arrival but said nothing. Instead, their attention remained to the south, towards the army of Lord Gebhard. Their gaze immediately drew Ludwig's attention, and he moved closer, peering through the crenellation to the fields beyond. Rosalyn came up behind him, the scent of her perfume wafting towards him.

"What is it?" she asked.

"Lord Gebhard has been busy," said Ludwig. "He's put up stakes to prevent your father from sending out a sortie."

"What are they building?"

"Catapults. Half a dozen of them, from the look of it."

"One of them"—she pointed—"appears to be much larger than the rest."

Ludwig paled. "That's no catapult. That's a trebuchet."

"What's a trebuchet?"

"A heavy engine of war. It uses a counterweight to hurl large objects over great distances."

"Large objects?"

"Yes," said Ludwig. "Primarily rocks or collections of stones, although they can also hurl flaming bundles as well. I've read their range can reach several hundred yards, well beyond that of your archers."

"How long will it take them to complete it, do you think?"

Ludwig strained to make out as much detail as he could. "Hard to say for sure, but my guess would be at least another week or so."

"Will they target the keep?"

"I doubt it. They'll be more interested in bringing down the curtain wall."

"How can you be so sure?"

He turned to face Rosalyn. "A weapon like that is stationary, which means they'll have to launch their stones from their present position. They are positioned to the south of us while the keep resides in the curtain wall's northeast corner, making it an improbable target. I suspect they'll bring down the south wall to allow them entry to the courtyard, then ask for your father's surrender."

"And the trebuchet can do that?"

"It will certainly help. The problem with that monstrosity is it takes forever to reload. Catapults, on the other hand, can discharge their smaller stones at a much faster rate."

"I suppose that means we're doomed," said Rosalyn.

"Perhaps I could negotiate a peace?"

"What makes you think that?"

"I've seen both sides of this conflict," said Ludwig. "I would hope that Lord Gebhard could be made to see reason."

"I fear there's no reason in the man. If there was, he'd have halted this assault some time ago. Instead, he has kept us bottled up here in hopes of starving us out."

"Yes, but now he's eager to see an end to it, hence the catapults. Something's changed."

"Like what?"

Ludwig returned his gaze to the field below. Something to the southeast caught his attention. "Those tents," he said as he pointed.

Rosalyn moved closer, pressing against him to see through the embrasure. "What of them?"

"There's a standard there. See it?"

"I do," she said. "What does it mean?"

"Can you make out what's on it?"

She leaned out farther until he was sure she would topple over. Instinctively, he reached out, grabbing her by the waist. If she took offence, she made no mention of it, instead merely speculating on the flag.

"It looks like a sword," she said. "Is that your mercenary company?"

"No," said Ludwig. "I think Lord Gebhard may have hired another group. Unless I miss my guess, it'll be the Blades of Vengeance. I know they were spotted in Torburg right before the tournament started."

"What do you think that means?"

"Baron Stein has obviously decided an assault is the only way to go. Why else hire more men?"

"We should tell my father," insisted Rosalyn.

"I'm sure he already knows," said Ludwig, "but I suppose it wouldn't hurt."

"What if you could suggest the idea of negotiating?"

"I thought you said Lord Gebhard wouldn't see reason?"

"I did," she confessed, "but all these engines of war have driven home the hopeless nature of our predicament. Lord Gebhard may be difficult for my father to talk to, but you… you might be able to make the man see reason."

"I'd certainly be willing to give it a try."

She climbed back down off the embrasure. "Come then, let's see what my father thinks of the idea."

Lord Wulfram Haas was in the great hall, poring over a map of the environs, and looked up as they approached, a smile creasing his lips, if only for a moment.

"I presume Ludwig has agreed to our terms?" he said.

"He has," replied Rosalyn.

"I see. And to what do I owe this visit?"

"Ludwig has an idea, Father. I think you should hear him out."

"Has he now? I don't suppose that would involve him being released, would it?"

Ludwig quickly intervened. "I assure you, my lord, I have no intention of escaping. I gave my word, and I intend to keep it."

"Excellent," said the baron. "Then come, explain this idea of yours to me."

Ludwig stepped closer, keenly aware of Rosalyn's presence beside him. "It seems to me this feud between you and Lord Gebhard has been taken to extremes."

"Clearly, but the man will see no reason."

"I thought he might be persuaded to give up his fascination with your destruction."

"I hardly think we're in a position to make demands," said Lord Wulfram. "He holds all the cards. From what position would we negotiate?"

"I think him a reasonable man," offered Ludwig, "but I fear the two of you are destined to butt heads."

"Then how would we arrive at a solution?"

"I would volunteer my own services to act as a negotiator, my lord."

"What makes you think you could do any better than I?"

"I was the one who proposed the last assault on this very keep," said Ludwig. "It also occurs to me it was Lord Gebhard's idea to wed his son to your daughter. Perhaps, if I can convince his son, Hagan, to argue the point, he might see fit to dismiss the suit."

"That's an awfully big if," said Baron Haas.

"Still, under the circumstances, what have you to lose?"

"And how would we arrange something like this?"

"I propose you lower me down from the wall. I shall carry a note, hand-written by you. At the very least, it would buy us some time."

"And you, your freedom."

"I can assure you I would return," said Ludwig. "For how else would I bring Baron Stein's reply?"

Lord Wulfram frowned. "I think you underestimate Gebhard's determination."

"You have nothing to lose. What's the worst thing that can result from this?"

"He could have you killed."

"Then you would be no worse off. In fact, you'd have one less mouth to feed. I urge you to let me try, my lord. Even if there's only a small chance of success, you must agree it's worthwhile? Think of your daughter. Would you have her killed in the siege?"

"Lord Gebhard would not kill Rosalyn," said the baron. "He wants her alive, remember? He can't very well marry his son off to a corpse." He turned to his daughter. "Sorry, my dear, I know how upsetting this must all be."

"Please, Father," she pleaded. "Listen to Ludwig."

"You may think your daughter safe," continued Ludwig, "but the truth is when those catapults begin bombarding, you'll have no control over who gets killed or injured. Do you care so little for Rosalyn that you would put her in harm's way?"

"Do not lecture me on my daughter!" shouted the baron. "She means everything to me. How dare you insinuate I would intentionally risk her life."

"And yet isn't that exactly what you're doing?" said Rosalyn. "I know you mean well, Father, I truly do, but when they start hurling stones at us, everyone is a target, including me."

"I understand, my dear, but you're asking me to trust the word of a stranger in our home."

"A stranger I may be," said Ludwig, "but I would have this conflict settled, and peace returned to the land."

Lord Wulfram stared at him. Ludwig felt the penetrating gaze boring into him as if examining his very soul.

"Fair enough," the baron finally said. "We shall try it your way. I'll write a letter. No, let's call it an invitation to Lord Gebhard proposing we meet to settle our differences. Do you suppose that will do the trick?"

"I would think so, my lord. I shall deliver it directly into his hands."

"I hope this works," said Lord Wulfram. "I would hate to meet him for a parley, only to find I've walked into a trap."

"I shall do all I can to prevent that," promised Ludwig. "And in any event, I'll return, whether he agrees to a parley or not."

"I wish you well, my young friend, but I fear you have a difficult task before you."

The next day saw Ludwig standing on the battlements while two of Lord Wulfram's men stood by with a rope. The plan was to lower him down to the ground and let him wade across the moat, the message in hand. To do this unhindered, they needed to make sure none of the besiegers were going to fill him with arrows, and so to this end, they stood by with a white flag.

The three of them watched the enemy lines for any signs of movement. The morning wore on until finally, a trio of individuals came forth, one of them towering over the others while a second was much shorter. Ludwig smiled, recognizing Sigwulf and Cyn. The third, however, astounded him, for it was none other than Hagan Stein.

Ludwig turned to face Wulfram's men and then backed out over the parapet, the end of the rope tied securely around his waist. They lowered him at a slow pace while his observers stood on the opposite side of the moat. Once he touched down, he untied the rope and watched as it was pulled back up the wall, then turned to greet his friends.

"You're alive, I see," called out Sigwulf.

"So it would appear," Ludwig replied. "I don't suppose you've had time to fill in the moat?"

Cyn chuckled. "You'll have to get your feet wet, and the rest of you as well."

Ludwig shrugged. "At least it's warmer today than the last time."

He pulled the note from his belt, holding it in the air to avoid getting it wet. He dipped his toe in, and then, content it wasn't freezing cold, the rest of him followed, taking his time to ensure his footing. It was still chest-high at its deepest, and he struggled to keep the letter safe, but as the water became more shallow, a large hand reached out, pulling him onto the other bank.

Sigwulf pounded him on the back. "By the Saints," the big man said, "we thought you dead. You gave us quite the scare."

Cyn punched him on the shoulder. "Yes, don't do that again."

Ludwig was smiling like an idiot, pleased to be amongst friends once more. His attitude soon disappeared, however, as his eyes took in Hagan Stein.

"You have a message?" pressed the baron's son.

"I do, Master Stein," said Ludwig, "but it's for your father."

"Then let us waste no further time," said Hagan. He pivoted abruptly and began making his way towards the village of Regnitz. Sigwulf followed, but Cyn, more interested in what had transpired, lagged behind, keeping pace with Ludwig.

"What happened?" she asked. "The last we heard, you'd been lost in the attack."

"You remember the Earth Mage?"

"Linden Herzog?"

"Yes," said Ludwig. "He opened up a small hole in the wall, and I had barely squeezed through when the defenders counterattacked and overwhelmed me. I'm afraid Linden perished in the attempt."

"We knew he was killed," said Cyn, "but heard naught of you. Lord Wulfram looks to have treated you well."

"He did, all things considered, but it was very nearly the death of me."

"Were you injured?"

"No," said Ludwig, "at least not seriously."

"Then what happened?"

"I fell ill. They threw me in the dungeon, and the cold almost did me in."

"Despite that, here you are, hale and hearty. How did you manage your escape?"

"I didn't," said Ludwig. "I volunteered to bring a message to Lord Gebhard."

"A clever ruse. Now that you're amongst us once more, things can get back to normal."

"I can't. I have to take a reply to Lord Wulfram."

"Surely you jest?" said Cyn. "Lord Gebhard is getting ready to reduce the place to rubble. You go back now, and you'll be killed."

"I gave my word, Cyn. In any event, I'm hopeful we can work something out between these two barons and cease this ridiculous feud."

"Well, it's good to have you back, if only temporarily."

"Thank you," said Ludwig, "and it's nice to see you and Sig looking the very picture of health."

"Don't use up all your niceties," warned Cyn. "You're going to need them for Lord Gebhard."

Lord Gebhard Stein sat at a table, a half-eaten plate of food before him. He waved the group forward, watching his son with a look of expectation on his face.

"Father," began Hagan, "this man comes from Lord Wulfram."

The elder Stein's eyes locked on Ludwig. "Aren't you the one who came up with that plan to capture the keep?"

"I am," said Ludwig.

"Well, I hope you're better at carrying messages than planning. That little escapade of yours was an unmitigated disaster. It cost me my one and only Earth Mage."

Ludwig wanted to tell the baron he had largely ignored the mage's presence during the entire campaign but thought better of it. Instead, he held out the note from Lord Wulfram.

"I have a letter here written by the Baron of Regnitz," he announced. "He proposes the two of you meet and discuss your differences."

"Does he, now?" said Lord Gebhard, holding out his hand. "Let's have it, then."

Ludwig handed over the letter, then waited as the baron perused it. He had not read it himself, but Rosalyn had assured him her father was earnest in his desire for peace.

The lord tossed the letter on the table. "What do you think, Hagan?"

After reading the letter, his son seemed to fidget. Was he embarrassed by his own opinions or trying to mollify his father? Either way, he was obviously being cautious.

"I think it deserves a look," Hagan said at last.

Lord Gebhard looked at Ludwig. "My son appears to agree with the sentiment of this letter. What do you think, Master Ludwig?"

"I am not familiar with its contents, my lord."

The baron frowned. "I have a hard time believing you have braved our lines and yet have no idea what this letter might contain. Tell me, what do you think is in this note?"

"A plea to meet?"

"Precisely. Now, what are your opinions on the matter? Surely you have some?"

"I do, my lord," said Ludwig.

"Then out with it."

"I think it worth pursuing, my lord. This feud has cost you both dearly. Perhaps it's time to put it behind you?"

"Our feud is hardly any of your concern," said Baron Stein.

"Having said that, you did ask for my opinion."

The lord shrugged. "I suppose I did. You've met Lord Wulfram, what do you make of him?"

"He's reasonable enough," said Ludwig. "Much like yourself, in many regards."

"How so?"

"He has great regard for his offspring. If I may be so bold, how would you feel if someone demanded your daughter be married to him?"

"I have no daughter," declared Lord Gebhard.

"True, but you have a son. Imagine if the duke arranged a marriage for him?"

The baron let out a snort. "I would welcome it. It's about time he settled down."

Ludwig decided to try a different approach. "I noted, my lord, you have hired another mercenary company."

"Yes, the Blades of Vengeance. What of it?"

"Such a famed company must have come at a significant cost."

"It did," said Baron Stein, "and I am proud to have them in my employ."

"Even so," continued Ludwig, "you are preparing for a siege, something that will take a significant amount of time. I trust you have deep pockets?"

He noted the look of irritation on the baron's face.

"Get to the point," Lord Gebhard commanded.

"I'm merely pointing out the fact that the longer this drags out, the more it will cost all parties involved. It is therefore in your best interest to consider what your worthy opponent has to offer, is it not? After all, what harm can come of it?"

"You have made a good point," said the baron. "I shall have you take back a reply. If our esteemed colleague, Lord Wulfram, is in agreement, then you will return to us to arrange things."

Ludwig bowed. "I'm sure His Lordship will welcome the chance, my lord."

23

PARLEY

Spring 1095 SR

I t took days of near constant back-and-forth communication to settle all the details of the parley. Lord Wulfram, wary of a trap, wanted his attacker to enter the keep, but Lord Gebhard, likely having his own fears, wanted everything done out in the open.

They finally agreed to meet on the field, which lay before the drawbridge. Baron Stein would be represented by a small group, namely himself, his son, Hagan, and three guards. Baron Haas, for his part, would be accompanied by Ludwig and three soldiers of his own.

There then remained arguments over every conceivable detail of the meeting, including which day, what time of day, even whether or not food would be served. All of this led Ludwig to pass back and forth over a dozen times. He finally got to the point where he would simply negotiate on behalf of Lord Wulfram and talk it out with the baron afterwards. In at least one thing, however, he considered himself fortunate, for he had convinced Lord Gebhard to use the Grim Defenders to act as his guard, thus significantly reducing the chance he might use the opportunity to attack his guest.

So it was that on a late spring day, Ludwig rode across the drawbridge with Lord Wulfram and three warriors. The horses' hooves echoed as they crossed the wooden planks, then they proceeded onto the field beyond where a small canopy had been erected to keep the sun off the two barons.

It was accompanied by four chairs and a small table, which held some goblets along with a few bottles of wine.

Ludwig dismounted, passing the reins to one of the warriors. Off in the distance he could make out Sigwulf and Cyn, along with a sour-faced Baldric. He nodded as his eyes met those of his sergeant, and then Lord Wulfram began walking to the table, breaking his attention and forcing him to catch up.

"What do you make of this?" asked Lord Wulfram. They were approaching the table, which was only about twenty paces from their present location.

"All is as it should be," said Ludwig. "You may rest assured, my lord, there is no treachery this day."

"I'll believe that once we're done and I'm safely back inside my keep." He took another step, extending his hand in greeting. "Lord Gebhard, good to see you this day."

His opponent wore the same smile. "And you, Lord Wulfram. Come, let us have some refreshment before we begin the day's discussions."

Ludwig marvelled at the insincerity of it all. These two men obviously loathed each other, but despite that, all was smiles and graces. They shared a drink, then got down to the business at hand.

"Now," began Baron Stein, "let us discuss the terms of your surrender. I am willing to let you leave Regnitz Keep, provided you leave Lady Rosalyn with us."

Lord Wulfram stared back. His face was calm, but Ludwig could see the tenseness in his neck muscles.

"I shall do nothing of the sort," said Baron Haas. "You, on the other hand, should consider withdrawing your troops back to Mulsingen."

"You are in no position to dictate terms," said Lord Gebhard. "After all, you're the one bottled up in his keep."

"If you think I'll let your whelp marry my daughter, you're sadly mistaken."

"Then I shall reduce your keep to rubble and force her to marry my son."

"She'd rather die!"

"On the contrary," said Baron Stein, "I'm sure she'd readily agree to marriage if only to prevent your own demise at my hands."

"You wouldn't dare!" shouted Lord Wulfram.

"Wouldn't I?"

"Gentlemen, please," interrupted Ludwig. "You serve no one by taking such a stance when we've only scarcely begun the process of discussion. Aren't there any items on which you can both agree?"

"Possibly," said Baron Stein, "but on the important issues, we are at loggerheads."

"Then I believe a discussion of those points is in order, provided you two can agree not to let your emotions get the better of you."

"How would you suggest we proceed?" asked Lord Gebhard.

"What if you were to start, my lord?" said Ludwig. "Present your argument while Lord Wulfram listens. Then, when you're done, he can present his own with no interruptions."

"Sounds reasonable. Where shall I begin?"

"With Rosalyn Haas."

Baron Stein took a sip of wine, then looked Lord Wulfram in the eyes. "You and I both know that family is everything. In order to carry on the name, our children must be allowed to have offspring of their own. Now, you are aware that there are few enough nobles in this area of a suitable age to marry."

"Hold on," said Ludwig. "Are you telling me there are no other suitable nobles in Erlingen?"

"Yes, nor in any of the neighbouring realms, it would seem. It, therefore, behooves us to seek an alliance through the marriage of Wulfram's daughter, Rosalyn, to my son, Hagan."

Ludwig turned to Lord Wulfram. "What do you have to say in response?"

"I'll admit there are few prospects for my daughter," said Baron Haas, "but I shall not simply order her to marry against her will. It seems I must cast a net over a wider area to find her a suitable match."

"Don't be absurd," said Baron Stein. "You know my son is a perfect match."

"Have you asked Hagan what he thinks?" said Ludwig.

"I beg your pardon?"

"Your son. What does he want?"

"That is immaterial. He needs to beget an heir. That's the plain and simple truth of it."

"We both know that isn't true," said Ludwig. "I'm sure you have plenty of male relatives who could inherit your lands when you both pass on."

"That's none of your concern. Look, we originally came here to ask for your daughter's hand in marriage. You were the one who rejected us, Wulfram, and you made it quite clear we were beneath you."

"I did no such thing," said Baron Haas. "Now you're just imagining things."

"Imagining things, am I? I'll show you what imagining is." Lord Gebhard stood, placing his hand on the hilt of his sword. Hagan stepped up and diffused the situation by grabbing his father's arm and steadying him.

"Not now, Father," he soothed. "Not here."

"Perhaps," offered Ludwig, "Lord Wulfram might see fit to apologize for his reaction."

"Yes," said Baron Haas. "At the time, I was overcome with emotion. I apologize if I gave offence, but you made a demand of me when you should have been seeking consensus."

"Demand?" said Baron Stein. "I did no such thing."

"Maybe," offered Ludwig, "you were merely overcome yourself. It was, after all, a highly contentious meeting, was it not?"

"On that, we can agree," said Lord Gebhard.

Baron Haas took another sip of wine, then nodded in acknowledgement. "Yes, agreed."

"There," said Ludwig. "Was that so difficult?"

"I suppose not," acknowledged Baron Stein as he sat back down. "So what do you say, Wulfram? Shall we discuss the idea with fresh eyes?"

"While I am willing to discuss the matter," said Lord Wulfram, "I must still stick to my scruples. I cannot, in good faith, ask my daughter to marry your son."

"Why ever not?"

"She is opposed to it."

"She may have any opinion on it she wants, but when it gets down to it, it's your wishes that count, not hers."

"Would you have your son marry a woman against her will?"

"Would you have your daughter become a spinster?"

"Gentlemen," chided Ludwig. "Surely you can do better than that. Have you nothing in common?"

"Nothing at all, apparently," said Lord Wulfram.

Ludwig felt like he was grasping at straws. "You both serve the duke. Surely that accounts for something?"

"My loyalty to His Grace is not in question," insisted Baron Stein.

"Nor mine," added Baron Haas.

"And what do you think the duke would make of this impasse?" asked Ludwig. "Do you believe he would approve?"

"The duke couldn't care less," said Lord Gebhard. "He's even said so on numerous occasions."

"Yes," agreed Baron Haas. "He delights in watching his lesser nobles fight amongst themselves. It's all purely amusement for him."

"I cannot believe that," said Ludwig. "Surely he wants a land at peace, as do we all."

"Who knows?" said Baron Stein. "But in the end, he is powerless to stop it. That's why he chooses to stand back and see old scores settled at the point of a sword."

"If I were duke," announced Ludwig, "I would demand that this type of behaviour cease."

"And were you the duke," noted Lord Gebhard, "you would have the right to do so, but the present circumstances are far from your idea of what a duchy should be. You must accept that which you cannot change."

"He is young," explained Baron Haas, "and is therefore subject to fits of dreaming. The future is for the young, Gebhard, not two old fools like you and I."

"Precisely why we must hammer out our differences," insisted Baron Stein.

"What if your son were allowed to court my daughter?"

"Court her? What do you mean, court her?"

"He could spend time with her at the duke's court. Dance with her, maybe even indulge in conversation with her. Who knows, in time, she may even learn to put up with him?"

"Put up with him?" said Lord Gebhard. "You make him sound like a buffoon."

"I'm sure that's not what he meant," added Ludwig hastily. "What do you think of the proposal?"

Baron Stein contemplated it for a moment. "I must admit the idea has some merit."

"Then you'll consider it?" asked Ludwig.

Lord Gebhard looked to be thinking about it for some time, but then Ludwig saw his jaw clamp down. "No, I'm afraid it's too late for that now," he announced.

"What's that supposed to mean?" asked Baron Haas.

"It means my mind is made up. You have insulted my son, Wulfram, and by your refusal to condone this marriage, you have brought all of this upon yourself."

Baron Stein slammed his cup down on the table. Ludwig absently noted the wine as it sloshed over the rim and splashed onto the table, staining the tablecloth red. Was this some portent, he wondered? A sign that further blood would be spilled?

"It appears," said Lord Wulfram, "our time here has been wasted. I shall withdraw back into the walls of my keep, sir."

"By all means," said Stein. "I shall grant you until tomorrow morning to prepare yourselves, then I will commence bombardment."

The two barons stood, then shook hands. It appeared that even as enemies, the rules of etiquette must be followed. Ludwig thought of all who would die to soothe the egos of these two men and felt an inner rage. He was about to turn to leave when he spotted Sigwulf and Cyn. What would they think of his failure?

Lord Wulfram saw his hesitation. "Why don't you take a moment and say goodbye to your friends?" he suggested.

"Are you sure that's all right?"

"Of course, I'll wait for you at the drawbridge." Baron Haas made his way back to his guards while Ludwig went over to his comrades.

"Have you decided to stay?" called out Cyn.

"No, I've come to say goodbye."

"I still don't see why you don't just remain here with us. It's not as if Lord Wulfram could force you to return."

"I gave my word I would not attempt to escape."

Cyn looked upset. "Is your word so important to you that you would face death to avoid breaking it?"

"Let him be," said Sigwulf. "He must make his own choices."

"Even if it means his life?"

"Yes, even then."

Cyn shook her head. "You men can be so stubborn at times."

Ludwig smiled to hide his nervousness. "I'll take that as a compliment."

"What will you do now?" asked Sigwulf.

"Return to my room," said Ludwig. "The baron has given me the freedom of the keep, but I don't want to get in his way."

"So you'll not resist the attack?"

"No, it's not my fight. I'll keep my word and remain neutral."

Baldric, who, until this time, had remained quiet, laughed. "Neutral? There's no such thing, Ludwig. If you're inside that keep when the assault comes, you'll be treated as the enemy, same as the rest of Lord Wulfram's men."

"I'm not your enemy," said Ludwig.

"We'll see."

"Why do you hate me so?"

Baldric moved in close, keeping his voice low. "You humiliated me. Now it's time I returned the favour. I make you this promise, Ludwig. When the keep finally falls, it'll be me who spills your guts onto the cobblestones. You mark my words."

"You don't scare me, Baldric. You attack me, and I'll do everything in my power to kill you, and it won't be a mock battle this time."

"We'll just have to wait and see." Baldric sneered, and Ludwig found the sight unsettling.

"Ignore him," interrupted Cyn. "He's all bluster."

"The assault will soon commence," warned Sigwulf. "It won't take long for our siege engines to reduce the walls. Stay safe."

"I will," Ludwig assured him. "They gave me in a room high up in the keep."

"Then we'll look for you once we're in," promised Cyn. "You just make sure you don't get yourself killed."

"I'll do my best," said Ludwig. "You two take care of each other. I'll seek you out once this whole affair is over."

"You treat this lightly," replied Cyn, "but it's no joke. People are going to die."

"I wish the barons understood that," said Ludwig. "I tried to make them see reason, but they were having none of it."

"It's Lord Stein's fault," said Sigwulf. "He's too stubborn to back down."

"Lord Wulfram is just as bad. If only he'd let his daughter marry Hagan, this would all be over."

"Marry Hagan?" said Cyn. "Is that what this is all about?"

"Yes, didn't you know?"

"No."

"It's not as if the baron confides in us," added Sigwulf.

Ludwig pointed at the canopy. "Did you not hear any of the negotiations?"

"Couldn't hear a thing," said Cyn. "It's the wind, you see."

"Wait," said Sigwulf. "Are you saying all this death is because his son was spurned?"

"You can't blame Hagan," said Ludwig. "He's never even met Rosalyn."

Cyn picked up on the name. "Rosalyn, is it? On a first-name basis with the lady, are we?"

Ludwig blushed. "It's not what you think."

"Oh? Tell me, what is it I think?"

"That there's something between her and me."

"And is there?" she pressed.

"Absolutely not. I can assure you my intentions are entirely honourable."

"You seem awfully defensive."

"See here, now," said Ludwig. "I resent the implications."

Sigwulf laughed. "Whether or not you agree with her observations, you must admit it looks suspicious."

Cyn clasped her hands together, holding them beside her face and making her best impression of a hapless maid. "Oh, Ludwig, save me!"

Ludwig turned beet red.

"Ignore her," said Sigwulf, "she's only teasing. Now, you'd best get going before Lord Wulfram thinks you've abandoned him."

Ludwig turned and, with a heavy heart, made his way back to the Baron of Regnitz.

Lord Wulfram, noticing his expression, waited patiently. "I trust all is well?"

"I fear the assault will soon be upon us," said Ludwig, hauling himself into the saddle.

They began riding back towards the gatehouse, the clatter of hooves echoing off the drawbridge once more.

"They have yet to reduce the walls," said Lord Wulfram. "That alone will take weeks."

"And then?"

"Then," said Lord Wulfram, "we shall match steel against steel, but that's hardly a concern of yours."

"And what of your daughter, my lord? What will be her fate?"

His Lordship turned and gave him a grim look of determination. "If things should turn out for the worst, I would have her take her own life. Better that than become the plaything of Hagan Stein."

"Surely not, my lord!"

They passed beneath the gates and into the courtyard. Ludwig could hear the drawbridge being raised, and then shortly thereafter the portcullis was lowered, locking them in.

Lord Wulfram dismounted, passing the reins to a waiting warrior. "I'm getting too old for this," he remarked. "War is for the young, Ludwig. Never forget that."

"That said, some of the greatest leaders of all time were older than you are now," Ludwig reminded him.

"True, but I find myself ill-suited to our current circumstances. Fear not, I shall do my duty, but things are looking grim."

"You see the outcome as inevitable?"

"I do," admitted the baron. "Don't you?"

"Then why fight? Surely it's better to surrender? At least you would still have your life!"

Lord Wulfram frowned. "And what kind of life would that be? I am a prisoner of circumstance, my friend. To back down now would be to admit defeat and face a lifetime of scorn. Better to die an honourable death."

"An honourable death? What is there about death that's honourable?"

"There's more than me at stake here, and well you know it."

"You speak of Rosalyn?" asked Ludwig.

"Of course. I would not have her watch her father rot in the dungeons of Mulsingen."

"Could you appeal to the duke?"

The baron shrugged. "It would do little good. The duke is only concerned with keeping his position. Without Regnitz Keep and the income that comes with it, I am of little use to him."

"But you have supported him for years?"

Lord Wulfram held up his hand. "It matters not. Nobles come and go with the seasons, my young friend, something you should become well aware of. Tell me, if your own king were not a cousin, would you be so loyal?"

"Of course," said Ludwig. "He's my king."

"Even so, you abandoned him."

"What makes you say that?"

"You're here, aren't you? You gave up any semblance of service to the king when you left Hadenfeld."

Ludwig felt the guilt hit him like a punch to the stomach. "I suppose I never thought of it that way."

"It happens all the time," said the baron, perhaps to soothe his captive's conscience.

"Not to me, it doesn't."

"If I may give you a piece of advice?"

"By all means, my lord."

"When this is all over, return home. I think you'll see things in a new light after your experiences here."

"I don't know that I can," said Ludwig. "My estrangement with my father—"

"Will fade in time, trust me. Now come, get off that horse, and let's go and have a nice dinner while we have no interruptions. Tomorrow the catapults start, and then we'll never have another opportunity for peace and quiet."

24

SUMMER

Summer 1095 SR

A nother rock struck the wall, sending shards of stone flying in all directions, the noise reverberating through the courtyard, adding an echo to the already ominous sound.

Summer had come, but not much else had changed. The endless assault on the walls continued, unabated, day and night, and the defenders were growing weary of it. Lord Wulfram had cut back on the food rations, the better to last through the siege. All within were a little thinner, but life carried on despite the army outside their walls, poised to destroy them.

Ludwig, high atop the keep, looked down at the confusion below. Even now, after many days of constant attack, Lord Wulfram's men were still skittish. Hearing footsteps approaching, he turned to see Rosalyn.

"Anything new to report?" she asked.

"No, the siege continues, though I daresay that crack in the wall doesn't bode well. It'll probably collapse sometime in the next few days."

She moved to stand beside him, gazing at the activity below. "Why do they not simply finish it off?"

"A catapult is not an accurate weapon," he replied. "They're lucky if two stones land within twenty feet of each other, let alone hope for hitting the same target."

"And when the wall falls?"

"Then they'll rush into the courtyard, but the keep will still be in our hands, and that's a formidable obstacle."

"How much longer can we last?"

"A good question," Ludwig said. "I would think your father has a better answer than me."

Rosalyn shivered. "If we are to die," she asked, "can you promise me something?"

Turning to look at her, he noticed the fear in her eyes. "What is it you would have me promise?"

"I can't be captured. They'll do unspeakable things to me."

"No they won't," he reassured her. "He wants you to wed his son. He can't do that if you've been… injured in any way."

"Still, I would rather die. Promise me you'll take my life and spare me the humiliation?"

"I cannot do as you ask," said Ludwig. "For to do so goes against every bone in my body. You'll survive this to see better days, I promise you."

Rosalyn's eyes turned cold. "Can you not do this one thing for me? I thought us friends."

"As did I, but what you ask is impossible."

"I love you, Ludwig. Can't you see that?"

Ludwig's eyes widened. "Love? What do you mean?"

"I've come to savour my time with you. Tell me you do not feel the same?"

"I…"

She moved close enough for him to feel the heat of her as she pressed against him. "Do you not yearn for my embrace?"

He grabbed her by the arms and pushed her back. "I cannot return your affection."

"Cannot? Or will not? Am I so unpleasing to the eye?"

"It's not that," insisted Ludwig. "Believe me when I say you are, I believe, the fairest maid I have ever laid eyes on."

"Then what is it?"

"My heart is not mine to give. To tell you otherwise would be dishonourable."

She stiffened beneath his hands. "Fine," she said, her voice clipped. "Then we shall speak no more of this." Rosalyn turned quite abruptly, taking the stairs back into the keep.

Ludwig let out a breath. His hands were shaking, and he felt as if his whole world had been turned upside down. Did Rosalyn truly love him? He doubted it, but as he looked back on his own past, he realized his love for Charlaine had grown somewhat unexpectedly.

Rosalyn was a wonderful young woman, but still... she was no Charlaine.

"I am destined, it seems, to spend the rest of my life alone," he admitted to himself.

"What was that, my lord?"

Ludwig jumped at the voice, then realized one of the bowmen was talking to him. "Nothing," he said. "I was only musing."

"That's about all we can do," said the archer.

"Have you served the baron for long?"

"Five years," the man replied. "I grew up in Regnitz village."

"And was your father an archer?"

"Saints, no. He was a carpenter. I tried the trade, but I don't have the hands for it."

"And thus you became a bowman?"

"Aye, I did. What of yourself? Did you always know you'd be a warrior?"

Ludwig chuckled. "I suppose I did. My father trained me in weapons from an early age. What else could I become?"

"And yet here you stand, a prisoner of Lord Wulfram. It must be galling."

"Not at all. I've come to find His Lordship a most interesting person."

"And his daughter too, I'll warrant."

"She is fair, to be honest, but a little on the thin side to my liking."

The archer looked insulted. "Are you saying the Lady Rosalyn isn't pleasing to the eye?"

"Not at all. Any man would be proud to call her his wife."

"Just not you?"

Ludwig smiled. "I see you understand."

"Then what is it? Is it her blonde hair? She gets that from her mother, you know."

"In truth, I can't tell you, for I don't know myself. There's just something missing between us. I feel as though she is destined for someone else."

"Does she know that? 'Cause from what I saw, she had other ideas."

"Yes, I suppose I should talk to Lord Wulfram about that before there's any misunderstanding."

"You do that," said the archer. "But if I were you, I wouldn't wait too long. She's likely to take your rejection badly. Women do that, you know."

"And here I thought you only an archer. You are a wise man, my friend. I shall do as you suggest. Now, I must be off if I am to see His Lordship."

Lord Wulfram sat in the great hall where the tables were empty, ready to be used to shore up the doors once the final assault came. He stared down at the meagre gruel that awaited him, deep in thought. As the Baron of Regnitz, he could take what food he wanted, but he preferred to eat the same as his men, the better to instill a sense of camaraderie.

He took a spoonful of the watery fare but tasted nothing as it slid down his throat. He set the spoon aside, the porridge uneaten, for the siege had crushed his appetite, along with his spirit. The approach of a familiar set of footsteps made him look up. Ludwig halted before the table, patiently waiting for Lord Wulfram to acknowledge his presence.

"Yes?" said the baron. "Is there something I can do for you?"

"I need to speak to you," said Ludwig, "on a matter of some delicacy."

"You have my attention. What is it? Has Stein begun his attack?"

"No, at least not that I'm aware of."

"Then out with it, man. I haven't got all day." The baron then let out a chuckle. "On second thought, I suppose I do. I find all this waiting to be quite tedious, don't you?"

"I do," said Ludwig, "though that's not what I'm here to discuss."

"Then best you get on to whatever the subject is."

"It's Lady Rosalyn, my lord."

"Oh?" said Lord Wulfram. "Is something wrong? She hasn't fallen ill, has she?"

"No, she's in fine health, as far as I'm aware."

"Then what is it?"

"I'm afraid I might have inadvertently given her the wrong impression."

"About what?"

"About my feelings for her."

The baron sat back in his chair. "And what are your feelings towards my daughter?"

"I harbour none, other than friendship, my lord."

"Then how is that a problem?"

"I fear she might have mistaken my intentions for something of a more intimate variety."

"Intimate? Are you trying to say she's falling in love with you?"

"So it would appear," admitted Ludwig. "I tried to dissuade her, but I fear she may have taken it badly."

"How bad?"

"I can't say for sure, my lord, but I'm worried she might prove hostile to further conversation."

Lord Wulfram leaned forward, unable to sit still. He rested his elbows on the table, steepling his fingers beneath his chin. "Now, that is very interesting. What, precisely, did she say that led you to believe she felt that way?"

"She told me she loved me."

"Well, I suppose that erases any chance it was a simple misunderstanding. Where did this happen?"

"We were up on the top of the keep, my lord."

"Look, Ludwig, if we're going to get through this conversation in a decent amount of time, you're going to have to stop calling me 'my lord'. Is that understood?"

"Yes, my... I mean, yes."

"What did you say in return?"

"That my heart was not mine to give."

"Meaning?"

"That I'm in love with someone else."

"Ah," said Lord Wulfram. "I presume that's the reason you left Verfeld?"

"It was."

"Might I ask what happened to this other woman? Did she die?"

"No, she joined the Church."

"Saint Agnes?"

"Yes," replied Ludwig. "As a Temple Knight."

"A Temple Knight? Truly?"

"Indeed."

"Well," said Lord Wulfram, "you certainly know how to pick them. I suppose she wasn't a member of the Church when you first met her?"

"No, she was a smith."

"A smith, you say? This story gets more and more interesting by the moment."

"I thought it best to be honest with you, Lord."

"Honest you may be, but obviously it's time to put aside your feelings for this woman. After all, she's beyond your reach now, isn't she?"

"I don't know that I can," said Ludwig. "She awakened something in me, something I didn't even know I possessed."

Lord Wulfram blushed. "Well, that's what women do, my young friend."

"No, that's not what I meant. What I was trying to say is she showed me a world full of possibilities, that I can chart my own path in life."

"She must have been a remarkable woman."

"She was," insisted Ludwig, "but I fear my remembrance of her will overshadow anything I might experience in the future."

"Perhaps it's time you buried the past."

"Pardon?"

"You are the son of a baron," said Lord Wulfram. "As such, you must marry and produce an heir."

"What are you suggesting?"

"My daughter would make an excellent match for you. By your own admission, she already holds you in high regard. Could you not learn to love her in return?"

"Possibly, in time, but I could not contemplate such a marriage in my present state. It would be unfair to her."

"You still have the passion of youth," noted the baron. "Eventually, you will come to see your duty."

"Duty," said Ludwig. "Why does it feel like such an onerous word?"

"It's what drives the nobility, my friend. Nobility without duty is nothing but chaos."

"You speak of duty, but what of your duty to your subjects?"

Lord Wulfram was taken aback. "Whatever do you mean?"

"Surely, as baron, you swore to protect them, did you not?"

"What gave you that idea?"

"Are you not charged by your liege lord to watch over your people?"

"Don't be absurd," said Lord Wulfram. "The only oath I took was to collect the taxes on behalf of the duke. My tenants are there to serve me, not I, them. You have such strange ideas for a baron's son. Is that the influence of this woman you spoke of?"

"I suppose it is," said Ludwig, "but I meant no offence."

"And I have taken none. Now tell me, what is it you think nobles are here for? Surely to rule?"

"Of course, but on behalf of their subjects. Were not the original nobles merely village leaders?"

"I have no idea," said the baron. "As far as I know, there has always been the nobility. Oh, the titles may have changed over the centuries, but the fact still remains we are, as a class, fit to rule by birthright. You wouldn't train a sheep to hunt, would you?"

Ludwig laughed. "No, of course not."

"Then surely you can understand things from my point of view. We are, as nobles, the only souls capable of leading humanity."

"What about the Halvarians?"

"What about them? Everyone sees them as the great enemy, but if you were to examine how they govern, I have no doubt you'd see they're much like us. After all, it's the rule of nature."

"Nature?"

"Yes," said the baron. "The strong rule the weak. Have you never heard the expression?"

"So you're saying commoners are weak?"

"From a certain perspective, yes. I'm not talking about physical strength, obviously, but mental acuity. They lack the capacity for rulership. It's not their fault, of course. They simply don't have the education."

"That poses a thought-provoking idea," said Ludwig. "If you were to raise a commoner as a noble, would they then be fit to rule?"

"That," said Lord Wulfram, "is a fascinating thought indeed, and one I have never contemplated. It would be interesting to see what might happen under those circumstances."

"They say the Therengians elected their kings."

"That's the most ridiculous thing I've ever heard. Of course, they didn't elect their kings. A king rules by the right of his bloodline, not on the whims of his subjects."

"I'm only repeating what I've read," said Ludwig. "I have no idea if it's true or not."

"Well," said the baron, "I think we can safely put that down to idle gossip."

"Maybe you're right. Information about them is scarce, to say the least."

"Frankly, I'm surprised you know as much as you do. The Therengians were eliminated hundreds of years ago."

"Eliminated? You mean none survived?"

"Well, the kingdom was killed off. There are still descendants out there, even as we speak."

"How would we even know?" said Ludwig.

"It's the eyes," said Lord Wulfram.

"The eyes?"

"Yes. Therengians look much like us, but they have grey eyes."

"You mean totally grey?"

"Saints, no," said the baron. "Their pupils are grey instead of brown or blue."

"I've seen grey eyes back in Verfeld, but I never connected them with Therengia."

"Well, it was a long time ago. There's likely more in these parts."

"Why is that?" asked Ludwig.

"Erlingen was within their borders. They say Torburg used to be one of their provincial capitals."

"Then why can they still be found in Hadenfeld?"

"I can only assume it was on the fringes of Therengia at one time, but I'm not an expert in such things. I rather gather they tend to stick with their own race."

"Their own race?" said Ludwig. "Surely they're Human?"

"I would have to disagree. The very fact that their eyes are different would lend credence to the idea they are, in fact, a completely different race. In that regard, they're likely similar to Elves."

"What do you know of Elves?"

"Only what I've read. They haven't been seen in this part of the Continent for centuries. In any event, it matters little. Therengians, Elves—they've all disappeared into the annals of history. This is the age of Humans, Ludwig, never forget that. It's people like you and me who will forge a new future. Well, maybe not me, for I shall die here, in Regnitz Keep."

"Your thoughts of death are a little premature," said Ludwig. "What if the duke were to intervene?"

"You have hope: that is commendable, but we must be realistic. The Duke of Erlingen has no interest in intervening. In fact, quite the opposite. The more we fight, the more secure he is in his own position."

"Are there any allies you could call on?"

"And how would I get a message to them?"

"I could escape and carry word to them."

"It is a generous offer," said the baron, "and one I greatly appreciate, but you've seen the army surrounding this place. You'd never get through, and if you were caught, you'd likely be executed as a traitor. After all, you still belong to the Grim Defenders."

"I would take that risk if it would put an end to this conflict."

"It might have worked had we thought of it sooner, but those who might come to my aid are weeks away at best. No, I'm afraid we must resign ourselves to our fate."

"Then you're giving up?" said Ludwig.

"Let's say I'm only facing the reality of the situation. I must accept that which I cannot change, as must you."

"Meaning?"

Lord Wulfram sighed. "My life is coming to an end, Ludwig, but yours is merely beginning, of that I'm certain. When the assault comes, you must stand aside, and let the affair run its course. Once that's done, you can return home and sort things out with your father before it's too late. Men don't live forever, you know."

"I can't stand by and watch them kill you."

"You must. Any interference on your part can only result in your own death."

"And what of my honour?"

Lord Wulfram smiled. "Ah, I see you're turning my own words against me. That's very clever. I suppose I should have expected it."

"You told me you considered me a man of honour."

"And I do. Nothing has changed that."

"Then allow me to intercede with Lord Gebhard on your behalf."

"We tried that," said the baron, "to no avail."

"I could beg him to spare your life?"

"To what end?"

"You could accept banishment," said Ludwig. "I'm sure I could convince my father to welcome you to Verfeld."

"To do what? Beg for scraps?"

"You know King Otto. Perhaps he would welcome you at his court?"

"I knew him years ago, as a spoiled young man, nothing more. I haven't spoken to him in decades. I can hardly show up at his door, uninvited." Lord Wulfram paused, taking a breath. "I know you mean well, Ludwig, but it's time to put such thoughts to rest. My fate lies in the hands of Gebhard Stein. I would not have him use threats against me to control my daughter."

"Is there nothing I can say to change your mind?"

"No," said the baron. "But you can make me a promise?"

"Of course," said Ludwig. "Anything."

"When the keep falls, see to it Rosalyn gets to safety."

"And where might such safety be found?"

"A town named Adelwel. It lies in the southwest corner of Erlingen. Lord Ewald Beck rules there. He'll take her in."

"I shall do all I can to honour your wishes," promised Ludwig, "but leaving a keep during a siege will be fraught with peril. I cannot guarantee she will survive, but I will do my best."

"That's all I can ask."

25

THE SIEGE CONTINUES

Summer 1095 SR

A loud crack echoed up from the ground, and then a section of the curtain wall crumbled into the courtyard. Standing atop the tower, Ludwig knew it wouldn't be long before the troops surged forward. Feeling a presence come up behind him, he turned to see Rosalyn a few paces back, but the distant cheering of the enemy drew her closer. Ludwig returned his attention to the courtyard below.

"They're coming," he said. "It won't be long now."

"How much time have we?"

In answer, his eyes looked skyward, examining the sun's position. "I fear they will be here before nightfall."

"That soon?"

"Look at the wall," he replied. "The cracks are widening. It won't be long before that entire wall collapses."

"What will my father do?"

He beckoned her. "Look and see for yourself."

She leaned out of the embrasure, steadying herself against the merlon. "He has a dozen men on the northern wall," she said. "Why?"

"They'll be able to send their arrows into the courtyard once the enemy crosses the breach."

"But they'll be trapped, surely?"

"No," said Ludwig. "He can run them along the wall to where it meets the keep, then down those stairs and through the front door."

"But won't that put them within range of the enemy?"

"It'll be close; that much is sure, but the archers are unencumbered by armour while the attackers will still have to navigate the rubble."

"And what of the gatehouse?" Rosalyn asked. "Will he try a similar tactic there?"

"I imagine he will. That structure juts out and flanks the collapsed wall. He can use that to harry them as they advance towards the breach."

"How do you know all this?"

Ludwig adopted a grim smile. "I've always been interested in military matters, though I can't say why."

"Was it the influence of your father?"

"My father never showed the slightest interest in army tactics."

"But as a baron, he must command troops?"

"Of course, but Verfeld has never been attacked, at least not in recent history. The garrison there is largely inexperienced in warfare. Oh, there might be a soldier or two who's seen battle, but by and large, they're a miserable lot."

"Miserable?" Rosalyn said. "You think them poor warriors?"

"I think they've grown too used to a quiet life. The biggest challenge they've ever had to face is the Midwinter Feast."

"And when you're baron, will that change?"

"When I'm baron?" said Ludwig. "What makes you think I'll ever return home?"

"I have a sense you know your duty. Now stop trying to change the subject."

He leaned on the parapet, considering her question. "I suppose I'd institute some form of training program. Not that I'm qualified to do that myself. I'd have to hire someone, I suppose. Someone with experience."

She noticed him break into a grin. "Something amusing?" she asked.

"I was just thinking I know the perfect people for such a task."

"You do?"

"Yes, a couple of friends of mine." Ludwig pointed southward. "They're out there, somewhere."

"Your friends are attacking us?"

"Yes. Strange, isn't it?"

"How can you remain so calm in the face of such danger?"

"You think me calm?"

"Yes," Rosalyn said. "You show no sign of fear."

"I can assure you I'm as worried as you. This is a dangerous situation we're in, even if neither one of us will be fighting."

Another stone hit the wall, causing a sizeable chunk to break free and crash to the courtyard, adding to the pile of rubble.

Rosalyn shivered. "What will happen once they secure the courtyard?"

"I imagine Lord Gebhard will ask your father to surrender."

"It won't do any good. I'm afraid Father's set on his own destruction."

"He's doing it for you, Rosalyn."

"How could throwing away his own life possibly benefit me?"

"He's worried Lord Gebhard will hold his life over you, forcing you to submit to his will." Ludwig noticed the look of shock on her face. "Does that surprise you?"

"That he would prefer to die than see me under the heel of Lord Gebhard? I suppose it shouldn't. He's always put my welfare above his own, ever since mother died."

"What do you remember of her?"

"Not much, I'm afraid," admitted Rosalyn. "What of you? What was your mother like?"

"She was a tender, caring woman," said Ludwig. "A far cry from my father."

"I assume he was strict?"

"To a certain extent, yes, but that I could deal with. What I couldn't stand was his aloofness."

"Surely he felt the loss of your mother as keenly as you?"

He nodded as the old pain resurfaced. "I suppose he did, but I was too young to understand at the time."

"And now?"

"I see some elements of him in your father."

Rosalyn chuckled. "Is that a good thing or bad?"

"I'll let you make that judgement. My father had a strong sense of duty, much as yours does. The main difference between them is your father truly cares about you, while mine..." He couldn't finish the sentence.

They stood in companionable silence for a while, and then another stone struck its target. A great cloud of dust rose into the air as a large section of the wall collapsed.

"This is it," said Rosalyn. "The moment we've all been dreading. We're doomed." Ludwig noticed the tears forming in her eyes.

"No," he replied, "there's plenty of fight left yet. Even with the courtyard in their hands, they'll have to take the keep, and that won't be easy."

"But can't they simply reduce us with the catapults?"

"Ah, but they want you alive, remember? They won't dare risk bringing the keep down on you, for fear you'd be killed in the collapse."

The roar of men echoing into the courtyard interrupted their conversation.

"Here they come," said Ludwig. "Watch closely, and you'll see how a man defends his keep."

Lord Wulfram stood with his bowmen, waiting for the enemy to swarm through the breach. From Ludwig's point of view, the attackers were hard to see, but he knew when they drew close, for the baron ordered his men to ready their bows.

The archers nocked arrows, pulling back their strings in preparation for loosing off their initial volley. Ludwig held his breath as warriors appeared in the breach, picking their way through the rubble.

A bark of command sent arrows sailing into the mass of men. Even through the dust, Ludwig could make out the carnage as warriors collapsed under the onslaught. One staggered into the courtyard, only to take an arrow to the head. Behind him, others were gathering their courage for a mad rush to overwhelm the defenders. He could well imagine their fear. Fighting a man was one thing, but running through a hail of arrows was quite another.

A couple of them turned and fled, seeking the safety of their own lines, but the bulk let loose with a roar of challenge and then began racing across the collapsed wall, heedless of the danger.

Ludwig admired their courage, for it took guts to rush into such danger. Another volley took down three more, and then Lord Wulfram led his men back along the wall, desperately seeking the safety of the keep.

A few crossbowmen were in amongst the attackers, and they halted, letting loose with their bolts. One struck an archer, and the poor fellow fell into the courtyard where he lay, unmoving.

As more of the attackers began swarming over the ruins of the wall, Ludwig wondered if they were the Grim Defenders, but the occasional glimpse of chainmail told him otherwise. He considered they might be the baron's men, then decided Lord Gebhard would never risk losing them. That could only mean they were the Blades of Vengeance.

Dozens of warriors now streamed into the courtyard while others were still climbing the obstacle behind them. An arrow sailed out from the gatehouse, taking one in the stomach. He screamed in agony, clutching the wound and falling to the ground, writhing.

A small group of Lord Wulfram's archers stood atop the gatehouse, buying time for their liege lord to return to the keep. Ludwig thought the effort might stall the attack, but then footmen swarmed up onto the roof of the gatehouse, cutting the bowmen down without mercy. One such attacker slew an archer with his axe then kept hacking at the corpse, splattering blood everywhere. Moments later, he lifted the decapitated head, and Ludwig, feeling his stomach heave, looked away, unable to bear witness to such a grisly act.

"The gatehouse is theirs," announced Rosalyn.

Ludwig could think of nothing to say. Footsteps on stone stairs drew closer, and then four men appeared on the top of the keep, rushing to the parapets with their bows.

One, bolder than the rest, put his foot on the embrasure and aimed at the distant courtyard, but just as he pulled the string to his ear, a crossbow bolt took him in the chest. He staggered back, then fell face down onto the stone roof, his arrow curving high into the air.

Another warrior pushed past them to toss a brick over the parapet, where it crashed into the courtyard, doing little damage.

Ludwig pulled Rosalyn back. "We must get you inside," he said. "It's too dangerous."

"No. My place is here."

The brick thrower took a bolt in the arm, twisted as he was hit, then lost his footing, toppling over the edge of the wall, his screams echoing as he fell.

"It's too dangerous," he insisted. "Can't you see that?"

"Look around you, Ludwig. There is, in truth, no safety anywhere within this keep."

"No, you're wrong. The walls below will protect you from those crossbowmen. Here we are both targets. Would you risk your own life so recklessly? What would your father think?"

She stared at him for a moment, and then a bolt narrowly missed her. "Very well," she said. "Let's get below."

They veritably flew down the steps and were halfway to the next floor when Rosalyn took his hand, pulling him to the side as two more archers ran past them on their way to the top.

"I'm sorry," said Rosalyn. "I regret that I have put you in this position."

"It was inevitable," said Ludwig. "It was my plan that failed to take the gatehouse."

"No," she corrected. "I mean about professing my love for you. It was a terrible burden to place upon your shoulders. I just assumed you were meant for me, that fate had brought us together. Never did I consider the possibility you were already spoken for."

"I should have been clearer on the matter rather than lead you on. It's my fault, not yours."

She forced a smile. "Honourable to the end? I should have known."

.   .   .

At Rosalyn's insistence, they made their way to the great hall where they found Lord Wulfram, directing his men to place the tables against the barred door. He noted their arrival, moving to intercept them.

"What are you doing here?" he asked. "You should be below, in the cellar. It's far too dangerous."

"I would see you, Father, before it's too late."

Ludwig could feel a lump forming in his throat. Was this also the last time he would see Lord Wulfram? Rosalyn moved quickly to her father's side, giving him an embrace. The baron, for all his stoicism, enveloped her in his arms.

"It shall be fine, Rosalyn," he soothed. "You will survive this."

"And what of you?" she sobbed. "How can I take refuge knowing you will die here, in this very hall?"

He placed her at arm's length. "See here now," he said. "We all have to go, eventually. Better for me to die a heroic death than waste away of disease."

Ludwig noticed her temper flaring.

"Heroic death?" she said. "There's no such thing. Death is final, Father, not something to be actively sought. You taught me honour was important, but I see no honour in dying needlessly. Surely it's better to live that you might see another day?"

Lord Wulfram clenched his jaw. "I don't expect you to understand," he said, "but a man cannot suffer the loss of his dignity."

"At the same time, I am to suffer the loss of my father? What dignity is there in that?" She turned to Ludwig. "And what of you? You stand here in witness. Can you honestly say his death is preferable to dishonour?"

Ludwig felt caught in the middle, struggling to come up with some form of compromise.

"Well?" Rosalyn urged.

Ludwig turned to the baron. "I cannot, in good conscience, approve of your decision, my lord."

Lord Wulfram's face dissolved in disappointment. "I thought I knew you better, my young friend. Have I taught you nothing?"

Ludwig grew defensive. "You taught me to fight for what I believe in, and my gut tells me you are wrong in this."

"Have you lost your mind? You know what Stein will do to me should I be captured."

"No, I don't, and neither do you. The truth is none of us know, but I find it very unlikely he would hold your life over Rosalyn. It would certainly not endear him to her."

"So I am to simply surrender?"

Ludwig was suddenly struck by an idea. "Surrender, no, but we must make his assault costly."

"What are you suggesting?"

Ludwig broke out into a smile. "It has just occurred to me, my lord, that we hold the advantage?"

"We do?" said Lord Wulfram. "It's certainly not clear to me."

"If Lord Gebhard merely wanted to destroy us, he could reduce the keep to rubble. Saints know he has enough catapults, but he wants Rosalyn alive and unhurt, and the only way to do that is to send his warriors into the keep."

"And?"

"I propose we let him in."

"How in the Continent will that help us?"

"It's quite simple, really," said Ludwig. "He can't batter down the walls. for fear the whole keep will collapse; that means he has to come through there." He pointed at the main door. "If we plan this right, we can funnel his attack so we can reduce his numerical superiority."

"How?" asked Rosalyn.

"The corridors are narrow," continued Ludwig, "and Baron Stein's men would be hard-pressed to get two men side by side. We, on the other hand, can pack the hallways with men armed with spears."

Ludwig watched as Lord Wulfram regained his enthusiasm. "Yes, and make them pay for every footstep."

"You also have curved stairs," added Ludwig.

Rosalyn looked confused. "Of what significance is that?"

"The stairs circle to the right when ascending," noted her father. "It means anyone attacking upwards has their right hand up against the central column, making it difficult to swing their swords."

"Yes," agreed Ludwig, "while the defenders would have their sword arms on the outside wall, allowing them freedom of movement."

"Unless they're left-handed," added Rosalyn.

Her father smiled. "Ah, that's a very clever observation, but the truth is there are very few left-handed warriors. I think on that score, we can rest assured the tactic is sound."

"It would also make it next to impossible for them to utilize bows," added Ludwig.

"But aren't your friends attacking?" asked Rosalyn. "Surely you don't want them killed?"

"I'm pretty sure Lord Gebhard will use the Blades of Vengeance once he's ready."

"How can you be so sure?"

"Several reasons, actually. First of all, they're expensive, and he'll want to get his investment out of them before he releases them. Second, they're relatively well-armoured, thus making it harder for us to kill them."

"Anything else?" asked Lord Wulfram.

"Yes," continued Ludwig. "They have a reputation for ruthlessness, and they're more numerous than the Grim Defenders, which will be important when they try to overwhelm us. I'm sure he'll send in his own men once the rooms are secure, but until then, I think it safe to assume we know what to expect."

"So we fight as we withdraw," said the baron, "leading them up as we go. I like the sounds of it."

Rosalyn smiled. "I thought you took an oath to remain neutral."

"Not quite," said Ludwig. "I promised not to attempt escape, not to interfere with the defence of this keep. I wouldn't call my suggestions interfering with the defence, would you?"

"But why?" asked the baron. "All you have to do is sit back and watch us fight. You're still a prisoner here. Why help at all?"

"Lord Gebhard's aggression is unjust," explained Ludwig, "and quite frankly, it really burns my bacon."

Rosalyn laughed. "Burns your bacon?"

"Sorry, it was the only thing I could think of that wasn't crude. The truth is, were it in my power, I would call him out and demand a duel."

"I'm afraid that would carry no weight here," said Lord Wulfram. "Such things are explicitly forbidden by the duke."

"Yet he allows a siege? Surely this is just as bad."

"Still, it's our way."

A pounding at the door drew their attention.

"Fear not," said Lord Wulfram. "The door is solid enough. It will take more than a few knocks to bring it down."

"How long will it take to prepare?" asked Rosalyn.

"Some time, I would imagine," replied her father, "but I'm sure Stein will try to talk me into surrender. That ought to buy us a little while."

"Then you must let me help," she said.

"Help? How in the Continent would you help? I won't have you wield a spear."

"Nor do I intend to, but I must be of some use, surely?"

"She is an intelligent woman," said Ludwig, "and understands the intent. Surely she could assist in the placement of obstacles, if only by directing where things are to go?"

"Very well," said the baron. "Now pick up the end of that table and let's get moving. We haven't much time."

26

DEMANDS

Summer 1095 SR

A rumble drifted to Ludwig's ears, and he moved to peer outside into the courtyard. They were on the second floor, where arrow slits provided the only means of observing their foe, but it mattered little. There could be no doubt as to what Lord Gebhard was up to, for a team of horses pulled a catapult through the gatehouse.

"I don't understand how you can be so smug," said Rosalyn.

Ludwig looked back at her in surprise but then realized she was talking to her father.

Lord Wulfram grinned. "He's bluffing, don't you see? All of this is only meant to intimidate us."

"And if you're wrong?"

"I'm not. Trust me."

Ludwig could see the lingering doubt on Rosalyn's face.

"How can you be so sure?" she pressed.

"It was easy enough to figure out," replied the baron. "He wants you alive. He can hardly guarantee that if he reduces the keep to rubble."

"Then why move the catapults into the courtyard?"

"As I said, it's meant to intimidate us, nothing more. Wouldn't you agree, Ludwig?"

"Certainly, my lord. The truth is, those weapons would be next to useless at this short range."

"Useless?" said Rosalyn. "Won't they be even more dangerous?"

"Catapults release their stones into a high trajectory," replied Ludwig. "They are not well-suited to such short ranges. If he meant to reduce the keep, he'd have been better off leaving them in the field that lies to the south of us."

"Yes," agreed Lord Wulfram. "So you see, my dear, it's little more than a bluff."

"If that's true," asked Rosalyn, "then how will they gain entry?"

"Likely by using a ram. There's little else that would serve their purpose."

"Yes, and that will prove difficult," added Ludwig, "for the main door is on the second floor. The steps leading up to it won't make it easy to get a ram into position."

"And who do we have to thank for that?" asked Rosalyn.

"Your great-grandfather's the one who oversaw the construction of the place," said the baron. "Quite clever, if you ask me. Of course, I never thought we'd need it. After all, who would attack us? It only goes to show you how dramatically things can change in a generation or two." He turned to Ludwig. "Can you see what they're up to?"

Ludwig returned his attention to the courtyard below. The team of horses had halted just inside, and he struggled to press his face up against the arrow slit to get a better view.

"Something's going on," he announced.

"What type of something?" asked the baron.

"It looks like one of the catapults has lost a wheel."

"How does one lose a wheel?" asked Rosalyn. "Surely they didn't misplace it?"

"I would guess it broke or fell off, but I can't tell which. In any case, they're unhooking the horses." The sounds of swearing drifted to Ludwig's ears, eliciting a smile. "They don't sound too happy about it, I can tell you. If curses could win wars, it'd be all over by now."

"As entertaining as this is," said Rosalyn, "all it's really doing is delaying the inevitable. Why does he not simply attack us?"

"I suspect his men are tired, and this will garner them some much needed time to rest."

"How much time?"

"I would think half the morning at least. How does one go about changing a wheel on a catapult?"

"That depends," said Lord Wulfram. "If it only fell off, all they'd have to do is lift the catapult and slip it back on."

"And how would they do that?" asked Ludwig.

"With a simple lever. Mind you, it would have to be strong. They couldn't use a spear, for it'd likely snap."

"And if the wheel is broken?"

"That presents a whole host of problems. For one, they'd have to make a new one. They don't keep spares for things like that."

Ludwig pressed his face back to the arrow slit in an effort to see more. "They've found a timber from somewhere," he said. "I think they seek to lift it."

"Possibly," said Lord Wulfram, suddenly alert, "but what if we slow them down a bit?"

"And how would we do that?"

"We still have a few arrows left," noted the baron. "I'll send a couple of archers to the roof. A few well-placed shots ought to keep them from completing their task." He rushed from the room, leaving Ludwig alone with Rosalyn.

"Why must they play these games?" she asked. "I wish they would just be done with it."

Ludwig's attention remained on the activity below, but he heard the worry in Rosalyn's voice. "We should be thankful for it," he replied. "The longer it takes to get that thing in place, the more time we have to prepare."

"Prepare? Is that what you call it? We've already shored up our defences. What more can we do?"

"We can pray," said Ludwig. He looked skyward to where dark clouds were gathering.

"To what end? We are facing a lingering death, trapped like rats in a barrel. It would be better to have done with it."

Below, a man gave a yell as an arrow struck him in the leg. It took only a moment for the rest to realize they were under attack, and then the work party fled into the cover of the gatehouse.

Ludwig chuckled. "That ought to keep them busy for a while."

"Why?" asked Rosalyn. "What's happening?"

"Your father's archers have let loose with a few arrows. One of them hit its mark."

More bellows came from below, including the distinctive voice of Lord Gebhard himself.

"Now what?" she asked.

"I'm not sure." Ludwig noticed men scurrying around, but to what end he couldn't say. Moments later, the answer presented itself.

"Archers," he said. "Crossbowmen, to be more precise. It appears Baron Stein has taken offence at his men being used for target practice."

Bolts flew into the air, several clattering against the stone walls of the keep. "I don't imagine he's done much damage to us, but your father's plan to harass the workers has come to a screeching halt."

"I didn't know Lord Gebhard had crossbowmen," said Rosalyn.

"I saw them earlier." He examined the new arrivals in more detail. "I believe they're actually mercenaries."

"The Grim Defenders, by chance?"

"No, they don't have any missile troops. If anything, they belong to the Blades of Vengeance. Either that, or he's hired even more men."

"I doubt that," said Rosalyn. "Lord Gebhard is notoriously tight with his funds."

"But despite that, he's hired at least two groups of mercenaries. I wonder how he can afford that?"

"That's simple. He expects his son to wed me. I'm worth a substantial dowry."

"Is that what this is all about? Wealth?" said Ludwig. "I thought this was about Stein's ego?"

"Greed might be a more apt description."

"He must have taken on a great debt by bringing his feud here. Now I understand why he wouldn't negotiate."

"And why he hasn't given up."

"That too," said Ludwig. "It also gives me hope."

"In what way?"

"Every day he remains out there is another day his expenses mount. Keep it up long enough, and we'll bankrupt the man."

"He deserves no less."

The morning wore on. Lord Gebhard ordered up more crossbowmen, piling them onto what remained of the curtain wall. Whenever anyone showed themselves at the top of the keep, they would loose a volley, driving the defenders back indoors.

Workers got back to repairing the catapult, and by noon it was being dragged into the courtyard. Even though it would be useless, Ludwig had to admit it was an imposing sight. By mid-afternoon, two others had joined it, resulting in a trio of siege engines waiting there with their deadly cargo.

Shortly thereafter, a lone rider advanced towards the keep, a white flag in hand. Ludwig recognized the face of Captain Gottfried Jager, Lord Gebhard's siege expert.

The man called out, demanding Lord Wulfram reveal himself. Moments later, the baron appeared. "Come along, Ludwig. It's time to have some fun."

"Fun?"

"Yes. Stein wants to negotiate. I suspect he's getting impatient for a resolution to this conflict."

"But surely it's you he wants to talk to," said Ludwig.

"Naturally, but you shouldn't pass up the opportunity to see something like this. It doesn't happen every day, you know."

"Very well, my lord."

Ludwig followed Lord Wulfram to the top of the keep where a warrior stood by, white flag in hand. At a nod from the baron, the man raised it, swinging it back and forth a few times to garner attention. His task complete, he stepped onto the battlement to peer down below, ensuring no bowmen stood ready to kill his lord.

"It's all set, my lord," the warrior announced.

Lord Wulfram waited for the man to back up, then took his place. Ludwig stayed behind a merlon, safe from enemy bolts.

"Tell Lord Gebhard I'm here," called out Baron Haas. "Let him show himself and make his demands known."

"I am here at his behest," yelled back Jager, "and am empowered to negotiate on his behalf."

"I shall not deal with an underling. If your master wishes to discuss terms, then he must do so in person, not send in a lapdog."

"I can assure you—"

"Get Lord Gebhard," commanded Baron Haas. "I shall speak with no other."

"Yes, my lord." Ludwig heard the hesitation in Jager's voice.

Lord Wulfram glanced at Ludwig and winked. The baron was enjoying this far too much.

"Is this wise?" asked Ludwig. "Should he choose not to recognize the sign of truce, he could have you killed."

"I think you overestimate their chances," replied the baron. "Don't worry, my friend, if I see any of their archers raise their weapons, I shall remove myself from their sight."

Lord Wulfram fell silent, and Ludwig, not daring to risk exposure, could only wait, unable to determine what was happening below.

"Ah, here we are," said the baron at last. "He has come like Demos to the Gods."

"Demos?" said Ludwig.

The baron gave him a quick glance. "It's from *Honour to the Brave*. Did you not read it?"

"I'm afraid my mind has been elsewhere, my lord."

"By the Saints, Ludwig. We're trapped in a keep. What else have you got to keep your mind so occupied?"

"To be honest, I've been reading the *Book of Mathew*."

"Where in the Continent did you find that?"

"In the library," Ludwig admitted sheepishly. "I hope you don't mind that I took it?"

"Mind?" said Lord Wulfram. "Why would I mind? Books are meant to be read, Ludwig. To ignore that would make them useless. Still, I sense a growing awareness of religion within you. See that it does not overwhelm you."

"The words comfort me, but I'm far from being overwhelmed. Do you fear the Saints' words so much?"

"No, but as in life, many take the words too far. I've seen terrible sins committed in the name of the Church. I would not see you turned thus."

Ludwig found himself caught off guard. He hadn't seen this side of the baron before. It appeared there was more to this man than he knew. Seeking to learn more, he opened his mouth but was interrupted.

"Here comes Stein," said the baron. "Now let's see what he wants, shall we?" He straightened his back, looking down on his foe with the most regal expression he could manage. "So we meet again, Gebhard."

Baron Stein's voice drifted up from below. "What is it now, Wulfram? You could just have easily dealt with Captain Jager."

"I wanted to see your smiling face," said Baron Haas. "You're the one who sought to make demands. The least you can do is make them face to face."

"Certainly," said Lord Gebhard. "I demand you immediately surrender and vacate this keep."

"And if I don't?"

"Then I shall reduce it to rubble with you inside."

"No you won't," said Lord Wulfram. "Do that, and you risk killing Rosalyn. With her dead, your entire reason for being here is gone with her."

"Then hand her over, and I shall leave with my army."

"I have a counterproposal."

"Of course you do," said Lord Gebhard. "Go ahead, then, speak your mind, and let's see what you suggest."

"Leave Regnitz once and for all and never set foot in my lands again."

"That's hardly an offer I would entertain. I might remind you that YOU are the one trapped here. It's only a matter of time before I get inside that keep, and when I do, the carnage will be great. You know what men are like when they get the fire within them, Wulfram. Would you expose your daughter to such horrific acts?"

"You're bluffing, Gebhard. You can't marry your son off to Rosalyn if she's been mistreated, and you know it. Your only solution is to give up this foolish quest. March your army away, and save what little dignity you have left."

Baron Stein's voice grew louder. "You dare to order me about! Surrender, this moment, or suffer the consequences."

"It's an empty threat. You'll not bombard this keep. You and I both know it. If you want to come and get us, you'll have to do it the old-fashioned way —through the front door!"

"Don't lecture me on tactics," warned Lord Gebhard, "or I shall reduce this keep to nothing but rubble, and Rosalyn can go to the Underworld for all I care."

"And throw away your chances of her dowry? I don't think you have it in you, Gebhard. Tell me, was this the plan all along, or did you actually think you could win her over?"

"I've had enough of your insolence. Now abandon this foolish resistance, while there's still life left within you."

"Foolish, is it?" said Baron Haas. "Next thing I know, you'll be demanding I pay you reparations for your attack on us."

"Don't think it hasn't crossed my mind!"

Baron Stein fell silent, and Ludwig had the distinct impression he was trying to soothe his nerves. Perhaps it was the strain of the situation, but when he spoke again, his voice was harsh and guttural.

"I've been civil with you, Wulfram. Saints know how hard I've tried to use reason, but you refuse to bend to the winds of change. Well then, bend no more. It's time for you to break."

"You may get into this keep," responded Baron Haas, "but it will cost you dearly."

"It will be worth it to be rid of you. My only regret is that innocents will die in the fight. I tell you what, old friend; send Rosalyn out, and I shall guarantee her safety while we two battle it out for supremacy. How does that sound?"

"Like an idea only an idiot would accept. What do you take me for, Gebhard? A fool?"

"If the shoe fits!"

Lord Wulfram fell silent. Ludwig shifted uncomfortably as the silence dragged on. A cool wind blew in from the east, ruffling his hair, and he looked skyward once more to see the clouds still gathering.

"Very well," said Baron Stein. "It's obvious this parley has been a complete waste of time. Ready yourself, Wulfram, for when the time comes, my men will be ruthless."

"Bring them on," taunted Baron Haas. "I am eager to put my sword to them." He stepped down from the parapet. "Fool," he swore. "Did he honestly think I would surrender so easily?"

Lord Gebhard could be heard yelling in the courtyard, a call quickly taken up by others and echoed back through the gatehouse.

"We must ready for an assault," said Lord Wulfram. "Gebhard does not appear amenable to my suggestions."

"So it would seem," said Ludwig.

Off in the distance came the creaking of wood echoing in the courtyard, and then Ludwig spotted a great rock flying through the air. It struck the battlements, dislodging a merlon and sending splinters of stone flying in all directions, along with a cloud of dust. Ludwig felt something sting his cheek, and then a trickle of blood welled up.

"Get below," he called out.

Lord Wulfram was already moving, rushing for the stairs that offered some degree of safety. Ludwig waited for the dust to clear and then peered south to where the great trebuchet was already being reset. He cursed himself for forgetting the mighty siege engine, then followed Lord Wulfram below, determined to see him to safety.

Rosalyn met them halfway down the stairwell.

"Father?" she called out. "What is it?"

"It's Stein," Wulfram replied. "He has grown fed up with our defiance. I'm afraid he's let that trebuchet loose against us."

"But you said he wouldn't dare reduce the keep?"

"It appears I underestimated him, my dear. I tried appealing to his sense of decency, but I fear it did no good. All I did was goad him on, and now he won't see reason."

"What are we to do?" she asked.

"Get yourself to the dungeon," he replied. "Gather the women and children and take them with you. I'm afraid our position here is about to get much more uncomfortable."

"And what of you?"

"My place is here," said her father. "I still have hope he'll come to his senses and attack our front door, but until then, I need you out of danger."

"And Ludwig?"

They both looked at the man who stood between them.

"It's your choice," said Lord Wulfram. "I have no control over your actions."

"Then I will stand with you and fight to the bitter end."

27

BREAKTHROUGH

Summer 1095 SR

T he very bones of the keep rumbled as it was struck again, while above them, Ludwig heard the sound of collapsing stone. It had continued all night, the trebuchet's great projectiles relentlessly wearing down the top of the keep. It was not a weapon that could discharge its missiles very quickly, and Ludwig was about to settle back down, determined to get some sleep before the next one came towards them, but then he heard a distinct sound, that of something battering the door.

Now, instantly awake, he stood, his hand instinctively grasping the hilt of his sword. Again came the noise, and then the front door shuddered, dust falling from its frame as a small portion of the wood buckled towards him, and he knew in a flash that they had come with a ram.

Lord Wulfram, of a similar mind, appeared from upstairs. "Find Rosalyn," he ordered, "and get her above."

"Surely not?" said Ludwig. "They have been hammering the keep all night. Wouldn't the dungeon be safer?"

"No, I have been inspecting the keep. The damage is mostly superficial, although we can no longer get to the roof. You need to get her to the upper floors, for only there can you take advantage of the stairwell."

Ludwig, seeing the wisdom in it, made his way to the dungeon. Rosalyn was there, huddled with the other women and children of the keep. At his approach, she rose.

"It's time," was all he said. She understood perfectly, crossing the room and following him upstairs.

"How long have we?" she asked.

"Not long. The door is already beginning to buckle, but at least the trebuchet is done."

"A small miracle. Even so, we must take what we can."

He led her through the great hall, past where the remainder of the garrison were taking up their positions to repel the enemy. They had ascended only two steps of the staircase that led to the second floor when a tremendous crash announced the front doors of the keep had failed.

Ludwig risked a quick glance to see the head of a ram poking through the wood. Baron Stein's men pulled it back, and two of Wulfram's archers loosed arrows through the newly vacated hole.

At least one man screamed out in pain, evidence that the volley was not misplaced. Ludwig was torn between his oath to protect Rosalyn and his desire to fight. He had to tell himself this was not his war, that he was one of the mercenaries who would soon be streaming through the door, yet something held him back.

He cursed at the necessity for the decision, then turned once more, pulling Rosalyn up the stairs. After half a dozen paces, he halted, hearing the sound of feet rushing up towards him. Expecting a fight, he drew his sword, but it was only three of Lord Wulfram's men, taking up positions to guard the stairs.

Ludwig halted in the small hallway at the top, placing Rosalyn behind him. Echoing up towards them was the sound of conflict, of steel on steel, a test of might between warriors. He wondered where Lord Wulfram might be found, but the thought was quickly taken from him as a group of warriors rushed up the stairs.

The attacker in the lead was quickly skewered, a spear taking him in the gut. The warrior who killed him tried to pull back his weapon, but it stuck fast, so he let go of the spear, allowing the body to fall, watching it slide down the stairs.

The fallen man was quickly replaced by another who stabbed out with a spear of his own. One of Wulfram's men took a tip to the chest and slumped to the floor.

"Get to the stairwell," he shouted to Rosalyn.

"What are you going to do?" she cried out.

"Hold the line, but I can't do that if I'm guarding you. Go, while you still can."

Even as he spoke, a hatchet flew forth, striking another of Wulfram's men in the face. The poor fellow sank back, clutching at the bloody mess and screaming. Ludwig saw the danger even as the man fell, for now only one of the baron's men remained between the attackers and him and Lady Rosalyn.

Ludwig, throwing caution to the wind, gave a yell and rushed forward, his sword clutched tightly. A spear lunged towards him, and he twisted, having the satisfaction of watching the tip scrape by, narrowly missing his chest. In answer, he swung down, cutting into an extended arm, and a cry of excruciating pain echoed through the corridor. Then Ludwig struck again, using his weapon's tip to extend his reach into a gambeson, tearing the fabric but failing to penetrate.

A mace struck his outstretched arm, knocking the sword from his grasp, and he quickly pulled his arm back as a pain shot up it. The warrior beside him attacked again with his spear, taking one of Baron Stein's men in the groin, but it was his last action, for even as he did so, another hatchet flew forth, sinking into his neck. Blood sprayed everywhere, splashing Ludwig in the face and temporarily blinding him.

He staggered back, desperate to clear his vision. A spear stabbed him in the chest, but his metal breastplate held firm, deflecting the blow. Ludwig grabbed the end of the spear as it passed him, then pulled as hard as he could, dislodging the weapon from his enemy.

Stepping back, he wiped his eyes with his forearm, and through the red mist, he saw two men rushing forward. He took down one with the butt of the spear and then reversed the weapon, stabbing out with the point. It glanced off the second's forearm, drawing blood, and then Ludwig risked a look over his shoulder. The stairwell to the keep's upper floors was now right behind him, so he took three quick steps backwards until he felt the first step against the back of his foot.

The spear was incredibly light in his hands, and suddenly he was struck by the remembrance of his training all those years ago when a fourteen-year-old Ludwig was first taught how to hold such a weapon. He stepped forward, spinning the spear and then stabbed forward once more, hitting nothing but causing the next group of warriors to back up.

They paused, but that all ended as one of them got up the nerve to lead an advance. With a roar, they surged forward, filling the short corridor with the echoes of their screams.

Ludwig skewered one, but the other two closed in, striking out with their blades. A tug to his own gambeson told him one had failed to penetrate his armour, but then he felt a stab of pain as a blade sliced across his thigh. It was a light wound, to be sure, but the suddenness of it took his breath away, and he dropped to the ground with the weight of his opponent pressing against him. Releasing his spear, Ludwig smashed out with his fist and pain shot through his arm as his knuckles connected with a helmet. One of his attackers pummelled his wounded leg, and all he could do in defence was lash out with his foot. He felt resistance, and then one of his attackers rolled to the side, grasping his knee, Ludwig's attack having done its work.

A face loomed over him while his attacker raised a dagger on high. Ludwig's hand clawed at his enemy's eyes, and a tortured scream erupted from the man's mouth as he rolled to the side.

Ludwig shuffled back on his arms and legs, desperate to put some space between them. His hand hit the stair, and he pushed himself upright as his eyes cast around for a weapon.

The enemy's initial attack had been blunted, but more approached even as Ludwig spotted his chance—a sword lying disused, its blade stained red with blood. He dove for it as the next warriors came for him. His hand reached out, grasping the handle with steely determination, swinging with the last ounce of strength he had left in him.

Into a shin went the blade, and he heard bone crunch as the sword penetrated the man's armour. His foe fell backwards, collapsing to the floor.

Ludwig was soon on his feet, eyeing his newest opponent with his sword held in a defensive stance. He stepped back, feeling once more the comfort of the next step. Up the stairs he went, slowly and deliberately, following the twist as he spiralled upwards to the top of the keep.

The air grew still, the quiet punctuated only by the occasional groans of the wounded. He heard the clash of steel on steel in the distance and again wondered what had happened to Lord Wulfram.

He kept backing up, moving slowly, trying to anticipate the next rush. A face peered up from below, using the centre of the column to hide the rest of the man's body. Moments later, Ludwig could hear them talking amongst themselves.

"We'll rush him," a man with a high voice suggested.

"You go right ahead," said a second, much lower. "I'll stand back and watch."

"Get out of my way, fools," snarled a third.

Ludwig braced, and then one came up the stairs, a seasoned warrior by the look of him, a shield firmly in his right hand, an axe in his left.

"By the Saints," said Ludwig. "It looks like I just can't win today."

"What is it?" called out Rosalyn.

"Of all the men in Stein's army, I have to get a left-handed one." Ludwig stabbed forward, but his sword only scraped along the man's shield. In response, the axe came down, narrowly missing to chip off a small chunk of stone from the step.

Ludwig saw his chance and quickly stabbed out, driving the point of his sword into the extended arm. He felt the blade penetrate the man's mail and sink into flesh, and then his foe pulled back, his axe now forgotten.

Their eyes met for the briefest of moments before the warrior backed down the stairs, his part in the assault finished. The other two were still somewhere below, muttering amongst themselves, just out of sight. Ludwig thought his fight over, but then slow, measured steps echoed up the stairwell.

"Where is he?" came a familiar voice.

"Baldric?" called out Ludwig. "Is that you?"

"Ludwig?" came the reply. "What are you doing here?"

"Protecting Lady Rosalyn."

"You can come down now. The fighting's over."

"And Lord Wulfram?"

"In Lord Gebhard's custody."

Ludwig felt relief flood over him, but then he remembered Baldric's last words to him. "Where are the rest of the Grim Defenders?"

"Waiting below," replied Baldric. "Come, let us waste no more time."

Ludwig descended the steps until he could see Baldric standing there with his weapon by his side, waiting for him. But something about his stance alarmed Ludwig, and while he was looking at the man's feet, they suddenly shifted.

Ludwig brought his sword up in the nick of time. Baldric's weapon struck it low on the blade, scraping up to the crossguard to force Ludwig back until his heel caught on the step, tripping him. He only managed to put his hand out at the last moment to prevent an injury.

Baldric moved closer, lifting his sword for another strike, but he'd forgotten about the stairs that circled above him. His blade scraped across the stone, and he let out a curse. A momentary distraction, yet enough for Ludwig to get to his feet and stab out with his own blade, doing little damage, though it bought him some time.

He retreated up the stairs, watching as Baldric slowly followed. Ludwig's mind was racing now, trying to think about how he could outmanoeuvre the oaf, but here, in this confined space, there was little room for such things.

"I said I'd come for you," boasted Baldric, "and here I am, ready to cut you into little pieces."

"You don't scare me," replied Ludwig. "You may be large, but you're slow."

Baldric laughed. "Come, face me in fair combat, and I shall make your death swift." He lunged unexpectedly, his sword stabbing out three times in rapid succession.

Ludwig was forced back, struggling to maintain his footing. Baldric, energized by his success, redoubled his efforts, rushing forward, his body slamming into Ludwig and driving him back against the wall, his forearm up against the younger man's neck.

Ludwig felt the air driven from his lungs, the force of his opponent's arm threatening to crush his windpipe. Dropping his sword, he gripped Baldric's arm, desperately trying to free himself. His head began to pound, and he felt as though his lungs would explode if he didn't get some air into them soon.

Baldric's putrid breath filled his nostrils. In his eyes, now only a hands breadth away from his own, Ludwig saw death coming for him. In a moment of clarity, he realized he was not ready to die. He would fight on, no matter what the cost!

His knee came up straight into Baldric's groin, and the big man crumpled, then slid down the stairs with an ear-piercing shriek.

Ludwig wanted to lash out, finish off his foe, but all he could do was gasp for breath as his head cleared. Forcing himself to continue climbing the stairs, he used his hands to steady himself against the wall. Up he went, taking slow, measured steps, feeling fatigue set in.

An open doorway came into view, the entrance to one of the upper floors, but Ludwig found it hard to focus. Was he on the third floor now, or the fourth? The stairs continued, but he paused, using the entrance to steady himself.

He had a brief glimpse of Rosalyn down the hall right as Baldric smashed into him, driving him to the floor. His knees struck the stone, and then the air was pressed out of him yet again as the full weight of his foe fell upon him. Ludwig tried to roll over, but a flurry of blows into his side caused him to curl up into a ball.

The sound of pottery breaking made him look up, and he saw Baldric staggering to his feet, his face cut and bleeding. Rosalyn stood defiantly, another plant in hand, poised to toss it like she had the first.

Ludwig seized the opportunity, rolling to the side and kicking out. His foot struck a knee, and the great man's leg buckled, smashing into the stone floor and eliciting a cry of anguish. Ludwig followed up by moving in close and grabbing his rival by the throat. This was his undoing.

Baldric, a much larger opponent, used his own arms to smash down on Ludwig's elbows, dislodging his grasp and clapping his hands around the younger man's neck, squeezing for all he was worth.

For the second time today, Ludwig found his breath cut off. Baldric stood, lifting Ludwig as he rose, dangling him in the air. He tried to punch Baldric in the stomach, anything to dislodge the grip of death, but to no avail. His knuckles hit metal, and he felt blood as something bit into his hand. Coming to the realization it was Baldric's dagger, he pulled it forth and drove the blade into the great man's belly. Again and again, he struck, and then finally, the fingers released.

Ludwig fell to his knees gasping for air as Baldric staggered back, clutching at his stomach. A final breath escaped his foe's lips, and then he fell to the floor where he lay, motionless.

Rosalyn called out to him, but Ludwig could do little to respond. Finally, he stood, still staring at the bloodied corpse of Baldric. Hearing footsteps coming up the stairs, he gripped the dagger tighter, his fingers aching from the force of it.

Through the doorway came Sigwulf, sword in hand. He halted as he saw the carnage.

"I surrender," gasped out Ludwig, dropping his weapon as his legs gave out, and he collapsed to the floor.

Sigwulf moved closer, cradling his friend's head. "Ludwig? Are you hurt?"

Ludwig heard the voice but lacked the energy to respond. Instead, his hands started shaking, and he wondered if he had been afflicted by some sort of curse. He tried to calm himself, but to no avail. Someone pried open one of his eyes, and he realized Cyn looking down at him.

"What's wrong with him?" came Sigwulf's voice.

"He's exhausted," she replied. "And no wonder. He looks like he hasn't slept in days."

"He killed Baldric."

"No," said Cyn. "He died in the assault. That's all we need to say. Now help me lift him."

Sigwulf grunted. "Let me do it. You'll only get in the way."

"And what am I to do?" she demanded.

"See to that woman."

Ludwig heard Cyn stand. "You're Lady Rosalyn, I presume?"

"I am," came the reply. Her steps grew closer. "Will Ludwig survive?"

"I don't see any reason why not," said Sigwulf, "but he'll need some rest."

"And then what?"

"What do you mean?"

"Is he to be a prisoner, like me?"

"No," said Cyn. "We merely rescued him. He was a prisoner, wasn't he?"

"He was," said Rosalyn. "What of me? Am I to be imprisoned?"

"That's not for us to say," said Sigwulf, "but we are in the employ of Lord Gebhard, so it seems likely."

"On the other hand," said Cyn, "His Lordship wants you in one piece to marry his son. I don't imagine he'll mistreat you in any way."

"No," said Rosalyn. "He'll merely force me to his son's bed. Better that I was dead."

"Don't say that," pleaded Cyn. "While there's life, there's hope."

"I pray that is so."

28

AFTERMATH

Summer 1095 SR

"Put me down," insisted Ludwig. "I can walk."

Sigwulf released him in the great hall, or what was left of it. So many bodies were strewn around, leading Ludwig to wonder how many had actually survived.

"Lord Wulfram?" he asked.

"Captured early in the fighting," said Cyn. "He was injured by an arrow."

"Not seriously, I hope?"

"He'll recover, providing Lord Gebhard doesn't kill him first."

Sigwulf shook his head. "All this death because of a woman."

"It's more than that," said Ludwig. "It's the dowry."

"I doubt there's much of that left now. It'll all be needed to repair this keep."

"On that, I think we are agreed. What of the Grim Defenders, did you lose many more?"

"Less than half a dozen, though we have a further nine with light wounds. We're the lucky ones. Baron Stein sent in the Blades of Vengeance ahead of us, and they suffered terribly."

"I suppose we'd best get outside. No doubt Lord Gebhard will wish to gloat."

"He will," agreed Sigwulf, "and I suspect he'll be pleased to see Lady Rosalyn."

"What will happen to her?" asked Ludwig.

"I have no idea. In any event, it's out of our hands. If you remember, we're only hired swords."

"It hardly seems worth it, looking back."

"Oh, I don't know," said Cyn. "We got paid. All in all, I'd say that's a good few weeks of work."

"Yes," added Sigwulf, "but I suppose that puts us out of a job now."

"What will the company do?" asked Ludwig.

"I imagine the captain will take us back to Torburg. There's likely a better chance of finding employment there."

"And in the meantime?"

"We'll probably camp here for a few days so Lord Gebhard can pay us. Speaking of which, we must be off. He's not a man you want to upset."

They wandered through the battered keep doors and into the courtyard. Lord Gebhard's troops were meandering around, gathering up weapons and seeing to the wounded while he was seated upon his horse, watching the door as people were brought out. At the sight of Lady Rosalyn, he smiled.

"There she is, Hagan, the jewel of Regnitz."

The baron's son looked up from where he was talking to a wounded man. Ludwig noticed the look of pleasure on the younger Stein as his eyes beheld the daughter of Lord Wulfram. Hagan moved closer, bowing at the waist.

"Lady Rosalyn," the man said. "I deeply regret the circumstances under which we meet."

"You are well-spoken, Master Hagan. If only your father were so well-versed in courtly manners."

Lord Gebhard glared at her but then looked to get his temper in check. Instead of yelling, he bowed his head slightly. "My dear Lady Rosalyn, I'm happy to see you safe."

"Why?" she asked. "So you can force me to marry your son?"

"Would that be so bad? After all, think of the alternative? I could always hand you over to my men."

"Father!" said Hagan. He returned his attention to Lady Rosalyn. "I must apologize for the harsh words," he said. "I promise you no such fate awaits you."

"Is it common practice for you to speak against your father thus?" Rosalyn asked.

"No, but in this case, I must insist."

"It will do you no good, sir, for I will not marry you of my own free will."

"Nor would I ask you to," said Hagan.

Lord Gebhard looked like he was going to say something, but then two soldiers exited the keep, Lord Wulfram between them. The Baron of Regnitz had a bloody bandage around his thigh, along with numerous bruises, cuts, and scrapes, but he was walking under his own power.

"There he is," said Lord Gebhard. "The vanquished finally reveals himself."

"Spare me the gloating," said Lord Wulfram. "I surrender to you, sir, and order all my men to lay down their arms."

"I'm afraid you're far too late for that, my friend. My men have captured or killed everyone in your employ. How does it feel to be utterly defeated?"

Lord Wulfram was defiant. "You may have defeated me, but you will come to rue the day you did so."

"Will I, now? I think it's you who will come to rue the day, sir, not I."

"Where do you want him, my lord?" asked one of Baron Haas's escorts.

Lord Gebhard smiled. "Bring him to me," he said. "I would see the look of utter defeat in his eyes."

The guards shoved Lord Wulfram forward, and he staggered a little but quickly recovered. Ludwig saw the pride in the lord. He might have been beaten in battle, but he was far from cowed. Lord Gebhard, on the other hand, could do little but gloat.

"Marvellous," he said, "simply marvellous."

He dismounted, then stood, waiting as the object of his scorn was brought closer. The Baron of Mulsingen locked eyes with his rival. "Kneel," he commanded.

"I shall do no such thing!"

Baron Stein's face grew red as he drew his sword, holding the tip to his captive's chest. "I said kneel!"

Lord Wulfram remained obstinate, causing his captor to look at his men. With a nod, the guards forced Baron Haas to his knees.

Stein smiled. "Now, plead for your life."

"I will not give you the satisfaction. If you're going to kill me, Gebhard, then stop mucking about and get it over with."

Ludwig noticed Lord Gebhard's arm tense. He half expected the man to plunge the blade into the chest of his rival, but something stayed his hand.

"No," he said instead. "Killing you is too easy." Baron Stein leaned down into a crouch, the better to look into his enemy's eyes. "I'm going to lock you up in the darkest bowels of Mulsingen, Wulfram. There, you'll rot until the end of time." He smiled, giving himself a chilling expression. "And while you're there, in the darkness, know my son will be rutting with your daughter."

"Father!" called out Hagan.

Lord Gebhard put his hand up, warning his son to silence, but kept his eyes on Wulfram. "What have you to say for yourself now, I wonder?"

The sound of hooves galloping across the drawbridge echoed through the courtyard, and then a trio of riders appeared. Ludwig had no idea who they were, but one of them carried an important-looking flag bearing a coat of arms.

Baron Stein obviously had no such trouble, straightening his back as soon as he spotted them. "My lord," he said. "What brings you to Regnitz?"

"What's going on here?" one of the newcomers demanded.

It was Hagan who supplied the answer. "Lord Anwald," he began. "My father has just captured Regnitz Keep."

Anwald looked like he was going to explode. "You what?"

"My son speaks the truth," said Lord Gebhard. "We have captured Regnitz."

"You will be lucky to retain your title after this," said Anwald. "I rode all the way to Mulsingen to tell you to raise your army, Stein, and what do you think I found?"

"To raise my army?"

"Yes, you fool. Erlingen is under threat of invasion, and here I find you're doing the work of the enemy! You've not only weakened your own forces on this ridiculous scheme of yours, but those of Lord Wulfram as well!"

Baron Stein was utterly taken aback. "But I had no idea, my lord."

"By the Saints, man, you're lucky I don't send you to the axeman."

"What can I do to make it up to His Grace?"

"You can start by releasing Wulfram."

Ludwig watched Lord Gebhard struggle with the decision. It was clear he hated doing it, but his loyalty to his duke was obviously greater than his desire to punish his rival.

Baron Stein turned on his men. "Release him," he snapped.

Lord Wulfram rose, then bowed to Lord Anwald. "Thank you, my lord."

"Don't thank me yet. There's much work to be done." Anwald returned his attention to Stein. "Assemble your troops, Baron. Your duke needs you."

"Of course," said Lord Gebhard. "To where do we march?"

"Torburg, and let's hope we're not too late."

"It's that serious?"

"I left the capital a week and a half ago, and at that time, we'd heard Andover was massing at the border. I pray this little sideshow of yours has not cost us too much time."

"And how may I serve?" asked Lord Wulfram.

"Do what you must here, then meet us in Torburg."

"I have only a few men left, my lord."

"Even a dozen is better than none," said Anwald. "It may very well make the difference between victory and disaster."

Lord Anwald looked around the courtyard. "Who are all these men? They don't look like yours, Stein?"

"They are mercenaries, my lord."

"Good. Bring them with you when you march."

"They are expensive, my lord."

"I'm sure His Grace, the duke, will compensate you for your investment," said Anwald. "Now, get your men moving. I want them on the road before nightfall."

Baron Stein bowed deeply. "Of course, Lord."

Lord Wulfram moved to his daughter, holding her in an embrace.

Ludwig wandered over, eager to have words with the man. "My lord," he started. "I would seek release from the terms of our agreement."

"I will gladly give it," replied Baron Haas. "You are an honourable man, Ludwig. I would be proud to have you in my service."

Rosalyn whispered something in her father's ear, and his face lit up. "What a marvellous idea," he said, turning to Ludwig. "You've proven yourself to be a man of exceptional qualities. Would you consider leading my troops, few as they are?"

Ludwig was overcome with emotion. "I…"

"Give him time, Father," said Rosalyn.

"Yes, of course," said the baron. "Please, take all the time you like."

"I would welcome the opportunity," said Ludwig, "but I fear I am still employed by the Grim Defenders."

"You can forget that," called out Sigwulf. "Captain Ecke struck you from the roster right after you were captured."

"Yes," added Cyn. "You can't really blame the man. After all, everyone thought you dead."

"Well, now," said Lord Wulfram. "It appears that impediment has been removed. What do you say, my young friend? Will you lead my men?"

"I'm flattered," said Ludwig. "I shall be happy to do my part to help repel the invasion, but eventually, I'd like to return home to Verfeld. I can hardly do that if I'm in service to a lord."

"Then serve me now, and when this war is over, I shall release you from your oath."

"In that case, my lord, I'd be honoured to lead your contingent."

"Good," said Lord Wulfram. "Now, someone give me a sword."

"My lord?" said Ludwig.

The baron looked around. "Anyone?"

Sigwulf stepped forward, drawing his blade. "Will this one do, Your Lordship?"

Wulfram smiled, taking the sword and holding it up to examine the hilt. "A fine weapon. Might I ask where you acquired it?"

"On the coast," said Sigwulf, "quite some distance from here."

The baron turned to Ludwig. "Kneel."

"My lord?"

"He said kneel," said Cyn. "He can't very well knight you if you're standing."

"Sure he can," said Sigwulf.

"You stay out of this," she replied.

Ludwig looked at Lord Wulfram in surprise. "Knighted? Me?"

"You've certainly earned it," said the baron.

"Very well." Ludwig knelt, bowing his head.

Lord Wulfram moved closer, holding the sword to his front and speaking in a loud, clear voice. "Gather all, and bear witness this day."

Lord Gebhard glared from across the courtyard, but his mercenaries and a good number of his own household warriors drew near to watch the proceedings.

"Since the days of our forefathers, we have bestowed titles and accolades on those who we deem worthy. The greatest of these has been that of knight: a warrior sworn to uphold the ideals of chivalry and honourable combat." He paused, letting the words sink in.

Ludwig kept staring at the ground, his heart feeling as though it would burst from his chest.

"As a noble sworn to the service of Lord Deiter Heinrich, Duke of Erlingen, I am empowered to award such titles and honorifics as I deem suitable. Normally, such rewards would be more fitting for a time of celebration, but due to the constraints of time and the threat of invasion lingering on our borders, I shall make an exception."

He placed the blade flat on Ludwig's right shoulder.

"Do you promise to be brave and upright that the Saints may look down on you with favour?"

"I do," said Ludwig.

"And will you always speak the truth," continued Lord Wulfram, "even if it leads to your death?"

"I shall."

"Do you swear to protect those who cannot protect themselves and to serve your lord faithfully until he releases you from your vows?"

"I do so swear."

"Then by the power invested in me by the Duke of Erlingen, I dub thee Knight of the Sceptre. Arise, Sir Ludwig of Verfeld."

Ludwig rose, overwhelmed by the ceremony. Lord Wulfram took his hand, giving him a heartfelt handshake.

"Congratulations," he said. "You've earned it." He looked around the courtyard, noticing the others nearby. "I'll let you talk to your friends now. Come and see me when you're done. We have work to do."

"Yes, my lord."

The baron backed up, taking his daughter's hand and leading her away. Cyn was the first one to congratulate him, giving him a lingering hug. She then held him at arm's length.

"Look at you," she said. "A real knight. Who would have believed it?"

Next in line was Sigwulf. He put out his massive hand, but Cyn gave him a light shove. "Not your hand," she said. "He's family. You're supposed to hug him."

The sergeant moved in close, awkwardly placing his arms around Ludwig, who returned the motion. They patted each other's back, then withdrew, both looking slightly embarrassed by the display of affection.

Cyn looked at Sigwulf. "Really? Is that the best you can do?"

He cleared his throat. "We have work to do."

"Very well." She winked at Ludwig, then followed Siggy to where the rest of the company was gathering.

Ludwig noted another's approach and turned to see someone in the livery of Lord Gebhard. It wasn't until the man spoke that he realized it was Karl Dornhuffer.

"Congratulations, Sir Ludwig, and well deserved if I may say so."

"Thank you," said Ludwig.

"It looks like we've both had a rewarding day."

"Oh? Why is that?"

"After the losses here at the keep, the baron promoted me to sergeant."

Ludwig smiled. "My compliments to you. Keep up the good work."

"I only wish it had been under different circumstances. I don't know what possessed the baron to go after Lord Wulfram."

Ludwig held up his hand. "Don't worry over things you can't control, my friend. You must pride yourself on doing your duty. That's all anyone can ask in the long run."

Dornhuffer smiled. "Perhaps I'll see you on the battlefield? It would be nice to fight alongside you, instead of against."

"I didn't fight for Lord Wulfram," Ludwig insisted.

"Of course you didn't," the sergeant replied with a smile. "Just as I didn't tell you about the warriors moss."

Ludwig laughed. "I'm glad we're on the same side."

"As am I." Dornhuffer glanced over his shoulder. "It looks like the baron's men are almost ready to march. Good luck, Sir Ludwig."

"And the same to you, Sergeant."

Ludwig watched as the man rejoined his new command. Soon afterwards, they marched off, passing through the gatehouse. The new knight looked around the courtyard, noting the damage. It would take months of work to repair the walls, and the top of the keep was in a frightful mess. Exactly how long he would be stuck here, he had no idea. As if reading his mind, Rosalyn approached, halting before him and curtsying.

"Sir Ludwig," she began, "may I offer my congratulations?"

"Thank you," said Ludwig, "and the same to you."

"To me? For what?"

"It would appear you have escaped the fate you so feared. Master Hagan has left, and you shall never have to see him again."

She gazed at the gatehouse to where the last of Baron Stein's troops were making their way southward. "I must admit Master Hagan was not quite what I expected."

"Don't tell me that after all you've been through, you're changing your mind about him?"

"I never had an opinion on him," she defended. "Remember, we were never acquainted."

"And now?"

She smiled. "He's very different from his father. Are you sure they're related?"

Ludwig laughed. "I only know what I'm told, although you must admit they bear a remarkable similarity from a physical point of view."

"You never told me he had manners."

"You never asked. I can't read your mind, Rosalyn."

She chuckled, and for the first time in weeks, it didn't sound forced. "It appears your Saints watched over us after all."

"My Saints?"

"You're the one who doesn't believe in fate. How else would you explain all of this?"

He looked around one more time, shaking his head at all the damage. "I don't mind the Saints interfering," he said, "but maybe next time they could do so BEFORE the place is completely destroyed."

"Come now, it's hardly destroyed," said Rosalyn. "Admittedly, the wall needs some work."

"And the keep," added Ludwig.

"Yes, all right, the keep as well." Her mood sobered. "I think the truly tragic thing about all of this is all the needless deaths."

"Let's not fool ourselves. Conflict leads to death. I'm afraid there's no way around it." He gazed skyward, possibly seeking some kind of sign.

"What is it?"

He brought his eyes back to hers. "There'll be plenty of fighting in the coming days, my lady. I'm afraid where the army marches, death will follow."

She reached out, touching him on the forearm. "Then I pray it shall not be yours."

29

COMMAND

Summer 1095 SR

L udwig stood atop what was left of the curtain wall, gazing off to the south.

"Your friends are well on their way," offered Lord Wulfram.

"Yes," agreed Ludwig. "I'm surprised Baron Stein kept them on the payroll. I imagine that was quite the expense."

"It is, but Gebhard is attempting to curry favour. More troops means more influence with the duke."

"Is influence so easily bought?"

Wulfram barked out a laugh. "No. Lord Deiter is not a man easily swayed, so it's most likely the other nobles who Stein's trying to impress. He's always thought of himself as a great man."

"He didn't look too happy about the arrival of the marshal."

"And why would he be? He'd just had victory snatched from his grasp. It'll take some time to get over that."

"Lord Gebhard has around two hundred men if you include the mercenaries. How does that compare to the other nobles of Erlingen?"

"About average, I would presume. The duchy is divided into twelve baronies, with a smattering of baronets thrown in for good measure."

"We don't have those in Hadenfeld," said Ludwig. "How do they work?"

"They're similar to knights but are hereditary titles. A baronet typically has a much smaller domain than a baron."

"Does that mean they're addressed as sir, or lord?"

"As sir. In a sense, they're not true nobles, and the duke certainly doesn't consider them as such."

"Then why have them?"

Lord Wulfram looked at him in surprise. "To look after the land, of course. There are many small villages and hamlets that are far too remote to rule efficiently from afar. Mind you, most of the men who are made into baronets are mere courtiers, so I suppose you could say it's used to reward the duke's followers."

"It seems like a waste of time to me."

"It's the way of things, I'm afraid."

"But it doesn't have to be," said Ludwig. "The duke could use them to effect change."

The baron smiled. "There you go, thinking again. It's an admirable trait, my young friend, but your energy is better spent on things you can affect, like my soldiers."

"Of course, I was merely—"

"Thinking. Yes, I know. Now, I've had what's left of the men assemble by the gatehouse. I would suggest you get down there and see what you can make of them. After all, you'll be marching them to the duke's aid."

"Don't you need some here?"

"I have decided to form a militia for that exact purpose."

"Won't you need people for that?"

"Yes, I will," said Wulfram, "but I've called in locals from the countryside. They're also going to help rebuild the wall, although that will take months. Your immediate concern, however, is looking after that bunch." He pointed towards the gatehouse.

Ludwig saw a sorry-looking collection of men, tired and hungry, the result of being on half rations for weeks on end, but they represented his first command.

"Well, don't just stand there," said the baron. "Get down there and get to work, Sir Ludwig."

Ludwig smiled. "Yes, my lord."

He walked along the curtain wall, heading for the stairs. All of his life, he had read of knights and armies, yet now, confronted with his own small command, he suddenly felt overwhelmed. Here he was, a man of only twenty-six years of age, trying to lead a group of seasoned veterans. Would they see through his bravado? He was determined to put on his best face.

Down the stairs he went, his footsteps echoing into the courtyard. The men, who milled about in a knot, looked up at his approach. Ludwig recognized most of them, for it was hard not to after spending so much time confined to the keep, but although he knew their faces, he did not yet know all their names.

"All right," he started. "Get into a line so I can have a look at you."

They shuffled into the semblance of a line, and Ludwig began examining them one at a time. They were, for the most part, well equipped. The foot soldiers had padded gambesons and kettle helmets along with a motley collection of swords, axes, and even a mace or two. Of the two dozen present, only six were archers, but their bows looked to be in good repair from what he could tell.

"Let's get you bowmen together over there," Ludwig said, pointing. He waited for them to move, then returned his attention to the footmen. "Do you have shields?"

"We do," replied an older man standing to his front, "but they're in the keep. Not much point in carrying them at the moment."

"Fair enough. Are you trained in spears?"

"To some degree."

"Have you a sergeant?"

"He died in the assault, sir."

"Then I'll promote you to sergeant. What's your name?"

"Krebbs, sir."

"Very well, Sergeant Krebbs it will be. How long have you served the baron?"

"Getting on twenty years, sir."

"Then you know these men well?"

The new sergeant grinned. "Better than I know myself, sir."

"Good. I'll expect you to name your successor come nightfall."

"My successor, sir?"

"Yes, the man who'd replace you should you fall. We can't have the men leaderless."

"And what do we call him, sir?"

"I suppose deputy sergeant will have to do."

"And will that involve more pay, sir?"

Ludwig was caught off guard, for pay was something he hadn't considered. "That's beyond my authority," he replied, "but I shall bring it to the attention of the baron."

"All right, sir."

"Follow me, Sergeant, while I inspect the other men."

"Inspect, sir?"

"Yes. We need to make sure everyone's equipment is up to scratch."

"I'm not sure I follow?"

"It's simple, really. Weapons become damaged, gambesons torn, so we need to make sure any repairs are complete before we march."

"Understood, sir."

Ludwig made his way down the line, looking over each one. The weapons were all in fine shape, a sign that these warriors knew their business. There were some rents in armour and tears in their gambesons, but nothing that couldn't be quickly dealt with.

As he reached the end of the footmen, he turned to Krebbs. "Have the men fetch their shields, Sergeant."

"To what end, sir?"

"I'd like you to pair them up and have them practice with their chosen weapons." He turned to the men. "I don't care what weapon you use in melee," he said, "so long as you know how to use it. For battle, you will be armed with spears, but once contact is made with the enemy, it may be necessary to discard them in favour of something else. That choice will be up to you."

One of the men held up his hand, and Ludwig spotted his new sergeant rolling his eyes.

"Not now, Arturo," said Krebbs.

Ludwig ignored the remark, looking instead at the man in line. "Yes?"

"Begging your pardon, sir, but why do we need spears? They're awfully awkward to carry."

"You'll be thankful for them when enemy horsemen approach."

"I doubt I'd be able to do much damage with a stick."

The other men chuckled.

"You don't attack with them," explained Ludwig. "Rather, you plant the butt in the ground and hold the tip out. It keeps the horses at bay. Have you never learned such things?"

Arturo looked at his fellow soldiers. "Prior to the attack here, few of us have ever been in a battle, sir."

"I thought you all veterans?"

"No, sir," said Krebbs, "although most have served the baron for years."

Ludwig felt light-headed. He had assumed these were seasoned warriors, but it now appeared he had vastly overestimated their capabilities. How, then, could he whip them into shape?

He turned to Krebbs. "Take the men to the armoury. I want each one back here with a shield and spear. I'll lead the training myself."

"Training, sir?"

"Yes, I'm going to show you lot how to properly use a spear."

"Don't you just poke the sharp end into the enemy?" suggested Arturo.

Ludwig smiled, pondering his own training under the tutelage of Kurt

Wasser. He wondered what his old mentor was up to these days, a recollection that was soon spoiled by the sergeant's cough.

"Shall I dismiss the men, sir?" asked Krebbs.

"Yes, but leave the archers here. I have yet to take their measure."

"Yes, sir."

Krebbs led the foot soldiers away as Ludwig walked over to the archers.

"I remember you," he said. "You were on the top of the keep."

"I was, sir. The name's Simmons."

Ludwig looked over the small group. "I must admit I'm not much of an archer, so I'll let your skill impress me. Have you any targets?"

"We do."

"Good. Set them up on the field between the keep and the village."

"Range, sir?" asked Simmons.

"I suspect a hundred paces would be a good indication of your skill, wouldn't you?"

"Yes, sir."

"Good, then make it so. Before you go, however, what do you carry for melee?"

"We're archers, sir," said Simmons. "We don't mix it up with footmen."

"True, but there's always the possibility the enemy might not co-operate. For that reason, we should always be prepared. Let each man carry a hatchet or short sword, depending on their preference, along with a knife. I'm sure the armoury will have any weapons you lack. Any questions?"

The men all looked at him, eagerness in their eyes.

"Very well, then. I'll see you on the archery range."

He watched them go, wondering if he should appoint them a sergeant of their own, but with only six of them, it would be an exorbitant cost for the baron. Instead, he decided he would let Krebbs take care of them.

The footmen were the first to assemble. Ludwig led them out in double file, crossing the drawbridge to enter the field beyond. A couple of his archers were struggling to set up a target to the east, so he led his footmen west, giving them ample space to manoeuvre. Finally, he called a halt, then took a spear from his new sergeant.

"This," Ludwig said by way of introduction, "is your first defence from charging horsemen." He drove the butt into the ground, angling the point away from him. "The trick is to anchor the end. Do that, and it'll keep the riders at bay. Trust me when I say no rider wants to bring his mount into a wall of spear tips. Of course, it works better when there's more of them."

"How many more?" asked Arturo.

"Ideally, enough for two ranks, but with our numbers, we'll only form one. After all, there's not much point in forming a line if the enemy can simply ride around you."

"Can't they do that, anyway?"

"They can, but that's where your allies come in. Remember, you won't be alone on the battlefield. There'll be troops on either side of you doing the same thing."

Ludwig hefted the spear, holding it up. "You first, Arturo. Let's see what you're made of."

Arturo nervously stepped forward.

"Sling your shield for now," said Ludwig. "We'll work on that later." He handed over the weapon, then pointed south. "Imagine the enemy is coming from that direction. Now plant your butt."

The men all laughed. "That's what my missus says," came a voice.

Ludwig chuckled. The men were in good spirits. Surprising, given the circumstances, but a good sign nonetheless.

"Like this?" asked Arturo.

Ludwig made a slight correction to the man's grip. "That's it. Now keep it steady." He walked to the front, then grasped the end of the spear right below the tip and pushed with all his might. Satisfied with the result, he looked back at his men. "As you can see, the spear is immovable. The placement is important. If the weapon slips, it could let a horseman through, and that would be the death of all of you. Now, the rest of you come forward and take up positions on either side. Let's see if we can't form a wall of spears."

They shambled forward, taking their time and examining Arturo's pose before settling into their own. Ludwig waited as they each took up their positions, then moved down the line, testing every spear as he went.

"Good," he said. "You've got the right idea. Now, in battle, things can happen quickly, so you'll have to be faster. Let's have you return to your previous position. When I give the command, I want you to form a line and set your spears. Are we clear?"

They all nodded. To Ludwig, this was like teaching children some new sort of game, but who was he to complain? In the end, this simple manoeuvre could make the difference between life and death.

"Set spears!" he called out.

The men formed line, but several struggled to find their place.

Sergeant Krebbs palmed his face. "This is never going to work."

"I see the problem," said Ludwig. "The men need to know where to stand. Let's line everyone up, tallest on your right."

They began moving around.

"Your other right," called out Krebbs. "By the Saints, I swear half these men don't even know their foot from their hand." He stepped forward, cajoling the men into place.

"Now," said Ludwig, "say hello to your new neighbours. From now on, whenever you line up, those same men should be on either side."

He watched as the soldiers shook hands and chatted amiably.

"Let's spread you out a bit, shall we?" He picked four men at random. "You four, move over that way."

He waited as they drifted over, then turned his back to the troops. Moments later, he turned around abruptly. "Set spears!"

The men rushed into line. They still fidgeted, and one or two had to change their position when they realized they were in the wrong place, but they were getting better at it.

"They're doing well," said Ludwig. "I want you to keep at them for a while longer, Sergeant. Do the same thing I did, mix them up, then have them form line. Ideally, they should be ready within, say, a count of ten?"

"Yes, sir," said Krebbs. "And where will you be, sir?"

"Over with the archers. I have yet to see what we've got to work with. They're in your hands now, so do me proud."

Ludwig felt altogether pleased with himself as he walked over to the archers. There was, of course, much more work to do than simply setting spears, but the men had responded well, and better yet, they appeared eager to learn, something he hadn't counted on.

The bowmen had set up three targets made of coiled straw placed on simple tripod stands. The archers themselves had already started loosing their arrows, taking time to line up each pull of the bow before letting go.

Ludwig watched them as they displayed their skills, having never developed a taste for it himself. Indeed, many nobles felt an aversion to the weapon, but it was considered essential on the battlefield, and there was no doubt these archers could hit a target. The real question was how effective they would be on the battlefield.

He waved them over. "Gather round," he called out. "Let's have a chat."

They were soon before him, curious as to what he might say. "You're good with target practice," he began, "but in battle, when the enemy is breathing down your necks, it'll be speed that's most important."

"Don't we need to hit the target?" asked one.

"You do, but when a mass of footmen is approaching, there'll be little chance of missing. In that situation, you'll want to empty your quiver as quickly as possible. Now, what I'd like you to do is form a line up along here"—he pointed along the ground—"facing the targets."

He waited as they took their places. "I want you to loose off three arrows in quick succession. The first you'll discharge on my command, with the others following as fast as you can manage."

"Ready bows," Ludwig called out, then drew his sword and raised it on high. All eyes were on him, not an easy thing as they had the bowstrings pulled all the way back to their cheeks.

"Loose," he shouted as his sword swung down.

The arrows flew downrange, each hitting its target. The next volley was ragged and less accurate, the third even more so.

Ludwig nodded in appreciation. "Good. Recover your arrows, and we'll try again. Let's see if we can't do a little better this time."

They repeated the exercise five times, each time getting a little faster. Ludwig couldn't help but smile, for the men's enthusiasm was infectious.

"All right, now follow me." He led them over to the footmen, who appeared to be doing well under the tutelage of Krebbs. On noticing his commander's approach, the sergeant turned, bowing his head slightly in recognition.

"Right," said Ludwig, struggling to decide on the next step. He thought back to his own experiences with the Grim Defenders, and everything fell into place. "You've done well so far today," he said. "We'll finish things off with a march."

"A march?" said Krebbs.

"Yes, we'll take the men around the keep."

"In the courtyard, sir?"

"No," said Ludwig. "We'll circle the perimeter from the outside."

"That's a considerable distance."

"Yes it is, but it's nothing compared to what the men will have to do to reach Torburg. Trust me when I tell you, you don't want to undertake such a trip unprepared."

"How would you like to proceed, sir?"

"Form up into twos and have them stay that way as we walk. Oh, and bring those spears and shields. We'll do a little more practice as we march."

A groan escaped one of the men.

"You may dislike it now," said Ludwig, "but come time for battle, you'll wish we'd done more." He set off at a brisk pace.

30

WARRIOR'S MARCH

Summer 1095 SR

Two days later, they were on the move. Each man was issued a loaf of bread and a bag of oats, not exactly enough food to see them through to Torburg, but better than Ludwig had expected.

To temper this, the baron had provided Ludwig with funds with which to purchase food, but it was unlikely there would be much left after the passing of Baron Stein's army. He had also been promised the duke would see to provisions once they were in the capital. The real trick would be to get there in one piece. With this in mind, Ludwig had convinced the archers to load up with some broad-head arrows in addition to their bodkins, the better to hunt if given a chance.

It was a risky idea, for technically, hunting the duke's deer was considered poaching, but Ludwig thought it unlikely to cause offence, considering these men would soon be under the command of the ducal army.

They set out under clear weather, with what remained of the village turned out to see them off. Ludwig thought this would be a send-off to fill the men with pride, but instead, the looks of dismay from the wives and children caused a lump to form in his throat. This was no game, he reminded himself, but the lives of living, breathing men.

He found himself praying. "Give me strength, Saint Mathew, that I might bring these men safely back to their loved ones."

Sergeant Krebbs, who was marching at his side, looked over at him. "Did you say something, sir?"

"No," replied Ludwig. "I was just thinking aloud."

"If you say so." The sergeant paused a moment before continuing. "Shouldn't you be mounted? You are a knight after all."

"Look at me. I scarcely have any armour, let alone a horse."

"But you were born a noble, weren't you? At least that's what the men say."

"Yes, a baron's son," admitted Ludwig. "And yes, before you ask, I once had nice armour and a horse, but I was foolish and lost most of it in a tournament."

"I bet that was a sight to see."

"Have you ever seen a tourney?"

"No," said Krebbs, "I've never been more than a couple of days travel from Regnitz."

"Then you've never seen the capital?"

"No, but I hear it's quite the place."

Ludwig glanced back at his men, noting the sad faces. "Tell me, Sergeant, do you have a wife?"

"Me? No, though I did come close once."

"Ah, I sense an interesting story."

"Not as interesting as you might imagine, sir. She married another."

"And there's been no one since?"

The sergeant blushed. "Well, I wouldn't say no one, but definitely not a wife, and not for lack of trying either."

"Oh? You must tell me more."

"She runs the tavern in the village."

"Really?" said Ludwig. "I didn't see anyone while I was there."

"No, you wouldn't have, would you? Most of the villagers fled when the word came of the approaching army. Some got inside the keep, but others ran into the countryside."

"Is that where your sweetheart went?"

"It was," said the sergeant with a wistful smile. "That's my Agneth."

"Agneth? Don't you mean Agnes?"

"It's the same name, but in the ancient tongue."

"How ancient?"

"They say it dates back to the old kingdom," said Krebbs. "Whatever that means."

"There was a kingdom here before the duchy?"

"Saints, no, that was centuries ago. No, it was those grey-eyed heathens who lived in these parts back then."

"The Therengians?" said Ludwig.

"Aye, that's them."

"Now you have my attention. Lord Wulfram indicated some still lived here in Erlingen. Are there many in Regnitz?"

"A few, maybe one in ten. You can't wipe out an entire people, sir, but a lot of them married outside their race, thinning out the bloodline. Although many still have the grey eyes."

"I thought they were feared?"

Krebbs shrugged. "Not by the common folk. The nobles, on the other hand..."

"What about the nobles?" asked Ludwig.

"I gather they're worried they might come back."

"What do you mean, 'come back'? Where have they gone?"

"I haven't the faintest, but every couple of years, the duke's men come round looking for anyone with grey eyes."

"To what end?"

"It's the mark of the old race."

"And what do they do when they find them? Arrest them?"

"Saints, no," said the sergeant. "They only take their names."

"I still don't see why?"

"I'm told they're not allowed to hold any position of power or influence," explained Krebbs. "Not that there's any need for it back in Regnitz. We haven't any positions for people to hold."

"And other than these grey eyes, they are exactly like the rest of us?"

"They are, but like I said, the duke gets worried about such things. This used to be part of their kingdom after all."

"I've heard as much. I always knew it used to lay somewhere within the Petty Kingdoms, but I never realized how close that was. You know, at its height, it was supposed to be unbeatable."

Krebbs laughed. "If that were true, they'd still be around. No, they were men, sir. Nothing more, nothing less."

"Still, it's interesting to speculate we might be treading the same ground they did."

The sergeant shrugged. "It means little to me."

"Is that why you haven't married this woman of yours, Agneth, wasn't it? Because of her eyes?"

"No, it's because I couldn't afford to keep her."

"I thought you said she owned the tavern?"

"She does."

"Then what's the problem? Does she not earn enough for the both of you?"

"That's just it, don't you see? A man wants to provide for his woman."

Ludwig laughed. "I expect you'll find that matters little to her. In any case, you're a sergeant now, and that comes with a substantial pay increase."

Krebbs broke out into a broad grin. "I suppose it does. I didn't think of that."

"There you go, another problem solved. Now, if only the enemy would be so accommodating."

That evening they camped by the side of the road but not before Ludwig led them through some more manoeuvres. He was determined to see them adequately trained by the time they arrived in Torburg, and so this was to become the regular routine after a day of marching. The next morning they set out early, eager to put as many miles behind them as they could.

He sent the archers out to either side in hopes of finding some game, and by evening, they had a pair of hares to supplement their meagre meal. It wasn't much, split as it was amongst two dozen men, but it certainly helped.

On the third day, they passed the keep at Mulsingen, Lord Gebhard's ancestral home. The mood was sour as they marched by, and Ludwig kept a close eye on them, lest they wander off and seek reparations against the baron's property.

The next day, he called for a day of rest. The men, unused to the marching, were most thankful for the break, and the bowmen managed to bring down a deer. That night, for the first time in weeks, they had full bellies.

A few days later, they came to a crossroads, along with a sign declaring Torburg was only some forty miles distant. After a brief rest, they continued on their way, following the road to the northwest. It was well travelled, which indicated the city was prospering, leading Sergeant Krebbs to become exceedingly loquacious.

"I hear the city is big," he said. "You've been there. What's it like, sir?"

"Much like Regnitz," replied Ludwig, "but with more buildings squeezed in together."

"I can't wait to see it."

"The first thing you'll notice is the smell, but you'll soon grow used to it."

"The smell?"

"Yes, it stinks because all their refuse is thrown into the streets. You can't go more than a dozen paces without stepping in something. Mind you, I doubt we'll be staying in the city itself. We'll likely be camped on the tournament field."

"Oh, yes?" said Krebbs. "And where's that?"

"To the south of the city. Don't worry, you'll be able to see all the buildings, just not up close."

"And will we have time to visit the place while we're there, sir?"

"That depends entirely on what the duke intends to do. I doubt we'll sit still for long. Then again, the army might have already marched, in which case we'll have to move quickly to catch up."

"Do you suppose the army will be large?"

"I have no idea. I've read all about them, but I'm afraid I have little practical experience."

"Nor me," said Krebbs. "But don't worry, sir, you're more than up to the task."

"What makes you say that?"

"The men look up to you, sir. You fought for the baron when all looked lost. They don't forget things like that. We might all die in battle, but none of these poor sods will regret marching with you, of that, you can be sure."

"Thank you... I think?" said Ludwig. "I'm still trying to understand if that's a good thing or not."

"Trust me, sir. It's good. There's only a handful of men who can inspire that kind of devotion, and you're one of them."

"They've hardly known me for long," protested Ludwig.

"True, but they know what you did, and if Lord Wulfram's willing to take you into his service, you must be good."

"Good? That's an interesting word."

"How so, sir?"

"It's completely subject to interpretation. Take our enemy, for example."

"You mean Lord Gebhard?"

Ludwig laughed. "No, I mean our neighbour, Andover. They're the ones who are threatening invasion. Do you suppose they see themselves as evil?"

Krebbs shrugged. "No, I suppose not."

"No, of course they don't. In their minds, they're the good ones, although why they're invading is beyond me."

"It's politics, sir. Beyond the understanding of simple folk like me."

"Who told you that?"

"No one," said Krebbs. "I just assumed. After all, such things are of little interest to commoners. It's not as if we can affect the outcome."

"Ah," said Ludwig, "but you are, don't you see? It's men like you who are marching to the duke's aid. Without you, there can be no army."

The sergeant straightened his back. "Well, I suppose, when you put it like that..."

"Never underestimate your own importance, Sergeant, and never take your men for granted."

"My men? Don't you mean the baron's?"

"These men are under our command at the moment. That makes them our responsibility."

"I suppose that's true," admitted Krebbs. "Tell me, sir, is the baron joining us at some point?"

"He is, as a matter of fact. He was due to set out three or four days after us, though, of course, I don't know if he stuck to that schedule. After all, he did have a lot of things to see to before he left."

"We'll have to keep an eye out for him in Torburg, then."

"That's the spirit, Sergeant."

The road they were now on saw far more traffic than that which led to Regnitz. As a consequence, it was not unusual to meet others along the way, typically merchants or the odd farmer. However, what they did not expect to see was a trio of warriors coming towards them wearing Lord Gebhard's livery.

Ludwig slowed the pace. "What's this, now?"

"I don't like the look of this," noted Krebbs.

As they approached, Ludwig noted the condition of their clothes. "They look like they've been living rough." When they were within a dozen paces, he called out, "You there! Where's your master?"

The trio looked up suddenly, as if only now realizing they were not alone. Their next action clearly explained their presence as they rushed into a nearby field.

"After them!" shouted Ludwig. "They're deserters!"

As his own men chased them, Ludwig caught the attention of one of his archers as he ran past. "Simmons, string your bow."

He watched his men scrambling across the field with an air of excitement, encouraged by the fact these were Baron Stein's men they were chasing after. He doubted they would be caught unscathed, for Lord Wulfram's men had suffered much during the siege, but Ludwig consoled himself that they had earned it.

Two of the deserters went down as they were caught, but the third, more fleet of foot, increased his lead.

Ludwig turned to Simmons. The young man had strung his bow and was notching an arrow. "Hit that man, and there's a coin in it for you."

The archer took his time, gauging the wind and leading his target. Ludwig was ready to complain about the delay, and then the arrow sailed forth, arcing into the air to then come down and take the deserter in the shoulder. The man gave a yell and dropped to his knees, clutching his wound and groaning in agony.

"That'll teach ya," shouted Simmons.

The rest of the men soon caught up to the fellow, dragging him to his feet and holding him steady until Ludwig reached them.

"Do we string him up?" asked Wahlman, one of the archers holding the prisoner's arms.

"No," replied Ludwig. "This man must be taken to Torburg, along with the other two. It's not our place to mete out punishment here. Rather, it is for their lord and master to decide."

"Tie him up," ordered Krebbs, "and let's get back to the road."

"What about his wound?" asked Wahlman.

Ludwig gazed at the prisoner, recognizing the defiance in his eyes. "Pull the arrow out," he ordered, "then bind the wound as best you can."

Krebbs looked at him in shock. "You can't do that, sir."

"Why's that?"

"The arrow didn't go all the way through. If we pull it out now, it'll likely do more damage than when it hit."

"What do you suggest?" asked Ludwig.

"It has to be cut out, sir, and carefully at that. I heard of a man who was shot in the leg. They got the arrow out, but it did such frightful damage being extracted that he lost the limb."

"Did he survive?"

"Only for a few days, then the stump turned sour."

Ludwig shuddered. "Well, we can't have that, can we?"

"We could always hang him."

"Kill him? Isn't that a bit extreme?"

"They'll hang him in Torburg anyway, sir. That's the punishment for desertion."

"I'll not have his blood on my hands."

Krebbs frowned. "But you already do, don't you see, sir? That happened the moment you chose to intervene."

Ludwig's heart raced. His impetuous action had now led him to a point where he must determine the fate of three men. This was not soldiering, far from it, in fact. He tried to envisage what his father, the baron, would do, and the answer came to him immediately. This was a duty he couldn't shirk, no matter how unpleasant it was. He looked around. All he saw were faces staring back at him in expectation.

"Very well," he finally said, "but I will allow each condemned man to speak in their own defence. We'll take them over there, beneath the trees. It will at least offer some respite from the heat. Bring the prisoners, Sergeant."

"Yes, sir," said Krebbs. His men bound the prisoners' arms, eliciting cries of pain from the injured man, then led them to the indicated spot.

Ludwig had the sergeant bring forward one prisoner at a time, but there was little they could say in their own defence. The injured man broke down, confessing to a multitude of sins, including the desertion. It appeared Lord Gebhard's men were not happy that their victory had been snatched from them at Regnitz. The injured deserter's pleas for mercy were lost on the men of Lord Wulfram, but Ludwig let him ramble on, determined not to curtail the last words of a man sentenced to death.

The other two were far less co-operative, choosing instead to remain mute, but it mattered little, for they were condemned by the confession of their wounded comrade.

A lump formed in Ludwig's throat as he pronounced sentence, and he had to pause a moment to calm himself. Once done, he now faced the prospect of how to actually carry out the sentences. He turned to his sergeant.

"How shall I execute them?" he asked. "By the sword?"

"Saints, no," said Krebbs. "These are commoners, sir, not nobles. They have to be hanged."

"We have no rope."

The sergeant cast his eyes about, finally resting on a distant farmhouse. "They'll likely have some over yonder, sir."

Ludwig dug into the small purse Lord Wulfram had given him. "Here," he said, handing over some coins. "Take two men and offer some coins in exchange for a length of rope. I'm sure you know how much we'll need."

"Of course, sir."

Ludwig watched them go, feeling numb. One of the prisoners was openly weeping now, and Ludwig felt brittle inside as if his very soul would snap like a twig. He came closer, kneeling before the condemned.

"Shall I say a prayer for you?"

The crying man nodded his head, as did the injured one, but his unwounded comrade remained defiant in the face of imminent death.

"Let us pray," said Ludwig, lowering his head. He interlocked his fingers and shut his eyes. "Saint Mathew, look down upon us this day. Here stands before you, three men condemned to death. I pray you forgive them their sins and guide them to everlasting peace in the Afterlife." The words felt so inadequate, yet they helped soothe Ludwig's own wounded heart. Did Saint Mathew truly look down on him? He found it hard to believe, yet the very thought of it gave him comfort.

"Saints be with you." As he concluded his prayer, he felt a warmth spread through him, an inner peace he couldn't explain.

"Saints be with us all," the three men repeated.

Ludwig glanced at the defiant one, only to see the fire of rebellion had finally been extinguished. In its place was only resignation.

Ludwig rose. "The road to the Afterlife is a long one. I would see you fed before you begin the trip." Into his own pack he went, extracting some of his food. This he passed amongst the condemned men, watching as they greedily consumed it.

By late afternoon the sergeant returned with the rope, then the nooses were formed, and the prisoners were hanged. Ludwig had seen a number of executions in his lifetime. After all, in Verfeld, it was the baron's responsibility to enforce the king's justice. Hanging to him had always seemed a quick and efficient method to end a man's life, but today, without an experienced executioner, the men dangled, kicking wildly as they slowly choked to death.

Ludwig felt his stomach rebel at the scene but managed to keep his food down long enough for the spectacle to conclude.

"Cut them down," he ordered through gritted teeth.

"Sir?" asked Krebbs.

"You heard me."

"They're deserters, sir. The practice is to leave them hanging as a sign to others."

Ludwig stared at the dangling bodies. "There's no one here to see them, Sergeant. The road is too distant. Let us put the bodies into the earth that they may not be food for the crows."

"I'll take care of it, sir."

Ludwig left the sergeant to his business, making his way deeper into the woods. Behind him, the men began digging with makeshift tools, but the sounds soon faded into the background, buried by the chirp of birds and the hum of insects. Ludwig leaned against a tree, and then the contents of his stomach finally heaved to the surface.

31

RETURN TO TORBURG

Summer 1095 SR

T he march into Torburg continued in silence. The executions had put everyone in a foul mood despite the right of it, and Ludwig had to wonder if his men were pondering their own futures.

The tournament grounds to the south of the city were littered with tents, guards, and campfires. Into this hodgepodge of soldiery walked Ludwig, determined to report his arrival to someone in authority. He halted his men, picking out a clear area for them to rest, then made his way towards a cluster of pavilions that held the standard of the duke.

As he closed the distance, a familiar voice called out.

"Sir Ludwig? Is that you?"

"Sir Galrath? I didn't expect to find you here."

The knight smiled. "Why ever not? I am, after all, in the service of His Grace. Will you partake of an ale with me?"

"I should like to," replied Ludwig, "but I have business with the duke."

"I'm afraid the duke isn't here."

"That's his pavilion, isn't it?"

"It is," admitted Sir Galrath, "but he had to go into the city on a matter of some import. What is it you seek? Perhaps I can help?"

"I've brought men from Regnitz, at the behest of Lord Wulfram."

"That's good news indeed. Might I ask how many?"

"Only two dozen, I'm afraid. We took quite a pounding at the hands of Lord Gebhard."

"Ah, yes, I heard something to that effect. Still, two dozen is better than none. I suppose you'll be wanting some food for them?"

"Yes, and a place to set up camp."

"Well, that," said Sir Galrath, "is easy enough. Simply pick any spare spot of ground."

"And the food?"

"For that, you'll have to speak with the duke's quartermaster. A man by the name of Wasser."

"Kurt Wasser?"

"Yes, you know him?"

"I'll say," said Ludwig with a grin. "He's the one who taught me how to fight."

"Then let me take you to him. This time of day, he'll be over yonder handing out loaves of bread and kegs of ale."

"He serves food now?"

Sir Galrath chuckled. "No, but he oversees the work. He's a smart man, keeps a close eye on things."

"Why is that so important?"

"It reduces pilfering. Before he came along, half the food was being whisked away to Saints know where probably to line some pockets with coins."

"Are you suggesting the duke's men are corrupt?"

"Of course," said the older knight. "It's the natural course of events when people are involved. The real trick, of course, is to not let it get in the way of things. Now follow me, and I'll show you the way."

Sir Galrath led them through the camp. "Over there, you can see the duke's knights. He keeps the horses together, making it much easier to feed them."

"It's an impressive sight," said Ludwig. "There must be hundreds of them."

"Yes, and that's only the ones under the duke's direct command. Some of the barons have their own knights as well. At last count, we had nearly five hundred horsemen. The bulk of the army is, of course, its footmen, but we also have quite a few archers. All in all, we have fifteen hundred but are expecting upwards of two thousand men when all the barons arrive."

"Impressive."

"Yes," agreed Sir Galrath. "Yet for all that, I wonder if it will be enough."

"You fear Andover outnumbers us?"

"I do. Their king would scarcely attack otherwise."

They halted at an awning where beneath stood a pair of women, taking loaves of bread from baskets and handing them to a line of warriors.

"Is Kurt Wasser about?" asked Sir Galrath.

"He's inside," the older woman replied, nodding her head in the general direction of the nearest tent.

"Come along, then," continued the senior knight. "Best if we don't keep him waiting."

An argument drifted out to greet them as they drew nearer.

"I don't care," came Kurt's voice. "Lord Helmer can only draw rations for those of his men who are present. Should any more arrive, then you can come back for extra."

"You haven't heard the last of this," came the reply. An older man stepped from the tent, almost colliding with Ludwig. Only the quick thinking of Sir Galrath saved the day as he grabbed his younger companion's arm and pulled him aside just in time.

"Who was that?" asked Ludwig.

"I'm not sure," replied Sir Galrath, "but whoever it was, wore the colours of the Baron of Galmund."

Kurt appeared at the opening, breaking into a grin. "I thought I recognized the voice. Ludwig, I'd wondered what happened to you. I see you've met Sir Galrath?"

"Yes," replied Ludwig. "He's the one who defeated me in the joust."

"You must tell me what you've been up to."

"I shall leave you to it," said Sir Galrath. "I have things to look after. Drop by later, Sir Ludwig, and we'll share a drink."

"Sir Ludwig?" said Kurt. "You're not still peddling stories?"

"No, I was knighted."

"Truly?"

"Yes, by Lord Wulfram, Baron of Regnitz."

"I sense a complicated story," said Kurt.

"Why would you say that?"

"Because with you, nothing is ever easy."

"I'm not sure whether to be flattered or insulted."

"I mean it in only the nicest way."

"In that case," said Ludwig, "I'll take it as a compliment."

"What brings you here?"

"I've come to get the food ration for the baron's men."

"How many did you bring?"

"A mere two dozen."

"Just send them over and get them to line up. Are they wearing the baron's colours?"

"They are."

"Then that will be more than sufficient."

"So tell me," said Ludwig, "how did you end up working for the duke?"

"It's a long story," replied Kurt. "Let's just say he recognizes talent when he sees it. Of course, I do much more than simply looking after food."

"Like what?"

"I'm one of his advisors."

"You?"

"Yes," said Kurt. "Why? Does that surprise you? It shouldn't. After all, I've got lots of experience when it comes to the intricacies of war. Look, why don't you come in and sit down for a while? We can catch up on things."

"I'd love to, but I have a duty to see to the baron's men."

"What's this, now?" said Kurt. "What have you done with that brash young noble I brought to Erlingen?"

Ludwig's face darkened. "That's not me anymore, Kurt. I've seen too much these last few months, things I can never unsee."

"Then we'll save it until we have more time. Look, I have to be at the duke's tent this evening. How about you drop by tomorrow afternoon? We'll catch up then?"

"Fair enough," said Ludwig, "but I'm warning you, I'll hold you to it."

Kurt chuckled. "As well you should. Now, get going. You've got men to feed."

As Ludwig left the area to seek the baron's troops, his mood lightened immeasurably.

With food in their bellies, Wulfram's men sat around a fire, staring into the flames. The entire area was eerily quiet, possibly a portent of things to come once they started marching. Ludwig poked a log, stirring up a few sparks that drifted into the starless night. The clouds overhead added to the general sense of gloom, and he found himself wishing he were back in Verfeld.

"What do you reckon, sir?" asked Krebbs.

"About what?" replied Ludwig.

"This here war."

He shrugged. "What is there to think on? We must do our duty to the duke. That's all there is to it."

"It's a strange one, though, isn't it?" added the sergeant.

"Strange in what way?" Ludwig leaned forward, intrigued with the sergeant's words.

"They say there was no warning from Andover, and they haven't even made any demands. Took His Grace completely by surprise."

Ludwig had to wonder who 'they' were, but he feared it was nothing but idle gossip. "What else have you heard?"

"Well, as everyone knows, there's been bad blood between Erlingen and Andover for years, and—"

"Wait a moment," said Ludwig. "Did you say bad blood?"

"I did, sir, although I suppose you wouldn't know of it, being a foreigner and all."

"Then you'd best fill me in on the situation."

"It all has to do with families," said Krebbs. "You see, the duke and the King of Andover are cousins of a sort."

"Of a sort? I'm afraid I haven't a clue what you're talking about."

"The duke's second wife was niece to the King of Andover."

"Wouldn't that bring the two countries closer?"

"Normally, yes," said the sergeant, "but after her death, the duke took up with a woman from Reinwick."

"That's a duchy," said Ludwig. "My stepmother is from there. It's on the northern sea, isn't it?"

"It is, sir, and that's the problem. Reinwick and Andover are rivals."

Ludwig struggled to understand. "Rivals in what way?"

"They both compete for trade, sir, and control over the ships."

"You mean seaborne trade?"

"Yes, that's it."

"But that's no reason to invade, is it?"

"No," said Krebbs, "but both realms are in dispute over a small portion of their border."

"Let me guess, the duke sided with Reinwick."

"That's what I'm told, sir. The king took it as a personal affront. A betrayal, if you will."

"There seems to be a lot of that going around," noted Ludwig. "First Lord Gebhard, and now the King of Andover."

"They can't help it, sir. They're both proud men."

"Proud? That kind of pride kills men. Doesn't that bother you?"

"We're soldiers. That's our lot in life."

"Do these people not care for the men under their command?"

Sergeant Krebbs looked at him as if he were a ghost.

"What?" said Ludwig. "Did I say something wrong?"

"Begging your pardon, sir, but it's not the way of things. Caring for your troops? I've never heard such a strange notion. We're here to fight and die. That's our role."

"You may rest assured, Sergeant, I would never ask you or the other men to risk their lives in battle without a chance of surviving."

"That's awfully decent of you, sir, but the decision isn't yours to make."

"I'm your captain," said Ludwig.

"Very true, sir, but it's the duke who'll make all the decisions about how the army will be used. I'm afraid you'll have little say in it."

"I would imagine the nobles have more influence."

"Only those with the most troops, sir. Our little group is terribly small."

"And who has the most troops?"

"That I don't know," said Krebbs, "but one thing is for certain, the barons are sure to spend lavishly to get the attention of His Grace."

"Does the duke have any troops of his own, or does he rely solely on his barons?"

"He has his own, sir, but the bulk of the army is controlled by his nobles."

"That must make it awfully hard to fight."

"I suppose it would," said Krebbs, "but I have little knowledge of such things."

"I shall have to remember to ask Kurt about it."

"Kurt, sir?"

"Yes, Kurt Wasser, the man in charge of the supplies. He and I are old friends."

"Good for you, sir. He could probably tell you more about the duke's army. Any word on when we're marching?"

"Not yet," replied Ludwig, "but judging from the number of men on this field, it can't be far off. If we stay much longer, we'll eat up every loaf of bread in the city."

"It won't be any easier on the march, sir."

"No, I don't suppose it will."

"I saw those friends of yours today, sir."

"Friends?"

"Yes, those mercenaries you used to work with. They're camped right over there," Krebbs said, pointing. "You might want to wander over and say hello."

"My duty is here," said Ludwig. "And in any case, they're likely camped with Lord Gebhard's men. I don't want to draw attention to us. There's too much bad blood already."

"Probably a wise move. When do you expect the baron will arrive?"

"I imagine he'll be here any day now. He must have set out from Regnitz some days ago, and I'm sure he'd be making much better time than us."

"Let's hope so, sir," said Krebbs. "I'd hate to have to march without him."

. . .

Lord Wulfram rode in the very next day with Rosalyn at his side while a wagon and driver followed in their wake, loaded up with tents, furnishings, and presumably other supplies such as food.

Word came to Ludwig soon after they were spotted, for it was the gossip of the camp. People were making wagers on what Baron Stein's reaction would be were he to encounter Lord Wulfram.

As soon as he heard of their arrival, Ludwig sought them out, finally locating them as servants were putting up their tent near the duke's own pavilion in amongst the other Lords of Erlingen.

Rosalyn was the first to notice Ludwig's approach. She tapped her father on the shoulder and pointed as a smile graced her features.

"Ludwig," called out the baron. "Is all well?"

"It is, my lord. The men are settled in, and their food taken care of. I'm sure they'd appreciate a visit if you have the time."

"I can't at the moment," said Lord Wulfram, "for I have to go and visit the duke, but I'll see if I can't get away this evening. In the meantime, perhaps Rosalyn can take my place?"

Ludwig turned to the baron's daughter. "My lady?"

"I should be delighted. Will you lead the way, Sir Ludwig?"

"Certainly." He guided her through the camp, steering her well clear of the refuse that was beginning to accumulate.

"Tell me," she asked, "do all camps smell this bad?"

"It's quite common, from what I've heard. Though admittedly, one gets used to it in time."

She held a kerchief to her nose as they walked. "They never warn you about such things when describing battles in books."

"You've read of battles?"

"To a degree," said Rosalyn, "although doubtless not as much as you."

"You surprise me. I've known few women to take an interest in such things."

"Nevertheless, are there not Temple Knights of the fairer sex?"

"Of course, but they are not common on the battlefield."

"I wonder why not?"

"For the same reason none of the other orders are here," explained Ludwig. "The Church does not wish to intervene in petty conflicts."

"Isn't their very presence meant to prevent such conflicts?"

"One would certainly think so, yet I have heard of no such expeditions in years," said Ludwig. He stopped suddenly, casting his eyes about.

"Is something wrong?"

"I must admit to having taken the wrong route. I'm afraid we must backtrack."

"Easily enough accomplished," said Rosalyn.

They turned around to retrace their steps.

"My lady?" someone called out.

They both turned to see Hagan Stein, who had been addressing a common warrior, but on their passing, had looked up to see the Lady of Regnitz Keep.

"Master Hagan," said Rosalyn. "I didn't expect to see you here."

"Why ever not?" Baron Stein's son replied. "After all, my father's army is here, as is yours, I presume."

"I stand corrected."

"My lady, allow me to apologize once more for the brutish behaviour of my father. Had I but known what he had intended, I never would have co-operated."

"Your words are soothing, Master Stein, but how do I know they are said in earnest?"

Hagan knelt, drawing his dagger and handing it to her, hilt first. "If I lie, then you may take this and plunge it into my heart."

She looked down into his eyes, although whether to gauge the truth of the man's words or merely to appreciate his good looks, Ludwig couldn't say.

"Very well," she said, taking the dagger. "I accept your statement as true, but I shall hang on to this..." She paused. "I may have need of it in the future."

"As you wish," said Hagan.

Rosalyn turned, ready to resume her steps, but the young man was persistent.

"Excuse me, my lady."

She returned her gaze to him. "Yes?"

Hagan struggled with his words. "Might I... that is to say..."

"If you wish to ask me something, Master Hagan, then you'd best make up your mind. Have you a question for me or not?"

"I do, my lady."

"Then out with it."

"I wonder if you might do me the honour of dining with me this evening?"

She stared at him for a while before finally replying. "And where, pray tell, would we eat? At your father's tent?"

Ludwig saw Hagan's face fall. The man was obviously well-intentioned but completely at a loss as to how to reply. Instead, he merely stared back, slack-jawed and open-mouthed.

"I thought as much," said Rosalyn. "Come, Ludwig. It's time we were away from here."

They turned from the humbled man, but no sooner had they taken three steps when he spoke once more.

"Torburg," he called out.

A hint of a smile floated across Rosalyn's face, and Ludwig had to wonder if she wasn't enjoying this a little too much. "What of it?" she demanded as she turned.

"There's a tavern there," said Hagan. "The Buck and Doe, do you know it?"

Rosalyn reddened. "I have heard of it, but I hardly consider it suitable for a lady of refinement, do you?"

"Of course not, my lady." The man was obviously struggling to find a solution, but Rosalyn, sensing his nervousness, decided to put even more pressure on the poor fellow.

"If you can think of no other, then I should leave."

"No," said Hagan, his voice taking on a desperate edge. "Name the place, and I shall take you there."

"A bold statement," she said. "I might pick somewhere expensive."

"No expense would be too great if it would allow me your company," said Hagan, his manner rushed, his face flushed.

Rosalyn smiled, allowing him to see her pleasure. "You can be exceptionally eloquent when needed."

"So you will consent to my invitation?"

"I shall give it some thought." She turned once more, and without so much as a goodbye, began walking away.

Ludwig, caught completely off guard, had to hurry to catch up. "What was that all about?"

"Whatever do you mean?"

"Don't play games with me, Rosalyn. You encouraged him. Are you sure that's what you want to do, considering who he is?"

"As you are fond of saying, he is not his father."

"Despite that, they share the same house, do they not?"

She halted, again catching Ludwig by surprise. "Why, Ludwig, are you jealous?"

"No," he replied, "only concerned for your well-being."

"Then perhaps you'd better accompany us as my chaperone?"

"Does that means you intend to take him up on his offer?"

"Yes," she said, "but I have work to do first."

"Work? Anything I can help with?"

"As a matter of fact, yes. I need to find the most expensive place to eat in all of Torburg."

32

DEBACLE

Summer 1095 SR

Ludwig wolfed down the barn bread, then sipped his watered-down wine. Provisions were growing scarce, so it was a meagre breakfast this morning. The duke's idea of food was bread and porridge, but the oats had run out, and now only the bread remained—slim fare for fighting men.

He spotted Lord Wulfram making his way towards him and stood. "Good morning, my lord."

The baron smiled. "Good to see you, Sir Ludwig. I trust you slept well?"

"I did, my lord. Did you come to visit the men?"

"Alas, no. I've been summoned to a council of war, and I thought to take you with me. Interested?"

"Most definitely," said Ludwig, "although I lack the wardrobe for such august company."

"It's a council of war, my friend, not a social event. Come as you are. You'll earn more respect for it. Best get your sword though."

"You think I'll need it?"

"Yes, if only to discourage insults."

"Insults?"

"Yes, when the duke's men gather, there's seldom harmony. You can expect a good deal of arguing, and I shouldn't like you to get caught up in all of it."

"Does it honestly get that bad?"

"Oh, yes," said Lord Wulfram. "I've seen steel drawn on several occasions despite the fact that the duke has outlawed such actions. Now, let's get over there before all the best wine is gone."

They picked their way through the tournament field, going around tents and campfires. They had to halt briefly, as a wagon rolled by, and then the duke's tent came into view.

"I should probably warn you before we enter," said the baron.

"Warn me about what?"

"The Barons of Erlingen can be a prickly bunch when it comes to station. As only a knight, I'd recommend you say as little as possible."

"Then I shall speak only if directly addressed."

"That's a sensible approach. I wish more thought as you do."

The guards eyed them as they approached, but they obviously knew Lord Wulfram, for they merely nodded at him. Ludwig followed the baron into the tent, an immense structure, rivalling the size of a tavern inside. The duke's coffers had spared no expense, and its interior was lavishly decorated. A small group of men nodded their heads in greeting as Lord Wulfram entered.

"There he is," said a considerably rotund individual. "Have any men left, Wulfram?" They all chuckled at the baron's misfortune.

"I do, Helmer, as well you know. You shan't keep me from serving my duke."

"That's it," spoke another. "Never say die!"

Lord Wulfram leaned over to Ludwig to whisper. "That's Rengard Pasche, the Baron of Rosenbruck. He and I go way back." He raised his voice. "Where's His Grace?"

"The duke will be here shortly," replied Rengard. "He's busy dealing with a personal matter."

"Personal matter?" said Wulfram.

"Yes, it looks like his new wife is not too happy about him going off to war."

"What's this, number three?"

"Four, if you include that one in his youth."

"That hardly counts," said Wulfram. "The Church never sanctified it." He turned to Ludwig. "Our duke likes his women."

"This new wife," said Ludwig. "Is that the one from Reinwick?"

The baron looked at him in surprise. "You've heard of her?"

"Only insofar as her birthplace is of interest. My stepmother is from the same place."

"Is she now? Will wonders never cease. You and she might be related."

"She's my stepmother, not my actual mother. That hardly makes us relatives."

"I suppose that's true, but still, imagine the strange fate it would be if you were."

"Are we onto fate again?"

Wulfram laughed. "I suppose we are. Sorry, I shall try to keep my mind on the subject at hand."

"Which is?"

"This war." Wulfram turned to Lord Rengard. "How many men did you manage?"

"Nearly two hundred," his old friend replied. "And you?"

"Only twenty-four. Still, it's better than nothing."

"Is it?" said Lord Helmer.

"Come now," said Rengard. "You should be more charitable."

"Well, I suppose someone has to fetch the wine."

"Ignore him," said Wulfram. "He's only showing off because he has one of the larger contingents."

"Larger? Try the largest," added Helmer.

"We'll see," argued Rengard. "Not all the nobles have arrived as yet."

"Oh?" said Wulfram. "Who's missing?"

"Hurst, and you know what he's like. I bet he's got more than anyone, the duke included."

The third man stepped forward. "Aren't you going to introduce us, Wulfram?"

"Of course, where are my manners. Gentlemen, this is Sir Ludwig of Verfeld. He has sworn to my service for the duration of this conflict."

"Pleased to meet you. I'm Lord Kruger, Baron of Grozen. You've met Rengard and Helmer here?"

"I have now," said Ludwig.

"So you're from Verfeld. That's in Hadenfeld, isn't it?"

"It is, my lord."

"Tell me, does King Otto still rule there?"

"He does, or at least he did when I left."

"Saints alive, he must be ancient by now."

"He's only slightly older than Lord Wulfram," noted Ludwig.

"There you have it," piped in Helmer. "The man's positively decrepit."

A tall, thin man entered the tent, the scent of flowers wafting along with him.

"Lord Hurst," said Wulfram, "we were just talking about you. May I introduce Sir Ludwig of Verfeld?"

"Nice to meet you," the new visitor replied, his voice high and nasally, then he immediately turned his attention to Helmer. "Has His Grace arrived yet?"

"I'm afraid not. He's dealing with a marital issue."

"That's what he gets for bedding a commoner."

"The duke's wife is a commoner?" asked Ludwig.

"Well," said Hurst, "from amongst the lower ranks of the nobility, but it's almost the same thing. Tell me, young Ludwig, are you married?"

"No, my lord."

"Then do yourself a favour, swear off women until a proper marriage can be arranged for you. It'll do you better in the long run."

"How so?"

"There can be no love in marriage. It only complicates matters."

"Don't be absurd," interrupted Wulfram. "That's probably the worst advice I've ever heard."

"We can't all have loving wives like you did, Wulfram. Some of us have more important things to take care of." Hurst looked into Ludwig's eyes. "Have you ever known love?"

Ludwig blushed.

"Good," continued Lord Hurst. "Now bury that feeling deep inside you. If you want to get ahead in life, you need to be ruthless. Look at me, I was once like these gentlemen, eking out an existence on a small parcel of land."

"And now?" said Ludwig.

"Now, I am the most powerful noble in all of Erlingen, with the possible exception of His Grace, of course. Speaking of which, where is the duke?"

"As I mentioned earlier," said Helmer, "he's—"

"Wait, don't tell me. He's dealing with marital issues. Doesn't he realize there's a war going on?"

"Of course I do."

Every single one of them turned at the proclamation. Lord Deiter Henrich, the Duke of Erlingen, was tall, with a flowing black beard braided on the sides.

"Is this everyone?" he asked, his voice deep and rich.

"I'm afraid so, Your Grace," said Kruger. "But I'm told the rest will be in Torburg within a matter of days."

"Then they'll have to catch up to us."

"Then we mean to march?"

"We do," said the duke. "And soon, before it's too late."

Ludwig's ears pricked up. "Have you news, Your Grace?" he asked.

The duke swivelled his gaze. "Sir Ludwig, I presume?"

"Yes, my lord. How did you know?"

Lord Deiter smiled. "I won a substantial amount because of you."

"You bet on me?"

The duke roared with laughter. "No, son, against you, at the tournament. By the Saints, I've never seen a man knocked so quickly from the saddle."

Ludwig reddened.

"Fear not, I shan't hold it against you. I understand you're now in Lord Wulfram's employ?"

"I am, Your Grace."

"Well, it's nice to see he's recruited someone with manners." He turned to the rest of the nobles. "Now, I suppose you're all wondering why I've called you here?"

"It had crossed our minds," said Helmer.

"Gentlemen, I'm afraid relations with our northern neighbour have soured of late." He held up his hands to forestall any argument. "Now, I take full responsibility for it. I know the circumstances surrounding my late wife's death led to some concern in the court of Andover, but that's in the past. What we must concern ourselves with now is defeating the impending invasion of our soil. To that end, we shall head for Chermingen in the morning."

"What shall be the order of march?" asked Lord Rengard.

"By order of seniority," replied the duke. "That means Hurst will follow my own troops."

"I have more troops than Rengard," insisted Lord Helmer. "I should, therefore, march before he does."

Lord Deiter turned his gaze on Rengard. "Is this true?"

The man nodded, too embarrassed to speak.

"I see. Consider the matter settled, then."

A challenge outside the tent caught the duke's attention. Moments later, Lord Gebhard Stein entered, looking incredibly flustered.

"Lord Gebhard," said the duke, his voice dripping with sarcasm. "How nice of you to join us."

"My apologies, Your Grace. It appears your aides did not inform me of the summons in a timely manner." Gebhard shuffled into the room, humbled by his tardiness.

"Now," continued the duke, "where was I?"

Kruger spoke up. "You were talking about the order of march?"

"Ah, yes, thank you. Now, let's see, Lord Wulfram will naturally be bringing up the rear, with Gebhard right in front of him."

"I must object, my lord," said Gebhard. "I have more troops than Rengard."

"Only because of those mercenaries," said Helmer. "You should be thankful you're not bringing up the rear like Wulfram here."

The duke simply let them argue the point, not deigning to provide a definitive answer.

"Speaking of mercenaries," said Hurst, "will you be taking on the cost of the Blades of Vengeance, Your Grace?"

"I can hardly leave it to Lord Gebhard to bear the expense. He's broke enough as it is." The lords all chuckled at the duke's remark.

Ludwig had to wonder at a ruler who would demean his own nobles so openly. He wanted to speak out, to complain about Baron Stein's treatment, but knew they wouldn't listen. Instead, he remained silent, aghast at the callous treatment being dealt out.

"And once we get to Chermingen?" asked Kruger.

"At that point," continued the duke, "we will have to assess the situation. We have reports of an army massing right across from Lieswel, but we have yet to receive any word of their crossing the border."

"So all this could be for naught?"

"One does not mass an army near the border only to make things inconvenient. If they choose not to cross into Erlingen, then we shall cross into Andover and deal them a blow from which they shall never recover."

All the lords were energized by the thought. "That being the case," said Lord Helmer, "are we to carry on and conquer all of Andover?"

"It's a distinct possibility," said the duke, "but it largely depends on whether or not we can defeat their army."

"My lord," said Rengard, "can there be any doubt? Our forces shall crush those of the enemy. Why, it should then be a simple matter to march to their capital."

"I wouldn't be so sure," offered Lord Kruger. "Defeating an army and conquering the land are two very different things."

"Yes," argued Helmer, "but the two are closely related."

"Indeed," added Hurst, "and no doubt there would be land aplenty for the victors. Who knows, even Stein might find his fortunes improving."

Lord Gebhard reddened but kept silent.

"Before I let you go," said the duke, "there's one more thing I'd like to discuss."

"Which is?" asked Kruger.

"The knights and their deployment."

"What is there to discuss; each knight shall serve under the lord who sponsors them. Is there any other way?"

"I thought we'd mass them all together," said Lord Deiter. "That way, they'd pack more of a punch."

Kruger paled. "But Your Grace, such a move would strip away our best warriors."

"Do you not have footmen?" asked Ludwig.

They all looked at the knight, distaste evident on their faces.

"And what would you know of such things?" asked Hurst.

"I have studied warfare since I was a child."

"So then that would make it, what, three years ago?"

Lord Helmer soon chimed in. "Yes, and you command... what was it? Oh, yes, two dozen men. It hardly makes you an expert on the matter. Try coming back when you've got some experience under your belt."

"Do not dismiss him so readily," warned Lord Wulfram. "He has rather recently been in a siege, as have I. That's more experience than most of you put together."

"I hardly think you're in a position to talk," said Lord Gebhard.

"Your Grace," said Hurst. "It appears the children are squabbling again. Might I suggest you send them to their rooms?"

"Don't patronize me," said Gebhard.

Ludwig felt the weight of his responsibilities. He had prayed to Saint Mathew to see his men returned safely home, but now it appeared the barons were more intent on fighting with each other than defeating the enemy.

The duke was content to stand back and let his nobles argue, so much so that while his barons bickered, he was helping himself to some more wine. Was there no end to this madness?

"What would the Church do?" interjected Ludwig.

The room fell silent.

"What was that?" asked the duke.

"The Church," he continued. "I was just wondering what the Temple Knights would do under these circumstances. I bet they wouldn't stand around arguing over who has the most men. They'd march towards the enemy and deliver a crippling blow."

"I suppose they would," said the duke, "but then again, we have no such men amongst our ranks."

"But you have knights," said Ludwig. "Are they not trained in the arts of war?"

Lord Hurst took a step towards him. "Do you dare to lecture His Grace?"

The duke held up his hand. "Let him speak. I would hear his words."

Everyone's eyes fell on Ludwig. He felt the pressure building until he could no longer contain his excitement. "The knights are the cream of your army, but you must hold them until the moment of greatest impact."

"I'm not sure what you're suggesting?" said the duke.

"I'm agreeing with your idea to mass them together, but I would go further."

"Go further, how, exactly?"

"Your command is fractured, Your Grace, with each of your nobles fighting over their place. I propose you organize your army by type, then designate experienced warriors to lead them."

"Don't be absurd," said Kruger. "They're our men, not the duke's."

"Yes," agreed Helmer. "What kind of nonsense is this? Do you seriously think we would agree to such terms?"

"But it could mean the difference between victory and defeat," said Ludwig.

"We will win through our superiority of arms," said the duke. "Let us not hear any more of this nonsense. Now, I dare say we've had enough for today. Return to your men, and get them ready for the march. We leave at first light."

The barons all grumbled, and Ludwig couldn't help but see them as petulant children, newly chastised by a parent.

"Sir Ludwig," said the duke, "I would have you stay a moment longer."

"Yes, Your Grace." He remained where he was, noting the look of concern on Lord Wulfram's face as the baron left the tent.

Lord Deiter walked over to a table, selecting a bottle, pulling the cork and sniffing the contents before pouring himself a cup.

"You know," he began, "I remember when I was your age."

"Surely not that long ago, Lord."

The duke turned to face him, drink in hand. He was smiling, but despite that, Ludwig couldn't help but feel it hid a temper.

"I'm sorry if I overstepped my place, Lord."

"It's understandable, given the circumstances." He swirled his cup, then took a sip. "You impress me, Sir Ludwig."

"I do, my lord?"

"Aye. The last I saw you, you were the worst jouster to grace the tournament in years. Now, here you stand, a few months later, the very model of a fighting warrior. I sense much has happened in that time."

"It has, Lord."

"Then share with me what has transpired. I need a tale to amuse me and give me some small respite from the burden I bear."

"Burden?"

"Yes, the burden of command. Are you familiar with the term?"

"Of course, my lord."

"Then come, speak to me of your exploits."

"Well, it all started when I lost that joust…"

Ludwig didn't leave the tent until well past noon. Lord Wulfram met him as he exited, concern written on his face.

"You were in there for quite some time. I hope he wasn't too hard on you."

"Not at all," replied Ludwig. "In fact, he was most gracious."

"The duke was? That's not like him. He's usually dreadfully antagonistic, even at the best of times. Why, I've seen him reduce a man to tears with nothing but a glance."

"Not so with me. I assume it's because I'm an outsider."

"I don't understand how that would make a difference."

"Don't you see? I ask nothing of His Grace, not land, wealth, or even influence, thus he bears me no ill will."

"What did you talk about?"

"I told him about everything that had befallen me in the last few months."

A look of horror crossed the baron's face. "Everything?"

"More or less," said Ludwig. "But don't worry, I had only nice things to say about you."

33

THE ARMY MARCHES

Summer 1095 SR

T he march began the next day, if march was the right word for it. Men assembled and horses were saddled, but they spent much of the morning doing little other than standing around waiting. Apparently, it was one thing to schedule an army to march, quite another to actually execute the command. The duke was to lead the army, but still, he himself did not rise till mid-morning, likely the result of too much time spent in the company of his new wife, or so the rumours claimed.

When he finally did appear, he looked hungover and tired, climbing into his carriage with little thought to issuing commands. His brief appearance complete, he left it for others to issue the actual orders for the advance to begin. Soldiers began moving, but their placement on the tournament grounds worked against them, creating log jams of men as they fought over who had the right of way.

By mid-afternoon, Ludwig's men were getting hungry. He ordered them to rest, knowing full well they were destined to bring up the rear. There was no sense in wearing themselves out when half the army still hadn't moved. Thus Lord Wulfram found them lounging on the ground, though if he was surprised, he gave no sign of it.

"Any news on when we can march?" asked Ludwig.

"I'm afraid not. There's been some kind of commotion about half a mile up the road. Apparently, Stein and Rengard have had a disagreement."

"Let me guess, it's about who goes first?"

"It is, as a matter of fact. If they don't sort it out soon, we may be here until nightfall, and I don't mind telling you I don't want to be marching in the dark."

"We may have little choice, my lord."

Lord Wulfram sighed. "I suppose that's true, but that doesn't mean I have to like it."

"Did you see the duke this morning?"

"No, did you?"

"Only from a distance. He didn't look well."

"Is he sick?"

"No," said Ludwig, "at least not that I know. I suspect he was hungover."

"Ah, yes, the new wife. I understand he drinks to excess when she's around."

"You've met her?"

"I have," said Wulfram.

"What's she like?"

"She is a handsome woman, with refined manners, most of the time."

"Handsome?" said Ludwig. "Not beautiful or pretty?"

Lord Wulfram smiled. "I can conceive of no other way to describe her. She's not a great beauty, yet she has a certain presence, a quiet dignity that can't be denied."

"What is she like as a person?"

"A difficult question to answer. I've only met her twice, and to be honest, I've never been in her presence long enough to form an opinion."

Ludwig laughed. "That's a guarded comment."

Lord Wulfram grinned. "I suppose it is, isn't it, but I must be charitable. After all, she is the duchess now."

"Out of curiosity, what happened to his last wife, the one from Andover?"

"Ah, now that was a genuine tragedy. She drowned, you see."

"Drowned? At sea?"

"No, more's the pity. She was out boating on the river, and the boat capsized. Such a terrible waste."

"How many died?"

"Only her," said Lord Wulfram. "It wasn't a big boat, you understand, just a small affair, with her and the boatman aboard. They were rowing out to a ship to say goodbye to the duke."

"She couldn't have said goodbye before he boarded?"

The baron blushed. "Well, he had been busy the night before."

"What does that mean?"

"He'd been in the company of another woman."

"Let me guess, his current wife?"

"Yes, how did you know?"

"Just a lucky guess," admitted Ludwig. "How long had she been at court?"

"Several months, although she only caught the duke's eye a few weeks before he set sail."

"Rather convenient, don't you think, my lord?"

"I must admit it's decidedly suspicious, but there's little that could be done about it. I suppose, looking back, I can see why the King of Andover was upset."

"It's more than that," said Ludwig. "It likely led to this war."

Lord Wulfram stared back at him, the words sinking in. "By the Saints, I suppose it did. I should have thought of it sooner."

"It would make little difference. It's not as if we could bring her back from the dead."

"No, I suppose not. Still, it would have been nice to know."

"You said the duke was combative. Is he like that with everyone in Erlingen?"

"Everyone except his wife."

"Was he always like that?"

"No, as a young man, he was outgoing and a delight to be around. He changed when he lost his first wife."

"You mean his first legal wife or the one the Church wouldn't recognize?"

The baron tried to hide his smirk. "I see you were paying attention. When he was a young man, he ran away from home and married a commoner. They set up house in a small village to the west of here, near the city of Grozen. Of course, that was long before he became duke."

"What happened?"

"They found him. You can't hide when you're the son of a duke, at least not in Erlingen."

"I managed it quite well," said Ludwig.

"Yes, but you're a baron's son and not trying to hide in your own land."

"What happened to his wife?"

"His father had the Church dissolve his marriage, and he was forbidden to set eyes on her ever again."

"That must have been hard."

"Hard? It broke him, took him years to recover. He remarried, of course; he had to, to continue the line, but I never saw any joy in his life after that."

"And now?"

"He seems to have found a little of his former spark since he took up with his present wife, though for the life of me, I can't understand why."

"He's in love," said Ludwig.

"Then more power to him," said Lord Wulfram. "He deserves at least a modicum of happiness. Saints know the rest of his life has been full of sadness. You know he's lost three children?"

"No, I didn't."

"Two from his first 'official' wife and a son from his second. If he doesn't father another soon, he'll have to pass on the duchy to his cousin."

"Is he ill?"

"No," said Wulfram, "but the pressure of court surely weighs on him. The people want to know the seat of power is looked after, and if he doesn't name an heir, his neighbours will begin to take an interest."

Ludwig shook his head. "So he has no real freedom."

"Not really. We all presume being a ruler is a fine thing, but frankly, no one stops to consider the cost it has on a person."

"I, for one, am perfectly content to be a simple baron's son."

Lord Wulfram smiled. "As you should be, but don't get too comfortable. Things can change quickly in the Petty Kingdoms. One day you're a baron, the next, you may be the sworn enemy of another."

"Speaking from experience?"

"I suppose I am. I still can't believe Stein took his quest for power to such lengths. I always considered him a reasonable man, but something turned him sour."

"I have an idea that the duke may bear some responsibility for that."

"You do?" said Wulfram.

"Yes, he encourages fighting amongst his nobles. Arguments are one thing, but sooner or later, it's bound to get out of hand as it did with you and Lord Gebhard."

"Let us hope that's the end of it."

A distant horn sounded, drawing their attention to the north, where the troops were finally moving.

Lord Wulfram smiled. "It looks like the roads have cleared up. Best get the men on their feet, Sir Ludwig. The march is finally begun."

Chermingen lay some hundred miles from the capital, necessitating a march of several days. It wouldn't have been bad had the army been properly informed of what was expected of them, but instead, the men set out not knowing how far they were to march each day.

Being in the rear had its own problems. Ludwig's men were constantly slowing, then speeding up as the army before them couldn't manage to keep to a steady pace. Add to that the inexperience of the army commanders, and the problems only magnified. On more than one occasion, he led his men into camp after dark, making even the simplest task of setting a fire that much more difficult.

He didn't see much of Lord Wulfram, for the baron was kept up front as part of the duke's entourage. Thus it fell to men like Ludwig to carry out the march.

They were four days out from Torburg when Ludwig next saw his liege lord. Having trailed into camp as the sun was low on the horizon, he was helping to get the fire going when the baron appeared, his horse lathered.

"There you are. I've been looking all over the place for you."

"We just arrived," said Ludwig. "Would you care for something to eat?"

"No, I don't have the time, and neither do you. We're wanted at the duke's tent."

"For what?"

"Haven't a clue," said Wulfram, "but we'd best not keep him waiting."

"I suppose I'd best clean myself up. I'm covered in dust."

"Don't bother. You're no worse off than the rest of us. I'll ride over there directly. It's just down the road, past that bend. Don't be long."

The baron left Ludwig to ponder his fate. Was he in some kind of trouble? He suddenly had a terrible feeling his father might have tracked him down. Was that it? Would he be sent home at the height of the campaign?

Sergeant Krebbs poked the fire. "I'll take care of the lads, sir. You'd best get along to see His Grace."

"The men have to eat," said Ludwig, "and I don't trust that fellow Kurt has handing out the rations. Last night he tried to stiff us."

"I've dealt with his sort before, sir. Don't worry, I'll take care of everything."

"Of course, but I expect a full report when I return."

"A report, sir?"

"Yes, a full accounting of how things went."

"Absolutely, sir."

Ludwig began making his way up the road. As the sun sank below the horizon, the campfires lit up the night sky, throwing shadows against the trees. Everyone appeared in good spirits, a far cry from how he felt inside— as if his entire world had suddenly been turned upside down. Mere days ago, he had been happy to march to war, had even talked of returning home once the campaign was over, but to be told he must leave now was simply too much to bear.

He tried to reason things through, but his own mind worked against him. What else could the duke want of him other than to send him home? He wasn't a formidable warrior, and his battle experience was limited to a brief fight in the keep. What else, then, could the duke want?

A soldier in His Grace's livery called out a challenge.

"Sir Ludwig, to see the duke," he replied.

The man ushered him on his way.

The road curved to the right, and then the tents came into view, well-lit by strategically placed lanterns. He was shocked by the sight, for here, the nobles of the court lived lavishly, while their men slept in the open, struggling to keep warm in the night air. True, summer was upon them, but the evenings had been chilly of late, and more than one warrior had been forced to spend the night warming himself by the campfire.

As he proceeded, he noticed movement off to his left. A well-dressed man had just relieved himself against a tree and was evidently returning to the duke's tent. He halted as they made eye contact.

"Are you Sir Ludwig?"

"I am."

The man extended a hand. "How do you do, sir? I don't know if you remember me, but I'm Lord Anwald, Baron of Zurkirk, and the duke's marshal. I've heard much about you."

"Good to see you again, but I'm afraid you have me at a disadvantage, my lord, for I am unfamiliar with your home."

"It lies to the west, past Anshlag. In any case, it doesn't really matter. Let's get you inside, shall we? We certainly don't want to keep His Grace waiting."

Lord Anwald led him into the largest tent where they found the duke waiting for them, along with Lord Gebhard and his son, Hagan. Lord Wulfram was also there, looking none too pleased.

"Ah," said the duke, "there you are. I was just talking to the barons here."

"My apologies, Your Grace. We were making camp," said Ludwig.

"Not to worry, you're here now." The duke turned to Lord Anwald. "Where was I?"

"You were discussing the baron's troops, Your Grace."

"Ah, yes, that was it. Lord Wulfram's forces are far too few to be of any consequence on the battlefield; still, I hesitate to not utilize them. As a result, I've decided to lump them in with the forces of Lord Gebhard."

"I must object," said Lord Wulfram. "I cannot, in good conscience, agree to such an arrangement."

"YOU cannot?" said Stein. "I'm the one who is being forced to take in those strays you call soldiers. I should have had them all executed when I destroyed your keep."

"You didn't destroy my keep," shouted Wulfram. "You couldn't even manage that. If it hadn't been for those mercenaries you hired, you'd still be rotting away outside my walls!"

"Gentlemen," said Lord Anwald. "I might remind you that you're in the presence of His Grace, the duke. Can you not act in a civilized manner?"

"It was not I who set out to invade my neighbour," said Lord Wulfram.

"But it was you who refused the marriage of my son to your daughter," returned Lord Gebhard. "What did you expect me to do, roll over and go back to sleep?"

The duke turned to the Baron of Zurkirk. "What say you, Lord Anwald? Have you an opinion on this matter?"

"I fear the animosity between their lordships may prove detrimental to the cause, Your Grace."

"Yes, I'm forced to agree." He turned back to face the two feuding barons. "Our land is under threat of invasion, my lords, so we must band together to defend what is ours. In order to do that, we must field as many men as possible. Can you not see reason, Lord Gebhard?"

"I agree," said the Baron of Mulsingen, "but they are, for the most part, men sworn to my service, and therefore should be under my command, as is my right."

"You have a son, do you not?"

Lord Gebhard looked at Hagan. "Of course, Your Grace. He's right here, as you can plainly see."

"And is he capable of exercising command in your name?"

Ludwig noticed the man fidgeting. "Of course, my lord. What, exactly, are you suggesting?"

"That your son assumes the position of captain of your forces. To balance things out, Lord Wulfram, your knight, Sir Ludwig, will become his aide. Would that be acceptable to you both?"

Lord Wulfram nodded, though whether he liked the idea or not was an entirely different matter.

"Good, then it's settled. Tomorrow morning, Sir Ludwig will gather his men and rendezvous with those under the command of Lord Hagan Stein."

The junior Stein preened at the compliment. To be named a captain was one thing, but to be addressed as Lord put him on an entirely different level of respect.

"I shall be honoured, my lord," said Ludwig.

"As will I, Your Grace," announced Hagan.

"Good. Now, as for you two," he addressed the two barons, "you shall remain close at hand, as my advisors. Is that understood?"

They both silently glared at him, defiance in their eyes.

The duke, not to be outdone, stared back. "I might remind you that as your duke, I am quite within my rights to strip you of your lands."

"You wouldn't dare!" said Baron Stein.

"Wouldn't I?" The duke glanced at Lord Anwald and nodded.

Lord Anwald made his way to a small table that sat nearby, on which were two rolled-up parchments. Picking them up, he then moved to stand beside the duke.

"Do you know what those are?" asked His Grace.

Ludwig noticed the sweat on Lord Gebhard's forehead and the nervous twitching of his leg.

"No, Your Grace," squeaked out Baron Stein.

"They are a proclamation, ceding all of your lands and titles to me for disbursement to individuals more deserving of such honours. Now, am I to issue these documents, or shall we all agree to honour my... suggestions?"

Baron Stein swallowed hard. "They are most acceptable, Your Grace."

The duke turned to Lord Wulfram. "And you? Do you also find them to your satisfaction?"

Ludwig had never seen his liege so pale of face.

"I do, Your Grace."

"Good, then it's settled. Now get out of here, the lot of you. I would have some peace and quiet for a change."

They all issued from the tent, Lord Wulfram stomping off while Lord Gebhard pulled his son Hagan aside to have words.

Lord Anwald, meanwhile, stood by Ludwig. "Well?" he said. "What do you make of this?"

"I have no objection, my lord. I have served Lord Gebhard once. To do so again is not so difficult."

Anwald lowered his voice. "Keep an eye on young Hagan. I fear he may be out of his depth."

"He and I are of a similar age, my lord."

"In years, perhaps, but in maturity, I would argue the point. In any event, the duke is counting on you."

"On me? I'm not the one in command."

"True, but you are a soldier, Sir Ludwig, while Master Hagan is not. He seeks position within the court, but you, as an outsider, hold no threat in that regard."

"So I am to be trusted because I have no political ambitions?"

Lord Anwald smiled. "I see you understand. Do this for His Grace, and you shall earn his friendship. Who knows, it may come in useful sometime in the future. One day you'll be the Baron of Verfeld, Ludwig, and having the ear of a duke, even a foreign one, may be advantageous."

34

THE NEW COMMAND

Summer 1095 SR

L udwig halted his men. Before them, Lord Gebhard's troops lay stretched out over the field, and beyond them, the Grim Defenders, all of whom would now be under Lord Hagan's command.

"There they are," he said.

"Are you sure about this?" asked Sergeant Krebbs. "The men aren't going to like it, sir."

"I don't imagine Stein's men will feel any better about it, but it's the will of the duke."

"We'll have to make the best of it, I guess."

"Best we get this over and done with," said Ludwig. "Come on, let's go and introduce ourselves."

Into the field he went, his men trailing along behind. Hagan was already there, walking amongst his own men, or rather, his father's, trying to look interested in all around him. In reality, he appeared uncomfortable, something as plain as day to the men under his command.

"My lord," called out Ludwig in greeting.

"Ah, there you are, Sir Ludwig. I was wondering when you'd get around to showing up."

"My apologies. We were some distance down the road."

Hagan waved away the excuse. "Don't let it worry you. I've only just arrived myself." He looked Ludwig up and down, paying particular attention to the mud on his boots. "Have you no horse?"

"I'm afraid not."

"Well, we'll have to do something about that. I have a spare you can use, a grey I inherited from our mage."

"You mean Herzog?"

"Yes, him," said Hagan. "Mind you, it's a finicky beast. I hope you don't mind."

"Not at all. Clay, wasn't it?"

"Wasn't what?"

"The horse. Wasn't Clay its name?"

"Yes, now that you mention it. I'll have it sent over in the morning, before we march. Better you should ride than walk. It lets the men see you."

"Thank you, I appreciate it."

Hagan, looking around to take in the campfires, seemed hesitant to talk.

"Where would you like to start?" asked Ludwig.

"A good question. What would you suggest?"

"I thought we might call all the sergeants together."

"Yes," agreed Hagan, "and Captain Ecke. After all, he still commands the mercenaries. I'll let you see to the details of that. We'll meet over there, by that large oak tree."

"By all means," said Ludwig. He turned to his own small command. "Sergeant Krebbs, have the men wait over there"—he pointed—"and then get yourself to that tree over yonder. I'll meet you there once I've rounded up the others."

"Yes, sir," replied the sergeant.

Ludwig scanned the camp. He knew Karl Dornhuffer had been made sergeant, and so he called out his name but was shocked to discover the man was almost directly behind him, his face hidden beneath his kettle helm.

"You looking for me, sir?"

"Yes, Sergeant. Join Sergeant Krebbs over by that tree. Your new captain would like a few words with you."

"New captain, sir?"

"Yes, Lord Hagan Stein."

Ludwig noted the look of disappointment on the man's face, but Dornhuffer soon recovered. "Yes, sir. Are you coming as well?"

"I'll join you shortly. I have to round up our mercenary friends."

"There's only the Grim Defenders left, sir. The duke took over the contract for the Blades."

"Did he now? Well, I suppose that will make things easier in the long run. Now, I'd better get moving, or Lord Hagan will be waiting all morning. Where are the Defenders?"

The sergeant pointed. "That way, sir."

Ludwig chastised himself, for their location should have been obvious to him, clearly marked out, as they were, by the neat lines of small tents.

He was soon amongst them. "Captain Ecke?" he called out.

"Here," came the reply. The mercenary commander stepped from his tent. "Sir Ludwig, this is a surprise. What can I do for you?"

"I'm here to inform you Lord Hagan Stein will be commanding the baron's forces, and that includes your men."

Ecke shrugged. "It makes no difference to me, as long as we're paid."

"I assume all financial arrangements will still be honoured," said Ludwig, "but I can check on that later if you wish. In the meantime, His Lordship would like to address his senior leaders. Can we have you and your sergeants join us over there?" He pointed.

"I'll gather them and be right over."

"Good. I look forward to seeing you there."

"One more thing," said Ecke.

"Yes?"

"Why are you here? You're not working for Baron Stein again, are you?"

"I am, in a manner of speaking. His Grace, the duke, has decided to merge the forces of Stein and Haas. The new, combined group will be commanded by Lord Hagan."

"And you?"

"I'll be his aide. Have you an issue with that?"

"No," said Ecke, "none at all."

"Good, then we'll see you shortly."

"You can count on it."

Ludwig joined his new commander.

"Did you get the mercenaries?" asked Lord Hagan.

"They'll be here shortly. The captain's gathering his sergeants."

"It looks like he already has."

Ludwig noted the approach of Ecke, followed by two of his mercenaries.

"What's this?" he called out, for Sigwulf was trailing his captain, joined by Cyn.

"This," replied Sig, "is our newest sergeant."

Hagan stood, open-mouthed, unable to articulate words.

Ludwig smiled, turning to his new master. "Are you ready to address them, my lord?"

"What is this woman doing here?"

"She's not a woman," replied Ludwig. "She's a soldier."

"Hey, now," said Cyn, "can't I be both?"

A chuckle ran through the other sergeants.

"That's quite enough of that," snapped Hagan. "I shall not have my leadership questioned."

"No one is questioning your right to be here, Lord," said Ludwig, "but Sergeant Cyn is an experienced veteran. We're lucky to have her."

Hagan looked her over, though his face still showed doubt. "A veteran, you say?"

"She's been a mercenary her entire life."

"I'll take your word for it."

Cyn was about to say something until Sigwulf placed his hand on her forearm. She remained silent.

"You wanted to see us?" prompted Captain Ecke.

"I'm your new commander," said Hagan, "and as such, I insist you show me the respect due my station."

"Of course, my lord," said Ecke. "Is there anything else you'd like to address?"

Hagan looked at Ludwig. "This," he said, "is Sir Ludwig, with whom I believe you're already acquainted. He will function as my aide, relaying orders as I see fit. Naturally, as commander, I shall be far too busy to look after the minutiae myself, so you should get used to seeing Sir Ludwig amongst you, carrying out my will."

"Minutiae?" said Krebbs.

"He means the small stuff," clarified Sigwulf.

"Now," continued the younger Stein, "I am needed at the duke's side. I shall leave you to it, Sir Ludwig."

Ludwig nodded his head. "Of course, my lord."

They watched him thread his way back through the camp.

"What in the Continent was that all about?" asked Ecke. "He didn't need to call us all together for that. He could have simply sent word."

"He's a man out of his depth," added Sigwulf. "Thank the Saints. Ludwig's here."

"That's SIR Ludwig to you," said Cyn.

The huge sergeant grinned. "So it is. So, SIR Ludwig, what are your orders?"

In answer, Ludwig turned to Ecke. "If I remember correctly, Captain, you have a few men who can use a bow. I'd like to group them all together, along with those from Sergeant Dornhuffer's group. I know they're crossbowmen, but I'd prefer to have all our archers together."

"I can do that."

"Good," continued Ludwig. "We'll add in Lord Wulfram's archers as well."

"Anything else?" asked Ecke.

"Yes, since we're now all part of one big company, we'll be marching together. For now, we'll keep Lord Gebhard's original men in front, with the Grim Defenders coming second. Lord Wulfram's will follow along afterwards."

Ecke smiled. "Keeping the enemies at bay?"

"More or less," agreed Ludwig, "but they'll eventually have to work together if we are to fight in battle." He looked skyward, trying to clear his thoughts, but found no inspiration. "If tomorrow is anything like the last few days, it'll be a hard march. We'll form up on the road at first light, but we won't begin moving until everyone is ready. Any questions?"

"What about camping tomorrow night? Do we still maintain separate campfires?"

"No, I want the men to realize we're all part of the same army. I'll give it some thought as we march, but I'm thinking we'll adopt the same technique as our mercenary friends."

"Sir?" said Krebbs.

"He means," said Sigwulf, "we'll organize the campfires in lines."

"Yes," added Cyn, "and post proper guards."

Ludwig smiled. "That's exactly what I mean. Now get back to your people. We have work to do."

A servant showed up just before daybreak, bringing the grey horse Hagan had promised. Ludwig took the reins, eager to climb into the saddle, but his muscles were soon complaining. It was not that the horse was difficult to handle, but his legs and back had not been riding for some time and rebelled against this recent activity.

He saw little of his new commander. Lord Hagan, as he now liked to be addressed, showed up at noon to see how the men were faring but offered little in the way of encouragement or even actual interest.

Ludwig was content. True, he had no end of issues to deal with, but he felt valued as if his mere existence now had meaning. Men would ask for brief rests, complaining their legs were sore, or they would beg for a water stop to fill their skins. His job was to keep them moving, though not to wear them out, for their strength must be conserved if they were to fight a battle.

By mid-afternoon, they topped a rise, revealing the army stretched out before them. To Ludwig's eyes, it was far larger than that which had set out from the capital, and he had to remind himself they had been expecting others to join them. He thought back to Lord Anwald. He had not been present when they had left Torburg, and so he must have met the duke's army on the road. Perhaps others had done so as well?

To him, the army was immense, easily numbering two thousand individuals. He couldn't imagine a force that could defeat them. What, then, could the enemy muster? Were his own men all marching to their doom? He hoped not.

Later that afternoon, they stopped to water themselves. Ludwig was walking his horse to a stream when he heard the sounds of an altercation.

"Get your filthy hands off our water."

"We have as much right to it as you do," replied the familiar voice of Arturo, the footman who liked to moan about everything.

Ludwig tied his horse to a tree and sought out the source of the dispute, arriving to see three of Stein's men, standing in front of the small stream, denying access to Arturo and his companion, the archer Simmons.

"What's going on here?" Ludwig demanded.

"These men are trying to steal our water," proclaimed the leader of the trio, a thin man with about as much muscle as an arrow.

"You own this river, do you?" said Ludwig.

"No, but we saw it first."

Ludwig moved to stand between the two groups. "Do you know who you're talking to?"

"Yes," he snarled.

"Yes, SIR," corrected Ludwig.

The thin man stared at him, venom in his eyes. "I serve Lord Gebhard."

"As do I." Ludwig moved in on him, forcibly pushing him back. In answer, the man's hand went to the hilt of his dagger. Ludwig drew his sword with lightning speed, taking the fellow by surprise by pointing its tip at his neck.

"Go ahead," Ludwig said, "pull a knife on me. Let's see what happens, shall we?"

The man turned pale. "Sorry, sir, I meant no disrespect."

"These men are part of the company now, YOUR company. Sometime in the next few days, there'll be a battle, and when there is, you'll need to stand next to each other and fight for your very lives. Do you seriously think it's a good idea to antagonize them?"

The man lowered his eyes. "No, sir."

"What's your name?"

"Hahn, sir, Gerrit Hahn."

"Get back to the company, Hahn. I'll have words with your sergeant."

"Yes, sir."

Ludwig turned on Arturo. "Get your water," he snapped, "and be quick about it." As soon as the words came from his mouth, he regretted them. It wasn't their fault. They were being asked to work with men who they had been fighting no less than a fortnight ago.

Ludwig felt the icy grip of despair. What if these men failed him on the day of battle? What if he couldn't get them to set aside their differences? He must strive to bring them together, yet he could think of nothing which could accomplish that feat. He resolved to take up the matter with Hagan at his earliest opportunity.

They didn't reach their next camp until it was quite late in the day. Without having spoken to his commander, Ludwig was loath to put the men together. So instead, he kept them apart, using the mercenaries to separate them, as they had on the march.

He issued special instructions to the Grim Defenders, ordering them to use force to keep the two groups apart should it become necessary. As it turned out, no one was willing to break the rules, so the evening passed without conflict.

Ludwig had just finished brushing down Clay when he heard the sound of approaching hooves. He turned, expecting to see Hagan, but instead, there sat Lady Rosalyn.

"Good evening, my lady," he said.

"And to you, Sir Ludwig."

"It's a bit late for a ride, isn't it? Did you come seeking me?"

She blushed, her face easily illuminated by the campfires. "I actually came seeking Lord Hagan. Is he here?"

"I haven't seen him," he confessed. "You might try up by the duke's retinue."

"I've just come from there. I'm told he commands the company at the back of the column."

"And so he does, yet I feel he spends too little time here."

"Is he ill?"

"Ill?" said Ludwig. "No, but I suspect he's unsure of himself. Tell me, did you ever have that dinner with him?"

Rosalyn laughed. "No, I never had the chance. The army set out the very next day."

"Perhaps you'll have an opportunity when we reach Chermingen?"

"One can hope. I've heard of your new assignment. Is it to your liking?"

"It is," he replied, "though I wish I knew more of such things. Some days it feels like there are countless issues to deal with. It's most distressful."

Rosalyn looked over at the nearby camp. "It looks peaceful enough."

He laughed. "Peaceful? You should have seen them earlier today. They were almost at each other's throats over the use of a stream."

"They need a firm hand, that's all. My father says simple men need a leader they can respect, and respect is earned through the infliction of discipline."

"Fine words, but I often find the reality is a far cry from what people say."

"Are you doubting my father's wisdom?"

"No," said Ludwig, "only wondering if it applies to me, in this particular situation."

"If his words do not bring you comfort, then you must find your own way to resolve the matter."

"Of that, I'm well aware. I'll give it further thought tonight."

"Maybe you should pray?"

He smiled. "Are you mocking me now?"

"No, but you have found solace in the words of Saint Mathew before, have you not?"

"I suppose I have, now you mention it."

"The Saints were wise people," said Rosalyn, "and their words meant to inspire, not control. There's much to be said for that."

"I see the truth of it, my lady. Unfortunately, I fear I did not think to bring the *Book of Mathew* with me."

She smiled, reaching into her bag slung across her horse's back. "Then it's good that I found you, for I have a gift."

"For me?"

"Indeed."

"I can't accept," said Ludwig, "for to do so would be seen as improper."

"Nonsense. I give it to you as a valued friend, nothing more." She pulled out a small book, its soft leather cover weathered and worn. "It's a prayer book of Saint Mathew. Not the entire *Book of Mathew*, I grant you, but still of value to those who believe in such things."

He took the book, holding it with reverence. "Where did you get this?" he asked. "It's quite the find."

"In Torburg. I discovered it in an old shop as I was looking for that expensive tavern. Of course, I immediately thought of you when I saw it." She smiled. "Consider it thanks for all you have done for my father and me."

"I have done no more than my duty, my lady."

"Your duty? You have done so much more than that, Sir Ludwig. I shall always think of you with kindness. You're like a brother to me."

"I'm only sorry I couldn't find Hagan for you. I really have no idea where he might be."

"It matters not. He can't hide forever."

"And when you do find him?"

She smiled. "I'll make him buy me that expensive dinner." She turned her horse around and rode off, tearing through the camp without a care in the world.

Ludwig smiled as she left. Moments later, he caught sight of a horseman under a nearby tree, his face clearly lit by the fires. As his eyes met those of the rider, he recognized Hagan Stein. The man stared at him for a moment longer and then, with a scowl, galloped off towards the front of the column.

35

RIVALS

Summer 1095 SR

B y the fifth day, he began wondering if they hadn't become lost. The trees they marched by all began to look familiar, giving him the feeling they'd been going in circles. Only after they passed a small hamlet did he let himself relax, for they were clearly making progress, after all, however slow it might appear.

That evening the camp was laid out much as before, with the Grim Defenders in the middle. Ludwig, desperate to escape some of the responsibility of command, wandered over to see what Sigwulf and Cyn were up to. He soon found them sitting before a fire, cups in hand.

"Well, well," said Cyn, looking up. "Look what the wolves dragged in."

"May I join you?" asked Ludwig.

"Certainly," said Sigwulf. "Care for some wine?"

"Of course."

"I warn you, it's barely tolerable."

"Yes," agreed Cyn. "In fact, it's disgusting, but anything's better than the water around here."

Sigwulf dug up a cup, pouring the pale liquid to the brim. "Here, it helps to gulp it down."

They both waited as Ludwig took a sip, then screwed up his face in disgust. "That was truly awful."

"What did I tell you?" said Cyn.

"Would you prefer water?" asked Sigwulf.

Ludwig caught his breath, the foul taste still on his tongue. "No," he managed to squeak out. "That'll do."

Sigwulf laughed, but Cyn wore a more serious expression.

"So," she said at last, "how do you like being a captain?"

"I could ask the same of you," Ludwig replied. "How do you like being a sergeant?"

"I asked you first."

"So you did," said Ludwig. "The truth is I feel overworked and underpaid."

"I suppose that makes you more like a sergeant," said Cyn. "I'd have to say the same thing."

He looked at Sigwulf. "You've been a sergeant for some time. Does it get any easier?"

"No, but the pay's better."

Ludwig raised his cup. "Spoken like a true mercenary."

They clinked their drinks, each taking a swig of the wine and making a face.

"That's foul," said Sigwulf. "It reminds me of the time Cyn here decided to brew mead from potatoes."

"Potatoes?" said Ludwig. "Don't you need honey for mead?"

"Normally," said Cyn, "but there was none in the area. You know us mercenaries, always trying to make do with what we have."

"What's that ever gotten us?" asked Sigwulf.

"Each other?"

He grinned. "Yes, of course, and I wouldn't change that for anything."

"Aw, he's so sweet."

Sigwulf blushed, sending Ludwig into a fit of laughter.

"Go ahead," the big man said, "laugh it up, Ludwig. Sooner or later, a woman's going to catch up to you, and then the boot will be on the other foot."

"Not me, my friend. That ship has sailed."

"Don't be ridiculous," said Cyn. "There's plenty more out there"—she waved her hand in the general vicinity of the wilderness—"somewhere."

A twig snapped in the direction she had indicated, drawing their attention. "See?" she added. "They're coming for you right now."

The distant echo of steel on steel drifted towards them.

"That's no ship," said Ludwig, his drink forgotten. He stood, tossing aside the cup, only to be followed moments later by Sig and Cyn.

"Alarm!" cried out Sigwulf, his voice booming through the camp.

"Come," said Ludwig. "Let's see what beckons."

Cyn raced past him, scooping up her mace. Others began taking up the call as men raced to arm themselves.

"It's coming from over there," said Ludwig. "What lies in that direction?"

"A stream," replied Sigwulf, "and beyond that, more of our own army."

"Then let's get there before our men kill some of our allies."

They crashed through the trees into a clearing where a small stream meandered its way through the forest, but the real problem lay in those fighting over its use. Two men, wearing the colours of Lord Gebhard, were lying on the near bank, their tunics stained with blood while a third battled the enemy.

Ludwig tried to discern who the man fought, but there was little to identify either side in the dim light of the moon. Cyn ran into their midst, striking out with her mace, taking one of their attackers in the thigh, sending him to the ground. Sigwulf gave a bellow and charged in behind her, his sword swinging wildly.

Others streamed through the woods behind Ludwig, and he saw Krebbs pass him, along with Arturo and two others. The fight grew more intense. Ludwig, giving up on trying to make sense of it, waded into the water, his sword striking out. There were at least twenty combatants now, with the numbers growing as word spread.

His sword scraped along a chainmail hauberk, and then someone stabbed out with the point of a spear. Ludwig twisted, avoiding the blow, then plunged the tip of his blade into the man's arm, eliciting a cry of pain.

He had a brief glimpse of Sigwulf lifting a man over his head, then throwing him to the bank. Cyn, meanwhile, was trying to push men apart from each other. Ludwig struggled to understand why, and then it hit him like a brick. These men they were fighting were the Blades of Vengeance.

Determined to stop the insanity, he called out in the loudest voice he could. "Stop, in the name of Duke Heinrich!"

At the invocation of their leader's name, the fighting ceased. Combatants glared at each other but lowered their weapons.

"Get back to your camp," ordered Ludwig, "or I'll get the duke's own men down here, and we'll begin executions."

The two sides separated, and men began hurrying back to their respective sides of the stream. Ludwig shook his head, not quite believing what he had witnessed. Instead of fighting amongst themselves, his men had decided to go after their allies. What could possibly be next?

Sigwulf and Cyn soon found him. The big sergeant was huffing and puffing, but his smaller counterpart was like a fox with a mouse.

"That was fun!" she said.

"Fun?" said Ludwig. "Is that what you call it?"

Sigwulf smiled. "Well, it wasn't a total disaster." He smacked Ludwig on the arm and then pointed. Ludwig looked to see a couple of Wulfram's men helping another back to camp, a man wearing Lord Gebhard's colours.

"It looks like all they needed was a common foe," said Sigwulf.

"I still say we could have taken them," said Cyn.

Ludwig smiled. "Likely, but we'll need them to fight the invaders."

In answer, Cyn looked at the retreating mercenaries of the Blades of Vengeance. She held up her hand, extending her middle finger. "This is for you," she yelled.

"You'd better get her back to camp," Ludwig told Sigwulf, "before she decimates them."

They returned to a far different scene. Soldiers now mingled freely, offering words of encouragement to the wounded and sharing drinks with their former rivals. The Grim Defenders, not to be outdone, told tales of their own, highlighting the unending dispute between themselves and the Blades of Vengeance.

Ludwig collapsed by the fire, feeling drained by the ordeal. All he wanted was to shut his eyes and fall asleep, but the approach of a horse interfered. Looking up, he discovered Lord Hagan Stein staring down at him.

"What was all the commotion about?" he asked.

"Nothing, my lord, merely the men being a bit rambunctious. It's all been settled."

Hagan scowled, an action that was not lost on Ludwig.

"Is something wrong, my lord?"

"No, nothing," the lord snapped. He paused as if wanting to say more but then clenched his mouth shut. Turning his horse, he sped off without another word.

"What was that all about?" asked Sigwulf.

"I don't know," replied Ludwig, "but I aim to find out."

He stood, but his legs felt weak.

"Sit," said Sigwulf.

"What's wrong with me?"

"Nothing," added Cyn. "It's only the wine."

Ludwig sat, his eyes seeking out his discarded cup. "What did you put in that?"

"Just the usual," she said, "except for some substitutions, of course."

"What kinds of substitutions?"

"Nothing too dangerous. You've had mushroom wine before, haven't you?"

"Mushrooms? I hope they weren't poisonous."

"No, of course not," said Cyn. "At least I don't think so."

"You don't THINK so?"

"Well, it was dark by the time we made camp, so I can't be sure."

"You mean you might have poisoned us?"

Sigwulf burst out in laughter. "She had you going there for a moment, but I can't let this continue. Relax, Ludwig, there's nothing dangerous about the wine."

"Then why are my legs shaking?"

"It's a side effect. Let's just say you'll sleep well tonight, shall we?"

"Then I must return to my blanket." He felt his eyes closing despite his best attempts to keep them open. The next thing he knew, he was lying on his side, a blanket laid over him, and then he fell into a deep sleep.

Ludwig opened his eyes to the bright morning sun glaring down upon him. All around him, the encampment was a bustle of activity as men gathered their gear and hastily downed what food they had. Ludwig sat up, instantly regretting his haste.

"He's awake," came Cyn's voice.

A shadow hovered over him. "Here," said Sigwulf, "have some water. It'll help."

Ludwig downed the cup, then rose, finding his legs up to the task this time. "Let's not do that again, all right?"

Sigwulf laughed. "Fine with me, my friend."

Everyone was full of energy this morning, eager to be on their way. Old enemies were now firm friends united in their distaste of the Blades of Vengeance. Who would have thought something like that was even possible?

"Let Captain Ecke know the men will march together, would you?" asked Ludwig. "Now, where's my horse?"

"Come on," said Sigwulf. "I'll help you find him, not that he's much of a mount though."

"He's all I've got."

"Where are you off to in such a hurry?"

"I must talk to Hagan," said Ludwig. "Something's up, and I need to get to the bottom of it."

It didn't take long to find Clay. The horse was standing in a field, nibbling away at some tufts of grass, ignoring the activity around him. Sigwulf helped saddle the beast, and then Ludwig was on his way, searching out Lord Hagan.

It took him some time to pick his way through the rest of the army, for not every company was so eager to be on the road. Ludwig had to investigate every group of horsemen he came across in his quest to find the younger Stein until he finally found his prey.

Lord Hagan rode with Lord Kruger while the baron's men marched behind them. Ludwig spurred on his horse, coming up alongside them.

"Lord Hagan," he called out. "I wonder if I might have a word?"

"What is it?" snapped Hagan. "Can't you see I'm busy?"

"My pardon, Lord, but there are matters which require your attention. You are, after all, commander of the company."

This statement appeared to mollify the man. "Very well, what is it?"

"I wonder if we might speak in private, my lord? It is of a delicate nature."

Lord Kruger smiled. "Go ahead," he said. "You can always catch up to me later. It's not as if I'm difficult to find."

"My apologies, my lord," said Hagan. "I shall return shortly."

"Take your time. There's no hurry."

Ludwig led him off the road and to the edge of the woods, far from prying eyes. Halting Clay, he turned to face his commander.

"I feel there's a distance between us," began Ludwig. "I would have it brought out into the open."

"To what end?"

"We are marching to battle, my lord. Is it not best to do so without distractions?"

"Speak, and I will listen."

"It's not I who must speak, but you, my lord. What is it that vexes you so?"

Hagan's face twisted into a fury. "You! You're the problem, Ludwig."

"Me? How am I the problem?"

"You're the one who gets everything your heart desires: knighthood, command, even women!"

Ludwig felt his heart jump into his throat. Women? What was Hagan talking about? He tried to reason it through and then remembered his talk with Rosalyn. This fool must have mistaken her conversation for an expression of love.

"Is this about Rosalyn?" he asked.

"You know it is," said Hagan. "I would know your designs on her."

"I have none, my lord, other than friendship. She is like a sister to me."

"I wish I could believe you."

"It is you who she desires, Lord, not me."

Hagan's face softened, but still, there was a threat lurking behind those eyes.

"I swear by the spirit of Saint Mathew, I speak the truth, Lord. I have no interest in her of a romantic nature."

Hagan visibly relaxed. "I'm sorry," he said, most unexpectedly. "I fear my heart rules where my head should prevail. I have never been so captivated by a woman in all my life. When I saw her with you the other day…"

"She was, in truth, looking for you," said Ludwig.

"But I saw her give you a present."

"A reward for saving her life back in Regnitz, nothing more." He reached into his tunic, pulling forth the book of prayers. "Here, see for yourself."

Hagan took it, flipping through the pages. He finally handed it back. "It appears I have acted churlishly. I do apologize."

"There's nothing to apologize for, my lord. Your heart was wounded."

"I envy you, Ludwig. You have such an easy way with the men."

"All of my life, I have dreamed of leading them," said Ludwig, "but now, I fear, I am not up to the task."

"How can you say that? You've brought the company together, while all I could do was run away and hide. It is I who have failed."

"It doesn't have to be that way," said Ludwig. "If you take a more active role in the company, I'll show you how to gain their respect."

"You think that possible? I'm not a knight, nor a seasoned warrior, and truth be told, not much of a swordsman either. The men would soon see through my inexperience."

"All the more reason for you to let me help you."

"You would do that?"

"Of course," said Ludwig.

"Why?"

"I beg your pardon?"

"Why would you help me? What could possibly be in it for you?"

"I'm not from Erlingen," said Ludwig, "nor do I have any desire to settle here. When this war is over, I'll return to my home, in Hadenfeld, to be reunited with my father. These men who march for us are simple folk. They don't fight for the duke. They fight for their families and their way of life. All they want is to return home alive and in one piece. I made a promise to myself that I would do my utmost to make sure that happens."

"You cannot promise such a thing," said Hagan. "It's beyond the purview of any one man."

"True," said Ludwig, "but I can do everything in my power to give them a fighting chance, and that's all they can hope for."

He could see the young lord's interest piqued. "Is that all it takes?"

"I wish," said Ludwig. "Look, there's more to leading men than simply wishing them well. We train them, teach them to use their weapons to the best of their ability. The more confident they grow, the better their chances of surviving."

"But I cannot fight," said Hagan. "Not with any real skill, that is."

"YOU don't have to. That's what the sergeants are for. All you have to do is take an interest. Watch them train, compliment their progress, even if you don't see it."

"To what end?"

"To encourage them, Hagan. What do you look for in a leader?"

"A man of power."

"And what does that mean, precisely?"

The younger Stein opened his mouth to respond but struggled to find an answer. "I suppose I don't really know."

"True leadership is about inspiring your troops, and that can take many forms. You'd be surprised what a single word of encouragement can do. Did your father ever compliment you?"

"He has, on occasion."

"And how did that make you feel?"

Hagan straightened in the saddle. "Proud."

"There you have it. Make the men feel proud, Hagan. That's the secret to leading them."

"And the rest? How do I make them fight?"

"Leave that to me and the sergeants."

"So you can reap the rewards?"

"It's not about the rewards," said Ludwig. "I'm leaving eventually, remember? The rewards, the honour, will be yours alone."

Hagan sat, mulling things over. Ludwig could imagine his brain thinking things through.

"These men are yours, Hagan, and you deserve a right to earn their loyalty." Ludwig held out his hand. "Let me begin by offering you the hand of friendship."

"I will accept your offer." Hagan reached out, and they clasped hands in a firm grip.

"I won't let you down," promised Ludwig. "Come back to the company, and I'll have the men following you to the ends of the Continent by week's end."

"And what of the Lady Rosalyn?"

Ludwig smiled. "I feel that situation will resolve itself in due time, but I'll put in a good word for you if you like."

36

CHERMINGEN

Summer 1095 SR

"What a strange city," said Ludwig. The streets of Chermingen were narrow, the architecture far different from that of Torburg, and he had to wonder why.

As if reading his mind, Hagan chose that exact moment to chime in. "It is, isn't it? You know, they say it's one of the oldest cities on the Continent, dating back to the Old Kingdom."

"What Old Kingdom is that?"

"Therengia, of course. I assumed you'd heard of it?"

"Naturally," said Ludwig. "In fact, I've read all I can about it, but I've never heard that term used before."

"It's common enough around here. We don't like to use their name, you see. Too much superstition surrounding it."

Ludwig was about to laugh but saw the serious look on his companion's face and stopped himself. "What kind of superstition?"

"There's always the fear that it shall rise again."

"By merely mentioning the name? I find that hard to accept."

"Not if you consider the facts," said Hagan.

"And what facts are those?"

"There are a lot of people in these parts that are descended from that ancient race. Recalling their name for the Old Kingdom could ignite the desire to recapture their former glory."

"Is that why the duke keeps them from positions of influence?"

Hagan looked at him in surprise. "You are a remarkably observant individual, Ludwig. I'm surprised you know of such things. Tell me, do you have any of them back home in Hadenfeld?"

"Possibly. I've never really looked."

"Never looked? How can that be? They are a dangerous people, my friend. You can't let them get organized, or you might find yourself facing a rebellion."

"Is that what the duke believes?"

"It's been the policy since the days of his grandfather, or so I'm led to understand."

"And what are your sentiments?"

Hagan paused a moment, obviously thinking things through. Ludwig waited, knowing the man would eventually make his mind known.

"I consider it a reasonable assumption," the young lord finally revealed. "After all, the Old Kingdom was a dangerous foe, and it took decades to finally defeat them. The last thing we want is for them to rise again."

Ludwig frowned. It appeared everyone in Erlingen was more concerned with keeping people in their place than looking after them.

"You don't agree?" asked Hagan.

"I don't. I'm of the opinion that the more you try to suppress people, the more they begin to resent it. If anything, you're only making the situation worse."

"Then what would you do, were you the duke?"

"Ah," said Ludwig, "but I'm not."

"Still, humour me."

"Well, I suppose I'd look at including them in positions of authority, rather than shutting them out entirely."

"Are you mad?" said Hagan. "Why on the Continent would you do that?"

"To make them feel like they're part of society."

"You do have some odd ideas, my friend. Where in the Saint's name did you ever come up with such thoughts?"

"From my mother," said Ludwig. "She would often talk of such things."

"Did your father not put her in her place?"

"Her place?"

"Yes, a woman's place is looking after the home, not talking of things she doesn't understand."

"And this is your idea of what women are like?"

"Of course. How else would I view the fairer sex?"

"How many women have you actually met?"

"Plenty," said Hagan. "Why?"

"In my experience, talking that way will only result in an empty bed. You wouldn't treat Lady Rosalyn with such discourtesy, would you?"

Hagan looked as if someone had hit him with a brick. "I... hadn't thought of that."

Ludwig chuckled. "That much was obvious."

"I must admit to having little experience in such things. It was my father who taught me a woman's place is in the home."

"And how does your mother feel about that?"

"My mother can be an ill-tempered woman at times. She's hardly the type to discuss such matters."

"Can you blame her? What would you do if you were relegated to the household all day long?"

He could tell Hagan was in over his head. The poor fellow struggled to come to grips with the concept, something which his upbringing had ill-prepared him for.

"What would you do?"

"Do?" said Ludwig. "About what? Your mother?"

Hagan laughed, then visibly began to relax. "No, I mean about Lady Rosalyn. I love her, Ludwig, and I would not see her mistreated."

"You love her? You hardly know her." As soon as the words left his lips, he saw the irony in them, for his own father had thought the same of him when he had met Charlaine.

"I cannot get her out of my mind, ever since I saw her at Regnitz."

"You never met her before that?"

"No, the betrothal was all my father's idea. I'd heard of her, of course. You can't live in Erlingen and not know the noble houses."

"If I were you, I'd learn more about her."

"Like what?"

"Her interests. Does she ride? Knit? Joust?"

Hagan laughed again. "Joust? What manner of woman jousts? Honestly, you're too much sometimes, Ludwig."

"I admit that jousting is likely not on her list of things she participates in, but she might like to watch. I know she likes tournaments."

"Does she? How interesting. Could be there's more to this woman than meets the eye."

"Isn't there always?"

"I assume you've some experience with women?"

"Well," said Ludwig, "I'm not an innocent if that's what you mean."

"And have you ever been in love?"

"Only once, but it didn't work out."

"I'm sorry to hear that," said Hagan. "Did she die?"

"Die? Why in the name of the Saints would you even suggest that?"

"I just assumed. I mean, there's nothing wrong with you after all. You're the son of a baron. Why wouldn't a woman find you irresistible?"

"I'm flattered you hold me in such high esteem, but the truth is it wasn't her choice, nor was it mine. My father objected to our union."

"Ah," said Hagan. "She was an unsuitable match then, according to your father."

"She was."

"Was she a commoner?"

"Yes," said Ludwig, "and not only that, she had a trade."

"A trade? Surely not."

"She was a smith, as was her father."

"Now you're pulling my leg. A female smith. What a preposterous idea."

Ludwig felt his temper flaring, but before he could formulate a response, they rode past the last of the buildings and into the field that lay to the north. Before them lay the army of Erlingen, an imposing sight, for it stretched on as far as the eye could see. They both halted, causing the men behind them to march around their position.

"Saints alive," said Hagan. "There must be thousands of them."

"Indeed," said Ludwig, "but the real question is where our men are supposed to camp? I don't see a spare section of field anywhere."

"There's someone up ahead, directing troops," said Hagan. "Let's hope he can tell us."

Ludwig halted the men, then joined his commander. They rode over to the man in question, who, having just finished dealing with someone, turned to greet them, revealing a familiar face.

"Kurt?" said an astonished Ludwig. "What are you doing here?"

His old comrade smiled. "Looking after the duke's business, what else?" He looked past them to see the warriors lined up on the road. "Are those all yours?"

"They belong to Lord Hagan Stein. I'm merely his aide."

Kurt consulted a list, then looked eastward, pointing. "You'll camp over there by the farmer's field just beyond that treeline."

"That far?" said Hagan.

"I'm afraid so, my lord," said Kurt. "I've been ordered to keep certain parties away from each other."

"To what end?" asked Ludwig.

"There are several rivalries that could lead to bloodshed. His Grace would like them to save that type of behaviour for the enemy."

"Rest assured, you won't have any trouble from us."

Again Kurt glanced at his notes. "That's not what it says here."

"I beg your pardon?" said Hagan.

"According to this, we've had reports of a run-in with a group of mercenaries. Do the Blades of Vengeance sound familiar?"

Ludwig blushed.

"That," added Hagan, "was a minor disagreement."

"That disagreement injured half a dozen men, my lord. A few more altercations like that, and we won't need an enemy army to destroy us."

Hagan cleared his throat. "You say the field was to the east?"

"Yes, my lord. Follow the path here, and it will lead you towards the treeline."

"Thank you."

Ludwig ordered the men eastward, through the muck and mire Kurt Wasser had called a path. So many had already trod the route that it was now little more than a road of mud that sucked at men's boots.

"Keep an eye on the rear of the column," said Hagan. "I shouldn't like anyone to be left behind."

"Yes, my lord," said Ludwig. He wheeled Clay around, trotting down the side of the column towards its back end. There, the archer, Simmons, already appeared to be stuck in the mud. Sergeant Krebbs was pulling on one of his arms, trying to extricate the man but with only limited success. Ludwig brought his horse closer, the intent being to assist, but as he did, the archer's foot finally pulled free.

"Walk on the side of the path," ordered Ludwig, "or it'll take us all night to get to our designated location."

"Aye, sir," said Krebbs.

Ludwig shook his head. He could well imagine what awaited them once they marched to battle. A muddy path was probably the least of their worries.

Kurt's voice drifted towards him in the wind. "You are not allowed," he was saying.

Ludwig gazed westward to where his old mentor was addressing a group of a dozen men. His interest piqued, he rode closer.

"But we want to fight for the duke," a man was saying. "Why can't you understand that?"

"I'm sorry, but by order of His Grace, you are forbidden from holding any rank, and that includes leading these men."

"Is there a problem here?" Ludwig called out.

The stranger turned to him, revealing grey eyes. "This man won't let us fight for the duke," he said.

"That is not what I said," argued Kurt. "I merely indicated you're not allowed to command them."

"What's your name?" asked Ludwig.

"Beornoth, and I've brought a dozen men to help the cause, but this fool won't allow them in."

Ludwig looked at Kurt, who merely shrugged.

"It's the duke's law," he defended. "Therengians are not allowed to hold any positions of command, especially leading troops, no matter how few their numbers."

"I'm sure he could make an exception here, don't you? After all, we need every man we can get."

"I cannot go against the wishes of His Grace."

Ludwig looked over the small group. They were armed with axes and shields, and at least half of them had helmets. "Can you fight?" he asked.

"We wouldn't be here if we couldn't," said Beornoth.

"I'll take them into Lord Hagan's group if they're willing."

Kurt looked at the Therengian. "Well? Does that suit you?"

"It does," said Beornoth. He turned to Ludwig. "Thank you, my lord."

"I'm not a lord," said Ludwig, "merely a knight, but in any case, you're welcome. We can always use more men, and yours look like they've seen a fight or two."

"That they have," the man replied.

"Follow me, and I'll take you to our camp. Did you bring any blankets?"

"For what?"

"To sleep on?"

"No, Sir…"

"Sir Ludwig of Verfeld."

"Never heard of it," replied the Therengian.

"Nor would I expect you to. I hail from a place called Hadenfeld. It lies some distance away."

"Might I ask what brought you here?"

Ludwig smiled. "It's a long story, so perhaps another time. What of yourself? I must say it's a little odd to see a group of your people looking so battle hardened."

"Our story is likely as long as yours, sir, and best told around the fire with plenty of drink"—he glanced around—"away from the ears of Erlingeners."

The statement immediately caught Ludwig's attention. "I understand completely. Now, if we can get through this mud, I'll show you to the camp."

. . .

By the time darkness descended, they were sitting before a fire. Lord Hagan, at first, was delighted more men had joined his command, but the news they were Therengians was not well received.

"You know the duke's wishes in this regard," he said, "yet you tempt his wrath?"

"They are warriors," defended Ludwig, "and seasoned ones at that. We'll need every man we can muster when we face the invaders. What does it matter the colour of their eyes?"

"Fine, but I shall hold you responsible for them. And don't even consider making any of them sergeants, do you hear me?"

"Yes, my lord." Ludwig watched as Hagan rode off, no doubt seeking out his father, then his attention returned to the men in the encampment. The newcomers, welcomed by the soldiers, gathered around the fires, likely telling stories as was often done. Obviously, the common soldier didn't care about a man's eyes so long as he fought alongside the others. Now, if only the nobles could be convinced to give up their prejudices.

He wandered over to one of the campfires where Sigwulf and Cyn were chatting with Beornoth and sharing a drink.

"Is that more of that disgusting wine?" Ludwig called out.

"No," replied Sigwulf. "Ale, if you can believe it. Care for some?"

"I thought you'd never ask."

"Hah," added Cyn. "You knew all along we'd offer it to you. Don't try to say otherwise."

"I confess you have the right of it. Now pass over that cup, or I might be forced to confiscate it."

She passed him a drink, and he took a tentative sniff. Content it was not tainted by mushrooms this time, he took an experimental sip. "Not bad. Where did you get this?"

"Don't ask," said Sigwulf. "It's best you don't know."

Ludwig took another swig. "Then forget I said anything. I see you've met Beornoth here."

"We have," said Sigwulf, staring back.

Ludwig could sense something else going on but decided not to press the issue. Sig would reveal whatever it was when he was ready.

"Well," said Beornoth, rising, "I should get some sleep. It's been a long day. Good night to you, Sir Ludwig, and to you two." He nodded to Cyn and Sigwulf, then left them to their thoughts.

Sigwulf waited until he was out of sight before speaking. "You do realize what you've done, don't you?"

"No, what? Hired a Therengian?"

"He's more than that."

"I'm not sure I follow."

"Did you note the man's torc?"

"I wasn't really paying attention to such things. Why?"

"It bears the symbol of Tauril."

"Who is...?"

"For Saint's sake, Ludwig," said Cyn. "Don't you know anything about religion? She's the goddess of the earth."

"So?"

"So the man worships the old Gods."

"It matters not to me," said Ludwig. "All I care about is the fact that he can fight."

"Then ask yourself this, my friend. How did a Therengian get battle experience? You know they're not allowed to form their own bands."

Ludwig shrugged. "I assumed he had served a lord of some type."

"But the nobles here don't like their type," piped up Cyn.

"That makes sense from what I've heard, but I still don't see what it is you're trying to intimate."

"Then let me say it plain and simple for you," she continued. "The man's a rebel."

"We're all trying to change things in one way or another."

"No," said Sigwulf. "She means they've fought against the duke's rule of Erlingen."

"What makes you say that?"

"You ask that knowing my history? Come now, Ludwig, you know I'm right."

"WE'RE right," corrected Cyn.

"I suppose it's possible," admitted Ludwig, "but what of it? They want to fight, and we need experienced warriors. It's a mutually beneficial arrangement."

"So it doesn't bother you you're harbouring criminals?" asked Cyn.

"Can you say the Grim Defenders are any different?"

"Of course there's a difference. We're mercenaries, not sworn to the service of some lord."

"But you are," argued Ludwig. "Go and ask your captain if you don't believe me. It matters little if you're on contract or a sworn man; you still fight for him."

"So this whole situation doesn't bother you?"

"I'll admit it's inconvenient."

"Inconvenient?" said Cyn. "It's far more than that, Ludwig. We could be hung for this."

"Hanged," said Sigwulf.

"What?"

"A person is hanged, not hung," corrected the large warrior.

"You know what I mean."

"Who else knows?" asked Ludwig.

"Likely only us. It's not as if he's displaying his religion out in the open. I only noticed it as he leaned over the fire."

"Good, then let's keep it that way. If you get a chance, have a word with Beornoth. Tell him I don't care what he worships, but there are others about who might. It would be in his best interest to keep his torc hidden, for all our sakes."

"I'll let him know," said Sigwulf, "but I can't tell you how he'll react."

"If he gives you any trouble, send him to me."

"What about the rest of his people?" asked Cyn.

Ludwig cast his eyes about, taking in the camp. "If they're rebels, as you say, then they'll be careful about revealing it to anyone here."

"Then why speak to them at all? If they were caught, you could always deny knowing anything about their background? After all, you're not even from Erlingen."

"No," said Ludwig. "I brought them into this company. That makes me responsible for them. I won't abandon them only to save my own skin."

"You know," said Cyn, "one of these days, you're going to make a good ruler."

"Don't be ridiculous. I'm only the son of a baron. How in the Continent would I become a ruler?"

"Stranger things have happened."

37

THE ENEMY COMES

Summer 1095 SR

E arly the next morning, word came that the commanders were to assemble in town, in a place called 'The Royal'. Ludwig had never heard of it, but Hagan definitely knew the name.

"It's a theatre," he announced.

"I've never seen one before," replied Ludwig.

"They're used to present plays."

"I'm fully aware of what they are. It's only that Verfeld was far too small for such a venue."

"Had you no cities nearby?"

"One, Malburg, but it had no theatre either."

"A pity," said Hagan. "They're quite the sight."

"Oh? Why's that?"

"The rooms are remarkably large, one might even say grandiose. I wonder what Rosalyn might make of it?"

"You should invite her," said Ludwig.

"I can't take her to one of the duke's briefings. What would people say?"

"No, I meant to see a play."

"Oh, yes," said Hagan. "Of course."

They turned up the street to see their destination.

"We're here," the young lord declared. "What do you think?"

Ludwig gazed at the structure, easily the largest building on the block, yet it looked old as if the wood and bricks had sat there for centuries.

"It's impressive," he said. "Have you been inside?"

"Not this one, but I've seen similar."

Carriages were there, unloading their passengers, while others milled about the establishment's front doors, crowding the entrance, which surprised Ludwig.

"How many are here?" he asked.

"I imagine all the barons and their captains. That alone accounts for dozens."

"Sergeants too, if that one over there is any indication."

"Let's get inside, shall we?" said Hagan. "I'd hate to have to stand."

They pushed their way through the crowd to find an interior with wooden benches lined up in front of a raised stage. A couple of barons sat waiting, surrounded by their bodyguards and captains.

"There's my father," said Hagan. "Shall we sit with him?"

Ludwig grimaced, eliciting a chuckle from Lord Hagan. "Do we have to?" asked Ludwig.

"We'll take these seats here instead, shall we?"

"By all means." They both sat, but Ludwig's eyes were roaming the room. "This place is amazing. What are those seats up there?"

"Those are balconies," said Hagan, "used mainly by the elite. That's where we'd normally sit if this was a regular play."

The doors opened, and the rest of the crowd from outside began streaming in.

"I'm guessing the duke has arrived," said Ludwig. "I assume we'll be starting shortly."

They sat in silence, waiting as the barons began taking their seats. Once situated, their captains began the same process, then the many sergeants who were also present. Everyone's eyes were on the stage when Lord Deiter Heinrich, Duke of Erlingen, made his appearance.

The room fell silent as he walked across the stage, his boots echoing on the wooden floor. He paused when he reached the centre, and then the whole room stood and bowed.

"Be seated," said the duke. He waited for the shuffle of feet to end and then began pacing back and forth, formulating his speech.

"Our numbers have swelled," he began, "thanks to the arrival of the barons of Hutfeld and Lieswel. I'm pleased to announce we now have close to three thousand warriors under the banner of Erlingen."

Some in the audience began clapping, while others cheered. The duke let them have their moment, then cleared his throat, causing everyone to fall silent once more.

"As you all know, we have been under the threat of invasion this last month. I am afraid it is with no pleasure that I inform you we received word a short time ago that the army of Andover has now crossed the border."

"Have they taken Lieswel?" someone called out.

"Yes, Lieswel has fallen despite our attempts to hold on to it. Lord Killian was forced to retreat here, to Chermingen in the face of overwhelming odds."

"How overwhelming?" came another voice.

"That," continued the duke, "is an excellent question. At the moment, we are estimating the enemy strength at between three and four thousand."

A collective gasp went through the audience, then people started peppering the duke with questions, so much so that little could be heard other than the general hubbub of conversation.

The duke used his hands to calm everybody. "I shall answer your questions in due course, but please, one at a time. Perhaps if you stood to speak?"

Several stood, and the duke looked past Ludwig to the man two seats to his rear. "Yes, Lord Baldwin?"

"How reliable is this information, Your Grace?"

The duke sought out one of the spectators. "Lord Killian, you were there. What do you have to say?"

The man stood, commanding the attention of the room. Clearly, he had only recently arrived, for his clothes were covered in dust and dirt.

"They came in overwhelming numbers, Your Grace. We held them as long as we could, but it soon became clear we were badly outnumbered."

"And what can you tell us of their troops?"

"Mostly foot and knights, Your Grace, with a smattering of archers, but no crossbowmen as far as we observed."

The duke scanned the crowd again as more lords stood. "You have a question, Lord Rengard?"

The Baron of Rosenbruck addressed his question to Lord Killian. "Are you sure of these numbers, my lord? They strike me as being awfully"—he fought to find the right word—"exaggerated."

"I can assure you my estimation is as accurate as my people could make it. I take no joy in informing you of it, but we must be prepared."

"How many knights has he?" called out Lord Hurst.

"I would estimate their numbers at close to five hundred, if not six."

Hurst quickly became irritated. "Which is it, man? Five or six? That's a significant difference."

"We were under considerable threat, Hurst, and lacked sufficient time to make a full appraisal."

Hurst opened his mouth to speak, but the duke intervened. "Sit down, man, and let someone else get a word in edgewise."

Lord Helmer quickly seized the moment. "What can you tell us of their quality?"

"Quality?" asked Killian.

"Yes, were they trained warriors, or merely a local levy raised to scare us."

"I can say with a fair degree of accuracy that these are well-trained and experienced troops. The few we engaged were armoured and knew their business."

The level of background noise increased dramatically as everyone debated the news.

"Lord Augustus?" said the duke. "You have a question?"

"Yes, Your Grace," replied the Baron of Salzing. "I wonder if you might share with us your plan to deal with this menace?"

"By all means. We shall remain in Chermingen enlarging our forces until such time as we can gain the advantage of numbers."

"Is that likely?"

"One can only hope. The problem is, if we advance, we could well be taken by surprise. By waiting here, we force them to come to us."

Ludwig, suddenly struck by an idea, stood, earning him some nasty looks from the barons. The duke, perhaps unwilling to take another question from one of his own nobles, looked directly at him. "Sir Ludwig, you have a question?"

"I do, Your Grace. I was wondering who would command the army should you fall."

The room fell into a hush. Ludwig looked around, trying to ascertain why, and then it dawned on him that he might have stepped over the line. All eyes turned, as one, towards the duke.

"I shall not fall," His Grace replied. "Far from it, in fact. We shall meet the enemy on the field of battle and send them packing."

"Then the strategy is to meet them in the field?" suggested Ludwig.

"Yes, although the precise timing and location of such an event is yet to be determined."

There was much more to be said, but the duke was clearly done. "That's all I shall say, for now, gentlemen. Return to your tents and pray for success. I fear we may have need of it. I'll convene another meeting once

I've had a chance to read over the latest dispatches. Until then, I bid you a good day." He turned, striding from the stage as if it were the end of a play.

Hagan joined Ludwig on his feet while everyone else began filing out.

"Was that it?" Hagan said.

"I suppose it was," said Ludwig.

"He didn't have much of an answer for you."

"No, nor for anyone else if the truth be known. I don't know why he insisted on bringing us all here for that."

"Because he can," said Hagan.

"What's that supposed to mean?"

"It means he's the duke, and as duke, he likes to exercise his power over us. He calls us here, and we're forced to appear. See what I mean?"

"It seems a petty thing to do."

"Ah," said Hagan, "but if you remember, the barons spend a lot of time fighting amongst themselves. This was a demonstration of the duke's power, plain and simple."

"And that's all there is to take away from this?"

"Not at all. But it's likely the most important thing, at least in his eyes."

"It felt like a waste of time to me," said Ludwig. "There was hardly anything to pass on."

"You mean other than we're outnumbered? I'd call that pretty important, wouldn't you?"

"Yes, but he appears indecisive. He talked of waiting here, then of marching out and fighting. Which does he intend?"

"I have no idea," said Hagan, "nor is it up to us. We are his vassals, Ludwig. We must do as he commands."

Ludwig looked at him, a gleam in his eyes. "Perhaps not," he said.

"What does that mean?"

"It means I have an idea. Come, we must speak to your father and Lord Wulfram."

"About what?" asked Hagan.

"My plan. What else?"

"Would you care to divulge what precisely this plan involves?"

"Not yet. I'm still working on it."

"My father's here. We saw him earlier."

"Yes," said Ludwig, "but here is not the place to discuss such things, and I'd prefer to have Lord Wulfram present as well. It will avoid having to explain it twice."

"Twice?" said Hagan. "I'm still waiting for you to explain it to me?"

"Then come, we'll discuss it on the way."

. . .

Finding Lord Gebhard's tent was easy, for Hagan had visited it the night they had arrived in Chermingen. Lord Wulfram, however, was more difficult to locate. Luckily, Ludwig thought to seek out his old swordmaster, Kurt Wasser, since he was the man who had been assigning locations for the nobles' tents.

A brief visit was all they needed to convince the man to accompany them, and so they set off, Baron Haas in tow to present Ludwig's idea. Lord Gebhard frowned as Lord Wulfram entered his tent, but at least he minded his manners.

"What's this?" he demanded.

"Father," said Hagan, "Ludwig here has a proposal. I suggest you listen to him."

"Really? And what's Wulfram doing here?"

"It involves his men as well. It's only right he gets a say in things."

"I suppose you're right," grumbled his father. "Very well, tell us of your idea, sir."

Ludwig found his mouth suddenly dry. He licked his lips, trying to gather his words.

"Is this about that meeting today?" pressed Gebhard.

"It is, my lord," said Ludwig. "In fact, the meeting is what gave me the idea."

"Go on," urged Lord Wulfram.

"It occurred to me we have next to nothing in the way of reliable information concerning these invaders."

"We know their numbers," said Gebhard. "Isn't that enough?"

"But we don't," insisted Ludwig, "at least not exact numbers. Lord Killian said between three and four thousand; that's a substantial variance. If we are to defeat them, we need more accurate information."

"Agreed," said Baron Stein. "What are you proposing?"

"I suggest he send a small group out to scout out the enemy positions."

"He hasn't enough horse," insisted Wulfram. "After all, you can't send knights out for such a task. They're too slow."

"I was going to suggest footmen," said Ludwig. "Specifically, our company."

"Are you mad?" said Gebhard. "They'd be overrun before the day was done."

"I don't think it likely. Hear me out."

"Very well, tell us more."

"The enemy is moving slowly," began Ludwig. "We know that because they've been massing for weeks yet have only taken Lieswel."

"I fail to see how that's relevant," insisted Baron Stein.

"It's my opinion they hope to draw us into battle. It's the only thing that makes sense. Think of it; how long does it take to march from Lieswel to Chermingen?"

"Three or four days. Why?"

"They could have taken this city by now. We were all the way back in Torburg when we heard tell of their army. And why mass on the border if only to wait? The answer is they wanted us to do precisely what we're doing."

"But if that's true," said Wulfram, "doesn't that mean we're walking into a trap?"

"It does."

"Then I'm afraid I can't see the logic in this. If it's a trap, shouldn't we hole up in Chermingen?"

"The city has no walls," said Ludwig. "We'd have to spread our army over a wide area to protect it while the enemy could concentrate on one section. We have little choice but to meet them in the field, and that means we need to know more about them."

"So then what's the purpose of this plan?" said Gebhard. "You can't be suggesting you can get close enough to count men?"

"My intent would be to infiltrate their army with a small force. Warriors look much alike on both sides. It shouldn't be too hard to send in half a dozen men, unseen. The rest of the company would search the area between here and Lieswel."

"To what end?"

"To learn about the countryside," explained Ludwig. "If we are to meet this threat, isn't it best to do so on land of our own choosing?"

Lord Wulfram looked at his counterpart. "Well, Gebhard? What are your thoughts?"

"The idea has merit, but it sounds difficult."

"Yes, and dangerous," said Wulfram. "It's not as if there would be reinforcements to back them up." He turned to Hagan. "What's your opinion?"

"I am in agreement on this," Hagan responded. "Ludwig's plan is sound, and I believe it worth the risk."

"Of course you do," said his father. "You're young and foolhardy. This is real danger, boy. You could be killed."

Hagan stood straight, his voice strained. "I'm not afraid, Father."

The senior Stein's face softened. "I don't mean to imply you are, but you're my son. I wouldn't have you throw your life away."

"Nor do I intend to, Father. We shall take every precaution."

"And if you are captured? What then, eh? I shudder to think what the King of Andover would do with you."

"I'm sure he'd be safe," said Ludwig. "The king means to conquer Erlingen; that much is clear. He'll need the goodwill of the people to rule, either that or he'll be forced to maintain a large-standing army."

"That's true," said Lord Wulfram. "You, on the other hand, aren't a native of Erlingen, Ludwig. That makes your life much less important to them."

"I'm willing to take that chance. I know this is a dangerous endeavour, but with so much at stake, can we honestly afford not to do everything in our power to defeat this invasion?"

Lord Gebhard did not look pleased. "What if we sent more troops? Could we borrow some knights?"

"No," said Ludwig. "A larger group is more difficult to hide. Stealth is our ally, my lord, not numbers."

"I still don't like it."

"He has a point," said Lord Wulfram. "Come, Gebhard, you know the man's right. If he manages to pull this off, we'll all come back covered in glory."

"Glory? What price is glory if it leads to the death of my only son and heir?" He moved to stand before Hagan. "I would not see you killed, Hagan. I know we've had our differences, but you're still my son, and I care for you greatly."

Ludwig noticed the tears in the baron's eyes.

Hagan hugged his father, words tumbling from his lips in a quivering voice. "I shall come back, Father. I promise."

Lord Gebhard held him at arm's length, coughing to hide his discomfort. "I know you'll do your best, Son, but that's not a promise you can make."

"I shall keep an eye on him, my lord," said Ludwig.

"Very well, but I'll have to take this to His Grace. Ultimately, it's not our decision to make."

"We understand, Father."

"Good," said Baron Stein. "Now, it's best you two return to your men, and get a good night's rest behind you. If the duke approves of your idea, you'll need to set out as soon as possible." He turned to Lord Wulfram. "I should like you to accompany me when I take this to His Grace."

"Are you certain?" replied Baron Haas. "Not so long ago, we were at each other's throats."

"And for that, I deeply apologize. It's only now, as I face the overwhelming possibility of losing my own son that I see how selfish I was concerning your daughter. She should be free to make her own decisions, Wulfram, just as my son must have the same choice."

"Well said, Gebhard."

"Then come, let us be off before I change my mind."

They left the tent, leaving Hagan and Ludwig alone.

"Are you all right?" asked Ludwig.

Hagan nodded. "I've never seen my father like that," he said, his voice still husky.

"People change. Mind you, it's taken an invasion for him to learn to appreciate you. It's a good thing you don't have any brothers or sisters, or we'd have to face an even larger force."

38

RECONNAISSANCE

Summer 1095 SR

The duke, pleased with the proposal, sent them on their way the very next day. Eager to be on the road, they set out at a fast pace, their spirits high despite the risk. There was pride in the men's steps, and Ludwig prayed it would carry them through the ordeal to come, for with the rising sun came his doubts the plan would work.

He said nothing to the others, yet Cyn could sense something was wrong. It wasn't until they took a brief rest, mid-morning, that she finally got around to confronting him about it. Ludwig had dismounted and was sitting on a rock, peeling off his boots when she found him.

"Something wrong?" he asked.

She smiled. "Does something have to be wrong for me to come and say hello?"

"I know you better than that, Cyn, and the fact that Sig's not here speaks volumes."

She crouched before him, balancing on the balls of her feet. "Something's troubling you," she said. "I can tell."

"What makes you say that?"

"Come now, Ludwig. You might fool the others, but I've known Siggy far too long to be deceived by the likes of you. You men are all the same, hiding away your fears. It's this mission you've volunteered us for, isn't it?"

He looked at her, feeling a sadness well up inside him. "Is this a fool's errand, Cyn? Am I condemning all these men to death?"

"They're soldiers," she replied. "Death is their stock-in-trade. You shouldn't be so hard on yourself."

"I can't help it. I have this feeling we're walking a knife's edge."

"That's a soldier's life. You're lucky. You're one of the people who makes the decisions. Most of us simply have to live with the consequences."

"Still," said Ludwig, "I can't shake this feeling I've neglected something."

"Of course you've forgotten something. No one has a perfect memory. What do you want me to do, soothe your conscience? Tell you everything will work out well? I can't do that, Ludwig, and neither can you. The sooner you realize that, the better. We must take what life throws at us and make the best of it."

"You're right."

"Of course I am," Cyn replied. "Now, get on your horse and show the men how confident you are. We can't afford for them to be skittish."

"Skittish?"

"Yes, flighty, scared if you like. The men need the example of your leadership."

"I'm no leader."

"Yes, you are. You still don't see it, do you? You have a gift for it, Ludwig. Men would kill for that type of presence."

"Even if it meant their deaths?"

"Soldiers die," said Cyn. "Nothing can prevent that. Your job, as the leader, is to keep their losses to a minimum."

He stared at her a moment letting the words sink in. Was he a leader? Part of his mind rebelled at the thought, yet there was no denying his presence had made a difference here, amongst the men who he and Hagan commanded.

Cyn wore a look of frustration. "What's going on inside that head of yours?"

In answer, Ludwig began pulling his boots back on. "You're right," he said. "I don't have time for such maudlin thoughts."

"Maudlin, is it now? Getting awfully uppity with your fancy words, aren't you?" She grinned. "Who do you think you are, the duke?"

"No, of course not," he bit back, then noted her look of amusement. "Very funny."

"You're mad, that's good. It means the old Ludwig is back. Now harness that energy, and get this band of yours on the road."

"They're not my band. They belong to Hagan."

"That might be true on paper, but I doubt these men would agree with you. You're the one they look up to, not that puffed up piece of nobility."

Now it was Ludwig's turn to laugh. "Piece of nobility? By the Saints, Cyn, you're learning to be diplomatic! We'll make an officer out of you yet."

She sneered. "No, thank you, I'm completely content as a sergeant. Now, let's get going, shall we? Before we waste away the rest of the morning."

Ludwig climbed into the saddle, watching as his men began gathering. He had issued no orders, given no indication of his desires, yet they instinctively knew what was required of them. He looked down at Cyn.

She grinned back. "See? What did I tell you?"

The road led westward towards its ultimate destination of Lieswel, and yet they would never reach that target, for their objective was to observe the enemy, not enter an occupied town. Instead, they would halt far short of the enemy army, sending in a small group to scout out their numbers. At least that was the plan. The difficulty lay in not stumbling into them by mistake. To that end, he had archers marching in front, some hundred paces or so beyond the main column, their intent being to alert the others should they spy any sign of the enemy.

He wondered if cavalry might not have been better suited to such a task but then dismissed it, knowing they would have been too easily spotted. In theory, it was Hagan's decision as commander of the company, but he had deferred to Ludwig, adding to the already heavy burden on his shoulders.

They made good progress on the first day, camping that night in a small woods. The men had complained, preferring a field, but Ludwig had been adamant. The woods, he explained, were far better at hiding the light of their campfires from prying eyes.

The next morning they rose early and were on the road in good time. This was, in all probability, the most dangerous part of the trip, for the news from Lieswel was old, and the enemy might be just past the next turn in the road.

When they halted at noon, the wind blew in from the west, bringing with it the scent of burning wood. It appeared the enemy encampment was close.

Ludwig sent out a few select men seeking a place of concealment and waited. It didn't take long for Simmons to return, bearing news of an abandoned building. They left the men in Captain Ecke's care while Ludwig and Hagan followed the archer back to his discovery.

Before them was a stone building, two stories in height, with a collapsed eastern wall and a roof that had half rotted away. Access to the second floor was by way of some rotted stairs. Whatever this building used to be, it was evidently extremely old, leading Ludwig to wonder why it was here in the middle of the countryside.

He dragged an old timber over to the stairs and propped it against what steps remained, using it to form a ramp. Up he went, testing his footing on the upper floor before committing fully to its support.

"What can you see?" called out Hagan.

Ludwig moved to what remained of the western wall, peering out through an old window. The sill had long ago rotted, leaving naught but the stone opening, but the view was magnificent.

"I see smoke in the distance," he said. "It's the Andover camp, by the look of it."

Hagan soon followed, taking considerably longer to climb to the upper floor until finally he crouched by Ludwig, looking westward.

"That's a lot of fires," said the lord. "Should we report this to the duke?"

"Not yet," replied Ludwig. "We still have no idea of numbers. For that, we'll have to get even closer."

"Closer? How do you propose we do that?"

"I'll pick a small group, no more than a dozen, and we'll move into their camp under cover of night."

"And the rest of us?" asked Hagan.

"I would suggest you bring them here. If things go badly, we'll need a defensive position, not that this is much of one."

"What do you mean?"

"This building gives us an excellent view, but the eastern wall is missing, and most of the southern one is little more than shin-high. This is not a good place to fight an enemy."

"Then shouldn't we withdraw?"

"It has the advantage of concealing us while we keep an eye on THEM." Ludwig pointed westward.

"Very well," said Hagan. "How can I help?"

"You need to keep a couple of horsemen ready. As soon as I bring word back, we'll need to send them off."

"We have no horsemen."

"You and I have horses. Somewhere amongst all these men, there must be two who can ride?"

"You expect me to give up my mount?"

"It's for the good of the army," said Ludwig. "And just imagine all the accolades you'll receive for bringing word of the enemy."

Hagan appeared to consider the idea for a moment. "Very well. Who will you take?"

"I have a few in mind, but I need to have a chat with some others. Let's get the rest of the men safely behind these walls. I don't want them being spotted."

"Anything else?"

"Yes," said Ludwig. "The men are not to build campfires tonight."

"Why ever not? Surely the enemy won't be able to see us from there?"

"The fires, no, but the light will illuminate the inside of this building, or at least what's left of it. Remember, the idea is to not draw attention to ourselves. Now, why don't you stay here, and I'll go fetch the men?"

"Very well," said Hagan. "I'll keep an eye on the enemy camp."

They settled in and awaited the coming of darkness. The afternoon dragged on, made all the longer by the knowledge that the army of Andover was so close. On the upper floor, they kept only a small group of men lest they risk being seen at the windows. It was there Ludwig found who he was looking for.

"Beornoth," he said in greeting. "Mind if I join you?"

"Suit yourself," the man replied, keeping his eyes westward.

Ludwig sat, his back to the ancient wall, looking around, taking in what was left of the building. "I can't help but wonder why this place is here?"

"It's a freeholder's house," said Beornoth.

"I'm not sure I'm familiar with the term."

"During the days of the Old Kingdom, men were given land in reward for their service to the Crown."

"You're saying this building dates back to Therengia?" said Ludwig. "I find that hard to accept."

"One only has to look at the way it's built to understand," said Beornoth.

"Yes, but that would make it over five hundred years old, wouldn't it?"

"Possibly, but remnants of my people lived on for some time before they, too, were hunted down. This building likely belonged to one such survivor."

"And your people built with stone?"

"Of course," said Beornoth. "Why wouldn't they? Did you think us barbarians, living in nothing but huts made of animal skins? Ours was a large kingdom, Sir Ludwig, the likes of which would put most of the Petty Kingdoms to shame."

"I'm sorry," said Ludwig. "I meant no offence."

"It's not your fault. Your people know so little of my race. Is that all you came to see me about? Or is there something else?"

"I was actually wondering why you're here?"

"You mean serving the duke I've sworn to destroy?"

"Precisely. Not that I'm not happy to see you; you certainly bring us a sorely missing skill set, but wouldn't you have been better off serving Andover?"

"I can see how you might assume that," said Beornoth. "But the truth is the treatment we receive at the hands of the duke is mild compared to that meted out by our northern neighbour."

"I'm not sure I understand."

"In Erlingen, we are shunned, the same as we are in many of the Petty Kingdoms, but in Andover, the penalty for being a Therengian is death."

"Just for having grey eyes?"

"Do you doubt my word?"

"No," said Ludwig, "of course not. I merely find it difficult to understand. Where I'm from, we don't see such attitudes towards your people."

"Your home is not part of the Old Kingdom. Erlingen, on the other hand, was founded in the heart of it. They have feared its return ever since."

"What is it your people hope to accomplish by rebelling against the duke? You can't possibly see it rising again?"

"No," said Beornoth. "There are too few of us left to do something like that. Instead, I fight for the rights of my people, to have them live in peace, as others do."

"A noble sentiment."

"Perhaps. Others would see it as desperate."

"I don't count myself amongst them. I admire what you're fighting for, even though I feel it unlikely you'll succeed. There must be a better way."

"Like what?" asked Beornoth. "Abandon our homes and flee eastward?"

"It might be safer."

"It could just as easily be worse. My people have been persecuted for generations, but at least here they are allowed to live, even if it's under the hand of oppression."

"I do not envy you your position."

"Nor would I expect you to, but come, let us speak of other things, or is it your intention to crush my soul?"

"Not at all," said Ludwig. "I'm putting together a small group of warriors to infiltrate the enemy encampment."

"To what end?"

"We need accurate information concerning numbers."

"I'm afraid my men would be too easily recognized. One wayward glance, and our eyes would give us away."

"I don't need you to enter the camp, merely to stand and assist when we leave, in case we run into trouble."

"We can do that," said Beornoth. "Tell me, who else is to undertake this fool's errand?"

"Sigwulf and Cyn, although I haven't spoken to them yet. I came to you first."

"They will agree," the Therengian replied, "else I'm a poor judge of character."

"Good. We'll leave right before dark. Now I must go and seek my friends. There's much to discuss."

"Then dusk it is," said Beornoth.

Ludwig climbed down to the ground floor. The other men of the company were strewn about what was left of the interior—a large area he imagined resembled the hall of some ancient warrior lord. Did heroes of the past gather here to hear the tales of history? He liked to imagine so, but his mind told him such accounts were little more than bedtime stories, meant to inflame the hearts of the young.

So intent was he on his ruminations that he almost bumped into the exact man he was looking for.

"Careful," warned Sigwulf. "You might hurt yourself."

"I was looking for you."

"It appears you've found me. What is it you want?"

"I'd like to discuss something with you."

"Like what? Sneaking into the enemy camp?"

"How did you…"

Sigwulf grinned. "What else would we be doing here? We can't get an idea of their strength by hiding in this ruin, can we?"

"Are all my plans so obvious?"

"Not all, but most of them."

"And your answer?"

"Need you ask?" said Sigwulf. "I'm in, of course, but we need to go and talk with Cyn."

"You think she'll agree?"

"Do you seriously imagine she won't? That woman has more guts than a badger."

"What is this fascination you have for badgers?"

"I don't know what you're talking about." Sigwulf quickly changed the subject. "Come on, Cyn's around here somewhere."

"It's not that big of a ruin. How could you lose her?"

"She's likely having a nap, and that means her face is turned away from people."

"Which means?" asked Ludwig.

"She'll be curled up in a corner somewhere."

"Like a badger?" He snickered.

Sigwulf turned on him, raising a finger. "Not funny!"

Ludwig held up his arms in surrender. "Sorry, I might have taken it a little too far."

They began their search, walking amongst the ruins, seeking out the faces of those who slept.

"You'd think this would be easier," said Ludwig. "I mean, how many women are in this camp?"

"Only the one," said Sigwulf, "and here she is." He halted, looking down at the sleeping form.

He stood there a moment, and Ludwig wondered why he didn't do anything. "Aren't you going to wake her?"

"I will, but it must be done carefully."

"Why?"

"Her first instinct will be to lash out."

Ludwig watched the woman sleep. She began to twitch, and then her leg kicked out involuntarily.

"She's dreaming," he noted.

"No, it's not a dream," said Sigwulf, a shadow falling across his face. "It's a nightmare." He knelt, placing his hand gently on her shoulder. "Cyn," he whispered, "come back to me."

Her legs jerked out again, and then her eyes opened. "Siggy?"

"It's me," he said. "We need you awake. Ludwig has to talk to you."

She sat up, rubbing her eyes. Ludwig noted the haunted look to them and wondered what might be the cause.

"Well?" she said. "What is it?"

"I'm looking to take Sig here into the enemy camp with me to have a look around."

"Not without me, you're not."

"That's what we're here to discuss," said Sigwulf. "You can't walk into the middle of their army without someone noticing."

"Then what do you expect me to do?"

"You'll come with us right up to the edge of their camp. We'll need you to keep an eye out for us."

"Who else is going?"

"Beornoth and his people," said Ludwig.

"Are you sure you can trust them?" asked Cyn.

"I am. They have much to lose if they're discovered."

"And what is our role in all of this?"

"When we leave that camp, we may be in a hurry. We'll need your help to elude anyone who might follow."

"You mean kill anyone who follows."

"Yes," said Sigwulf.

"Good," said Cyn. "Then I'm in. What time do we leave?"

"Right before sunset," said Ludwig.

"Fine, then I'll return to my nap."

Ludwig noticed the concern on Sigwulf's face. "You weren't sleeping well," the big sergeant added.

"Then come and lie by my side, Siggy," said Cyn, "and keep me safe."

39

AMONGST THE ENEMY

Summer 1095 SR

L udwig edged up the side of the gully. They had followed a dried-up riverbed and were now within a few hundred paces of their target. Peering over its lip, he took in the view while beside him came Beornoth, his breath visible in the chill of the evening.

"What do you make of it?" asked Ludwig.

The Therengian grunted. "Pretty typical camp," he replied. "They have a few guards out against intruders, but we can make short work of them."

"No!" insisted Ludwig. "That might alert them to our presence. Our objective is to get as close as possible, even inside if we can. The last thing we want to do is raise the alarm. Do you see any easy way in?"

"No, but maybe downwind?"

"Why would you say that?"

"An army is a lot of soldiers," said Beornoth. "Soldiers who eat food, and you know what food does once you're done with it."

"So we're looking for waste pits? Do they even have them?"

"This isn't a Church army, so I doubt they'll have set aside an area for such a use. They'll still have to go, though, and that means likely a wooded area downwind, where the smell won't bother them too much." The Therengian wet his finger, then held it aloft. "The wind is coming from the west, which means we want to be farther east."

"Towards our own camp," said Ludwig. "How convenient."

"Do you want to get in or not?"

"I do. Lead on, and the rest of us will follow."

Ludwig waited until the man had started on his way to motion for the others to follow. They crept along, exiting the gully and making their way eastward. It felt like they were backtracking, but then Beornoth turned northward, and they passed through a copse of trees before halting. Everyone went quiet, and then voices drifted towards them.

"They're just ahead," whispered Beornoth.

Ludwig moved up, crouching as he went. Ahead of them, he heard something crashing through the trees and then the distinct sound of someone urinating into the underbrush. He waited until whoever it was began making their way back to the camp, then looked over at Sigwulf and nodded.

"This is it," whispered Ludwig. "The rest of you stay here and keep your eyes open. We'll be back as soon as we can."

Ludwig and Sigwulf both stood, making their way through the trees, emerging to see the edge of the encampment scarcely a stone's throw away.

"Shall we?" he asked.

Sigwulf nodded. "After you."

It was a strange feeling walking amongst enemy troops. Closing his eyes, Ludwig almost felt as though he were back with the army of Erlingen, yet if any here were to guess at his allegiance, he would be killed. They passed by a paddock crammed with horses.

"Knights," grunted Sigwulf, "and a substantial number of them if the horses here are any indication."

Ludwig, too busy counting heads, merely nodded. His tally complete, he halted, looking to the north. "Over there is a group of tents," he said. "I want to see what troops they command."

"Then shouldn't we look for their footmen?"

"In their eyes, they're in enemy territory," said Ludwig. "That likely means they have guards on their tents."

"And?"

"If you were a noble, who would you want guarding you, your best troops or the rabble?"

"I see your point," said Sigwulf.

As they advanced towards the tents, Ludwig kept running the numbers in his head, trying to commit his count to memory. Writing things down would have been more accurate, but to walk through a camp with a quill and paper in hand would have aroused too much suspicion, not to mention the necessity for ink. Instead, he had to rely on his recollections.

A well-dressed man stepped out of one of the tents as they passed by. Ludwig felt anxiety swell within his breast as the man looked at him, but all he got was a nod and a brief, "Good evening," and then the man carried on with his business.

In this area of the camp, the guards were equipped with padded gambesons. Some even had chainmail shirts—a far cry from what the knights might be expected to have, but still of concern, nonetheless.

Next, they passed by archers, most of whom slept on the ground, with threadbare blankets, much as the duke's army. The similarities to their own forces were striking. Ludwig had to remind himself it was, doubtlessly, the same amongst all the armies of the Petty Kingdoms. Would Elves or Dwarves be similarly equipped, he wondered?

"Over there," said Sigwulf, nodding to the northwest, where another group of horses was clustered. Not the knights' large destriers, but smaller, more nimble mounts. "What do you make of those?" he asked.

"Let's get closer," suggested Ludwig.

As they approached, trying hard to look like they were merely wandering around, they spotted the horsemen. Sigwulf immediately recognized them.

"Mercenaries," he said.

"Do you know their band?"

"No, but I know their type. They're raiders, used to pursue a beaten enemy."

"Then we shall have to ensure we don't run," said Ludwig. "How many would you say they have?"

"At least a hundred, I would guess. I can't be sure of the exact number. It's too dark."

Ludwig brought them to a halt. "I think we've seen enough, don't you?"

"Enough to get a good feel for numbers," agreed Sigwulf, "though I fear it doesn't bode well for the duke."

"Agreed. Let's start making our way back the way we came. The last thing I want to do is get lost in the dark."

The task was easier said than done, for they had been so consumed by the desire to count men, they had paid little attention to where they had wandered. As a result, they found themselves in an unfamiliar area of the camp, and Ludwig had to fight down his impending sense of panic.

As luck would have it, they were inadvertently saved by an enemy noble. Passing by his tent, they heard him mention he needed to relieve himself, so they quickly ducked into the shadows. The man headed off towards the trees with Sigwulf and Ludwig following.

All looked well until a guard decided to challenge them.

"You there," he called out.

Ludwig turned, feigning innocence. "Who? Us?"

The guard came closer. "Who are you with?"

"The mercenaries," said Sigwulf.

"Which ones?"

Sigwulf turned pale.

"The Bent Swords," said Ludwig, moving closer to the man

"Who?"

Sigwulf picked up on the diversion. "The Bent Swords?"

The look of confusion was soon replaced by shock as Ludwig's fist slammed home. Blood exploded from the guard's nose as he fell.

"Run!" shouted Ludwig.

"Guards!" called out the fallen soldier. "Alarm, intruders!"

The call was soon taken up by others. As Ludwig rushed past Sigwulf and into the trees, his foot snagged on a plant, and he tumbled to the forest floor. Sigwulf quickly pulled him to his feet, and they both rushed through the trees, their faces stung by the low-hanging branches.

"Where are they?" called out Ludwig.

"Cyn!" shouted Sigwulf but nothing came back in reply. They slowed, now deep in amongst the trees. Ludwig was trying to get his bearings, but one group of trees looked much like the next.

"We're lost," he said. "I can't even tell which way's east."

"Nor can I," admitted his companion. "I suspect we were heading south when we entered the forest."

"Yes, but we've followed the path of least resistance. We could have got completely turned around for all I know."

Ludwig felt the desperation building. All this work to collect vital information, and now they had no way of getting back to the duke. What a colossal waste of time!

"This way," said Sigwulf.

"Are you sure?"

"No, but unless you have a better idea, it keeps us moving."

"All right, but take it slow. I don't need to lose an eye on all these branches."

They tried to keep to a straight line, but the underbrush and the darkness made it difficult. Wandering for what felt like forever, they finally reached the edge of the forest, only to spot the enemy camp stretched out before them.

"Saints alive," said Sigwulf. "We're back where we started."

To make matters worse, a large group of soldiers were carrying torches, heading almost directly towards them.

"Back this way," said Sigwulf. "At least we'll be moving away from them."

They heard crashing as the enemy began searching, the light of their torches flickering off the boughs of the trees, casting an eerie glow throughout the forest behind them. Ludwig cursed when Sigwulf managed to snap a twig, the sound a direct beacon to their location.

"Over there," yelled someone, as the torchlights grew brighter.

"Let's split up," said Sigwulf.

"No," said Ludwig. "If it comes to a fight, we're better off to stand together."

"Then you go. I'll stay and delay them."

"I can't do that."

"You have to. The information is too important."

"And leave you to fight them off alone? What would Cyn say?"

"Very well, then we'll both run." Sigwulf dashed forward, but in the darkness, he smashed into a tree. Ludwig heard the grunt as he struck, and then the great man staggered back. "That hurt," he said.

"Slow down," said Ludwig, "or we'll kill ourselves."

"If we slow down, we won't have to kill ourselves. Those men will gladly do it for us."

A horse neighed, and they both froze.

"This way," whispered Ludwig. The enemy was so close now that the trees' boughs reflected the light, illuminating the surrounding woods. They pressed on, determined to put as much distance as possible between themselves and their pursuers.

Ludwig halted and drew his sword as the horse drew closer. Sigwulf pulled out his own weapon, and then they stood, side by side, ready for anything that might come.

The first rider had just appeared to their front, bearing down on them, when something flashed out of the trees and struck the man on the head. Next they knew, the rider fell, an axe protruding from his helmet.

The mount ran past them, but Ludwig ignored it, for not a moment later, two more horsemen appeared. Out of nowhere came Beornoth, swinging his axe overhead, bringing it down into one's chest, and knocking the man from the saddle to crash to the ground.

The third rider halted, then drew his sword, his eyes scanning the area when a bush suddenly exploded with action. Cyn's mace smashed into the man's shin, the blow so hard you could hear the bone break. The cavalryman screamed out in agony, reaching down to clutch the wound and then

Cyn silenced him forever. He fell back, still in the saddle, but no longer alive.

She reached up, pulling him down, then took hold of the reins. Behind them came screaming, the underbrush coming alive with the sounds of men rushing to battle.

"This way," she yelled, racing past them, a horse in tow.

Ludwig had a brief glimpse of Beornoth retrieving his axe, and then they were all fleeing in the wake of the riderless horses. One of the beasts had halted its headlong flight, choosing instead to nibble at some plants. Ludwig grabbed the reins and hauled himself onto its back, then kicked with his heels, forcing the beast to rush forward, carrying him along with it.

They soon cleared the trees, and Ludwig could finally make out his surroundings. A field opened up before him, but the most welcoming sign was the gully they had originally followed to get to the camp in the first place.

It led them in a meandering manner to the south and then farther east, opening up into a shallow depression. From here, it was only a short distance to the ruins, and by the time the sun was starting to make its appearance, they were back amongst the rest of the company.

Ludwig set about quickly writing a letter and then dispatched it to the duke with all haste. They sent three riders, mounted on the captured horses, to carry word to the army of the enemy's strength. Once they had left, he and Hagan met out of earshot to determine their next move.

"What are your thoughts?" asked Ludwig.

"That we should retreat," replied Hagan. "Our task here is done. We have discovered the enemy's numbers and passed word back to the duke. What else is there to accomplish?"

"I would suggest we remain awhile longer. I know the risk of discovery is great, but the duke will need to know should the enemy begin to march."

"They are aware you infiltrated their encampment. Won't they come looking for you?"

"It's a reasonable assumption," said Ludwig, "but I think it worth the risk."

"Very well, we shall remain here, but we'll come up with a plan for withdrawal. We may have to retreat with little notice."

"A wise precaution."

Hagan stared westward to the distant smoke of the campfires. "It won't be much longer now," he said. "The enemy will march, and then a mighty battle will be fought. I hope we have the forces to defeat them."

"We are outnumbered," said Ludwig, "yet I feel we have a chance provided we can pick the terrain."

"Even against such numbers?"

"It wouldn't be the first time a smaller army defeated a larger enemy, but it's rare."

"You've read of battles," said Hagan. "Tell me, what is it that allows the weaker to defeat the stronger?"

"It's hard to say, but at a guess, I'd say spirit."

"Spirit?"

"Yes," said Ludwig. "The ability to fight on despite losses, to stand your ground when all appears lost. Battles are won and lost not through inflicting losses alone but by breaking the morale of the enemy. If we can defeat their will to carry on, we will have won."

"You make it sound so easy. Is there a secret to breaking their will?"

"Inflicting casualties can certainly help, but it's more about denying the enemy objectives."

"What kinds of objectives?" Hagan asked.

"Something like a defensive position. People can get fixated on one thing to the detriment of others, and that's something we, in particular, are going to need."

"Why? What's wrong with us?"

"Our army is fractured, Hagan. The duke's rule has led to nobles who argue and fight amongst themselves. If the enemy realizes that, they can sweep us from the field. For Saint's sake, all they'd have to do is defeat the two top barons, and the rest would collapse. It would be like pulling the legs off a table. Tell me, who are the two most powerful barons?"

"That would be Hurst and Baldwin. Of course, the duke himself has more troops, but I suppose those will be held in reserve."

"As they should be," said Ludwig. "I imagine he'll need them to fill in the lines as men die."

"Is it truly as bad as all that?"

"You've seen the numbers, and it isn't good. By my reckoning, the enemy has close to four thousand men. That's about a third again as many as we've been able to muster. What do you know of Andover?"

"What, in particular, would you like to know?" asked Hagan.

"Is their king anything like our duke?"

"In what way?"

"Does he encourage his nobles to fight amongst themselves?"

"Not that I'm aware of," said Hagan. "My understanding is he's a ruthless ruler who doesn't put up with any kind of dissent."

"That would fit with his attitude towards the Therengians."

"Why? What does he do to them?"

"I'm told he executes them."

Hagan shrugged. "I suppose that's one way to deal with them."

Ludwig stared at the man, not believing his ears. "Dealing with them? We're talking about living, breathing people. How can you be so callous towards them?"

Hagan wore a blank expression. "They're not like us, Ludwig. They're an entirely different race, like Elves or Dwarves."

"Would you have the same attitude towards those elder races?"

"Of course. After all, they're not Human."

Ludwig was at a loss for words. He shook his head, trying to make sense of it, then an idea came to him, unbidden. "It matters not the colour of our skin or the appearance of our face. We are one people, united in our desire to live in peace. Those are the words of Saint Mathew, written over a thousand years ago, but still full of meaning. Do you consider yourself a religious man, Hagan?"

"I do, and I am humbled by your words. This war, and the events surrounding it, have brought out only the worst in most of us. You, on the other hand, have remained pure of heart and stout of soul. I thank you for the reminder we are all one people"—he grinned—"conceivably even the Dwarves and Elves."

"You talk of race, but Mathew only refers to people. It is, I think, an important distinction."

"It is, and one I'll strive to bear in mind. I'll remember those words in the future. I promise."

"And the Therengians?"

"I shall endeavour to accept them as the Saints would wish. Of course, I can't disobey the duke's law in that regard. They are still banned from holding office."

"True," said Ludwig, "but one day, you'll be the baron, and your influence at court may sway the opinions of others."

"Yes, and the duke can't live forever."

A call from Simmons drew their attention to the west. It appeared the enemy had decided to march.

40

WITHDRAWAL

Summer 1095 SR

T he first sign of trouble was a small group of horsemen trotting across the field, heading directly for the ruins.

"Do you think they know we're here?" asked Hagan.

"I doubt it," replied Ludwig, "but this place is likely of interest to them if only to see what it contains."

"I'm not sure I follow."

"He means plunder," said Cyn, moving up beside them. "Soldiers don't make much and are always on the lookout for any sign of valuables."

"What could possibly be of value in an old building like this?" asked Hagan.

"You'd be surprised," she replied. "Many's the farmer who buries their treasures, then fails to retrieve them."

"We can't let them find us."

"We have little choice in the matter," said Ludwig. "It appears they're going to investigate this place whether we want them to or not." He scanned the interior, looking over the men. "We should prepare to withdraw."

"With cavalry out there?" asked Hagan.

"It's only a small patrol," said Cyn. "I say we lure them in and take care of them."

"And by take care of them, you mean..." Hagan's voice dropped off.

"Kill them, of course. What else would you do with an enemy soldier?"

Hagan paled. "But that would be murder."

"This is war, my lord," said Cyn, "and I might remind you they're the ones trying to invade YOUR land."

"Yes, of course."

"She's not asking you to do the job yourself," added Ludwig. "We have plenty of men for that."

Hagan looked mollified by his remarks.

Ludwig turned to Cyn. "Spread the word. Everyone is to remain quiet but vigilant. Get the archers up here, to the second floor. It'll afford them the best view."

"What shall I do?" asked Hagan.

"For now, simply remain still, but once we've taken care of that lot, the rest of the army won't be far behind."

"How do you know this isn't just a patrol?"

"Simple," said Ludwig. "The smoke from their campfires has ceased. That means they're on their way."

The men took up their positions. Ludwig marvelled at how strange it was that more than a hundred of them could remain so silent when needed.

The enemy horsemen came closer as Simmons, who would occasionally peek out of the window, relayed their progress in hushed tones until finally he flattened himself against the wall and went silent.

Ludwig heard the muffled sounds of the horses' hooves as they trotted through the grass, then slowed, nearing their target. Their harnesses jangled, and then at least one of them dismounted, making his way towards the south end of the structure.

Simmons nocked an arrow but waited to draw back the string, shifting slightly to get a better view. The horseman reached the end of the building, rounding the corner to come face to face with Sigwulf. The big man reached out, grabbing the rider by the throat and forcing him to the ground. The man never knew what hit him. His legs thrashed about as the life was slowly choked from him, but Sigwulf's grasp on him prevented him from alerting his companions.

The body went limp. The other riders, showing no concern for their comrade, began chatting, and at least one of them laughed about something.

Ludwig motioned two more archers to the window. Joining Simmons, they drew back their strings, while down below, Sigwulf and the others watched their leader for a sign.

At a nod from Ludwig, they struck as one. The archers took a step forward, sending their arrows flying through the windows. One rider went down immediately, an arrow digging into his collarbone from above. The other two missed the riders but hit a horse, causing the poor creature to rear up in pain. Simultaneously, Sigwulf led a group of men around the corner of the building, and they were soon amongst the enemy, their swords and axes glistening with blood. It was all over in a matter of a few heartbeats.

Ludwig turned to Hagan. "Go," he said. "Get the men moving as quickly as you can. We won't have much time."

Beornoth appeared at his side. "I have an idea."

"I'm listening."

"You need time to make your getaway," said the Therengian. "Leave me some spare spears, and my men and I will hold them off to buy you some time."

"That's suicide. You can't hold off an entire army with only a dozen men."

"True, but I can slow them."

"At the cost of your lives?"

"You're a good man, Sir Ludwig. The Petty Kingdoms need more like you, but the truth is the time of the Therengians has passed. We must make way for those who follow."

"I don't suppose I can change your mind?"

"No," replied Beornoth. "Let us make this last stand and remember us for it. I pray our sacrifice this day will change the duke's opinion of my people."

Ludwig felt the weight of this decision on his heart. "Very well. Fight well, Beornoth the Therengian, and may the story of your heroism be remembered in the annals of history." He turned away, unable to meet the gaze of the doomed man.

They gathered spears and placed them around the building, their tips extending past ruined walls to give the illusion of more men. To this, they added some helmets, standing on sticks and visible from windows and such.

All the while, Hagan began moving the men eastward towards what they hoped was the approaching army of Erlingen.

Ludwig looked at Sigwulf. "Can you ride?"

"Of course," he replied.

"Then gather those enemy horses, and put that poor injured creature out of its misery."

"Wait for me," called out Cyn.

"You can ride?" said Sigwulf.

"I don't know, but I'm willing to try. How hard can it be?"

Ludwig dismissed the archers, watching them climb down to ground level. "Bring up the rear," he ordered, "and look for any signs of the enemy. I'll be along shortly."

He turned his attention back to the window. Off in the distance, he saw a grey line. As he waited, it grew more distinct, revealing the soldiers of Andover, their footmen in the lead, with what Ludwig guessed were light cavalry on the flanks. They appeared to be moving southeast towards the road, but then someone must have spotted movement, for they changed direction, heading instead for the ruined building.

Ludwig turned to Beornoth. "Good luck," he said.

"Goodbye," the Therengian replied. "We shall not meet again."

"Then I shall drink to the memory of your deeds."

The Therengian smiled. "As it should be."

Ludwig climbed down from the upper floor and mounted Clay, waiting while Sigwulf and Cyn joined him. Turning eastward, they rode off, the spare horses in tow, galloping as fast as Cyn could manage. Ludwig resisted the urge to look back, knowing he would waver in his resolve. Would Beornoth's ruse work, or was it folly? Only time would tell.

The retreat was swift, for no one wanted to fall into the hands of the advancing enemy. They found the duke's army on the road outside of Chermingen, having taken up a position on a slight rise before a relatively clear field, determined to deny the invaders access to the city. Only the presence of an old farmhouse disturbed the weeds that dominated the area.

The duke had deployed his army in a long line that stretched across the road, using the height to his advantage. Ludwig had to admit it was an imposing sight with its gaily coloured banners rising above the men's heads. However, upon closer examination, he came to the conclusion it was not as impressive as he first thought, leading him to turn to Sigwulf.

"I don't like this," he said.

"Like what? The army is massed and ready for action. That's good, isn't it?"

"Yes, but with no thought to tactics. The cavalry is all over the place, and where are the archers?"

"In amongst each noble's retinue, I should think."

"Is that how it's always done?"

"It is," said Sigwulf. "What other way is there?"

"I thought the duke was going to mass his cavalry."

The sergeant shook his head. "The barons would never agree to that. They value their independence far too much."

"Even at the risk of losing the entire kingdom?"

"You'll be a baron yourself one day. Would you willingly give up control of your own warriors?"

"For the good of the realm? Of course."

"Then you are the exception, my friend. Most nobles in the Petty Kingdoms would resist such an idea."

"If that's true," said Ludwig, "then how in the Continent did they defeat the Old Kingdom?"

"My understanding is things weren't as rigid back then."

"And so we've weakened ourselves over generations to the point we're at now? It feels like such a waste."

"The system works," said Sigwulf. "One has only to look at the Petty Kingdoms to see how effectively."

"Yes, but the Petty Kingdoms are constantly fighting amongst themselves. It makes them ripe for being conquered."

"Does it? I would've thought just the reverse. Constant warfare leads to a professional army, doesn't it?"

"I would have thought so too," said Ludwig, "but looking at the troops arrayed before us this day, I have to wonder."

"You'd best ride ahead. You'll want to be there when Hagan reports to the duke."

Lord Deiter Heinrich's tent was easy to find, for even from the outside, Ludwig could hear the voices of dissent within.

"I say we withdraw into the city," Lord Rengard was saying. "It's much more defensible."

Hagan stepped through the doorway first.

"Your Grace," he said by way of greeting. "I trust you received our report?"

The duke wheeled around, a smile creasing his lips. "Yes, Lord Hagan, I did. You've done a magnificent job these past few days. I must congratulate you."

"We only did what we thought was best, Lord."

"Come, join us. We were discussing how we should handle the army of Andover. Lord Rengard here says we should withdraw into Chermingen."

"I believe that a mistake, Your Grace," offered Ludwig.

Lord Rengard turned his icy glare to the knight. "I hardly think your opinion matters."

"Let him speak," said Lord Hurst. "It would serve us well to hear a fresh take on things."

"Very well," said the duke. "Sir Ludwig? Your observations?"

"The enemy is numerous—" started Ludwig.

"We know," interrupted Lord Helmer. "Lord Hagan's report said as much."

"Let him speak," insisted the duke, his irritation plain for all to see.

"The city has no walls," Ludwig continued, "and we would have to defend every street, fortify every building."

"What of it?" demanded Lord Helmer.

"Most of the buildings there are wooden, my lord. Easy targets for fire."

"Are you suggesting they would burn the city?"

"To dislodge an army? I'm sure of it."

"Well," said the duke, "we can't allow that. It appears our decision is made for us. We shall make a stand here, as I have already suggested."

"They shall rip us to tatters," said Helmer. "Can you not see that?"

"They outnumber us, that's true," continued the duke, "but we cannot let them advance unopposed. To do so is to concede defeat."

"So, instead, we shall let most of our noble lines end in a catastrophic failure?"

Ludwig felt his anger rising. "Would you so easily abandon your liege lord?" he demanded.

"It's easy for a foreigner to make such an accusation," Helmer replied. "It's not your family who would be wiped out."

"I stand with the duke, as should you. Where are your loyalties, sir? To your rightful leader, or your own wealth?"

"Enough," roared the duke. "The decision has already been made. We shall fight. The only thing to discuss now is how we shall conduct the battle." He gazed around the room, but his barons avoided his gaze. "Have none of you any thoughts on the matter?"

His eyes once more fell on Ludwig. "What of you, Sir Knight? Have you anything you'd like to contribute? Other than insulting my barons, that is."

"I noticed the old farmhouse, Your Grace. Have you any warriors stationed there?"

"I have not. The position is too exposed."

"I would suggest you change that."

"To what end?" asked Lord Anwald. "Wouldn't such an act only be throwing away good men?"

"On the contrary," said Ludwig. "The building is needed if the enemy is to advance unhindered. It is, therefore, a strategic location. A single company could hold off their attack for half a day at least, longer if we fortified it."

"Fortified it?" said Lord Rengard. "With what? We have no stone with which to build new walls."

"True, but we could cut timber; even logs can impede the enemy. Stakes would be even better."

"How far behind you are they?" asked the duke.

"Half a day, maybe less."

"Then send word. I want trees felled and the logs brought to that house. Sir Ludwig, you'll oversee the construction of the defences."

Hagan stepped forward. "It is my command, Your Grace."

"Good, then you can do yourself a favour and listen to your knight." His eyes scanned the barons. "I want a dozen men from each of your retinues to head to the trees, gentlemen. We need those logs cut and dragged into place by sundown."

There was grumbling but no real argument.

"Good, this meeting is adjourned. Now, get out there and get to work. There's much to be done."

Hagan decided to visit his father, leaving Ludwig to return to the company alone. He was halfway there when Rosalyn appeared.

Ludwig halted, turning to face her. "My lady? What are you doing here?"

"I'm here with my father."

"This is a battle, Rosalyn. It's no place for a woman."

She bristled. "My place is by my father's side. Would you deny me that?"

"No. My apologies. I merely meant, as you're not a warrior, it might be safer for you to stay in Chermingen."

"I may not be trained in the art of weapons, but I can at least inspire the men."

"And how do you intend to do that?"

"These men are fighting for their families. By showing myself, I remind them of that."

"Very well," said Ludwig. "Let me take you to them."

"Is Hagan there?"

He noted the hint of a smile and decided to have some fun. "Lord Hagan?"

"Or course Lord Hagan. Who else would I mean?"

"I have no idea. Hagan may be a popular name amongst your people."

"My people? What's that supposed to mean?"

"You know, your countrymen. I've heard tell some names are used a lot. Take William, for example…"

"That's enough already," said Rosalyn. "Now, is he there or not?"

"Not, I'm afraid. He wandered off, seeking his father, Lord Gebhard."

"A pity," she added. "I was hoping to have words with him."

"That sounds ominous."

"Why? Merely because I wish to speak with him?"

"Having words with someone sounds more like they're in trouble. Is that your intention?"

Ludwig could tell he'd hit a sore spot, for she pouted.

"I'm a little curious as to why he didn't accept my invitation," said Rosalyn.

"Invitation to what?"

"Why, dinner, of course."

"And when did you send this invitation?"

"The day before yesterday. Would you believe he didn't even deign to answer? How rude can a man be?"

Ludwig couldn't help but laugh.

"What's so funny?"

"Lady Rosalyn, there was no way Lord Hagan could even have received your letter. The entire company has only recently returned from scouting out the enemy. Did your father not inform you?"

"He most certainly did not!"

"Ah, well, doubtlessly for good reason. I don't suppose he wanted you worrying about anything."

"Was it dangerous?"

"Very," said Ludwig, "but Hagan acquitted himself quite well."

"Hagan did?"

"Yes, why? Does that surprise you?"

"I suppose it shouldn't, yet the more I learn about him, the more fascinating he becomes."

"Are you going to tell him?"

"Tell him what?"

"That you're in love with him?"

Rosalyn reddened. "I never said any such thing!"

"Maybe not in so many words, but your face lights up at the mere mention of his name, not to mention you're full of energy when he's around."

"I..."

"Don't try to deny it, Rosalyn," said Ludwig. "You know it's true."

"Does he feel the same?"

He smiled. "You mean does his face light up like yours does?"

"Stop teasing, Ludwig. You know what I mean."

"I believe he does, my lady, but the influence of his father is still strong. I have, admittedly, been chipping away at that exterior. In time, I think, we'll see more of the relatively decent fellow who's buried beneath the rough exterior."

She chuckled. "You make him sound like a statue."

"And so he is, to an extent. Men like Hagan are shaped by those around him, and he has led a somewhat sheltered life."

"Unlike you?"

"Precisely."

Her face grew serious. "You must consider me frivolous to speak of such things the eve before battle."

"Not at all," said Ludwig, "but make no mistake, there will be a battle tomorrow, or possibly the day after, and men will die. There are no guarantees in war, Rosalyn. If you wish to tell Hagan of your love, you should do it now, before it's too late."

She paled. "And if he were to die?"

"Then he would do so knowing he is loved. Can a man wish for more?"

"And what of you? If you were to die tomorrow, would you be content?"

Ludwig thought of everything he'd experienced these last few months. "I would," he said. "For all I've been through has brought me here, to this spot, at this time. You may laugh at the idea, but I'm beginning to sense I came here for a purpose."

"Yes, to win a joust, remember?"

"No, it's more than that." He looked her straight in the eyes. "It's my destiny."

"Or the will of the Saints?"

"Perhaps. Who can say? In any event, for the first time in my life, I feel as though I'm exactly where I need to be."

41

THE BATTLE BEGINS

Summer 1095 SR

L udwig crouched behind what was left of a low stone wall. At some point in the past, there must have been a pathway leading south, but it had long since become overgrown with weeds. To his right sat the old farm, packed with men of Lord Gebhard's company along with the Grim Defenders. To their front, they had dug in sharpened stakes to dissuade the cavalry from closing, but there had not been enough time to complete the task, and the northern portion had been left unfinished.

Hagan Stein was in the building, commanding its defence, while Ludwig led those behind the low wall. Though the stones afforded some protection, he still felt exposed and was well aware that should cavalry bypass them, they would be cut off from any help. To that end, he had stolen Sigwulf and Cyn, leaving Captain Ecke with the rest of the mercenaries inside. It had been a difficult decision, but the group outside would have to adapt far faster to the changing battlefield, and he needed his best sergeants for the task.

Lord Hagan seemed more than satisfied with the arrangement. Clearly, the poor fellow was out of his depth, but Ludwig was careful to make it look like the troops' dispositions had been his commander's idea.

By late in the day, Ludwig could take solace in the fact there would not be enough daylight left to determine the ultimate victor. Instead, this battle would likely last two days, with initial contact occurring sometime before nightfall.

He walked along the wall, checking on his men. They were nervous but ready, determined to do their best.

Sigwulf nodded westward. "Here they come."

A wall of men filled the horizon. The enemy appeared to be keeping their horsemen in reserve, although Ludwig doubted that would last long. They would likely close the distance, then take up a line opposite, ready for the morning's battle. Only then would they be able to discern the enemy's true intentions.

"What do you make of them?" asked Sigwulf.

"They're hiding their horses," said Ludwig. "A wise move, considering what they're up against."

"Yes, the Knights of the Sceptre are a fearsome bunch, the best warriors in all of Erlingen. By rights, you should be amongst them yourself, but I suppose this little command of yours is more important."

"Are you objecting to my presence?"

Sigwulf grinned. "Not at all, but I imagine the duke's knights will play a decisive role in the coming battle."

"If he doesn't waste them," warned Ludwig. "You know what some of his barons are like."

Cyn came up beside them. "What are we looking at?"

"The enemy," said Sigwulf.

"They don't look so scary. Hit them with a weapon, and they'll die like anyone else."

Ludwig grimaced. "I only wish there wasn't so many of them."

"Regretting your suggestion to hold here?"

"Not at all, but that doesn't mean it's going to be easy."

"It's the cavalry that scares me," said Sigwulf.

"They're not so bad," said Ludwig. "We've built up our defences, so they won't get in here so easily."

"It's not only that," said Sigwulf. "At the battle of Krosnicht, it was the cavalry that decimated my family."

"I thought you weren't there?"

"I wasn't, but my brother was, along with my father."

"It was that bad?"

"Let's just say the king didn't take prisoners."

"I doubt that'll be the case here," said Ludwig.

"I wouldn't be so sure," said Cyn. "If I was going to conquer a country, I'd want all the old nobility out of the way. That way, I could put in my own people. That's not so bad for people like us, but Lord Hagan might feel otherwise."

"Best not tell him your theories, then," said Sigwulf. "We don't want to alarm him."

"There, to the south of their line," said Cyn. "Do you see it? The king's banner."

Ludwig could make out the white and green background. Something was emblazoned on its front, but the wind had died down, making it hard to tell what it was supposed to be. He squinted, hoping it would help but found all it did was aggravate him.

"It's meant to be an eagle," said Sigwulf.

"Is it? It looks like it has two heads."

"And so it does. It represents the fact that the kingdom looks both to the sea and land."

"Andover has ports?"

"Yes," said Sigwulf. "It's on the Great Northern Sea. Did you not know?"

"I knew they commanded a great deal of river traffic, but I had no idea they were on the coast. How far away is the sea?"

"Within a few hundred miles."

"I'd like to see it someday, providing we live long enough."

Sigwulf shrugged. "There's not much to see, just a lot of water and a cold wind blowing in from the north."

"Don't listen to him," said Cyn. "He's simply missing home."

"It's not my home anymore!" defended the huge man. "The King of Abelard saw to that."

"You may see it again," said Ludwig. "A lot can happen in the span of a decade or so."

"The Underworld would have to freeze before I set foot in that wretched place again. My home is here, with Cyn."

This pleased her no end. "Aw," she said. "Now he's making me all teary eyed."

Ludwig returned his focus to the king's flag. "We never actually saw the king's retinue," he said. "Does he have an order of knights like the duke?"

"He does," said Sigwulf, "though they're said to be more numerous. At least that's what I heard from the locals."

"The locals?"

"Yes, Baron Stein's men. Sorry, I suppose they're Lord Hagan's men now."

"How do they know about the king's guard?"

"They know a lot more than they let on. Word travels quickly in an army camp, and the barons aren't shy about expressing their opinions."

"Well," said Ludwig, "let's hope he doesn't decide to use them to attack our position here. I don't fancy fighting men in full plate armour, do you?"

"No," agreed Sigwulf. "Mind you, it wouldn't be so bad if I had a hammer, or maybe an axe, but swords are almost useless against that kind of protection. In any event, I doubt they'll come up against us."

"Why's that?" asked Ludwig.

"Knights are nothing but glory hunters, present company excluded of course. They'd prefer to run around the battlefield fighting their peers, more chances of earning ransom."

"I hadn't thought of that."

"They're halting," said Cyn.

"I can see that, but why?" said Ludwig. "Don't they want to get closer?"

"No," she replied. "They fear the duke's knights. Their entire army is forming into a long line."

"Why are there gaps?"

"I expect that's to let their own knights through when the time comes."

"Where are their archers?"

"Likely formed up behind their foot," offered Sigwulf. "The royalists did the same thing at Krosnicht. I thought you would have known that—you read a lot."

"I do," admitted Ludwig. "Unfortunately, the bowmen get short shrift in such accounts."

"That's because the nobility doesn't like them. They consider them cowardly for fighting at a distance."

"But in spite of that, they still employ their own."

"True," said Sigwulf. "They're not complete idiots. They'll employ anything that can give them an advantage against the enemy, yet rail against those same tactics when employed by their foes."

"Such is the nature of war."

Cyn was looking eastward, back towards the duke's army. "Something's happening."

Ludwig turned to see a group of knights riding forth.

"What is he doing?" he asked.

A gap had opened in the duke's line, and now a large group of horsemen were riding forth, their armour glittering in the afternoon sun. Ludwig felt his heart swell with pride, for it was an inspiring sight, yet his mind told him it would end in disaster.

He watched them advance. "By the Saints, they're a magnificent sight."

There must have been close to two hundred of them passing the farmhouse to the south, stretched out into a long line advancing at the trot.

When they were almost even with Ludwig's position, they drew swords as their mounts picked up speed.

Ludwig struggled to understand their haste, for they still had hundreds of paces yet to go before contacting the enemy.

Sigwulf's hand rested on his shoulder. "Look," he said, pointing westward.

The King of Andover had responded with cavalry of his own. The duke's knights now faced half again as many enemy horsemen. Ludwig could feel his heart racing, his pulse quicken, and, for a brief moment, he wished he were with them, tearing down on the enemy, ready to wreak havoc.

The lines struck each other with a mighty clash. The closest part of the melee was less than a few hundred paces from Ludwig's position, and he watched in awe as steel met steel, unable to tear his eyes from the carnage. To him, they were heroes of myth, battling the enemy in a life or death struggle. Lines began to disintegrate, merging to become hundreds of individual duels, the bright tabards of their heraldry blurring into a riot of colours.

Even as close as he was, it was now impossible to tell friend from foe. Only the clash of metal told of the fight. Around the outside of this melee, individual knights rode, seeking an opportunity to strike. Then a trio of enemy knights spotted Ludwig and his men.

Ludwig stood. "Archers, draw!"

Closer they came, picking their way carefully through the stakes, not yet realizing what awaited them.

"Loose!" he shouted.

A ragged volley flew forth, several striking true, but metal armour protected their targets. It did, however, convince the enemy knights they were better served by re-entering the melee that raged nearby.

Ludwig turned to Cyn. "Get the rest of the bowmen out here as fast as you can. If those knights come back, I want them taken down." She ran off to the farmhouse like a madwoman, no thought to her own safety.

Ludwig was frustrated, galled even, to have to sit back and watch the battle unfold, unable to take part in it. He turned to Sigwulf, who appeared content to watch.

"We must do something," urged Ludwig.

"What would you have us do? Charge forward and be cut down like blades of grass? Our time will come, my friend, but you must be patient."

The fighting began to slacken, the sounds of battle now dull in the distance. The combatants were tiring, the field churned up by the horses' hooves. Even as Ludwig sat there, he saw a small group of riders break off from the melee, riding eastward, desperate to escape the clutches of the king's army. They didn't get far.

Ludwig watched in horror as a knight of Andover caught up to them, bringing a mace crashing down onto a helmet. The rider slumped, then slid from the saddle to lie, unmoving. The second victim took a blow to the arm and lost control of his reins. His horse kept moving, but the rider twisted, desperate to parry another blow. He got his sword up, but the manoeuvre was weak, and the mace crashed down, ruining the man's shoulder. He screamed in agony and fell from the saddle to land with a thud as his horse ran off in a panic.

The knight of Andover continued his chase, calling out at the last of the duke's men. To his credit, the Knight of the Sceptre turned around, meeting his fate with courage and determination. They gazed at each other and, with a nod, urged their horses into a head-to-head confrontation.

They rode past each other at the gallop, their weapons held on high. The Erlingener struck with the sword, but his foe deftly deflected the blow, then countered with a backward bash as they passed, catching his target in the lower back. The mace dug in, only denting the armour, but the weapon had done its job. The duke's man fell from the saddle, screaming in agony, his spine likely crushed by the force of the blow. The Knight of Andover slowed his pace, turning to chase after the lost mounts, ignoring the cries of anguish.

Ludwig looked away, sickened by the sight. It was one thing to die in combat, quite another to suffer such a grievous wound. Death would be a long time coming for the poor fellow, pain his constant companion. Ludwig felt the contents of his stomach rebel and fought hard to keep them in place.

Finally, the fighting ceased. The enemy horsemen began turning their mounts around, seeking the safety of their own lines once more. Behind them lay the dead and dying, their cries of agony gut-wrenching.

"We must do something," said Ludwig.

"There's nothing we can do," said Sigwulf. "Go out there, and those knights will turn around in an instant and be amongst us. What chance would we have to survive that?"

All his life Ludwig had read of battle, yet nothing had prepared him for this horror. In place of elation, he felt only revulsion and dread. Was he destined to lie, mangled and in pain, only to die a slow, horrible death?

"Saints preserve us," he mumbled.

"It's not the Saints who will save us," said Sigwulf, "it's men."

At that moment, Cyn returned, a dozen of Hagan's crossbowmen in tow. She deployed them at the southern end of their position, ready to ward off any horsemen who might get too close.

Ludwig stared out at the carnage, sickened, and yet at the same time, he couldn't tear his eyes away from it. He wanted to offer solace to the dying, to put them out of their misery but knew Sigwulf was right. Any attempt to help them would only lead to their own inevitable deaths.

The two sides appeared to be content to stare at each other across the battlefield as the light waned, the night soon to be upon them. With it would come a brief respite, but Ludwig knew that morning would bring more slaughter.

The sun sank in the west, casting its red hue across the field of battle, making the place look like a nightmare from the Underworld. A lone horse staggered out of the mass of dead and injured, then collapsed, its dying call echoing across the meadow.

Ludwig found himself praying to Saint Mathew, not a conscious act, yet the words came to him unbidden. "Keep me safe, oh Blessed Saint, that I may survive the coming day. Watch over me as I do thy bidding and welcome me to the Afterlife when my time has come." He halted the litany, feeling a calming peace fall over him, knowing what he had to do.

He turned to Cyn. "Gather men," he ordered. "A dozen should do."

"For what?" she asked.

"We're going to go out there," he said, "amongst the dead."

"To what end?"

"We shall bring the wounded back here."

"Are you mad?"

"No," said Ludwig. "Those who cannot be saved shall be given a merciful death, be they friend or foe, but the rest we'll bring here, out of harm's way."

"You seek to bring the enemy here?"

"Would you do any less were your own men dying?"

Her face fell, and he felt sorry for berating her.

"Pick the quietest men you can find," he continued. "We shall have to move stealthily, lest we alert the enemy to our presence."

She nodded, then moved down the wall, tapping men on the shoulder.

"What shall I do?" asked Sigwulf.

"I'll need you to keep an eye out for the enemy. The last thing we want is for them to attack us in the middle of evacuating the wounded."

"You're crazy, Ludwig. Has anyone ever told you that?"

He smiled. "I'll take that as a compliment."

The sun dipped below the horizon, throwing the field into darkness. Ludwig waited for his eyes to adjust to the moonlight. By this time, Cyn had returned, alongside a dozen individuals.

Ludwig looked at the group. "Out there," he began by pointing, "lay the dead and wounded. Our task this night will be to bring back those who can be saved. If you come across a man who looks like he won't make it, then finish him off. Better to give him a quick death than make him suffer. If you're in doubt, ask Cyn or me."

"What about the enemy?" came a voice.

"What's your name?" asked Ludwig.

"Velton, sir."

"Well, Velton, the same rules apply to the enemy. If they have a chance of surviving the night, we bring them here. Otherwise, you dispatch them cleanly. I don't want anyone to suffer unnecessarily. Now, is everyone ready?"

He looked at their faces. They were all staring back at him, and he suddenly felt a chill in his bones. How many of these same faces would be staring at the sky in death by tomorrow night?

"Come," he said, leading them out from behind their cover. He passed by the outer edges of the battle, looking for any signs of movement. A horse shifted to his right, and he turned towards it. As he neared, he saw the poor creature rearing up its head. A nasty gash had been torn into the creature's rear leg, breaking bone and sending a flood of blood that had drenched the beast's abdomen, making it look black in the moonlight.

Ludwig pulled his dagger and moved to the horse's head, trying to soothe it. It looked at him with wild eyes, shifting its head in fear. He drove his weapon through the creature's ear and into the brain, taking it out of its misery. Bile rose in his throat, and he turned aside, emptying the contents of his stomach.

His men started spreading out, and he caught a glimpse of a dagger rising and falling, and then the last gasp of a dying man. He shook his head, trying to keep it clear. There was work to be done, he told himself; this was no time for sentimentality.

Ludwig moved south, checking bodies as he went. Kneeling by a knight, he removed the helmet to see if he lived, but as soon as he did so, he saw the terrible wound that had been inflicted on the side of the man's head. Despondency threatened to overwhelm him, and then he heard a gurgling noise.

He froze, trying to ascertain from where the sound came, for the body before him lay still; surely, the man was dead? It was only then that Ludwig saw an extra arm protruding from beneath. Someone had fallen prior to this knight and lay covered by the corpse.

He waved the nearest one of his warriors over, and together, they heaved the dead man to the side. Beneath was the crushed helmet of a knight, its visor jammed closed, likely the result of a blow from a hammer or mace. He tried to remove the helmet but to no avail. The poor fellow was covered with mud, and in the darkness, Ludwig could see little.

"Help me get him up," he said.

They took the man's arms and pulled, hearing a sucking sound as he came free of the mud. "Drag him to the house," he said. "We'll examine his wounds back there."

He moved on, searching for others, determined to save as many as he could. Six men were already being helped back to their defensive position, then Ludwig heard a noise that turned his blood to ice. Men were coming from the west. That could only mean one thing—a nighttime assault. He abandoned the search, ordering his men back to their positions.

42

NIGHT ASSAULT

Summer 1095 SR

L udwig crouched behind the wall, his helmet removed to better hear
the enemy's approach. At first, there were the small sounds: the snap
of a twig or the smack of a boot hitting a puddle, but then came the sound
of scabbards slapping against legs, of men struggling to advance in the dark.

"Archers," whispered Ludwig. "Draw bows."

The command was carried down the line. Men rose, pulling arrows
back to ears while crossbowmen stood ready, their weapons pointing
westward.

"Aim waist-high," he added, then waited again.

Finally standing, he moved beside his archers, lest he impede their aim.

"Loose!" he hissed.

Bolts and arrows flew forth, disappearing into the darkness of night. He
heard grunts and then a roar of voices as the enemy broke into a run.

"Man the walls!" Ludwig called out. Warriors stood, their spears at the
ready as he peered past them into the darkness. He could hear the
advancing enemy well enough, but still the darkness hid them, and he
wondered just how close they had gotten.

All was revealed within moments as a wall of men came into view, the
moonlight reflecting off chainmail coifs and kettle helms.

The archers moved up to the wall, filling in the gaps and let loose with
more arrows and bolts. This volley was much more accurate, and he saw

half a dozen of the invaders go down. The enemy screamed out their defiance as they rushed the last few paces.

Spears stabbed out, playing havoc with their assault, and then men were everywhere. He stabbed out with his sword, taking one in the gut. His foe fell forward, threatening to land atop him, and Ludwig twisted, narrowly avoiding the fate. A spear scraped off his breastplate, and he struck out, slicing into a man's arm.

His sword scraped along that of an enemy, smashing into the crossguard. In defence, his foe tried to sidestep, following up with a quick jab, but Ludwig was quicker, his sword catching the man under the arm, digging deep. He pulled his blade free, letting the body drop, then struck to his left, feeling the steel sink into flesh.

There was no time to think as another spear came at him, slicing through the fabric of his sleeve and pushing his arm backward, throwing him off balance. His foe followed his weapon, pressing forward until Ludwig went down beneath the onslaught.

The man loomed overhead, grinning in triumph, determined to drive his weapon into Ludwig's skull as a mace smashed into the side of the invader's head, knocking him sideways. Cyn pushed forward, driving the man to his knees before finishing him off with a second strike to the skull.

Ludwig got to his feet, trying to get his bearings. His men, pushed back from the wall, were in danger of being overwhelmed, and then he heard a roar. Captain Ecke led a group from the house, slicing into the enemy like a scythe cutting down wheat.

The enemy broke, fleeing westward as if the denizens of the Underworld were nipping at their heels. Ludwig turned to his own men, counting heads. Captain Ecke came towards him, looking quite pleased with himself and then a whistling sound made them look westward, where a burst of arrows flew out of the dark. Ludwig instinctively dove behind the wall. There he lay, pressed up against the stone wall, desperate for cover as screams erupted from all around him. A body fell against him, and he turned on the man with a curse, only to see the face of Captain Ecke, an arrow protruding from his eye.

"Saints save us," Ludwig called out.

Sigwulf crawled up beside him, cursing in a low voice. An arrow had taken him in the arm, and he clutched it as blood seeped forth.

"Where's Cyn?" shouted Ludwig.

Sigwulf pointed. "Over there, crouched behind that stake."

More arrows flew, littering the ground as they fell.

"Get yourself into the building," ordered Ludwig, "and have someone look at that wound."

"It's nothing."

He gripped the big man's hand. "Get inside," he repeated. "That's an order. I'm going to need you in fighting shape when those men come back."

Sigwulf got ready to rise, but Ludwig heard a noise. "Wait till after the volley, then run."

True to his word, another shower of arrows descended, peppering the ground. No one was hit this time, but it made moving difficult. Sigwulf ran, disappearing into the farmhouse.

When the next volley came forth, Ludwig began counting. At twenty, another onslaught of arrows rained down.

"Wait for the next volley," called out Ludwig, "then gather what arrows you can. You will only have to the count of fifteen before more come." He could feel the eyes of his men upon him, and he started to sweat. What if his count was off? Was he dooming them to death?

Another volley. "Now," he called out and then started counting as they leaped from cover, seeking out arrows where they lay. Handfuls of the things poked up from all over the place, leading Ludwig to conclude at least a hundred archers lay to the west, loosing arrows in the dark in a vain attempt to hit anyone who might stray out into the open.

When his count reached fifteen, he shouted, "Cover." They all sought a place of concealment, then more arrows came forth. The men cheered, for they had cheated the enemy of targets.

Ludwig wondered how many arrows they had collected, but looking around, it was apparent they had plenty to spare. The real question was, how many more volleys must they endure?

More arrows struck the ground, and again he counted. This time he reached twenty-five, and still no arrows flew.

"Prepare," he ordered. He poked his head over the wall, looking westward. Sure enough, the familiar clatter of armour drifted to his ears. "They're coming."

He spotted Sigwulf at the door to the house. "Remain where you are," he ordered, "and gather some men. Once they overrun us, I want you to counterattack." A nod came back in reply.

Cyn peered over the edge of the wall. "I see them," she said.

"Call out when they're within twenty paces," said Ludwig. He turned to Simmons. "Pass the word. On Cyn's command, I want the archers to stand and loose off as many arrows as they can, crossbowmen as well." He looked over at his footmen. "The rest of you stand by. The archers will back up when threatened. That's your sign to move in."

"Now!" called out Cyn.

The archers rose, drawing bows and sending a volley westward. The enemy was packed so closely together there was no chance of missing. Arrows dug into armour, and men went down by the dozens.

"Keep going," said Ludwig. "Loose in your own time!"

He stood behind them, drawing his sword. The first rank of enemy footmen had gone down, their screams echoing across the wall. Browbeaten by their sergeants, the others pressed forward until he could make out the details of their armour in the moonlight.

"Archers fall back," he commanded. "Foot to the front!"

Someone amongst the enemy threw a spear, and it sailed past Ludwig, burying its tip into the ground. Ludwig stabbed out, causing the warrior before him to hesitate. Something came over him, a type of frenzy, and he seized the opportunity, jumping up to the top of the wall and hurling himself at the enemy, striking out as he went, his sword blade taking out a man's throat. His teeth bared, he struck again, driving his blade deep into another's thigh. A scream of agony followed, and then Ludwig moved past, now in amongst the soldiers of the king, his sword seeking a target as if possessing a will of its own.

An enemy came up on his left, only to have his head explode. Ludwig had a brief glimpse of Sigwulf, his sword dripping gore, and then he had to parry, blocking a strike that would doubtlessly have ended him had he not moved quickly.

Out of the corner of his eye, he saw Cyn duck as a spear was thrust over her head. She responded by smashing her mace into her foe's groin. Ludwig heard the scream, and then the man went down, clutching what was left.

A sword scraped along his cheek, and he cursed, for he had been so busy listening for the enemy he had not thought to don his helmet. He suddenly felt vulnerable as if the next blow might well do him in.

A strange noise drifted to his ears, and then he realized it was Sigwulf. The man was singing, swinging his sword two-handed like a hero of yesteryear fighting the chaos of the Underworld.

The opposition began to falter, and then they were all running westward towards the safety of the enemy's lines.

"Back," yelled Ludwig. "Back to the wall and prepare for another barrage!"

He jumped the wall as more arrows came sailing from above. Two of his men went down, and he cursed. He had let the battle get him fired up, acted impulsively, endangering his men. He swore to not be fooled the next time.

Again, they collected arrows, and then the enemy returned. Over and over came the attacks, each time a series of volleys followed by foot soldiers. Ludwig felt the adrenaline coursing through him as the pattern repeated until he thought it would never end. Was he stuck in the Underworld, doomed to repel attacks for the rest of eternity? It certainly felt like it.

He soon lost track of how many waves they fought. They slaughtered the enemy's troops by the dozens, yet the king's men kept coming, each time whittling down the defenders. Arrows came aplenty, allowing his own archers an unlimited supply. But with each new assault, their numbers weakened, if not their resolve.

Ludwig's arms felt like lead, his legs even more so. He was barely able to stand, yet he and his men fought on valiantly. His voice grew hoarse and raspy, yet still he would not give up. He called on more reinforcements from the house, only to find none were left.

He considered withdrawal, but his stubborn streak kicked in, refusing to let him. On and on they fought until the wee hours of the morning.

Dawn broke over a bloody field of battle, revealing the dead and injured. Had he not been so tired, Ludwig would have gone out to see to the wounded, but he consoled himself by admitting he could not chance another attack. In that instant, he would have gladly given a fortune for the opportunity to sleep, but it appeared it was not to be.

"By the Saints," said Sigwulf. "We must have killed hundreds."

The stench of death drifted to their noses, and Ludwig retched. Even here, in this fortified position, the wounded outnumbered the living. Ludwig would have killed for something to drink, but there was none left.

"Lord Hagan?" he asked.

"Inside," said Cyn.

Ludwig stared at the farmhouse, no more than two dozen paces away, yet to him, it felt like an uncrossable gulf. He forced himself to his feet, feeling weary beyond belief. "What are our losses?"

"Half the company at least," she replied. "It might be easier to count who's left standing."

He turned to Sigwulf. "Anything to add?"

"Yes," the big man replied. "Lord Hagan is wounded."

"Wounded? I didn't even know he'd been fighting."

"He was indeed. While we were busy charging the enemy, another group tried to gain entry from the north."

"How bad is he?"

"You'll have to judge that for yourself."

Ludwig shut his eyes for a moment, trying to summon the energy to continue. "Mathew, give me strength," he said, then began moving towards the house.

He entered the structure to be assaulted by the smell of untreated wounds. The men had done their best to make the injured comfortable, but there was little anyone here could do to save them. Most would bleed out. Indeed, several had done so earlier this morning, but to do nothing was unconscionable.

He was directed over to Lord Hagan, who sat, his back supported by the outside wall, his chest bloodied and his face pale, yet his eyes were clear. He noted the approach of his aide.

"Ah, Sir Ludwig. I'm afraid you'll have to take command of the company. It appears I am no longer able to stand." He stared down at his legs.

Ludwig saw more blood. It looked like arrows had done him in, and he wondered how, when the house would have protected him from such things.

"He led a charge," explained Sergeant Dornhuffer, the tears coming freely. "You would have been proud of him, sir. He showed true courage."

Ludwig turned to the sergeant to see a bandage around the man's head, also soaked in blood. His gaze moved elsewhere, determined not to show his sorrow. He saw nothing but death, for there lay Arturo, his most argumentative soldier and beside him Krebbs, who he himself had raised to the rank of sergeant. He could well imagine the tears when Agneth, the tavern keeper, heard the news. Was this all worth it? He doubted it.

"Gather what wounded you can," said Ludwig. "It's time we vacated this building."

"I'm afraid we can't, sir."

"Why? Is there no one left?"

"It's not that, sir."

"Then what?"

"It's the enemy, sir. They've begun the attack."

"They're attacking us again?"

"Not only us, the whole army."

Ludwig found the strength to walk over to one of the windows. The army of Andover was advancing from the west in a wide front, ready to overwhelm the duke's army, which lay to the east of his position.

"For Saint's sake," said Ludwig. "Can't we at least get a moment to rest?"

"You should go," said Hagan, his breath laboured. "Go while you're still able. Leave the wounded here if you must, but if you stay, you'll be overwhelmed."

Ludwig felt like an animal caught in a trap. On the one hand, he could flee, but that meant leaving the wounded behind, something he wasn't willing to do. On the other, he could stand and fight, but that would likely result in the death of everyone. "What to do?" he muttered. "What to do?"

"I beg your pardon, sir?" asked Dornhuffer.

Ludwig looked at the sergeant. "Nothing, I was simply thinking. Call the men to me. We'll make a last stand here, inside the building. How much time do you reckon we have?"

Dornhuffer looked out the window. "Not long, sir."

"Get the wounded inside." He looked around the room, his gaze falling on a couple of men. "You two, lift that timber. I want it by the door, over there. We'll block up the entrance once everyone's inside." His voice grew more confident. "Archers, gather what arrows you can, then get to the windows. See if a couple of you can get onto what's left of the roof. I imagine it'll give you a good view of the area. Sig?"

"Here," came the reply.

"You take the north door. Block it up to the best of your ability. Cyn, you'll take the south. Move those wounded men to the eastern wall. I want them out of the way as much as possible."

"Right away, boss."

"You men, collect as much loose stone as you have time for and stack it against the south wall. I also want those two timbers laid against the wall."

"To what end?" asked Dornhuffer.

"I want the top of that wall knocked down. We'll put men up there to throw debris at those below attempting to gain entry."

Ludwig's passion energized the men. Tired though they were, they found the strength to act.

His gaze fell on a knight. The unknown man had been dragged in here earlier, his helmet a mess, but little had been done for him since. Ludwig crouched by his side. "Can you hear me?"

"Yes," came the answer, faint though it was.

"I'm going to try to remove your helmet, do you understand?"

The knight nodded.

Ludwig examined the damage. The visor had been crushed, pushing the bulk of the metal back in on the man. He wasn't eager to see the damage but knew it must be painful. Reaching under the helmet, he sought the chin strap, but none could be found, so he bent closer, examining the visor. Under normal circumstances, it would swing up from the chin, but the hinges had become damaged, making such an act all but impossible.

Digging out his dagger, he paused a moment to consider how to proceed. The lower part of the visor was protruding out from the helmet, so he carefully set his dagger beneath it, using the edge of the helmet to pry it up. At first, it resisted, then the hinge popped, and the visor came loose. Beneath was the bloodied countenance of none other than Sir Galrath.

43

THE BATTLE OF CHERMINGEN

Summer 1095 SR

L udwig stared down at the battered face. "I don't understand," he said. "You're not wearing your colours?"

Galrath coughed, spitting up blood. "The duke forbade me from fighting."

"But why? You're a knight of renown. Surely he would have wanted you there?"

"Ah, but's that's just it, don't you see? So great was my fame that he feared me falling into enemy hands. He wanted me by his side, not risking all for honour and glory."

"Don't speak to me of glory. I've had my fill. War is a thing to be avoided, not embraced."

"There's no hope for me, Ludwig," said Galrath. "I'm wracked with pain, and I can't feel my legs. I doubt even a Life Mage could help me now. Never, in all my life, did I imagine I would die here, in a ruin in the middle of a field even the Saints have forsaken."

Ludwig took the man's hand in a firm grip. "The Saints have not forsaken you, Sir Galrath." He felt tears welling up in his eyes. "They wait to take you to the Afterlife. No doubt there you will find plenty of adoration for your accomplishments."

The man smiled, but so torn up was his face that it began to bleed anew.

Ludwig felt the knight's grip tighten. "Ludwig, you are a good man and well-deserving of the title of knight. I would have you take what was mine, for I have no further use of it."

He wanted to object, but Galrath was adamant. "Promise me..." he coughed. "I have no family, no one to inherit. I would see it put to good use."

"It's not right," said Ludwig. "I haven't earned it."

"You're wrong, my friend. You've had a rough start, it's true, but in the short time you were amongst us, you touched us all, setting an example of what it means to be noble. Take what is mine, and use it to show the Continent what is needed."

Ludwig was overcome with emotion. Unable to speak, he merely nodded.

"Good," said the knight. "I can now die, knowing my life has not been wasted." He lay back and closed his eyes, his breathing ragged. Even as Ludwig watched, the man who had set him on his path to knighthood let out his last breath. Sir Galrath of Paledon was dead.

Ludwig released his grip, then laid the knight's hands on his chest. He hadn't known the man for long, but his example had been an inspiration, and Ludwig swore to keep his memory alive for as long as he could.

He stood, looking down at the body, his mind in turmoil. Panic was growing inside him, setting his nerves on edge, but then a sense of calm enveloped him. He turned to where Sigwulf and Cyn were organizing the defence. "I have an idea."

Ludwig examined their work. Dead bodies lay strewn around the interior of the house, packing the floor from north to south. Beneath them, bits of dust and stone littered the area, along with fragments of fallen timbers and old thatch.

Taking up his position behind a section of collapsed wall, he crouched, listening to the distant sounds of the approaching enemy. His mind struggled with his idea. It had come to him unexpectedly, and now that he waited, he wondered if he had done the right thing. It was dangerous, but then again, the same could be said of the battle that put them front and centre in this conflict.

Curiosity got the better of him, and he peeked out from behind cover. Everyone was still, except for the wounded. The only sounds permeating what was left of the interior were those one might expect amongst the injured.

Outside, the noises of an army drew closer. The enemy had been determined to be over four thousand in number, and the racket created during their advance made it sound like they would all descend upon Ludwig's position. He knew it wasn't true, of course, but he couldn't help but feel he was about to be overwhelmed.

There had been little time for planning, but his choice had seemed clear. Now, however, he began to wonder if he'd done the right thing. He pulled his head back to safety and shut his eyes. The army was entering the ruins now, their footsteps echoing as they carefully trod through the debris. Ludwig began his silent count, forcing himself to slow down for fear he would act too soon.

Finally, as he reached fifty, he rose to his feet to see at least thirty enemy soldiers within the room, each examining bodies as they went. Ludwig's presence was not noticed until he lunged forward, stabbing out with his sword. He took one by surprise, driving the tip of his blade into a leg, and the man fell back with a scream.

Now the enemy drew swords and began moving towards him. Ludwig's mouth was dry, his nerves shaking, yet he attacked again, a wide swing that took one in the arm. Armour stopped any actual damage, but it caused the others to focus their attention on him.

"Now!" Ludwig screamed.

All around the room, his men stood, covered in blood, guts, and debris, but it was all for show. They stabbed out with daggers, swords, and axes, taking the enemy completely by surprise.

The men of Andover turned to face these new foes, but confusion reigned supreme. Ludwig had ordered some of his own men to don the garb of the wounded enemies in their care, making it all but impossible for these new invaders to tell friend from foe. It was a delay that cost them dearly.

Swords struck out, axes chopped down, and Cyn's mace wrought terrible damage. The fight was all over in a matter of moments. Sigwulf ran to the north door, while Cyn took the south seeking any sign that their trap had failed, but outside, the king's army marched on, unaware of what had transpired.

"Strip those bodies," ordered Ludwig. "It worked once, so let's hope it can again." The men of Andover all wore a blue surcoat over their armour, the better to identify themselves in battle.

He knew it was a long shot, but with the numbers arrayed against them, it was likely the only way to save the day. The King of Andover was getting ready to swamp the duke's forces. Only a desperate act could save the army of Erlingen now.

"Better take this, sir," said Sergeant Dornhuffer. "Your sword won't do you much good where we're going."

Ludwig looked down to where a war hammer was offered. "Thank you," he said, examining its head. One side was the typically flat surface of a hammer, while the other consisted of a spike of metal, ideal for penetrating armour.

He moved to the south to where Cyn was watching the enemy march by. She turned at his approach.

"By the Saints," she said, "there are hundreds of them. Are you sure this is going to work?"

"There's only one way to find out," he replied.

He exited the building, falling in behind the soldiers of Andover who were flooding past them. The men of the company followed along, forming up into a rough column. They moved slowly, letting the rest of the army get ahead of them while Ludwig kept his eyes to the south.

The King of Andover was close, overseeing his army as it marched forward to crush the duke's men. He had only a small guard around him, a dozen armoured knights who were far more concerned with the enemy ahead of them than a small group of their own men who had emerged from the ruins.

Ludwig's heart was pounding frightfully, so much so that he would have sworn others could hear it. His fatigue was forgotten as they drew closer to their quarry. He glanced over at Sigwulf to see him grasping a halberd, with Cyn beside him, cradling her mace like it was a sacred relic, while everyone else kept glancing the king's way.

Closer they drew, and then Ludwig knew it was now or never. He looked at Sigwulf and nodded, then broke into a jog. The company picked up its pace as he wheeled them towards the king's entourage. They were only fifty paces away when they began to close the distance. Soon it was forty, and Ludwig was convinced they would be found out.

Something was happening to the east, holding the king's attention, and then they were thirty paces away. Ludwig found he was holding his breath and forced himself to exhale.

At twenty paces, one of the king's knights noticed them and opened his mouth to speak, but a trio of crossbow bolts sailed forth. Two bounced off the man's plate armour while the third wedged itself into the shoulder, right below the pauldron. The knight yelled something, but as the words issued forth, so, too, did a cry from Ludwig's men as they surged forward, running full tilt.

The king turned to see a group of his own men coming after him and froze, not quite grasping the danger. This was his undoing. An arrow struck his horse, causing it to rear up. The king, not expecting it, was thrown, landing in the churned-up mud where only yesterday the knights had fought their bloody encounter.

The king's guards drew swords, but Ludwig swung first, driving the head of his hammer into a kneecap where it struck plate, bending the metal and puncturing clean through to the flesh beneath. Pulling it free, he attacked again, this time with the back end, plunging the spear-like tip into a hip. He felt the armour part, the scraping of steel on steel as the weapon dug in, then blood spurted forth, showering him as he withdrew his weapon from the wound. The knight leaned forward in the saddle, although whether to attack or because he was in pain was anybody's guess. In any event, this was his last move as three different men struck out with spears and halberds.

Ludwig had a quick glimpse of the one who had been hit by a bolt trying to push his horse forward to protect the king, but the other knights were so intent on repelling the assault that they got in his way.

Ludwig, spotting a knight bearing down on him, waited, ready to leap to the side to avoid the attack. As the knight drew closer, Sigwulf appeared out of nowhere, bringing his halberd down onto the horse's head. As it struck, it made a noise like a melon, and then the beast went down, throwing the rider from the saddle. Erlingeners swarmed the body, and the knight was dead before he could make another move.

Ludwig saw Cyn dodging an enemy blow, then using her mace to smash into the horse's leg. Rider and mount fell, threatening to crush her as they went, but she leaped aside, finishing off the knight with a series of rapid strikes to the head.

Dornhuffer went down, a savage cut nearly separating his arm from his shoulder. Emile, Baldric's old chum, came out of nowhere, leaping onto the back of a knight's saddle, stabbing out repeatedly, using a dagger to find the gaps in the armour. That tactic was good, but the fool wasn't paying attention, and another knight sliced into his back. Emile screamed and fell to the ground, only to be trampled by the horses.

Ludwig swung his hammer, missing his mark as a knight rode past. He looked around, seeking the king, but too many horses blocked his view— the knights were everywhere, slaughtering his men. Sigwulf roared off to his right, and he turned, moving as fast as he could. The big man was in a test of strength, his halberd holding his foe's sword at bay. Ludwig rushed forward, smashing the head of his own weapon into the knight's leg. Sigwulf's halberd crashed down as the enemy knight lost his grip, the blade burying itself in the man's shoulder.

Ludwig swung again, his hammer deflected by the shaped armour. The clang of metal connecting with armour rang out as they both took turns smashing their weapons onto their opponent. Despite their efforts, the knight still managed to strike out, his blade slicing Sigwulf's tunic but causing only a surface wound.

Sigwulf twisted his halberd, exchanging the blade for the spike and smashed it down onto the knight's helmet with the last of his strength. The knight went limp, slumping in the saddle.

Ludwig tried to catch his breath while the chaos still surrounded him. Someone grabbed his arm, and he swung around, expecting the enemy, but it was only Cyn.

"Over there." She pointed.

Ludwig saw the king standing, shin-deep in mud, trying to climb up behind a mounted knight holding out his hand to help him up. Ludwig broke into a run, with Cyn right behind him, his anger building as he went. Harnessing its power for one final push, he screamed out, his voice harsh, his words lost to the sound of battle, yet still he ran, his feet carried by his rage at all they had endured.

The King of Andover had grasped the knight's arm, ready to be hauled up right as Ludwig attacked, his hammer swinging high above the king's head to take the knight in the bicep. The armour held, but the damage had been done, and the proffered hand was knocked from the king's grip.

Ludwig rushed forward, dropping the hammer, his focus now solely on the king. Into him, he ran, tackling His Majesty and driving him back into the mud. Royal hands came up, seizing Ludwig by the throat, but the grip was weak, and he knocked them aside. Ludwig landed a blow on the king's face, then reached for his dagger.

He heard the sound of a mace striking plate and knew Cyn was there, taking care of the mounted knight. Ludwig was on top of the king now, his knees on the prone royal, his dagger halfway out of its scabbard, but the King of Andover was no slouch. Realizing the danger, His Majesty had grabbed the same weapon by the hilt, and now a test of strength ensued.

Ludwig was weak, for he had slept little in the past two days. The King of Andover, on the other hand, was in good health and well-rested. Realizing he was in a no-win situation, Ludwig did something completely unexpected; he leaned down and head-butted his opponent. The king's grip slackened, and then Ludwig whipped out his knife, pressing the tip to his foe's throat.

"Surrender!" he demanded.

"I yield," came the reply.

"Louder!" Ludwig pressed the knife closer, depressing the skin on the king's neck.

"I order my men to yield!" the royal shouted.

The fighting slowed, then halted as all eyes turned to Ludwig. The knights began shifting, trying to surround him, but then Sigwulf and Cyn moved into position, watching to either side, weapons at the ready.

"Come any closer," said Sigwulf, "and the king dies."

"Then you will soon follow," claimed one of the knights. "It's an empty threat."

"We're not afraid to die. However, if you wish your sovereign dead, then come at us and be done with it."

The king's men all backed up.

"Lay down your arms," said the king. "I command it."

There was hesitation, but eventually, the knights complied. The few of Ludwig's men who survived moved in, picking up the weapons. With Sigwulf's help, Ludwig rose, lifting the King of Andover to stand before him.

"You have outwitted us, sir," said the king. "Might I know your name?"

"Sir Ludwig of Verfeld, Your Majesty." He bowed, although it felt strange doing so in front of a prisoner.

"And what would you have of me now?"

"You shall send word to halt the attack, Your Majesty, then we will all go and visit the duke."

"Very well, but tell me, if you would, why a foreigner such as yourself would intervene in this conflict? Of what possible interest is it to you?"

"This is an unjust war," said Ludwig. "You have invaded Erlingen and brought immense suffering to its people. Is that not reason enough?"

"You would not say that if you knew of the events that brought about this conflict."

"You mean your niece? Her death was accidental, was it not?"

"I find the circumstances surrounding her demise to be most peculiar. I asked Lord Deiter to investigate further but was refused. Surely you can see I had little choice left?"

"Not in the least. I can understand your distress, Your Majesty, but you had many other options available. At the very least, you could have insisted on a meeting between you and the duke. There you could have ironed out your differences."

The king wore a surprised look. "I must admit the thought never occurred to me. The duke has a reputation as a vain and stubborn man."

"Can you say any less of yourself?"

"You dare to speak thus of a king?"

"I might remind you," said Ludwig, "it is you who is MY prisoner, not the reverse. I think, under the circumstances, I may address you as I please."

The king glared, then turned to one of his knights. "Order the army to withdraw."

"Your Majesty?" the man retorted.

"I said order the withdrawal! We shall discuss things further once I have conversed with the duke."

"Yes, My King."

Orders were sent, bringing the attack to a grinding halt.

"You can put away that dagger," said the king. "I give you my word of honour. I shall not attempt to escape."

Ludwig sheathed the blade.

"You are a remarkable man," said the king. "My sense is we shall hear of you again. Let us hope by then we shall be on the same side."

Ludwig smiled. "I should like that, Your Majesty."

44

TO THE VICTOR, THE SPOILS

Summer 1095 SR

L udwig made his way through the camp looking for what remained of his command. He soon found them huddled together beneath the shade of a large oak. His heart sank as he counted heads.

"Is this it?" he asked.

Sigwulf nodded. "I'm afraid so, less than twenty men standing."

"A terrible price."

"But light considering what the army would have suffered had the attack continued."

"Yes," added Cyn, "and the duke owes it all to you. You should get a big reward for this. Fancy becoming an earl?"

Ludwig shook his head. "There's nothing they could give me that I would accept. This is not my home, nor will it ever be. I wish nothing from His Grace."

"Well said," said Sigwulf.

"I suppose," said Cyn, "but I wouldn't be opposed to a hefty reward. Surely they could afford that?"

"You still have Sir Galrath's belongings," Sigwulf reminded him. "Did you get a chance to look them over?"

"I did, as a matter of fact."

"And what had he?"

Ludwig laughed. "Most of the rest of my armour, but little else."

"No coins?"

"A little, maybe enough to have a drink in his memory."

"Can a man ask for anything more?"

"He certainly can," said Cyn. "What about the love of a good woman?"

Sigwulf made a show of scanning the area. "Why? Is there one nearby?"

She gave him a light tap on the shoulder, but he smiled at her, softening her features.

"What of the Grim Defenders?" asked Ludwig.

Cyn shook her head. "They're gone. The few who survived have sworn off the mercenary life."

"And you two?"

She looked at Sigwulf. He nodded, and she turned her attention back to Ludwig. "We'll keep our eyes open and our ears to the ground. Something will come along."

"Yes," said Sigwulf, "perhaps we'll become bodyguards. It's likely less dangerous."

"What about you?" asked Cyn. "What will you do now?"

"I'm not sure. I suppose I'm still sworn to Lord Wulfram, so until he releases me from my pledge of service, I'm not going anywhere. That reminds me, where's Lord Hagan?"

"Being looked after by the lay brothers," replied Sigwulf. "They're right over there."

"I'd better check in on him."

"Look for the brown banner with the axe on it," said Cyn.

Ludwig smiled. "I know the symbol of Saint Mathew."

"Good luck," said Sigwulf. "I hope we meet again."

Ludwig was about to leave, but then Cyn ran up to him, grabbing him in a tight embrace. She held on to him for a moment, then whispered in his ear. "Take care of yourself, Ludwig. Your destiny awaits."

He nodded, too overcome to respond. Cyn walked back to Sigwulf, then they stood hand in hand, watching Ludwig with smiles on their faces. It was hard to leave them, but despite that, Ludwig knew his duty. He turned, leaving them standing there, the image forever in his memory.

The Brothers of Saint Mathew were trained in the healing arts, though none here had the use of magic. As a result, there was much they could do in terms of cleaning wounds and applying bandages but could offer little more than prayers for the more seriously wounded.

They had set up their mission in the shade of the trees, the wounded laid out upon pallets of straw. Lay brothers made their way amongst their patients, assessing wounds and offering comfort where they may. There were few to tend to this day, for Ludwig's mad plan had seen the enemy king captured before much damage could be done.

Ludwig found Lord Hagan lying on a pallet of straw, his head resting on a rolled-up blanket. Someone was bent over him, ministering to his wounds, and Ludwig assumed it was a lay brother. As he drew closer, however, the person stood, revealing it to be Lady Rosalyn.

He halted, not quite sure how to proceed. After some deliberation, he decided to wait, not wishing to interfere in what was clearly an intimate conversation.

"Strange how things work."

The words made Ludwig jump. Lord Wulfram stood beside him, gazing at his daughter, revealing a soft spot for his rival's son. "Incredible, isn't it?"

"What is?" said Ludwig.

Lord Wulfram smiled. "It wasn't so long ago she refused to even consider the idea of marrying the son of Lord Gebhard, and now, here she is, chatting away as if they've known each other for years."

"Tragedy has a way of bringing people together."

"So it does." The baron looked at him. "How are you? Recovered from your ordeal?"

"A day or two of sleep wouldn't go amiss, but other than that, I'm in one piece. Why?"

"I've been sent to fetch you. The duke would have words."

Ludwig looked down at his clothes, rent with cuts and stained with blood. "I'm afraid I'm not dressed for it, my lord."

"I dare say you're correct, but I doubt it matters. You turned over the King of Andover to his knights. Lord Deiter now wishes to see the man who saved the day."

"I only did what I thought was best."

"Humble to the last," said Wulfram. "You do yourself proud, my young friend, but it's not a request; rather, it's a command, and I might remind you that while you're sworn to me, he is still your duke."

"Very well," said Ludwig, "then let's get it over with, shall we? Sleep calls me, and I would find a bed once we're done."

Lord Deiter Heinrich, Duke of Erlingen sipped some wine as Ludwig entered along with Lord Wulfram.

"Ah, there he is," said the duke. He stepped forward, extending his hand. "By the Saints, you've done us a good turn this day."

"I've only done my duty, Your Grace."

"If only my own nobles were as dutiful, we should have an invincible army."

"And has the king agreed to leave Erlingen soil?"

"He has indeed as well as pay a heavy price for it. Why, his ransom alone will keep the court fed for months."

"A toast," called out Lord Hurst.

Silence fell as servants hurried to pass out cups of wine. Ludwig took his in hand, then waited as everyone looked to the Baron of Anshlag for his words.

"With Your Grace's permission?" said Hurst. The duke nodded.

"We are gathered today to honour the man who won us the war, Sir Ludwig of Verfeld. Your memory, sir, shall be cherished for generations to come."

Ludwig held up his hand. "It was not my idea," he said. "You must give credit where credit is due. The idea was that of Sir Galrath of Paledon. It is his name that should live on in your annals."

This brought a round of astonished looks from the gathered nobles.

"Sir Galrath?" said the duke. "Are you sure?"

"Without him, there would have been no attempt to capture the king, Your Grace."

"Astounding."

"Instead," continued Ludwig, "let us drink a toast in his name and remember the loyal knight who saved the duchy." He raised his cup. "To Sir Galrath."

"Sir Galrath," they all echoed.

"Our brave servant, Sir Galrath, perished in the battle," said the duke, "but you, Sir Ludwig, have survived to bring us salvation. I would know what reward you would have."

"I desire none," said Ludwig, "save the knowledge that Erlingen prospers." He had thought his words complete, but a trick of the light played a reflection across the duke's eyes, making him think of something.

"Is that all?" asked the duke.

"Perhaps one other thing?" added Ludwig.

"Then speak, and whatever it is, I shall do my best to give you."

"I would have you stop persecuting the Therengians."

A gasp escaped the nobles. To demand this of their sovereign lord was clearly unthinkable.

Ludwig continued. "Were it not for a man named Beornoth, we would have failed to escape the clutches of the army of our enemy, Your Grace. He and his fellow Therengians gave their lives to save this land. I would ask that you honour that sacrifice by removing the restrictions on his people."

"They are descended from those of the Old Kingdom," said the duke, "and as such, represent a threat to my power."

"No," said Ludwig. "They wish only to be given the same treatment as the rest of your subjects. Include them, and I have a feeling you will find less resistance to your rule. This is the boon I would ask of you."

"Ridiculous," said Lord Rengard. "Who does he think he is?"

"Who indeed," said the duke. "I'll tell you who he is. He is our saviour, plain and simple." He returned his attention to Ludwig. "You could have had anything: a title, land, riches beyond your wildest dreams, and despite that, this is all you ask? Why?"

"Because it's right," said Ludwig. "Even the Saints talk of such things."

"I cannot promise all will be peaceful," said the duke, "but I will do what I can to honour your wishes."

"That's all I can ask, my lord."

"Now, having settled that issue," continued the duke, "there's another matter I must address."

Ludwig looked up in surprise.

"When Lord Wulfram informed me of your true lineage, I was honour bound to notify your father of your whereabouts. I have, therefore, sent riders to Verfeld Keep, informing your family of all that has transpired. I know such a trip will take time, so I invite you back to Torburg where you will be a guest in my palace until such time as arrangements can be made for your safe transport." He looked at Lord Wulfram. "Baron?"

Lord Wulfram stepped forward. "I hereby release you from my service, but know you shall always have a home in Regnitz should you ever return." He extended his hand. "Let us shake hands in friendship."

"Gladly," said Ludwig.

"Good," said the duke. "Now that's out of the way, let us celebrate our victory!"

EPILOGUE

Autumn 1095 SR

Ludwig stood off to the side, waiting as Lord Hagan Stein and his new bride, Rosalyn, stepped from the Cathedral. The crowd cheered, parting as they made their way down the steps to the waiting carriage. Servants rushed forth, placing a small step to assist them in climbing aboard, and then the coachman cracked the whip, and the horses began moving.

He watched them head down the street, then turn a corner, disappearing from view. Lord Wulfram descended the steps, coming to rest beside Ludwig.

"I hear you're leaving us," said the baron.

"I'm afraid so, Lord. I received word yesterday that my father is ill."

"When do you intend to depart?"

"Today. I delayed only to watch the ceremony."

Lord Wulfram smiled. "Perhaps one day you'll have a marriage of your own. If you do, I'd be honoured to be invited."

"And if that day ever comes, Lord, I shall be sure to include you on the guest list."

"I wish you well on your travels, my friend, but be warned, the road from here to Hadenfeld is a long one, and danger lurks at every turn."

Ludwig looked at where his horse, Clay, sat waiting for him. "Fear not, Lord. I have taken precautions."

"Oh?" The baron leaned forward, looking past him to where his horse stood. Beside Ludwig's mount waited two others, each with someone in the saddle.

"Now," said Ludwig, "I must be off if I am to reach a roadside inn before nightfall. Good luck to you, Lord."

"And to you, Sir Ludwig."

Ludwig strode across the street to where Clay stood, climbing into the saddle without a word. He wheeled his horse around and began the long trek south. His companions soon caught up to him, taking up positions on either side.

"So," said Cyn. "What's Hadenfeld like?"

"Yes," said Sigwulf, "and more importantly, how much ale do you have there?"

This was going to be a long trip.

Read the prequel Tempered Steel

If you liked *Warrior Knight*, then *Ashes*, the first book in the Internationally Best Selling *Frozen Flame* series awaits your undivided attention.

Start Reading Ashes Today

SHARE YOUR THOUGHTS!

If you enjoyed this book, I encourage you to take a moment and share what you liked most about the story.

These positive reviews encourage other potential readers to give my books a try when they are searching for a new fantasy series.

But the best part is, each review that you post inspires me to write more!

Thank you!

CHARACTERS, PLACES, AND ITEMS OF NOTE
FOR WARRIOR KNIGHT

Cast of Characters:
Nobility of Erlingen:
Duke of Erlingen - Deiter Heinrich
Baron of Anshlag - Hurst Radler
Baron of Galmund - Helmer Becken
Baron of Grozen - Kruger Prochnow
Baron of Lieswel - Killian Bockler
Baron of Mulsingen - Gebhard Stein
Baron of Zurkirk - Anwald Kesselman
Baron of Rosenbruck - Rengard Pasche
Baron of Regnitz - Wulfram Haas
Baron of Hutfeld - Marten Drachmann
Baron of Salzing - Augustus Strappe
Baron of Adelwel - Ewald Beck
Baron of Chermingen - Baldwin Classen

Grim Defenders
Baldric - Mercenary sergeant, reputation as a hothead
Cynthia 'Cyn' Hoffman - Female mercenary sergeant
Dorkin - Mercenary, cook
Emile - Mercenary, brother to Quentin
Kerwain - Mercenary
Odo - Mercenary
Quentin - Mercenary, brother to Emile
Sigwald 'Siggy' Marhaven - Mercenary sergeant
Ludwig Altenburg - Son of Lord Frederick Altenburg, Baron of Verfeld
Waldemar Ecke - Captain

Lord Wulfram Haas, Baron of Regnitz's Men:
Arturo - Foot soldier
Horst - Soldier
Krebbs - Sergeant
Lothar Haas(Deceased) - Older brother to Lord Wulfram Haas
Rosalyn Haas - Daughter of Lord Wolfram Haas,
Simmons - Archer
Wahlman - Footman

Lord Gebhard Stein, Baron of Mulsingen's men:
Gerrit Hahn - Soldier
Gottfried Jager - Siege expert
Hagan Stein - Son of Lord Gebhard Stein
Karl Dornhuffer - Soldier
Velton - Soldier
Beornoth - Therengian soldier
Linden Herzog - Earth Mage

Knights:
Galrath of Paledon - Knight in service of the Duke of Erlingen
Haren - Knight in tournament at Toburg
Hendrick of Corburg - Knight in tournament at Toburg
Ludwig Alwise of Garmund - False name used by Ludwig Altenburg
Nathan of Feldmarch - Knight in tournament at Toburg

Others:
Adler Bonn - Spice merchant and former employer of Dorkin
Albrecht Hoffman(Deceased) - Captain of Crossed Swords. Cyn's father
Allard(Deceased) - Poet and philosopher from long ago.
Berthold Altenburg - Stepbrother to Ludwig
Brother Vernan - Lay brother of Saint Mathew
Charlaine deShandria -Master Smith, past lover of Ludwig
Demos - From the book, *Honour to the Brave*
Ebert (Deceased)- King of Deisenbach
Frederick Altenburg - Baron of Verfeld Ludwig's father
Kasper Piltz - Baron of Verfeld's right-hand man
Konrad III -King of Ulrichen
Kurt Wasser - Master swordsman, Ludwig's past sparring partner
Marroch(Deceased) - Poet and philosopher from long ago
Millie - Server at the Hammer
Otto - King of Hadenfeld
Rossdale - Lord from Ulrichen
Volkard - King of Andover

Places:
Abelard - Kingdom on the northern coast
Andover - Kingdom north of Erlingen
Verfeld - Barony of Hadenfeld
Braymoor - Kingdom on northern coast
Deisenbach - Petty Kingdom, northern border of Hadenfeld

Erlingen - Duchy ruled by Lord Deiter Heinrich
Eidenburg - City in Duchy of Talstadt
Eversham - Petty Kingdom
Hadenfeld - Kingdom ruled by King Otto
Halmund - City in the Kingdom of Novarsk, far to the east
Harlingen - Capital of Hadenfeld
Krosnicht - Town in Abelard
Lieswel - City in Erlingen, north of Andover
Lonkirk - City in Eversham
Marston - Petty Kingdom
Neuhafen - Petty Kingdom, broke off from Hadenfeld
Novarsk - Petty Kingdom far to the east
Paledon - Town in Talyria
Reinwick - Petty Kingdom on the northern sea
Rosenbruck - Village in the kingdom of Zowenbruch
Kurslingen - Capital of Zowenbruch
Talyria - Petty Kingdom to the west
Therengia - An ancient Kingdom now defunct
Torburg - Capital of Erlingen
Walgarten - City the Crossed Swords once found themselves in
Ulrichen - Petty Kingdom, borders on Erlingen
Verfeld - Barony in Kingdom of Hadenfeld, home to Ludwig
Zowenbruch - Petty Kingdom, borders on Erlingen

ITEMS OF NOTE:
Blades of Vengeance - Mercenary company in the Duchy of Erlingen
Ferengeld Saga - Story of a knight who travels about righting wrongs
Grim Defenders - Mercenary company
The Crossed Swords - Defunct mercenary company
Honour to the Brave - Book
The Book of Mathew - Religious book
Knight of the Sceptre - Knightly Order in the Duchy of Erlingen

A FEW WORDS FROM PAUL

When I first envisioned Ludwig's story, I knew I needed to write about his journey from a somewhat arrogant, spoiled noble to a true warrior. In the first book in this series, Temple Knight, we meet Charlaine deShandria, who just emerged from a year's worth of training in the Temple Knights of Saint Agnes. Ludwig, on the other hand, has no such training, and so his emergence as a leader is a direct result of his experiences. The one saving grace he has is his insatiable desire to learn. As a youth, he read all he could about battles and the warriors that fought them, but actually participating in a fight for survival is something he's never had to face before.

Just as Sister Charlaine has her Danica, so, too, does Ludwig have his own comrades in the form of Sigwulf and Cyn. They will join him when his adventure continues in Warrior Lord: Book Four, while Charlaine's story resumes in the next book in the series, Temple Captain.

I owe a debt of gratitude to many people, including, most of all, my wife, Carol, without whom this book wouldn't have seen the light of day. I should also like to thank Christie Kramburger, Stephanie Sandrock and Amanda Bennett for their support, along with our group of gaming friends, Brad Aitken, Jeffrey Parker, and Stephen Brown.

As usual, my BETA team has provided some great feedback that has helped make this book a better tale, so thanks go out to Rachel Deibler, Michael Rhew, Phyllis Simpson, Don Hinckley, James McGinnis, Charles Mohapel, Lisa Hanika, and Debra Reeves.

My writing would have ended long ago if it weren't for you, my readers, who continue to delight me with your encouragement and feedback. So thank you, and I hope you enjoy Warrior Knight.

ABOUT THE AUTHOR

Paul J Bennett (b. 1961) emigrated from England to Canada in 1967. His father served in the British Royal Navy, and his mother worked for the BBC in London. As a young man, Paul followed in his father's footsteps, joining the Canadian Armed Forces in 1983. He is married to Carol Bennett and has three daughters who are all creative in their own right.

Paul's interest in writing started in his teen years when he discovered the roleplaying game, Dungeons & Dragons (D & D). What attracted him to this new hobby was the creativity it required; the need to create realms, worlds and adventures that pulled the gamers into his stories.

In his 30's, Paul started to dabble in designing his own roleplaying system, using the Peninsular War in Portugal as his backdrop. His regular gaming group were willing victims, er, participants in helping to playtest this new system. A few years later, he added additional settings to his game, including Science Fiction, Post-Apocalyptic, World War II, and the all-important Fantasy Realm where his stories take place.

The beginnings of his first book 'Servant to the Crown' originated over five years ago when he began running a new fantasy campaign. For the world that the Kingdom of Merceria is in, he ran his adventures like a TV show, with seasons that each had twelve episodes, and an overarching plot. When the campaign ended, he knew all the characters, what they had to accomplish, what needed to happen to move the plot along, and it was this that inspired to sit down to write his first novel.

Paul now has four series based in his fantasy world of Eiddenwerthe, and is looking forward to sharing many more books with his readers over the coming years.

HOW TO GET BATTLE AT THE RIVER FOR FREE

Paul J Bennett's newsletter members are the first to hear about upcoming books, along with receiving exclusive content and Work In Progress updates.

Join the newsletter and receive *Battle at the River*, a Mercerian Short Story for free:

PaulJBennettAuthor.com/newsletter

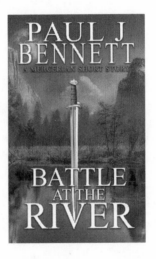

An enemy commander. A skilled tactician. Only one can be victorious.

The Norland raiders are at it again. When the Baron of Bodden splits their defensive forces, Sergeant Gerald Matheson thinks that today is a day like any other, but then something is different. At the last moment, Gerald recognizes the warning signs, but they are outnumbered, outmaneuvered, and out of luck. How can they win this unbeatable battle?

If you like intense battle scenes and unexpected plot twists, then you will love Paul J Bennett's tale of a soldier who thinks outside the box.